The Midnight Secret

By Karen Swan

The Wild Isle series
The Last Summer
The Stolen Hours
The Lost Lover
The Midnight Secret

Other books
Players
Prima Donna
Christmas at Tiffany's
The Perfect Present
Christmas at Claridge's
The Summer Without You
Christmas in the Snow
Summer at Tiffany's
Christmas on Primrose Hill
The Paris Secret
Christmas Under the Stars
The Rome Affair
The Christmas Secret
The Greek Escape
The Christmas Lights
The Spanish Promise
The Christmas Party
The Hidden Beach
Together by Christmas
The Secret Path
Midnight in the Snow
The Christmas Postcards
Christmas by Candlelight
All I Want for Christmas

The Midnight Secret

Karen Swan

MACMILLAN

First published 2025 by Macmillan
an imprint of Pan Macmillan
The Smithson, 6 Briset Street, London EC1M 5NR
EU representative: Macmillan Publishers Ireland Ltd, 1st Floor,
The Liffey Trust Centre, 117–126 Sheriff Street Upper,
Dublin 1, D01 YC43
Associated companies throughout the world
www.panmacmillan.com

ISBN 978-1-0350-5159-5 HB
ISBN 978-1-0350-5160-1 TPB

Copyright © Karen Swan 2025

The right of Karen Swan to be identified as the
author of this work has been asserted by her in accordance
with the Copyright, Designs and Patents Act 1988.

All rights reserved. No part of this publication may be reproduced,
stored in a retrieval system, or transmitted, in any form, or by any means
(electronic, mechanical, photocopying, recording or otherwise)
without the prior written permission of the publisher.

Pan Macmillan does not have any control over, or any responsibility for,
any author or third-party websites referred to in or on this book.

1 3 5 7 9 8 6 4 2

A CIP catalogue record for this book is available from the British Library.

Map artwork by Hemesh Alles

Typeset in Palatino by Palimpsest Book Production Ltd, Falkirk, Stirlingshire
Printed and bound by CPI Group (UK) Ltd, Croydon, CR0 4YY

MIX
Paper | Supporting
responsible forestry
FSC
www.fsc.org
FSC® C116313

This book is sold subject to the condition that it shall not, by way of
trade or otherwise, be lent, hired out, or otherwise circulated without
the publisher's prior consent in any form of binding or cover other than
that in which it is published and without a similar condition including
this condition being imposed on the subsequent purchaser.

Visit **www.panmacmillan.com** to read more about all our books
and to buy them. You will also find features, author interviews and
news of any author events, and you can sign up for e-newsletters
so that you're always first to hear about our new releases.

For Daphne and Colin Hydes,
who so richly deserve their happy ending

S.T KILDA

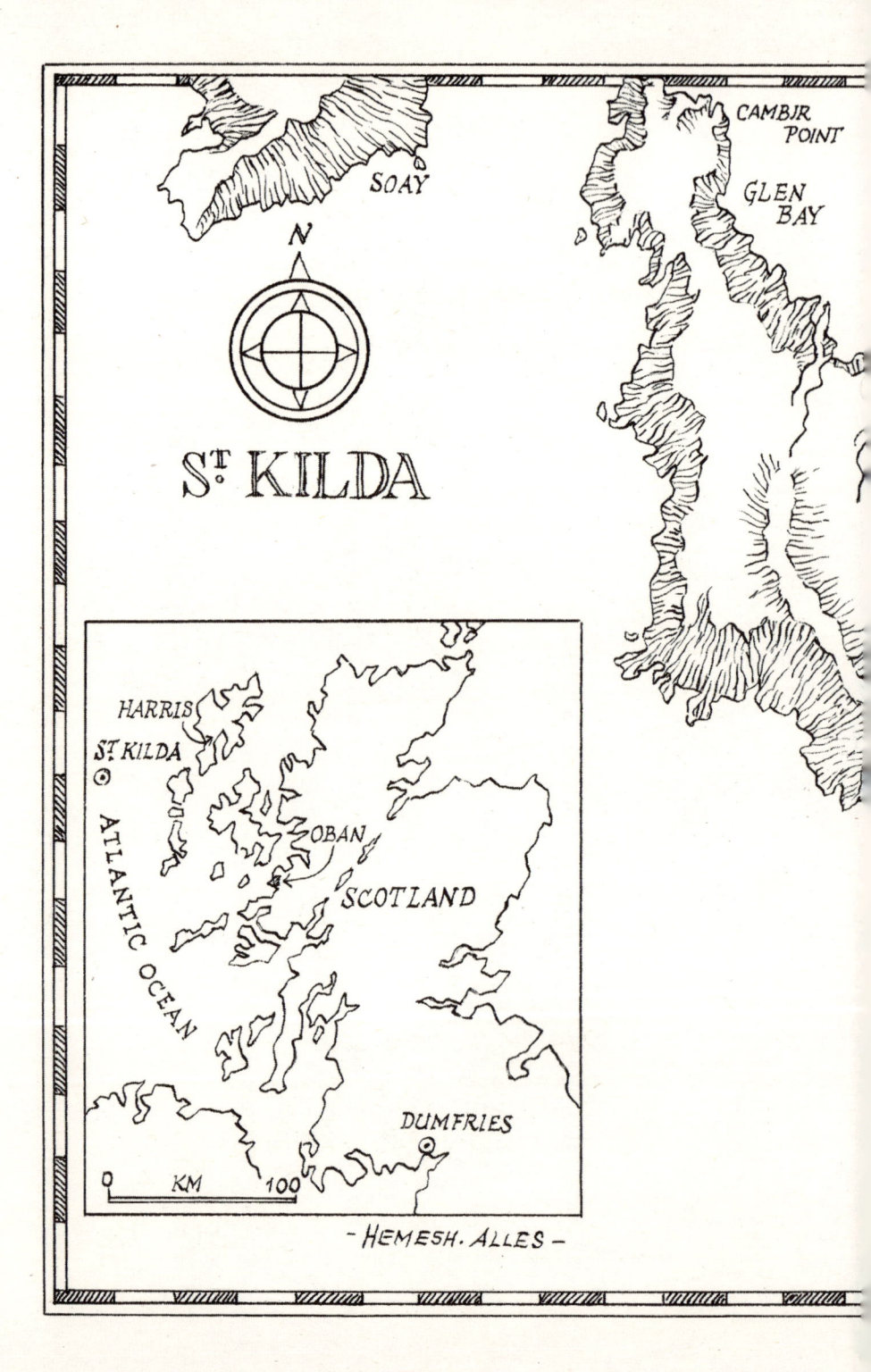

SOAY

CAMBJR POINT

GLEN BAY

HARRIS
ST KILDA
ATLANTIC OCEAN
OBAN
SCOTLAND
DUMFRIES
KM 100

- HEMESH. ALLES -

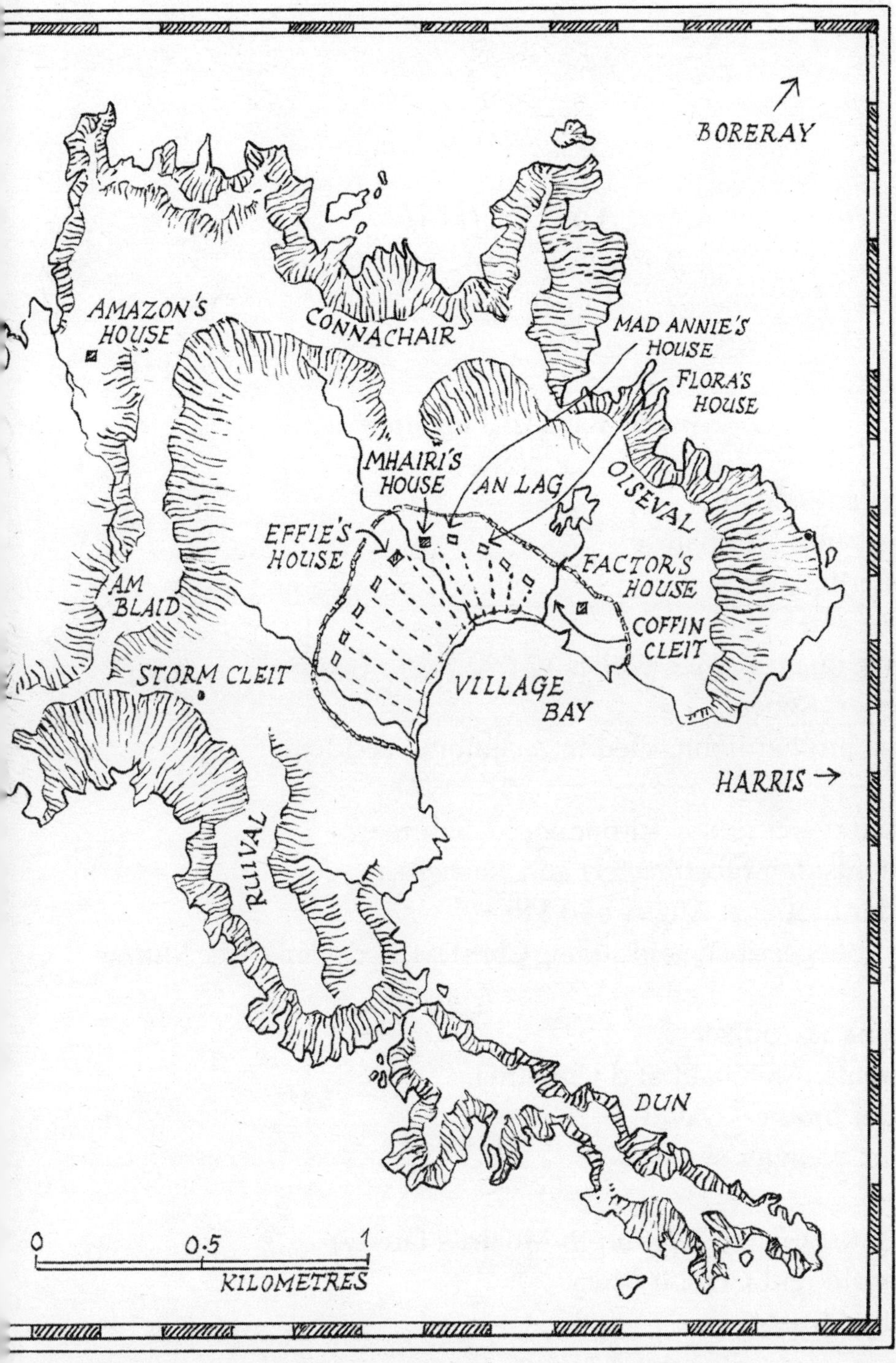
BORERAY
AMAZON'S HOUSE
CONNACHAIR
MAD ANNIE'S HOUSE
FLORA'S HOUSE
MHAIRI'S HOUSE
AN LAG
OISEVAL
EFFIE'S HOUSE
FACTOR'S HOUSE
AM BLAID
COFFIN CLEIT
STORM CLEIT
VILLAGE BAY
HARRIS
RUIVAL
DUN
0
0.5
1
KILOMETRES

Glossary

St Kildan Families

JAYNE FERGUSON
Husband: Norman
Sister-in-law: Molly

EFFIE GILLIES ('Wee Gillies')
Father: Robert
Late brother: John, died in a climbing accident

MHAIRI McKINNON (pronounced Vah-ree)
Parents: Ian (postmaster) and Rachel
Elder brothers: Angus and Fin
Six younger siblings, including Christina, Red Annie, Wee Murran

FLORA MacQUEEN
Parents: Archibald and Christina
Elder brother: David
Four younger siblings

McKINNONS (no relation to Mhairi's family)
Donald and Crabbit Mary
Baby Struan

The Midnight Secret

BIG GILLIES
Hamish (brother of Robert) and Big Mary
Five children

VILLAGE ELDERS
Ma Peg
Mad Annie
Old Fin

LORNA MacDONALD
Nurse from the mainland, now settled in St Kilda

Dialect

ARCHIPELAGO OF ST KILDA: Hirta (principal isle), Boreray, Soay, Dùn
BLACKHOUSE: a traditional, single-storey, grass-roofed dwelling
BLUFF: a cliff, headland or hill with a broad, steep face
CEILIDH: traditional Scottish dance event
CLEIT: a stone storage hut or bothy, only found on St Kilda
CRAGGING: climbing a cliff or crag; a **CRAGGER** is a climber
CROTAL: a lichen used for making dye
DINNER: taken at lunchtime
EIGHTSOME: a Scottish reel
EVENING NEWS: daily walk down the street sharing news
FANK: a walled enclosure for sheep, a sheepfold
HOGGET: an older lamb, but one that is not yet old enough to be mutton
LAZYBEDS: parallel banks of ridges with drainage ditches between them; a traditional, now mostly extinct method of arable cultivation

PARLIAMENT: the daily morning meetings on St Kilda, outside crofts five and six, where chores were divvied up for the day
ROUP: a livestock sale
SECOND SIGHT: traditional Celtic term for clairvoyance
SMACK: boat
STAC: a sea stack (a column of rock standing in the sea) usually created as a leftover after cliff erosion
STAC LEE: a sea stack outside Village Bay, where villagers would hunt for gannets
WAULKING: a technique to finish newly woven tweed, soaking and beating it

Earth's crammed with Heaven
But only he who sees takes off his shoes

Elizabeth Barrett Browning

Prologue

3 November 1926

Village Bay, St Kilda

It was raining, but that was auspicious, they said.

Not that Jayne needed luck. She was marrying the handsomest, tallest man on the isle, a man who made her stomach cartwheel whenever she looked at him. His eyes were the colour of a June sky, his glossy dark hair worn a little longer – shaggy, Mad Annie had said once, 'like the sheep in moult' – than the other men. He had broad, flat shoulders and long arms and legs, standing a whole head taller than all the men except for Angus MacKinnon.

That he was the most handsome man on the isle was never disputed. Jayne could still remember the stunned silence that had fallen on her when Norman had first approached her after kirk in the summer, asking if she'd like to join him for a walk. She had been so sure he was going to ask their new nurse, Lorna, whose arrival was all the women talked about as they did the washing in the burn. Lorna had only recently come to the isle – 'New blood!' Ma Peg had happily exclaimed – and at twenty-six, she was four years older than Norman. 'A woman of the world,' Mad Annie had said with rare admiration. She was serious-minded but pretty with it, educated and clever and able to help people in all the ways Jayne, just turned eighteen and brilliant at nothing, couldn't. Anyone could see that Lorna was a finer prospect for the village's most eligible male. And yet, it was Jayne he had wanted!

Their first walk had been awkward, there was no denying it. Jayne had caught Rachel MacKinnon and Christina MacQueen's astonished looks as she and Norman had peeled away from the others and headed for the rocks. Neither of them had known what to say, either talking over one another or lapsing into silence at the same time, but he had been careful to keep her within sight of the village. People were going to talk and he wouldn't compromise her virtue, even though she had no family left to care.

Her father had left for Australia after her mother's death, taking her two younger brothers with him. He hadn't believed Jayne when she'd said she wouldn't leave with them. Even as he climbed aboard the whaling ship that would take them to the mainland he still expected her to relent 'from this nonsense' and follow. But then, he had never understood his own wife either, nor the burden of the curse both mother and daughter carried: to go into the wider world and expand their community was to risk the visions increasing, and those were bad enough in a village of forty. And so he had stared back at Jayne with open-mouthed dismay as she stood, white-faced, on the shore with everyone else, waving them goodbye.

When the ship rounded the headland, everyone had turned back to their cottages and walked in a tight huddle, their footsteps darning the hole left in their wake. It was Ma Peg, seeing Jayne tremble on the shore amid her own self-imposed abandonment, who had reached for her hand and taken her back to her croft for supper – and Jayne had never left. Lorna

The Midnight Secret

had moved into Jayne's former home when she had arrived this summer, two years later, and so the wheel of village life had kept turning: a little bit different, but still the same.

But today Jayne would be leaving here. Within the hour, she would be Mrs Norman Ferguson and tonight she would sleep beside her new husband in Cottage number two. He lived there with his younger sister Molly; the two of them had been orphaned when he was fifteen and Molly just nine, and he was fiercely protective of her. None of the village boys dared pull *her* hair or leave cow pats on *their* front doorstep!

The two girls had grown close in recent months, in spite of their age gap. Molly had been quick to ask her if she would walk with Norman again, even though he wasn't a sentimental man. She had told her all his favourite things so they had something to talk on the next time – and it had worked, easing the stiffness between them so that their walks became regular.

'There, I knew I still had it somewhere,' Ma Peg said, straightening up slowly from where she was reaching into the chest, one hand on her back, the other holding a thin chemise deeply wrinkled and yellowed with age. The only things in its favour, so far as Jayne could see, were that it was a much lighter cotton than their usual garments – even their summer shirts – and a faint lilac floral pattern could just be discerned. 'I wore this on my own wedding night,' Ma Peg said, pressing it against her ample body. 'Of course, I was a lot more spry in those days,' she chuckled. 'It fit me like a dream back then. I can still remember my Hamish's expression . . .' Her face softened with the memories and she nodded to herself in silent reminiscence.

Jayne waited anxiously for more. She needed more. Tonight, Molly would be sleeping here so that Jayne and Norman could spend their first night together alone, and she had no idea what to expect. She had tried asking Ma Peg what she 'should do' and her response had been to let things take their natural course – but if even conversation hadn't come naturally to her and Norman, she didn't know how *that* would.

Her face must have betrayed as much because it had prompted the old woman to get down on her hands and knees and start rummaging through the blanket chest.

'. . . Just make sure to stand by the firelight, lassie,' Ma Peg said, looking back at her with a knowing smile. 'That'll have him running to y'.'

Jayne was confused. 'The firelight?'

'Y'll see,' Ma Peg nodded, pushing the garment into Jayne's hands just as the door opened and young Mhairi MacKinnon peered in.

'He and Molly have just left!' she said excitedly. Mhairi and Flora had been on watch, intently surveilling the groom's cottage for the past forty minutes as if making sure he didn't flee (Jayne wasn't sure exactly where he *could* escape to on a two-mile island in the the Atlantic). Meanwhile, Effie Gillies was 'stationed' by the church door to make sure he actually went in. Poor Norman, Jayne thought with a smile. The girls would make sure he married her whether he wanted to or not!

'Oh, Jayne!' Mhairi gasped. 'You look so pretty, just like a fairy!'

Did she? Ma Peg had brushed her light brown hair with a hundred strokes to bring up the shine before intricately threading it with daisies and buttercups. There were no trees on the islands, so a crown of blossoms had never been an option, but this wasn't the season for wildflowers either. Daisies and buttercups were the best they could muster, and the girls had been out picking them for her all morning.

The Midnight Secret

'Let me see,' Flora said, bursting through after her, eager to see the bride. '. . . Oh! You're the most beautiful bride I've ever seen!'

Jayne didn't like to point out she was the only bride Flora had ever seen as the young girl's hands clasped over her heart, her hazel-green eyes shining at the thrill of it all. Even at fourteen, Flora was a prodigious beauty, surely destined for a far brighter life than St Kilda could provide. Jayne had a sense that *her* wedding would be more sensational than anything this small isle had ever seen.

'Thank you,' she said quietly. She would have to take their word for it that she looked . . . presentable. Sometimes it felt daunting, the prospect of marrying such a good-looking man, and she had to remind herself that *he* had chosen *her*; that he had seen something in her that he liked. 'Y're a fine young lass,' Ma Peg would always say as they sat by the fire in the evenings, knitting and talking over the day's events; but that felt hard to believe when Jayne had been overlooked her entire life. People kept their distance with her, as they had with her mother. *There's a look that comes into their eyes when they see us, child. They'll still smile but they're always wary, frightened of what we might have seen.*

It felt to Jayne like wearing a shroud – it was what people saw first, the 'gift' of second sight always a step ahead of her so that she was perpetually in its shadow. She didn't know how it felt to have the sun on her face.

'Effie Gillies, look at the state o' you!' Ma Peg scolded as Effie tore into the cottage moments later. 'Your feet are black!'

'Aye, it's raining,' Effie panted, looking completely unconcerned.

'And could y' not have put a brush through y' hair?'

The girl frowned. 'Why? *I'm* not getting married.'

'Honestly,' the old woman tutted, despairing.

'What's that?' Effie asked curiously, seeing the chemise bundled in Jayne's hands.

Jayne's cheeks reddened, as if it was obvious to everyone that this was how she would seduce her husband tonight.

'Never you mind that!' Ma Peg said crossly, taking it back from Jayne and wagging a finger at the girls. 'You're supposed to be in the kirk!'

'Aye. And I've come up to tell you Norman's there, and he's wearing his suit.'

'I should hope so!' Ma Peg said huffily, checking over the bride again. Jayne couldn't remember a time when she'd been so fussed over. Certainly not since her mother had died. 'Now be off with y', Effie, and take these rascals with you too.' Ma Peg's gaze fell upon Flora and Mhairi's impish faces. 'We'll be there in a few minutes. Make sure one of you's by the door for taking off Jayne's boots. I'm too old for all that bending down.'

'I can do it—' Jayne began, but Ma Peg stopped her.

'Nonsense. Whoever heard of the bride taking off her own boots? Besides, I don't want these flowers falling out.'

'Bye, Jayne,' Mhairi beamed as Ma Peg bustled them out. 'We'll sing the hymns extra loud for you!'

Jayne walked after them through to the kitchen, listening to their laughter carrying down the street as they skipped over the stone slabs, arms linked. The whole island was ready for a party, irrespective of the weather. Ma Peg had made Jayne her favourite oatcakes for breakfast – a parting gift – and the plates were still sitting on the side, waiting to be taken to the burn for washing. Jayne felt the itch of habit to do them herself; there had been little time for the women to get to their usual chores today when they'd all been so busy with preparing the dinner. The men had slaughtered a hogget this morning and it was cooking on the spit outside, a few sheep's hides stretched overhead between washing lines to keep the rain off. After the vows they would feast, and later they would dance a ceilidh.

And then, finally, the door of number two would close and there would be no more eyes upon them, no more planned conversations. Jayne and Norman would be alone at last. She would stand in a chemise in the firelight before the man who made her nervous and excited all at once. He had yet to kiss her – he was honourable as well as reserved – and she tried again and again to imagine his mouth upon hers. Flora, with her usual precociousness, had shown her how to practise on her own arm. As if she knew! Jayne had laughed and swatted her away, but in bed that night, lying in the darkness, she had tried it anyway.

Ma Peg bustled back in, satisfied the girls were running ahead to the kirk. Her gaze travelled over Jayne with grandmotherly affection and she made a final adjustment to some of the daisies wound in her hair.

'He's a lucky man, that Norman Ferguson.'

'I'm the lucky one.'

'Oof! He'd like y' to think that, that's for sure,' Ma Peg chuckled. 'That man's got a high enough opinion o' himself as it is.' She disappeared into the bedroom and re-emerged a moment later with the chemise. 'And we mustn't forget this,' she said with a knowing look, as if the finer details of the seduction had been agreed.

Jayne held out her arm to help Ma Peg balance while going down the step, and they walked together through the deserted street. All the cottage doors had been left open, of course, fires flickering with low flames. The smell of burning peat mingled with the aroma of the lamb cooking slowly on the grass.

The tide was in, the sea a heavy grey, but there was little wind for once. A trailing mist was trickling over the summits of Oiseval and Ruival, the hills that flanked either side of Village Bay like sentries. The rain was soft, and she hoped it settled like a dew upon her cheeks, diamonds on her lashes.

They stopped at number two on the way past, and Jayne hurried in with the chemise, excitedly laying it down on the unmade bed. She bit her lip, feeling her heart pound harder at the illicit visit. She had never been inside his bedroom before, and she allowed herself a moment to take in the sight: his tweed cragging breeks were thrown upon a rush-seated chair – discarded as he'd changed into his Sunday best – a blanket Molly had knitted strewn along the end of the bed, his musky smell lingering as if he'd only just left the room. Within the hour, this would be her room too . . . She wished time would speed up and spirit her into the future like a fairy on the wind.

It took less than two minutes to arrive at the kirk, and Jayne heard the babble of conversation within die down as they came and stood in the doorway.

Molly was waiting for her with bright eyes. In marrying Norman, Jayne knew she was gaining not only a husband but a sister as well. From today, she would have a family again. She would belong.

'You're an even more beautiful bride than I dreamt you'd be,' Molly whispered as she set about untying Jayne's boots.

Jayne gave a shy smile. She knew she was no great beauty, but all the girls' excitement was infectious and she was beginning to believe she might, perhaps, look pretty today.

There was no introductory music to cover the short pause as Molly worked on her laces – no organ, not even a stained-glass window. As Jayne looked through into the familiar, tiny whitewashed chapel, it was completely unadorned but for the daisies in her hair.

She saw the rows of villagers awaiting her, and she could tell every single person by the backs of their heads. This was the landscape to her life; she knew everyone's story, everyone's secrets.

Throats were cleared, someone blew their nose . . . and then, silence.

Jayne saw Norman turn, his beautiful black-ringed blue eyes fastening upon her so that the butterflies in her stomach took wing. He didn't smile at her excitedly the way the girls had just now, but of course he was neither a teenage girl nor a sentimental man.

Ma Peg squeezed her arm, and Jayne realized that somewhere along the way they had traded places and it was no longer her supporting Ma Peg, but Ma Peg supporting her.

'You're sure now?' Ma Peg whispered, holding her arm tightly as they looked past all their neighbours towards the minister standing at the end of the aisle, beside her groom. Waiting.

Jayne nodded. She'd never been more sure of anything, and she boldly took her first step down the aisle, eager to get to her destiny.

Chapter One

JAYNE

Four years later – late August 1930

Village Bay, St Kilda

Jayne stared down at the humble cross, tacked together from driftwood that had washed up on their single shore long ago and been stored in the coffin cleit, ready for the next death.

Despite their best efforts, it wasn't much to honour the memory of a girl who had been so radiant in life. Jayne, Effie, Flora and Mhairi had each taken a turn with Effie's paints, picking out Molly's name in swirling letters and decorating the spaces with flowers and a tiny motif of the St Kilda wren whose songs she had loved so much.

Jayne sank to the ground and pressed a hand to the lush grass; buttercups nodded in bright greeting but they still made her blanch, even now. She could never forget how they had rained from her hair on her wedding night, daisies and buttercups shaken loose and falling, one by one, until nothing beautiful had remained.

She looked away. She couldn't believe she was leaving her young sister-in-law behind. It felt like losing her all over again,

The Midnight Secret

for there had at least been solace in visiting her grave every day. Jayne had taken to bringing her knitting up to the burial ground and sitting beside the little cross, protected from buffeting winds and prying eyes by the high stone wall that encircled the oval space like a mother's arms. She sat there most days and kept the girl she'd loved as a sister up to date with all the village news, chatting like they always used to over the kitchen table: Flora and Mhairi were summering with the flocks in Glen Bay; Crabbit Mary was – finally – with child, due any day; Donald had had a nasty fall when they went over to pluck the sheep on Boreray, but he'd recovered well; Effie had fallen in love with an earl's son who had then, of course, broken her heart . . .

So much life had been lived since Molly's death, even here on their tiny isle where supposedly nothing ever happened. Jayne simply couldn't envisage what awaited them on the other side of the water. She could scarcely believe the evacuation was happening at all. It had seemed like a trick when the news had come in May, everyone stunned. Yes, they'd come to an 'all or none' consensus in the weeks that had followed Molly's passing last November, when Lorna – fuelled by guilt or rage – had argued that no one should die of pneumonia in this age; that if they'd only had the right resources and aid, Molly could have lived. Didn't they deserve more, better, Lorna had asked?

More and *better* weren't words in the St Kildan vocabulary; but then, Lorna MacDonald was a St Kildan by choice, not by birth. And somehow, as the argument wore on through those dark nights of winter, it had become a petition for evacuation to the mainland.

The islanders had been split when the thought was first mooted: the elders wanting to stay, the younger generation enticed by the comforts found on the other side. There was no denying their number, now down to thirty-six, had dropped to a critical level. Half the population was either aged or juvenile, and they needed strong young men to climb the cliffs to catch the very birds and their eggs they lived on; they needed strong young women to birth the future generations of St Kildans, especially now that Mhairi was betrothed to a farmer on Harris, Flora to her gentleman from Glasgow, and Effie, a wild thing, was no more suited to marriage than the wind was meant for a box. Molly had been the worst possible person to die, for so many reasons.

Jayne had collapsed when she had first seen Molly's face in a vision; she'd felt her insides turn to dust. There had been no one she could tell, no one with whom she could share her horror. Though everything in her being had wanted to scream desperate warnings, to somehow alter the future and deceive fate, it would have been an unconscionable cruelty to utter them. Her mother had warned her of the futility of trying to ever change what was already foreseen.

The horror of that day lingered still, and as she sat by the grave, flashbacks still tormented her. *Picking Molly up from the floor and carrying her to her bed . . . Norman paling at her sudden deterioration, praying to a God he didn't believe in . . . Lorna working with fast hands and a grim look . . . the darkness buffeting and gathering around them, a rolling energy that was spiriting Molly away like she was a ball of rags . . .*

'Come on, Moll!' Lorna urging her patient to rally, to respond, her hands moving faster and faster as time began to run out.

'Oh God,' Norman crying, sensing it too. 'Moll, no!'

Molly's shallow, grasping breaths drawing out ever longer, pauses outweighing little desperate hiccups for oxygen. Silences steadily becoming ominous – and then deafening.

The Midnight Secret

'Moll?' Norman's voice breaking on the whispered word. The big man sounding small. He had vowed to protect his sister, thinking it meant a rich husband and a house on the mainland; never knowing they would be imperilled by sheep in a snowstorm.

Lorna turning to them, ashen-faced. 'She's gone.'

'No!' Norman reaching past her, pulling his sister into his arms. 'Wake up, Moll!' His hollow gasp as Molly's head dropped backward in dreadful proof.

A creak of the latch, footsteps . . . David MacQueen stopping at the sight of Jayne, Lorna, Norman and Molly positioned like marble figurines. His legs buckling, staggering backwards, his face becoming a Greek mask – tragedy pulling down on a gaping mouth, eyes bulging – as Norman moaned a ghostly sound, his soul being dragged from his innards. But it was worse than that.

A man could live without his soul. But his heart?

Norman's eyes finding hers, sorrow turning to rage – because she had known all this. Foreseen and not stopped it. Given no warnings.

Her body weakening, knowing there would be consequences. There always were.

'I thought I might find you here.'

The voice pressed over her memories, pushing them back down into the depths of her psyche, and she looked up to find David standing before her. The sun pressed at his back so that he glowed, his edges black and blurred against a bleached sky.

'Of course,' she smiled as he sat beside her in his usual way, looping his elbows over his knees as he looked down the hill, back towards the bay. She knew he felt the same as her. Leaving Molly was going to be the worst part about leaving here. No matter the comforts they might find elsewhere, it was only in this spot right here that either of them felt at peace.

This had become their meeting place in the nine months since Molly had gone. Not intentionally, of course; it had never occurred to her that they might become friends (David was three years her junior, for one thing). But they had each needed to feel close to Molly and had found themselves drawn back here, day after day. At first, they had been at pains to give one another space – David had been Molly's sweetheart, Jayne her sister-in-law. But over time, instead of scattering, they had begun to sit here together and talk about times past with the girl they had both loved. Sharing their memories had become a way of grieving, a new ritual. Jayne recounted the quiet companionship of cooking with Molly at the stove, washing the sheets in the burn, knitting by the fire. David's reminiscences were more lively: dancing all night at the ceilidh, Molly's cheeks flushed and eyes bright; how they would flirt in the kirk, hiding messages in their prayer books. He remembered what had turned out to be their last day together, stealing kisses in her bedroom as they hid from Norman, holding themselves back from temptation in the mistaken belief that they had a future waiting for them and all the time in the world. But where had their patience and virtue got them?

'Is the madness abating?' Jayne asked now, picking up her knitting.

Everyone had been packing up for days. Mad Annie had been practising walking up and down the street with her spinning wheel on her back, ready for embarking the boat. Effie had been checking the climbing ropes, brushing off all reminders that they wouldn't be needed on the mainland. Ma Peg's windows shone even though in two days' time, no one would look through them again.

'Only getting worse,' David tutted. 'Old Fin's adamant he

The Midnight Secret

hid a sovereign up the chimney thirty years back, but he can't find it.'

'How did he come by a sovereign thirty years back?' Jayne frowned. Theirs was a barter economy of chores, errands and favours swapped between families. The rich visitors who sometimes sailed in, offering shillings in exchange for photographs or woollen socks, had only been coming in any number since the Great War.

'Says he won it off a captain. Arm wrestling.'

Jayne smiled. Old Fin was in his twilight years now, but thirty years ago? There were few men who could match a St Kildan's arm strength. The islanders' survival depended upon cragging; even challenging one of them to a thumb-wrestle was ill-advised.

'He reckons he'll need it at last, so he tried to send Wee Murran up the chimney looking for it.' David rolled his eyes. 'Suffice it to say, Rachel was not pleased.'

'I thought I heard a racket,' Jayne nodded, smiling. It would mean another round of scrubbing shirts in the burn before they got on the boat. 'Did you see Norman anywhere?' Her husband had scarce been home the last two nights.

'Aye, down at the factor's house. Thick as thieves, they were. I think he'll be the only person not to be glad to see the back of Frank Mathieson.'

'Aye. I can't understand it myself,' she murmured, although she thought perhaps she did. To the rest of the village, the landlord's rent collector and 'man on the ground' was a bully. He lorded it over them all and, some of the men were convinced, pocketed the hefty difference between the rates at which he bought from them and sold on to others. But her husband was an ambitious man; he had proved as much when he'd denied his sister her heart's wish to marry David.

News of the evacuation had excited him. With Molly gone, he had become ever more dissatisfied with life here – with her – and he now saw a chance for the *more* and *better* Lorna had promised.

Unlike everyone else, Norman viewed Mathieson as his equal; he saw himself as a man of the world, not of the soil. He knew the factor had seen things and been places, and although her husband was too proud to ask for advice, he absorbed Mathieson's vainglorious boasts and stories like a sponge. He was learning from him; he wanted to know as much as possible.

'There's Mhairi,' David murmured, his eyes fixed up the slopes of Oiseval. Jayne followed his gaze towards the distant, flame-haired figure heading for the fanks on the An Lag plateau. A flock of sheep trotted before her, herded by two dogs, one of which was Poppit. Jayne's eyes automatically scanned for Effie too, for she and Poppit were never parted. Sure enough, she was up ahead, arms wide as she channelled the animals into the correct enclosure. There was vivacity in her movements and Jayne could tell, even from here, that Effie was glad to be with her friend again. Mhairi and Flora had trialled summering on the distant pastures, and if Jayne herself had felt the loss of their company, poor Effie had been as lonesome as a ghost.

She watched as the flock grouped in nervous clusters against the stone walls. They were moving easily and breathing freely now, but it had been very different on the day of the snowstorm back in November. How could something so innocuous have turned so deadly? At first, it had been Mhairi who was almost lost; but there she was now, standing in the sun, while Molly lay in the ground here beside them. The reversal of fortune had come as a shock to all but Jayne.

The Midnight Secret

She looked away sharply, David doing the same, and she knew they were sharing the same thought. It happened a lot.

'What will we do on the other side, when we can't come here?' David murmured.

Her chest tightened at the question. It was something she had been asking herself in the quiet hours, but her voice was calm and level when she spoke. 'We'll still talk, you and I, just in a new place. We'll find somewhere special Molly would have loved.'

She smiled with encouragement, but a small frown puckered his brow. 'But what if they don't keep us all together?'

'They have said they will try, and I . . . I choose to take them at their word,' she replied after a moment, unable to bear the alternative. She knew that like her, he had no one else to talk to about Molly. The villagers, their friends, had already moved on; Molly was still beloved, but her name was already infrequently mentioned as the seasons began to run one into another, and she would be left even further behind once they sailed from these shores. There was no time to dwell on death on St Kilda when they had to work so hard at staying alive.

'But what if they don't, Jayne?' he persisted.

She swallowed. 'Then I hope we can write to one another and continue to talk that way.'

He looked over at her, and she saw it was an inadequate solution. So much of what they shared went unsaid, sitting together in silences crowded with thoughts and memories. How would that translate on a page? For the first time, she realized that it was not just Molly she might lose, but David too. Life could part them with the same ease as death. Their new friendship was like a glass bubble, strong and fragile all at once: it floated here, but would it shatter on the mainland?

He was still staring, as if reading her thoughts, before he looked away abruptly and tightened his grip around his knees. Neither of them spoke for several moments. 'Jayne, I came up here because . . . well, there's something I wanted to put to you.'

'Oh?'

'I wondered if we might stay with her here together, on the last night? I . . . I don't want her to be alone.'

'You mean to *sleep* here?'

'Under the stars, aye. Molly's never going to have our company again. I can't bear to think of her alone for all the nights to come, when this place is silent.'

Jayne felt a sob come to her throat and pulse there at the thought of it too. Complete abandonment. There would be no human life treading the grass any more, only bones in the earth.

'So?' he prompted.

Still she hesitated. How would she explain to her husband that her last night on St Kilda would be spent here and not in their bed? She knew he would not take it well, but she saw the plea in David's eyes and nodded. For his sake, for Molly's, she would make it happen. Norman could join them if he so chose – Molly was his sister, after all – but she knew only too well that he was not sentimental. 'I think that would be a lovely way to say goodbye,' she murmured.

'Good. I'm glad you agree,' he said, getting to his feet and brushing the grass from his trousers. 'I'd best get on. Pa wants me to help him with bringing down the loom.'

The looms, cumbersome items that took up half a room, were stored in the rafters through the summer months and their removal to the ground was a sign they were in the lee of the move. Tomorrow, SS *Dunara Castle* would drop anchor in the bay and they would begin the process of moving their household belongings and animals aboard. The day after that, the HMS *Harebell* would come for the villagers themselves, and the evacuation would be under way.

Jayne couldn't bear to think of the island falling silent. After two thousand years of human settlement, their ancient rock was being left to the wind and the waves, the birds and the sheep. There would be no more evening news along the street; the chimneys would no longer puff with peat smoke. Sailors harbouring from a storm would find no friendly welcome on the beach.

She watched David walk away, past the many other rudimentary crosses stuck in the ground. He was fully grown now, tall and rangy with an easy lope that was clearly discernible even at a distance – at least, it was to her. His almost-black hair had a curl at the collar and his hazel-green eyes were always kind. It occurred to Jayne that his future was far brighter than he could see from this spot; his heart was still tied to Molly, in part because there was nothing more here for him, but there would be plenty of girls on the mainland who'd like the look of such a fine young man. He had prospects even if he couldn't see them yet, and Jayne felt her own heart ache for Molly. She was going to lose him for good on the other side.

They both would.

'You're back,' she said, looking up from the stool as Norman walked through. He was sunburnt from the long and relentless days outside recently, his linen shirt tucked inside the waistband of his trousers like a rag. He looked especially handsome, but if her heart still skipped a beat at the sight of him, her body withdrew.

She watched as he bent to wash himself in the bucket, muscles rippling with careless grace. Their marriage had come to balance on an uneasy point, a strange tension formed between distrust and lust, despair and resignation. Over the years, she had come to understand why he had proposed to her, plain Jayne: she was little more than a shadow in the room, pale warmth in the bed. He had married her precisely because she was the bare minimum, taking up no room in his life.

'Y' make it sound like I have somewhere else t' go,' he replied.

She watched as he splashed water on his face from the pail before running a wet hand through his hair. 'I only meant that I've scarce seen you the past few days.'

'It seems to me you're the only one with time to sit down.' His eyes flashed in her direction. Had he seen her sitting in the burial ground with David? He had taken against David for being indelibly intertwined with the moment of Molly's death: Norman had lost control of his emotions and David had witnessed his weakness. She knew Norman would never forgive him for it. 'All the others are frenzied trying to get done but you're on y' backside darning socks.'

Jayne looked around the spotless cottage. They owned precious little as it was – certainly less than those with big families – but she had folded their blankets, sheets and spare clothes into the wooden chest, she had taken down the curtains at the windows and polished the glass to a shine. The hearth was swept, her spinning wheel and bundle of yarns already sitting by the door. The pans were gleaming; the butter churn scrubbed . . . But she knew better than to plead her case.

'Well, your tea's ready to eat,' she said instead, getting up and reaching for the stove door. She had cooked roasted puffin as a last treat. Lorna had told her it wasn't so readily eaten over the other side – why would it be, when they had a daily butcher's choice of lamb, beef, pork and chicken? Jayne had

The Midnight Secret

listened on with wide eyes, wondering if perhaps one day, they might look back at their sparse diet here with something like nostalgia. It seemed hard to believe.

'In a while. I've to help Mathieson with some jobs.'

She straightened up. 'Again? But weren't you helping him earlier?'

'Aye, in between moving the fulmar oil down from the top for ourselves.'

'But what does Mr Mathieson have to do that requires so much help? Surely he's here just to collect the rent and oversee the move?'

'Jayne, I know you are simple-headed but surely even y' can understand that he has work to do on behalf of MacLeod? Hirta is being closed up, and he needs to check the cleits and all over the isle to make sure nothing is missed. We'll be lucky to get it done, the two of us, in the time that's left.'

'Then surely the other men can help as well? It's not fair for the burden to fall to you.'

His gaze came to rest upon her. 'They don't have the time. They all have families to look after.'

She heard the silence beat after the words, the accusation hanging inside them of her inability thus far to bear him a child. Jayne looked away. He was free enough with his fists but it was his tongue that often caused the most hurt: *barren, dry, fallow*, those were the taunts that lingered long after the handprints had faded. Was it true? Or was her biology denying him in ways her body could not, knowing she wasn't safe? Even Crabbit Mary and Donald had succeeded where they had failed – and everyone knew those two could scarce share a room together, much less a bed.

'Who do I have, but for you?' he shrugged, walking into the bedroom.

Jayne stared at the floor, hearing him moving around, his footsteps falling still, then breaking into loops around the room as he found everything had been packed up, nothing in its rightful place any longer. A moment later he was back in the doorway. It had always struck Jayne as the cruellest irony that he was never more handsome than when he was at his most dangerous.

'Where's my knife?'

'What do you need that for?'

Norman frowned. 'I don't answer to y', woman! Where is it?'

She hurried over, squeezing past him in the doorway and feeling his eyes upon her as their bodies touched. For a moment, she thought he might clasp her wrist and stop her in her tracks, as he sometimes did; but she slipped past, liquid as water, over to the wooden trunk and opened it. The knife, along with his climbing rope, lay atop the linens and blankets. 'Here.'

He took it from her palm, his gaze still heavy upon her. He had come to bed so late these past few nights, she couldn't even be sure he'd come to bed at all, rising again with the light before she awoke, and she knew he was battling himself. He was a man with needs but he was also a man with ambition, and if he felt he had an opportunity to ingratiate himself with the factor, he would not pass it up. Not even for that.

'Have tea ready for when I return,' he muttered finally.

Her mouth opened to ask him when that would be – to tell him it was already ready – but she closed it, watching as he slipped the knife into his waistband and headed outdoors again. He would be back when he was back. That was all she needed to know.

*

The Midnight Secret

The bed creaked as Norman moved on top of her, his breathing ragged in her ear. She watched the usual spot on the ceiling and waited, knowing that in a few moments it would be done for the night. Her body was passively compliant as his pace quickened, groans beginning to gather in his throat as he lost himself, the bully growing defenceless until finally he stiffened, stilled, then collapsed upon her. His full weight pressed her deeper into the horsehair mattress for several seconds before he pushed back on his arms and rolled off her with a sigh.

They never spoke during the act, nor after, and barely two minutes passed before she heard his breathing slow and grow deeper. Jayne pulled the blanket tightly around her shoulders and turned her head towards the window. The curtain was thin, no match for tonight's full-bodied moon, and she tried to imagine its view back down at their tiny landmass, a lambent speck in the midnight ocean. It helped her to visualize their insignificance, as if their smallness could somehow scale down the pain and loneliness that often felt overwhelming to her. 'This is nothing,' she would whisper to herself in the darkness. 'We're nothing.'

She closed her eyes and tried to sleep, to fall into the easy oblivion her husband enjoyed, for he was never troubled with bad dreams or wakeful nights. But rest wouldn't come. She felt strangely disquieted, and as she blinked again into the brightness, she understood why.

The room was beginning to blur, golden shadows flickering across her eyes.

Oh God, no . . .

She tried to move, as if it was something she could dodge, but the portent settled like a lead cloak, holding her down. She felt the tingle begin to hum in her fingers and the growing heaviness in her soul, as if another spirit was clambering over her and sitting upon her own.

Time stopped.

She became aware of nothing but the thud of her own heart, the future showing itself in her mind's eye, indecipherable images offering a flashed glance behind the curtain. It was always difficult to understand what she was seeing at first; the sights that floated before her eyes were often little more than impressions, only growing distinct as the moment drew near. But this time a face appeared with perfect clarity, and she felt a dread even worse than when she had seen Molly's – because she understood this was going to change everything. They were standing in the shadow of their departure, but the Fates weren't done with them yet.

Death was coming again to St Kilda.

Chapter Two

Jayne watched from the rocks as the men brought over the last of the animals to board the *Dunara Castle*. They had been going back and forth in the smack for two days, bringing down the sheep from An Lag in small groupings, and Hamish had caught a black eye off one particularly angry ewe who kicked while he rowed. Now they were towing the cows behind the small boat, ropes looped around their horns as they mooed in bleak protest. Jayne had never seen such a curious sight, and she wondered what the animals must make of it all; they had no context for the historic event of which they were a part. They didn't know the beginning of the end had begun.

Wooden trunks now sat outside every door, looms and spinning wheels were set against the walls, the slates cleaned in the schoolhouse, the hearths gradually growing cool. Every family was down to one cooking pot, one wash pot, their beds and tables and chairs. The rest of their worldly belongings were packed, and for the first time in their lives the villagers felt themselves held in a state of abeyance – no longer fully here, but not yet left. She saw how everyone kept looking out to the bay, as if checking the cargo ship was still there or else keeping an eye out for the *Harebell* that was coming to spirit them away tomorrow. She sensed they were half expecting a message to come that it was all off, a misunderstanding; they'd be staying here after all.

But with every passing hour, that likelihood was fading. Amid the teeming activity in the glen, realization was sinking in that this really was their final day in their ancestral homeland.

That there was no chance of rain made the transition simpler. The skies were baked a deep sapphire blue, the late summer sun pulsing down on a languid sea. Jayne looked around as she knitted, watching the buttercups and pink thrift nodding in the meadows, hearing the wrens singing loudly from hidden crevices in the dyke, and thought St Kilda had never looked more beautiful. Was this her goodbye? An apology for the harsh winter and all the others before it, which had taken so much from them? Or perhaps she was trying to make them stay, beguiling them with warmth and comfort and pretty views.

Only the seabirds were unmoved, whirling in their thousands in a white lattice in the sky and shrieking at one another as they dived for fish to bring back to the colonies on the cliffs. For them, life would grow easier now too. After tomorrow they would be predators and not prey; no more men on ropes snatching their eggs or grabbing at their necks.

Jayne heard footsteps, the rustle of a skirt, and looked back to see Rachel MacKinnon making her way over the rocks. 'Of all the things I shall miss about this place, one shall be this familiar sight of you on the rocks,' the woman said with her apple-cheeked smile.

'Rachel,' Jayne grinned. 'No wee ones?' Rachel had nine children in all, the youngest being only eleven months. It was so rare to see her without them, it was like she was missing a limb.

Rachel settled herself on the smooth rock beside her, tanned feet and slim ankles peeking from her skirt. A look of calm settled upon her face as she looked out to sea and gave a happy sigh. She tossed her red hair back and looked over at Jayne. 'Ian's taken them up to the gap for a last look . . . He said it's for them to remember, but really it's for him.'

'Aye. Norman's been the same. He's been out almost every hour for the past few days.' She had heard him stir from the bed a few hours after their nightly ritual, when he had supposed her asleep. He'd moved soundlessly for a big man, only the click of the latch on the front door telling her he'd gone back outside as the moon shone. 'He says he's helping Mathieson, but whenever I catch a sighting of him he's up a slope, taking in the views.'

'And he was one of the keenest to leave, too!'

'He was,' Jayne nodded. 'I think the service tonight will be fair heavy in spirit.'

'Aye,' Rachel sighed, watching closely as the Gillies' cow was hoisted, helpless, onto the boat. 'The Reverend's not stepped outside today.' She gave a small groan. 'I imagine he'll be wanting this sermon to frighten the devil from our heads, with all the temptation we've ahead of us now.'

Temptation: it was an alien concept for a community that had only ever focused on existence. Lorna's promises of more and better, once only a mirage, were slowly beginning to take on solid forms. For the younger men, that meant the new lassies they would soon meet, while the older men talked of earning a wage and feeling the weight of coins in their pockets; the children wanted to see motor cars and go to the pictures; the women dreamt of a wireless, hot running water and private lavatories.

The two women sat in companionable silence for a while. Jayne had – uncharacteristically – dropped a stitch on the last row, and she went back, rehooking it on the needle. Of course, she knew perfectly well she no longer needed to knit any socks. There would be no more tourists to buy her wares before they departed now, and the rent quotas for MacLeod had been fulfilled, the barrels of fulmar oil and sacks of sheep wool, tweeds and feathers assessed already by the factor in the featherstore and now loaded onto the ship. But knitting was the only way she knew to quell her restless spirit. It concealed her shaking hands and gave her body something to do as she waited for the clock to run down and fate to run its course. It was the only way she could appear normal as she alone anticipated the swing of the blade.

'Your Mhairi's been working hard on the high slopes,' she said. 'She and Effie have done a fine job of bringing the flocks over.'

'Aye. I've missed her, but it looks like Donald's plan to send the girls over there for the lambing wasn't so harebrained after all. They only lost three in total and there were plenty of triplets. Did I hear right, we're twenty-eight over last year?'

'That's what Norman told me.'

'So then we'll make some coins at the roup between us all. We needn't have fretted so much after the sheep drama—' She stopped herself, her hand shooting out to Jayne's arm in quick apology.

'It's all right,' Jayne said. 'I know what y' meant.' Over sixty sheep had been lost in that snow storm, but the successful lambings this spring had more than made up the numbers. It meant Molly's death had been needless; they could have all stayed indoors that fateful day and they'd have still come out with a profit this summer. 'No sign of Flora, of course.'

'Aye,' Rachel said in a sombre tone. Terrible news had come in the past few days, which had laid the girl low. Flora's fiancé, James Callaghan, a rich businessman from Glasgow,

The Midnight Secret

had been on an expedition to Greenland, but word had come that his ship had been caught and crushed in the ice. 'Lorna says she took the news awful bad. It must have been made all the worse by the fact that she was so close to being reunited with him. She was right on the cusp of stepping into her new life.'

'Has Christina been over to see her?'

'She tried, but Mhairi told her Flora's gone to Cambir Point. She wants to be alone for a while.'

'She didn't even want to see her own mother?' Jayne asked, surprised. Flora and Christina had always been so close.

'That's what Christina was told,' Rachel shrugged. 'And with things so busy here, it was difficult anyway to spare the time to get over there. At least she'll see her tomorrow, no matter what. And Flora's got Mhairi with her, so she's not alone over there.'

Jayne started on a new row of stitches.

Rachel lay back on her elbows, enjoying the sea view. 'Did y' hear Mary's tightenings have started?'

'No!' Jayne gasped. 'Will the baby come today?'

Rachel shrugged again. 'Lorna's been monitoring her most of the day but she says her waters are still intact, so she's probably a way off yet. Y' know what it's like with firstborns; they tend to drag their heels.'

Jayne didn't know – she was versed in deaths, not births – but she let the comment pass. Rachel loved to gossip and she often forgot her audience. 'So then it could come tomorrow instead?' Was that even worse? 'How would we get her on the boat?'

Rachel pulled a face. 'If they can get the cows up, they'll get Mary up too.'

Jayne hoped they wouldn't have to lash her with ropes and

hoist her. 'But a boat's no place to have a bairn,' she said. 'If I was her, I'd be crossing m' legs and holding on till we land tomorrow.'

'The way Mary holds a grudge, I'm sure she could hold on for another month,' Rachel grinned. 'What's twenty-four hours?'

Jayne smiled at the joke, but she looked back out to sea, hiding her eyes from scrutiny. She knew exactly how much could – *would* – change in the space of a day, but it wasn't her place to warn her friends. Nor to frighten them.

The silence that fell had lead weights in its skirts, pulling down from the rafters of the old kirk and settling heavily upon the villagers as they knelt on their cushions, praying into clasped hands. Jayne glanced around, not a hair on her head stirring as she took in her neighbours' white knuckles, tears falling past scrunched-shut eyes, whispers hovering on moving lips. Even the Reverend, standing in full power at his pulpit, had run out of words. His sermon done, his warnings spent, all any of them could do now was hope that this was for the best after all, and that a bright new beginning really was coming on the back of this ancient goodbye.

Almost every seat in the tiny chapel was occupied. The smallest of the children sat quietly for once, and even Mad Annie – notorious for her resolute abstinence from God's house since the drowning of her husband fourteen years prior – was sitting stiffly on the wooden bench beside Ma Peg and Old Fin. Her lips didn't move and she wouldn't bend her head, but nonetheless she was here, reluctantly surrendering to forces even greater than her indignation. Only four villagers were absent: Mhairi and Flora still in Glen Bay, and Crabbit Mary and Lorna. Mary's waters had broken after all, and

The Midnight Secret

Donald was sitting in the pew alone, wearing the apprehensive expression of every expectant father.

There was a stranger among them, too: Mr Bonner, a reporter from *The Times* in London, had come over on the *Dunara Castle* to bear witness to the 'historic event'. He was staying at the Manse with the reverend and his wife, and in the space of a day had made a nuisance of himself, wanting to ask the villagers questions while they finished packing up and cleaning their homes. No one believed him when he said the evacuation had caught the public's imagination. Why should anyone care what their thirty-six souls did or didn't do?

Jayne looked past him as she scanned the congregation, taking in the faces young and old that she knew as well as her own, and trying to memorize this moment. Never again would they sit here as a community, praying to the God whose mercy had been but a thin skin protecting them from the full might of Mother Nature.

Next to her, Norman cleared his throat; it was an innocuous gesture but she knew her husband too well and recognized the impatience it contained. He was a man of action, not of contemplation, and there were still jobs to be completed before they could step onto the boat in the morning.

Stirred by the prompt, the minister's voice rose into the silence, the islanders sitting back on the benches in a muted symphony of rustling tweeds and creaky joints as he invoked a final blessing upon their souls. None of them were ignorant, now, to the mortal temptations awaiting them on the other side of the water; he had made sure not to squander this opportunity to terrify his flock into moral obedience.

They watched with lowered gazes as he strode down the aisle and took his position by the door. There was a pause, then the villagers rose, turning to one another and beginning to talk in low voices. Usually there was a rush for the doors, but tonight was different. This was the final time they would ever walk out of here.

Jayne looked around at the simple white walls and beamed roof of the kirk they were leaving behind. There was no master stonemasonry here or dazzling stained-glass windows. Take out the pews and the altar and, to anyone else, it could be a schoolroom. Only the St Kildans themselves knew of the hope that had breathed colour into this space: marriages and christenings marking the high days; frantic prayers uttered as the crops failed, the seas rose, the winds blew and the babies died. Lockjaw and smallpox had bludgeoned their community in times past, but it was comfort and ease – or at least the promise of it – that was finally propelling them away from here.

That and a needless death.

Jayne stared down at her feet, shuffling on the wooden floorboards in a slow-motion stampede as everyone talked around her without quite seeing her. She stole a look towards the MacQueen pew, where Archie and Christina MacQueen had bookended their boisterous brood. David, as if sensing her stare, looked up and caught her gaze; his lashes were wet, his cheeks flushed. She knew it was a struggle for him to contain himself. If he had been able to find Molly anywhere, it had been in here . . . but now, no more.

She smiled, trying to remind him with her eyes that they still had tonight to say goodbye too, and his head dipped fractionally, confirming the plan, but she saw no comfort in his face.

She glanced over at Norman. He was a step ahead, talking with Neil Gillies about the bother with getting the cows onto the boat earlier. She hadn't yet found the opportunity – or words, or courage – to explain the plan to him, and her

The Midnight Secret

nerves pitched. What if he said no? Defying him, even arguing with him, was impossible to consider.

They were almost outside now, and she could feel the cool night breeze whickering past the doorframe, peering in like a curious cat but not quite able to curl inside. She felt clammy and a little dizzy, for reasons other than the heat, and she needed to gulp down some fresh air.

'Norman. Jayne,' the minister said, shaking Norman's hand and nodding his head at her. 'I trust you found comfort in the sermon? You were in the forefront of my mind when I was making my selection about leaving our loved one—'

'Aye, thank ye. Keep us in your prayers, Reverend,' Norman said briskly; he had a way of saying the right thing and yet somehow undercutting it too. Jayne knew it suited him to have someone to pray on his behalf. He had never been a natural churchgoer and he had resented the power the minister had wielded over their island community; but like the factor's, the minister's power was now on the wane here. As of tomorrow, he would no longer be the guardian of their souls.

'Thank you, Reverend,' Jayne said, smiling apologetically for her husband's curt manner as he stepped past the churchman without further ceremony or thanks. 'It was good of you to remember us on such a momentous occasion.'

'One might argue this evacuation is all but happening in Molly's name, and of course your loss is still fresh . . .'

Raw was a better word, she thought, still smiling politely.

'. . . I know it shall be difficult for you to leave her behind.'

'Aye, but we'll carry her with us in our hearts,' Jayne said quietly, squeezing her hands to suppress the tingles. She felt a shadow pass over her.

'Honour her memory through good deeds. I know you will, Jayne.'

'I'll try,' she said, stepping out into the night. Though it was only just past nine, the days were already growing short and the stars were beginning to peep above them, distant galaxies winking in a white haze. The tide was out and the curlew moon threw a silver shadow onto the water.

Norman had already gone ahead, oblivious to her absence at his side. Ahead of him she saw Effie's father, Robert Gillies, limping along the street with his brother Hamish, and it struck her that although she and many of the villagers were leaving behind the dead, some would be parted from the living too. The Gillies brothers had spent their entire lives – fifty years or more – never more than thirty yards apart. But tomorrow, when the majority of the islanders disembarked at Lochaline, Hamish and his family, along with Donald and Mary McKinnon, would continue on to Oban, further down the coast. The rupture was already beneath their feet, the first tremors beginning to be felt.

Many of the villagers were already halfway back up the street now, their voices carrying over the hiss of the sea sinking into the sand. She could see the youngsters – having dodged around legs in the kirk – were now tearing over the grassy path and jumping onto the low stone wall, knowing tonight was no ordinary night. Ahead of them, Lorna was standing by the door of the McKinnons' cottage, watching the villagers heading back. Was there any further news on the baby?

She looked for Donald, wondering if he had seen the nurse too, but she caught sight of him peeling away from the crowd instead and heading somewhere with a determined look. She watched as he strode over to where Effie was standing; she was in conversation with someone hidden by the coffin cleit – only, conversation wasn't the right word. Argument looked more like it. She was standing rigid, her arm outstretched,

The Midnight Secret

though she was pulling back, and it was only dropped as Donald made his fierce approach.

Jayne stared as hot words were exchanged between them briefly, before Donald took Effie away from the confrontation with a black-eyed look. But he didn't see Effie turn back and nod to the other person, reluctantly though almost conspiratorially too.

Jayne frowned, confused by the encounter, and as she passed by the coffin cleit a few moments later, she glanced over to her right and saw Frank leaning against the stones.

Another shadow passed over her, her heart quickening as indistinct images surfaced – or were they memories? She looked again at the islanders walking back towards their cottages for the last time: Donald hastening Effie away; Effie's furtive look back; Lorna standing in the McKinnons' doorway . . . Jayne had a sense that nothing was quite as it seemed.

Only that players were already moving into position, and that the ending had begun.

Every cottage door was open, amber lights blazing through the windows as if the tiny isle was trying to announce itself to the moon, now high in the sky. They were approaching the midnight hour, the sea shushing its lullaby, but though the number of people lingering on the street had finally dwindled away, still voices carried through to outside, as if the villagers were restless and unnerved in their denuded homes. No one knew quite what to do with themselves. All evening Jayne had watched the comings and goings from the rocks, shrouded in the darkness as she knitted socks she didn't need. Waiting.

She had seen Norman and Frank heading up earlier towards the cleits on Ruival, heads together as they strode out; she had watched as the Gillies brothers sat on the street wall, smoking their pipes. Effie had streaked towards the Am Blaid ridge like a white moth, flitting and darting and glancing back as she headed to see her friends in Glen Bay. The curtains had been drawn on Crabbit Mary's bedroom window all evening – the only curtains still up in the village – but Lorna hadn't come again to the doorway; too busy within? And she had seen David kiss his mother on the cheek and slip around to the back; away from the cottages, he was lost to the darkness, but she knew exactly where he was heading. She slowed her stitch rate, knitting several more rows to give him some time alone with Molly before she decided to head back to number two.

She slowly walked the grassy path, barefoot in the moonlight. If she had been in more of a rush, she wouldn't have caught sight of Frank Mathieson's stocky silhouette as he walked along the top of Mullach Bi, backlit by stars, and it stopped her in her tracks as she watched him heading for the ridge. The rush of static came again, flooding through her veins and rooting her to the spot.

It felt so unnatural to know what he did not, the stalled vision of his face, blood, rocks and a rusty knife flashing behind her eyes. It told her only who – not when, where, how or why.

Where was Norman? The question pressed into her consciousness and she swivelled her eyes, locked in a body that could channel but not direct. There was no sign of him that she could see from here, but the island had fallen into an inky immersion with only a narrow strip of lighter sky along the top of the cliffs. He could be anywhere on the moor, walking around on the far side in Glen Bay, or out of sight around Ruival by the Lover's Stone, or meeting up with Frank on the saddle of the Am Blaid ridge.

Or heading back here alone, right now, their work done for the night.

The Midnight Secret

She realized the thought frightened her – not of him catching her gone, but catching her here and stopping her from going at all. A sense of desperation emboldened her now that they were standing in the shadow of their dying hours here.

She ran the rest of the way home, and was grateful to find it still empty. Hurriedly, she left a message on the slate on the table: *I'm at the burial ground if you need me. J.* Beside it, she left a small stack of oatcakes, in case he should be hungry when he returned; she was hopeful that if he did come back, a weary body and full stomach would override any anger at her absence.

Grabbing the knitted bed blanket, she silently crept through the crepuscular pause, past the dyke and circling around to the burial ground gate. The high bowed walls rebounded the worst of the winds and contained within them a distilled silence, almost perfumed in its sweetness. She saw a dark shadow stir as the gate creaked on its hinge.

'It's only me,' she whispered, already recognizing David's lean, nervy silhouette as he pushed himself back up to sitting. She imagined him lying with his cheek on the ground, his tears spilling into the earth that now held his sweetheart.

'I thought you'd changed your mind,' he said in a low voice, watching as she picked her way between the crosses towards him.

'I was waiting on everyone going inside – and staying there. There's a nervy air tonight.' She threw her blanket on the ground and settled herself upon it, on the other side of the domed grave from him.

'But why did you need to wait for them to go inside?'

She gave him a bewildered look. Did he really not see the impropriety? 'Because us, sleeping out here together, isn't exactly . . .' She swallowed. 'Usual.'

A deep flush – of anger, she supposed – rose to his cheeks. 'But we're not . . .'

'Of course we're not,' she said quickly, not wanting to hear the vehemence of the refutation. 'But you know the gossip's mouth is the devil's postbag.' She arranged her skirts, eager for the distraction. It felt impossible to look at him while discussing this. The thought had clearly never occurred to him that she was a married woman. Another man's wife. The thought of 'only Jayne' at the heart of a scandal was probably ludicrous to him.

'So then what did you tell Norman?' he asked after a moment.

She swallowed. 'I didn't. He's still out working, but I left a note saying where he can find me if he needs to.'

'Does he know I'm here too?'

'. . . No.' She felt David's eyes scanning over her, perplexed by her evasiveness. To him she had only ever been Molly's sister-in-law, and even as she had slowly become his unexpected new friend and confidante, he still didn't fully see *her*. She wasn't sure anyone ever had. Her so-called 'gift' kept people at bay, a magnetic field that repelled them whether they realized it or not. 'He's been on a short fuse all week. I'm not looking for reasons to make him lose his temper.' She was well aware of the village's pity for her when Norman's sporadic storming rages saw him move out of the cottage to the byre. No one seemed to have any idea that he was so much worse when he was quiet. 'Did you tell your family you were coming here?'

'Of course.'

'And did you tell them I'd be here too?'

His eyes flickered in her direction and away again. 'Well, actually, no . . . There didn't seem any need to mention it.'

The Midnight Secret

He plucked at the grass as she raised an eyebrow. Neither Christina nor Archie had tempers on them. 'So what's Norman still doing out at this hour anyway?' he asked after a pause.

'Helping the factor.'

'. . . With what?'

She shrugged. 'He says MacLeod is making Mathieson check all the cleits to make sure nothing is left behind.'

'As if anyone is going to want our salted fulmars!' he snorted.

She shrugged again, unable to admit that it suited her this way: Norman being kept busy made for a quieter life for her. She picked a long-stemmed dandelion from the grass and wove it between her fingers; in lieu of her knitting needles to occupy her hands, she needed something else with which to distract her body. She felt heavy and leaden, sure it must be visible in her clumsy movements. The golden shadows were flickering increasingly across her field of vision now, her own private aurora that no one could ever see or even know about. Not even her only true friend.

They were quiet for a few moments. 'Well, we've nothing to hide if he does come here.'

'. . . Norman?'

'Aye. We're doing nothing wrong. I asked you to join me tonight because we both loved Molly.'

'Aye, we did. We *do*. And Norman does too, in his way.'

David's eyes hardened. He would never forgive Norman for keeping him apart from Molly in her final months. They were different beasts, motivated by different values.

'Not the same, though.'

'No,' she agreed.

'You're the only one who understands.' David looked over at her, his elbows slung over his knees, and she felt that spring of panic again at the thought of losing him – this – tomorrow.

They might end up living two miles apart or ten; they had no way of knowing till they got there. 'Jayne, I want you to know that whatever happens—'

But he was stopped in his tracks by a sudden commotion. Someone was running . . . sprinting . . . their breath coming heavily as they flew down the slope, past the cleits and the burial ground. David looked back at Jayne with wide eyes and pressed his finger to his lips as the figure tore past in a whirlwind. From their seated position on the ground, below the curved stone wall, they couldn't be seen; nor could they see who it was darting back through the dyke and into the safe-holding of the village confines again. But Jayne caught sight of a streak of corn-blonde hair above the stones, and she heard the lightness of the footsteps . . .

'Effie,' she whispered, seeing his apprehension. 'She went up earlier to see Flora and Mhairi.'

'Ah.' He looked a little rueful. Had he thought it was Norman? She could have told him her husband would never run so fast, nor sound so desperate, looking for her.

They straightened their backs to peer down the slope towards the small village. They couldn't see the dyke while still seated, it was too close to here, but from this distance the square amber pools of light from the cottages spilled onto the street in a crooked smile. The smile was becoming snaggle-toothed as, one by one, the doors were finally closed and the St Kildans' last night in two thousand years finally yawned.

They watched together as their home was swallowed into darkness and silence. The moonlight shimmered on the mirrored bay, the grassy slope now stripped of its flocks. All around them birds were sleeping in crevices and ledges, whales and seals slipping through the water like inky shadows, but somehow they felt utterly alone. The vista was jet-black

The Midnight Secret

and midnight-blue and silver – but the golden glimmers stole Jayne's peace, robbing the scene of its beauty.

With a frustrated sigh she lay back, pulling the blanket around her. She wanted to be in this moment with David and Molly, but her mind felt untethered from her body, a balloon that kept pulling away.

'What is it?' David asked as she clutched the blanket beneath her chin.

She shook her head. 'Nothing,' she whispered, staring up into the fathomless galaxy of stars and feeling the scale of her solitude. She was exhausted, her body physically spent from the effort it took to channel the energy of the visions.

Beside her, she heard David lie back too and do the same. They blinked in the darkness, the sky seeming to grow brighter with every breath, another world coming alive as their own subsided into slumber.

'. . . You know, Jayne, I disagreed with the minister tonight.'

It was a controversial statement. No one ever disagreed with the minister. 'Which part?' she asked. 'Avoid the evil and it will avoid thee?'

It had been the recurring theme in his polemic. David chuckled lightly.

'I do worry about his worry for our souls. Why does he so terribly fear the worst for us?' she asked.

'Because temptation has never been within reach before.'

But that wasn't wholly true. Jayne knew it had sat upon David and Molly's shoulders when they hid, kissing, in her box room; she knew that it had danced around Flora as her fiancé once secretly landed his seaplane in the northern bay; and she had seen how Effie had thrilled in the earl's son's grip as he had taught her to swim. Other villagers would have had their temptations, too – some secrets were better kept than others, but temptation was everywhere. Even on a rock in the Atlantic.

'So what did you disagree with, then?' she asked.

'It was when he was speaking of the final judgement, saying our bodies, being united to Christ upon death, will rest in their graves till the Resurrection.'

'You disagreed with that?' It was a fundamental tenet of Presbyterianism.

'Aye. I believe our spirit does separate from our bodies at the moment of our deaths – but not that it goes to God. It goes . . . somewhere out there.' His gaze roamed the skies as if searching for Molly's face. 'Where else could a countless number of souls reside but in infinity?'

Jayne blinked, understanding in a flash. David had spent the past few months trying to stay with Molly here; it made the thought of leaving her here unbearable. Abandonment in its truest form. But if her spirit was up there, then it wouldn't matter where he was in the world, he would always be able to look for her.

'You could be right.'

She heard his hair rustle against the ground as he turned to look at her. 'Do you really think that or are you just humouring me?'

'When have I ever humoured you?'

There was a pause, then another rustle as he stared at the stars again. 'It makes better sense to me.'

'And it comforts me,' she replied. 'To think we could still be with her, wherever we are.'

'Aye.'

A golden flash dazzled her, blinding her suddenly, and she closed her eyes tightly, knowing the moment must be drawing close now. She turned onto her side, facing him, giving a

The Midnight Secret

shiver as she pulled the blanket tighter around her shoulders. Clear skies always turned chilly at night.

'Cold?' he asked, lifting his head to see her better.

'I'm all right,' she murmured. 'Just tired.' She placed a hand on the grassy dome that lay between them, as if patting Molly.

'Goodnight, then,' she heard David say as he too turned inwards, his own hand reaching out and accidentally covering hers. 'Sorry.' He pulled it away sharply, positioning it somewhere else instead.

Jayne stared into the darkness, jolted momentarily by the unexpected touch. His hand was warm and rough, not as large as Norman's, nor as cruel, and she realized she couldn't remember the last time anyone other than her husband had touched her hand. Her arm. Her hair . . . Any part of her, in fact.

She wished he would cover her hand with his again, the both of them covering Molly and protecting her. They were here to lie with her in companionship, after all – so why was it Jayne who felt so alone? She didn't want to sleep. She knew there would never come another night like this, when she could lie under the stars and talk to her friend; her nights were so very different. She wanted to stay awake all night, to search for Molly in the stars until the sun broke cover. Was that what David wanted too? She had thought she heard regret in his voice as he wished her goodnight . . . But she was subject to forces he couldn't possibly understand, and her eyelids fluttered heavily, dragging her under and away from this, into a place of darkness.

The sound had been indistinct – a stone rolled out of position on the ground, perhaps; a distant dog's bark or a stray bird squabbling on a ledge. But something had woken her.

Jayne sat up slowly, her entire body leaden as if she had

woken into dreamland. Was she, in fact, still sleeping? She looked around, disoriented. David was still lying on his side, his arm slung over the grassy grave like a strap, the blanket twisted at his waist, sharing an intimacy in sleep that had never been afforded to him when Molly was alive.

Another sound came, this one more like a grunt, and she got to her knees just in time to peer over the wall and see a figure heading down the slopes towards the village. It was difficult to see clearly before they slipped through the dyke and were almost hidden from view again; she could make out only a head and shoulders. But the houndstooth check of a lambing shawl seemed distinctive as the figure crept past a window before turning out of sight.

Jayne sank back onto her heels, trying to make the connection, but the fugue was still heavy upon her and she slowly sank back to the ground, the grass rising up in a soft embrace.

Whispers, so quiet by day, could slice through the night like knives, and if her eyes were closed, her ears were open. Jayne stirred again, sitting up in a trance. The moon had moved its position slightly on the water; David had rolled onto his back. This was the same act as before, but a different scene. How much time had passed? It was after midnight, she knew that.

The whispers came again, and she tried to rouse herself more fully to escape the delirium that had her pinned between worlds. Her body moved clumsily, her balance off as she got to her knees in time to see two figures moving through the narrow gap in the dyke. Both heads were bent with concentration, but one of the figures was propping up the other. Were they injured? Could she help? She must help . . .

But she couldn't move, her limbs as useless as if the bones had been snapped.

The Midnight Secret

No. The protest, strong in her mind, made no register in her throat and she felt her heart rate quicken as the terrible vision flashed through her mind and stayed there. Surely this was it now? Fate had swung its mortal blade, and she was free of the bonds that had captured her these past few days?

But her eyelids fluttered again and she felt herself slump, still caught after all. She was like a fish in a net, hoping to be thrown free, but instinct telling her there was worse still to come.

Heavy breathing. Just air upon air, the clash of hot breath into the cool as the dark night lengthened and stretched. She could tell they had entered the dead of night now, and Jayne swayed, her body moving by rote as she got to her knees, peering over the wall back down to the village and waiting for the next figure on the stage.

But the sound that came next was behind her. She was looking the wrong way. Staggering around, her skirt catching under her knees, she turned and looked up the slope to find a figure heading for the ridge. Arms swinging, they would have marched right past her and David here. Had they peered in and glimpsed them hugging the grave? Or did they believe themselves to be fully alone in the witching hour? No witches here . . . ?

Jayne watched the figure stride strong and solid over the grass, instantly recognizable even though it was also . . . inexplicable. She frowned in her half-wakened trance. It made no sense to her.

But then, it didn't need to. She was given images, not narratives. She was only a witness, not a judge.

The figure disappeared into the shadowy moor and she felt the darkness engulf her once again, her head hanging as she placed her hands on the grass and sank back into oblivion.

It was all over, finally. Or about to be.

Chapter Three

'Jayne?' She felt pressure on her shoulder, a warmth on her chilled, dewy skin. 'Jayne, wake up.'

Her eyelids fluttered open and she had to squint as the brightness of the dawn fell upon her face. David was crouched beside her, moving slightly so that his shadow covered her, his dark hair falling forward as he smiled down. 'It's time. They're here.'

'. . . Who?' For a moment she felt befuddled; the visions often left her drained afterwards.

'The Royal Navy,' he chuckled.

'Oh. Of course.' She felt foolish, as lethargic as if she'd drunk a sleeping potion. Lorna had many remedies in her medical bag and had given one to Norman to calm him after Molly's death; when he had woken the next morning, he too had been in a stupor. It had taken him several minutes to remember what had happened – and Jayne's role in it.

'Look.'

She sat up slowly. David was pointing to the huge ship now dropping its whaler in the bay. The scale of it stunned her: masts and rigging both fore and aft, a giant smokestack and several decks. How could something so huge move so silently?

'So then it's real,' she murmured. 'They actually did it. We're leaving here.'

The Midnight Secret

David swallowed, his gaze falling to her and then the grassy grave beside her. 'Aye.' He rocked back on his heels for a moment, hugging his knees contemplatively, before he rose to standing, holding out his hand for her. She gripped it tightly as he pulled her up and they stared out to sea together, seeing the naval men in their white ducks moving on the deck as a rowing boat was lowered down to the water.

In the village, people were stirring. Jayne saw Old Fin step out of his cottage in his long johns and lean with his hands on the wall, watching intently. She wondered whether he had slept at all. It was no secret he had wanted to stay.

Jayne looked for the sun's position in the sky and calculated the time to be no later than five. She had had maybe four hours' sleep. Interrupted, of course. Murky images rose from her muddied mind.

David glanced at her. 'We should probably get back.'

'Aye, before . . .' Before anyone notices, she had been going to say. Even though they had nothing to hide. They had come here for Molly.

She realized she was still holding his hand, or he hers, and she pulled away. David stepped back, watching as she bent to retrieve her blanket, but her gaze fell to the grave and she sank to her knees with a sudden rush of emotion, pressing her palms to the grassy mound.

'I love you, Moll,' she whispered desperately. 'I'll never forget you. I promise I'll always look for you in the stars.' She bent forward and lightly kissed the hand-painted cross. 'I'll keep you with me, sister.'

She closed her eyes and said a silent prayer before she pulled back, looking up and seeing tears in David's eyes. She stood again, clutching her blanket in one hand as she pressed the other to his arm. 'I'll go.'

He looked panicked. 'Why? You don't need to.'

'Aye, David. You should say your goodbyes in private.' She could see the pain in his eyes; this was going to be harder for him than he had anticipated, but she knew he had to say goodbye in his own way, without the worry of being watched. 'Take your time. We've several hours here yet.' The *Dunara Castle* had already left with the majority of their belongings, but all the beds would be coming back with them on the HMS *Harebell*. 'I'll see you back down there.'

She walked away, feeling his eyes on her back. She knew he wanted her to stay, that there was comfort in company. But today wasn't going to be easy for anyone, and in her own best interests she had to get back before Norman woke. The thought of his anger at finding her out all night chilled her blood, and her mind raced as she walked back quickly towards her home. Perhaps if she was in the kitchen when he awoke, she could make him believe she'd come in late and slept beside him after all?

She slipped through the narrow opening in the dyke and headed left, past the backs of the cottages, just as she had come. It would be best to stay hidden from sight till she could put down her blanket; she didn't want people to guess she had slept out.

She was passing Donald and Mary McKinnon's cottage when an unmistakable sound stopped her dead – the mewl of a newborn.

Mary had had her baby?

Her mouth dropped open as she realized this was either very good news or very bad: if Lorna had come calling for Jayne in the middle of the night, needing extra hands for wet towels, fresh sheets, sustenance, then Norman would know that she hadn't come home. On the other hand, if Lorna hadn't

The Midnight Secret

come by – or at least, if she'd called *before* Norman had returned – Jayne could tell him she had been here with the other women all night.

It would be a bald-faced lie to her husband and she didn't like it, but she could do it; she was used to keeping secrets.

She moved quickly, hearing voices beginning to drift as more and more people stepped out. She went round the far end of her own cottage, holding the blanket at her back and slipping in through the front door, unnoticed. Everyone's eyes were upon the ship.

She let the latch drop and stood for a moment in the bare croft, her body straining for clues as to her husband's whereabouts. She had long ago learned to keep her back to the wall.

No sound came from the bedroom, and as her eyes travelled she could see the slate and the oatcakes still out, exactly as she'd left them. They were untouched. With a frown, she moved further into the room and saw that the bedroom door was wide open, the bed sheets tucked in and unrumpled.

Norman hadn't come home either? *He'd* been out all night?

If she was confused, she still didn't hesitate. She knew opportunity when it came knocking and he would be back at any moment now. She rubbed the message from the slate and ran into the bedroom, stripping the bed of its sheets and folding them down into a final bundle.

Her heart pounded with relief. There was nothing now to indicate her own absence from the marital bed, and even better, she wouldn't have to lie about it. He wouldn't ask after her final night here.

She plucked a few stray grass stems from the blanket and carefully placed it with the sheets, thinking of David still sitting with Molly as the sun steadily rose into a peerless blue sky. They, at least, were getting to have a proper goodbye;

but for her . . . ? She looked around at the four stone walls of the bedroom. There had been precious little joy here and certainly never any love.

She dropped the linen bundle on the front step and walked out without looking back, going to stand with her neighbours by the wall. The sun was at their backs as they watched the sailors row across the bay. Coming for them . . . The dogs, of course, were barking on the beach. They had always been St Kilda's first line of defence.

She cast her gaze around for a sighting of her husband, but he was still nowhere to be seen. Her eyes rose up to Mullach Bi where she had last seen the factor striding out alone. The men had been separated by then, but that didn't mean they hadn't met up again minutes later, or even hours. She felt an anxious tightening in her gut as to what it all might mean when the vision had been clear this time.

Norman hadn't come home. What had he been doing all night?

She looked away sharply, pushing the thoughts down. He wouldn't do such a thing, she told herself. For all his faults, he wasn't capable of *that*, surely?

But her body was on high alert – heart pounding, nausea rising in her throat. She knew what her neighbours did not. She had seen the rage that gleamed in the back of Norman's eyes some nights. He wasn't a man to be crossed.

She looked over at Ian MacKinnon, Angus and Fin; at Hamish and Neil Gillies, Archie MacQueen. What would they do to Norman if she shared her fears?

And if she was wrong, what would Norman to do to her? Last night had been a delirium, swirling with confused images and imaginings. What had been real and what a dream? No one yet knew that tragedy had even struck.

The Midnight Secret

She took a deep breath, trying to steady herself. She was allowing her fears to get the better of her. She would not think about what lay on the other side of that ridge, and she would not sound the alarm. She must keep to herself, as she always had.

But for someone who hadn't wanted to leave here, suddenly escape couldn't come soon enough.

It was thirty minutes past the seventh hour and the last of the furniture had been loaded. The cottages had been locked, the front steps swept and Bibles left open on the surfaces that remained. The younger children, mothers and elders were already on board, and Jayne stood on the jetty awaiting her turn.

Beside her, David, Fin MacKinnon and Neil Gillies stood as silent as statues, their wet trousers dripping onto the stone. Drowning the dogs had been a distressing but necessary final chore. The islanders hadn't the means to pay for the dog licences that were obligatory on the mainland, and without any natural prey on the isles for the dogs to hunt, the only mercy available had been to kill them quickly.

Jayne could see from the anguished looks on all three of the men's faces that they wouldn't forget it quickly.

'Effie Gillies!'

Robert's voice resounded around the glen. From here Effie was but a bright spot on the bluffs, but even at this distance, they could see how she clutched Poppit tightly to her as Angus MacKinnon and Hamish Gillies began to climb the cliffs. There could be no exceptions. Not even for the girl whose dog was family, her most constant companion – the only friend she had known this past summer, with Mhairi and Flora in the other glen and the earl's son long gone over the horizon.

'Miss?'

Jayne looked down to find the sailors had moored next to the jetty again, one of them holding out a hand to help her down.

She glanced back at Mullach Mor, then at the three young men she had known her whole life. 'But Norman—' she protested.

'Is coming. Stop fretting. There's no one wants to get away from here more than him,' Neil said.

She knew he was right on that score at least. Norman had finally made an appearance an hour earlier, striding along the street and manhandling Mr Bonner, claiming he had found him 'hiding out' in one of the cleits. The reporter had protested he had merely been 'exploring' the isle, but Norman had been adamant he found him crouched in the far end, trying to stay hidden and out of the light.

Quite why the reporter should want to do that, Norman couldn't explain. He would have been risking his life. With all their paltry crops lifted from the ground and the livestock removed to the mainland, there was nothing left here to sustain a man – not unless he could crag a cliff like the St Kildans, and from the look of his shiny leather shoes and coat, that didn't seem likely. The *Dunara Castle* was scheduled to make a tourist trip several days after the evacuation to what they were now touting as 'the ghost isle' but it was entirely weather dependent; there were no guarantees of a sailing, and therefore, of rescue.

Mr Bonner had been dispatched back to HMS *Harebell* with the first of the bed deliveries and Norman had gone off again, seeming to forget he had a wife. He didn't come back to their cottage for a 'last look' and he hadn't offered any explanation for his absence last night. Jayne had caught pitying looks

The Midnight Secret

between Mad Annie and Old Fin as he'd headed round the back and disappeared once more, but that wasn't what bothered her. His rage at the reporter had been disconcerting. Her husband clearly wasn't himself.

'Miss,' the sailor said again.

Jayne accepted his help and stepped carefully into the boat. It frightened her, going out on the water. She couldn't swim, and it was usually only the men who rowed out into the bay to the visiting ships. Jayne herself had only stepped foot off St Kildan rock once, when she was a child and her father had allowed her to join them on a row for the postbag.

The three men, well versed in jumping into the smack and the wallowy feeling of bobbing on the waves, leapt in after her. She gripped the sides as the boat rocked, swallowing down a gasp and unable to understand why none of them were terrified. Fin and Neil were positioned right in front of her, David beyond them, his gaze pinned back to shore. She knew it wasn't Effie he was staring at as the sailors released the tethering rope and they began to row towards the ship.

The children on board were either gathered at the bow rails or running around the bulkheads as the mothers clustered together, talking intently. Mr Bonner was standing apart, his gaze fixed firmly upon the drama unfolding on shore. Would he write about it in his newspaper report? What had he been hoping to achieve by staying back here?

'Welcome aboard,' a naval man said as they drew alongside the stern. Jayne was disembarked first. She only realized her hands were shaking when the sailor took them to steady her as she stepped on deck.

Ma Peg was singing a lament, Mad Annie puffing on her pipe and looking back at her home through slitted eyes. Jayne caught sight of Mhairi and Flora sitting together and talking in whispers, as if they had been separated the entire summer and not in fact sequestered together. She supposed they had grown even closer during that time. It was hard not to think once more of Molly, left behind now in every way possible.

Automatically, she looked around to see where David had gone. Drowning the dogs would have been a terrible duty for him when he had such a gentle nature. She found him at the far end of the deck, his hands gripping the bow rail as he stared back to land, and she turned in his direction.

A piercing scream tore suddenly into the sky.

Everyone paused their singing, talking, playing as the scream was followed by more. The sound was heartrending.

'Oh my goodness! Who—?' Rachel gasped.

'What was that?' Christina asked. But they knew it could only have come from Effie.

The villagers rushed to the side of the ship, looking for a sighting of her. Every pair of eyes scanned the bottom of the cliffs, finding no trace of her anywhere, even though both Angus MacKinnon and Hamish Gillies could be seen still scrambling up the bluffs.

Rachel and Big Mary looked at one another in horror. Had their son and husband, charging up the cliffs after her, provoked a fatal error in Effie? A desperate leap? Effie had been guarding her dog with her life. They all knew she would never give Poppit up.

For several minutes no one spoke as they tried to make sense of what was happening back on shore.

Jayne felt a hand on her shoulder and looked over to see Flora had come to stand beside her. The young woman was pale beneath her sunburnt skin, her eyes puffy and red-rimmed with tears. Jayne didn't know if she was crying for her lost lover, for leaving here, or out of fear over Effie's fate. But she

The Midnight Secret

took Flora's hand and squeezed it, trying to reassure her as they looked back towards the Ruival cliffs again.

Angus and Hamish were getting to their feet now, the bluff scaled, but there was movement to their right and Jayne could make out another two figures: just pale dots against the grass, coming down the slopes. Effie's bright hair shone like glinting glass in the sunlight. From her lurching gait, it was clear she was being dragged along.

It was a moment before Jayne noticed Poppit was nowhere to be seen. Effie's shadow, she was usually never more than a few feet away from her mistress.

Jayne felt her stomach drop as she realized the reason for the scream – and the reason Flora had come over to console *her*. Angus and Hamish had been too far away to have been involved. Norman was the only one other person left on the isle who would have done what had to be done.

Her husband had never been a sentimental man. But she couldn't say he wasn't also a bad one.

The last of the villagers climbed aboard just before eight o'clock, the crew swinging into action as the whaler was slowly winched up and the smokestack began to puff. Big Mary had taken up singing the lament now, but the passengers were otherwise silent, every set of eyes trained upon Effie as she walked barefoot, without her shadow.

Instinctively Jayne's hand went out as she passed. 'Effie, I'm so sorry.'

The girl looked at her, but her eyes were blank. She was hollowed out with shock. She had lost too many that she loved recently and the pain sat upon her like a gauze veil.

Jayne's hand fell back. What good was her apology when she was married to the man who had done this to Effie?

Without a word, Effie staggered over to where Flora was sitting and the two young women collapsed into each other like folded petals, just as Flora and Mhairi had done earlier. Jayne felt not just Molly's exclusion from the three girls' close bond, but her own too. She sat apart from everyone – too old for the girls but too young (and childless) to fall in with the mothers.

'So there y'are,' Norman muttered, coming to sit beside her as if she was the one who had been missing all night and almost all morning. As if he hadn't just committed an act of atrocious cruelty.

It took her a moment to find her voice. 'Did you finish what you were doing?' she asked, seeing the dark expression he still wore. He was outwardly composed but she knew him too well; his spirit was agitated.

He gave a small grunt. 'Well enough.'

'That's good then,' she said lightly. 'We can leave with no regrets.'

Norman looked down at her but she had turned away. The anchor chain was rattling loudly, the sailors running through their drills, the vibration of the engines beginning to hum beneath their feet as they powered up. There was a collective pull of tension as the St Kildans realized the moment was finally, truly here.

They were leaving. They were really going.

Everyone rose and looked back to shore as slowly the ship began to pivot, pushing away huge volumes of water that rolled in waves to crash upon their beach. It was impossible to believe that the cottages now stood empty, the chimneys cold, the cleits cleared. Jayne's gaze rose over the slopes, cliffs, moors and crags they knew so well, the birds flying in their thousands overhead, as yet unaware that all this was now theirs.

The Midnight Secret

From this vantage point, the islanders could finally see how very small their home truly was. A two-mile-long rock in the Atlantic, unable to bear crops or trees and surrounded on almost all sides by precipitous sea cliffs, had somehow sustained human life since the Bronze Age.

Until today.

None of them knew what they were sailing towards. Norman was dreaming of riches and position, but all Jayne wanted was security: close neighbours and a good friend nearby. For the first time she was facing the prospect of living truly alone with her husband – and it terrified her.

She looked around, seeing how every islander was lost in their own thoughts. David still stood alone, his eyes trained upon the distinctive oval wall of the burial ground; Flora was weeping silently as the wind rippled her dark hair, Effie shell-shocked beside her; Lorna was below deck with the McKinnons, helping them adjust to life as new parents. Celebrations for the baby's overnight birth had had to be largely 'postponed', although with the new family travelling on in the minority to Oban, it was unlikely anything would come of it. The villagers' salutary visits to the McKinnon cottage following the birth, just after midnight, would have to suffice.

To her relief, no one had asked Jayne where she had been, just as none of them seemingly noticed the glaring absence in their midst. Frank Mathieson hadn't been seen all day, and she alone knew why. Of course, everyone was highly distracted, she knew that – there were several decks on the ship, so the islanders were scattered, or *could* be, if they so chose. The drama with Effie and Poppit had diverted attention too, and the high emotion as they pulled away was driving everyone into introspection. They weren't thinking about what they couldn't see. Not yet, anyway.

But Norman, who hadn't let the man out of his sights for the past few days, hadn't uttered Mathieson's name once. And he was gripping the bow rail with blanched knuckles, his gaze trained on a distant spot, out of sight. She watched his finger tap-tap-tap impatiently on the chrome until the giant anchor finally burst out of the water like a whale's tail and they all felt the ship come free, untethered now from the island's last grasp. The rudders shifted, the vessel gaining traction as they began to splice through the bay.

She watched her husband's hands loosen their grip, becoming relaxed at last, and she stole a horrified glance at his beautiful, brooding profile. She already knew he had blood on his hands this morning from his altercation with the reporter, his casual violence towards Poppit . . . But more than that?

She stared at the open horizon where their future lay, with one question on her mind.

What exactly was her husband capable of?

Chapter Four

EFFIE

Three months later – early December 1930

Dupplin Castle, Perthshire

'Why can't we do *Private Lives*?' Bitsy Cameron complained from her stretched-out position on the four-poster bed. Her toenails were painted scarlet, vivid even through her stockings, and she didn't care that a button on her silk blouse was missing, flashing a slice of pale stomach. 'Everyone in London says it's a riot.'

'God, I miss London,' Peony Lovat sighed, looking bored and beautiful.

'We're not doing a Noël Coward when I've spent the past week writing this *especially* for us,' Veronica Maudsley replied without looking up, biting her lip as she scribbled an amendment at the dressing table. 'Wait till you hear the punchlines to the jokes. I managed to put one in about Gerry's shooting accident with the peacock.'

'Old hat,' Peony sighed. 'I don't know why we have to do a play at all.'

'Well, it's either rehearse for this or stand as peg dollies in the mud all week.' Veronica's pointed look at the mention of mud made Peony turn away with a shudder.

Effie stood at the window, watching the driving rain pound into the ground like glass bullets and wishing she could be standing in it. She offered no comment on their choice of activities as she looked out at the grounds; she was more preoccupied with the realization that these castles all began to seem very alike after a while. Turrets, grand staircases, draughty rooms, formal gardens criss-crossed with ornamental parterres . . . This was their third in as many weeks.

News of their engagement had spread like wildfire since Sholto had returned from Dumfries House with his parents' blessing – Effie had remained in Oban with Mhairi and Donald for an extra day – and, ever since, they had been on what could only be described as a celebratory tour, staying with his friends. He was keen for her to meet everyone, he said, but she sensed something more below the surface: he wanted her to be accepted. He knew as well as she did that the match would be controversial – a point proved by the fact they had received invitations from seemingly every duke's son in the country, as everyone clamoured to see the woman who had bedazzled one of Scotland's most eligible bachelors.

Effie lived in perpetual fear of disappointing them. She wasn't a dazzling beauty of Flora's order; indeed, her hair was always tangled, and she didn't see the point in putting powder on her face. It was her effervescent, indomitable spirit that Sholto had fallen in love with, but girlish stubbornness and defiance didn't play so well in country-house drawing rooms, and she could feel herself becoming tamed. She was quickly learning that it was better to remain quiet and reserved in company. Saying the wrong thing, even just the wrong *word*, marked her as an outsider, which was difficult when these people did so love to talk.

She had always thought Rachel and Christina could blether, but the women here seemed to live for gossip. Scandal was the highlight of their day, and no one gossiped more than the girls in this room. They had greeted her like an old friend with kisses on the cheek, showering her with compliments, but Effie knew heightened good manners were the aristocrats' armour: their smiles were bulletproof, and cool gazes quenched inner rage. She knew her every move was being studied, stored and filed for future reference.

Still, Bitsy, Peony and Veronica couldn't talk behind her back while she was sitting directly opposite them, and their days here had acquired a certain louche rhythm: rising late, a cooked breakfast, followed by the men going outdoors for some sporting pursuit while the women remained indoors, talking, preening and planning the next party.

Distantly, Effie recalled Lorna calling for *more* and *better*. She had assumed that this applied only to the St Kildans, but now she understood that even Sholto's gilded circle wasn't immune to want. In fact, his friends arguably wanted more than she and her friends ever had: finding a 'good' husband (which meant rich, landed and noble) was their primary focus, but while they waited, they were always on the hunt for more fun! More champagne! More parties! More jewels! Novelty seemed to be what they craved most, and she had certainly given them that these past few weeks.

Sholto tried to be reassuring, telling her his friends loved her, that everyone found her a breath of spring air. But he didn't understand how many unspoken rules there were for her to learn. He had been born into this world – he didn't even know he knew what he knew! – whereas she found herself laughing at the wrong things, or else not laughing when she should. She hadn't read the books that had formed their minds, nor could she formulate an opinion on dresses or shoes. In company, Sholto helped shelter her from the worst of her ignorance, standing by her side like a kindly referee; she had a suspicion he had asked the girls to 'look out for her' too, and they were always ostentatiously welcoming in public. But when it was just the ladies alone, as now, hers was an almost silent presence. Like a child, she was seen but not heard.

With relief, she saw the men walking through the grounds, returning early from playing golf as the weather closed in. Sholto had been playing in a pair with their host, Viscount 'Gladly' Dupplin, against Tarquin 'Colly' Colquhoun and Ferg Campbell. Their tweeds were soaked, raindrops dripping off the peaks of their caps, and she wished she could be out there with them instead of in this powder-dry room. She wished her puppies could be here with her instead of remaining back with her father. She wished many things that weren't possible. She watched until they walked into the lee of the castle, disappearing from view.

Veronica looked up at Peony with an earnest expression. 'I say, does that piper play the trumpet?'

'Why are you asking me?' Peony pouted, a defensive flush springing to her cheeks. 'You know, you really shouldn't believe everything you hear, Veronica!'

'I'd have him whipped and shot if I could.' Bitsy rolled her eyes. 'Every single morning! It's insufferable.'

'Hmm, it would just have so much more . . . *gusto* if we came on in the first act to the trumpet . . .' Veronica thought hard for a moment. 'I shall ask Gladly if we can borrow him for the show. Although bagpipes could work too.'

The Midnight Secret

Effie watched as they all talked at, but not to, one another.

Veronica scribbled something down in the margin of the top page. 'I think this will suffice for a first draft,' she said, pushing back her chair and handing out the typed scripts.

'What's it about?' Peony asked, flicking through the pages without bothering to read them.

'Think *Swan Lake* meets *A Farewell to Arms*,' Veronica said after a moment's pause.

Bitsy's eyes narrowed. Neither reference meant anything to Effie, of course, but Bitsy was sharp of mind as well as sharp of tongue, and Effie was learning the nuance of most things by observing her waspish wit. 'A princess disguised as a swan falls in love with her lover's friend?'

Veronica gave a small huff. 'No swans, but lots of doomed romance. It's a story of love and betrayal during a time of war.'

'Oh well, that story's *never* been told before—'

'But with comedy!' Veronica protested. 'I wanted to keep it light-hearted.'

'Good idea. Important to laugh through the mustard gas.'

Peony giggled as Veronica threw a velvet cushion at Bitsy. Bitsy gasped and threw one back, her eyes wide. Within moments, a pillow fight had erupted; even Peony was roused from her languor to take part. Feathers and sheets of paper danced through the air. Effie watched, open-mouthed and smiling, as the young women jumped on the bed, squealing and laughing, suddenly alive. Were they really so very different from Flora, Mhairi and Molly? Their dresses were finer, the surroundings grander, but at heart, weren't they also carefree young women waiting for their lives to start? It felt like the first spontaneous thing she'd seen them do.

Effie grinned, picking up a cushion on the chair beside her, and threw it at Bitsy – currently straddling Veronica and swiping wildly through the air – with a strong aim. A lifetime of snagging puffins in traps and cragging on sheer cliffs meant she had precise hand-to-eye coordination. The cushion hit her victim square in the face, knocking a tortoiseshell comb from Bitsy's coiffed hair as she fell backwards on the bed, knocking her head on the headboard on the way down.

'Oh!' Effie squirmed as a horrified silence fell upon the room and she realized direct hits were not, in fact, the intention. 'I – I'm so sorry.'

Looks were shared as everyone dropped their weapons. The game was over as suddenly as it had begun. Peony smoothed her dress as Bitsy replaced her hair comb with a look of irritation. Effie had the impression they were checking their tempers with her, holding back the words they always felt quite free to launch at one another as old friends; the fact they didn't, with her, only made her feel more of an outsider.

'Why don't we go downstairs and have a rummage in the dressing-up box?' Veronica said with forced cheer. 'One of the characters needs an opera cape and I seem to recall Gladly had one last year.'

'Who wears an opera cape during a war?' Bitsy muttered, still smoothing her hair as they headed for the door.

Effie trailed after them, feeling chastened, her heart heavy in her chest as they wound down from the tower room to the castle's imposing reception hall. Housemaids in black dresses and white pinafores fluttered like moths along the corridors, always just out of sight, slipping silently behind hidden doors that led back to the servants' quarters. Effie caught herself wishing she could disappear into the innards of the castle too; only a few months ago, she had been a member of 'below stairs' herself. But now, wearing Sholto's engagement ring with a silk blouse and finely tailored woollen trousers, she belonged on this side of the castle walls and she was obliged to follow Bitsy, Veronica and Peony down to the old playroom.

Like all the other rooms in the castle, it was vast. Her old home could easily have fit inside it and still not touched the sides. Floor-to-ceiling shelves lined the walls, with wooden toys as well as books set along them. There was an oak desk and chair, several sagging sofas arranged in small groups, the fireplace unlit. The windows gave onto the east lawn and it was so cold that frost still sat inside the glass.

At the far end, tattered pea-green silk curtains were swagged above a small, low stage. A deep-red velvet Victorian chaise longue stood askew upon it beside a lamp table, left over from the last production. Naively painted panels of a drawing room created a backdrop that didn't seem in keeping with Veronica's plotline. Perhaps she could help paint a new one, Effie wondered. She wasn't entirely hopeless with a paintbrush.

Veronica headed straight for a large domed leather trunk in the corner and opened it with intent; she seemed to know exactly what she was looking for, rifling through piles of old costumes. Then again, this was an annual tradition of theirs, old friends gathering here for the Dupplin house play in the weeks before Christmas.

Bitsy rang the bell. 'It's freezing in here,' she said, shivering.

Peony idly set the stylus on the gramophone and music filled the room. Effie hovered again, unsure where to put herself. She was surrounded by bored women and careless beauty, and she realized again that she had become the girl she'd envisaged that night in the featherstore on St Kilda last spring, when Sholto had entered her life by just a few hours. She would never have believed she'd end up here, nor that if she did, it would feel like this: empty and dull, everything somehow flat. If Flora were here, she would know just the thing to say or do, to somehow bring a sparkle to the group. But Effie had always been a creature of the outdoors, better suited to doing than to talking.

'My ladies,' a maid said, coming into the room and seeing with horror that the fire was laid but unlit. She hurried over and put a match to it, flames leaping into life and enlivening the room.

'That's hardly going to help us now, is it?' Bitsy snapped at the girl. 'It's perishing in here. Why wasn't the fire set hours ago?'

'I'm sorry, m'lady,' the maid stammered. 'We didn't think the room would be used today.'

'Not used today?' Bitsy was incredulous. 'But we always do the show during this week. Everyone knows that. The preparations take days. Are we to rehearse in our furs?'

'I'm so sorry, m'lady. It's my first month here. I didn't know.'

'First and last, if you ask me.'

The maid gasped, horrified at the threat. Effie felt the same. She looked at the others: Peony was leaning against the back of a chair, looking more interested than she had been all day, and Veronica was still kneeling by the dressing-up trunk, trying on a Venetian mask.

'What would the viscount think if I were to tell him of your negligence, hmm? We're his guests! His oldest, dearest friends, and you'd have us shivering and catching our deaths?'

'I'm so sorry, m'lady. Please don't tell him,' the maid beseeched. 'Let me make it right.'

'And how exactly are you going to do that? This room will take at least an hour to heat. That's an hour wasted while we wait around for something you should have done hours ago.'

The Midnight Secret

The girl stared down at her shoes, her face pale, as she awaited sentencing.

There was a long silence as Bitsy regarded her, seeing how she trembled. Her appetite for blood abated as quickly as it had come on. '. . . Oh, don't look so feeble. Bring us some tea,' she said finally. 'At least we might warm our hands around our cups.'

'Yes, m'lady. Straight away.' The maid turned to leave the room.

'. . . But before you go, what is your name?'

The girl swallowed. She was like a mouse caught under Bitsy's sharp claws. 'Matilda.'

'I see.' Bitsy nodded. 'Hurry along then, *Matilda*.'

Effie looked away as the girl scuttled out. She could imagine her running through the passageway in tears, the other servants flocking to learn the cause of her distress. But would they condemn or console her? The below-stairs world was just as much a political maze as this one.

'Here it is!' Veronica's triumphant cry made them all look over as she wrapped a black taffeta cloak around her shoulders and twirled extravagantly. She appeared oblivious to Bitsy's heinous bullying. 'It'll be just perfect.'

'What's the feathery thing there?' Peony asked from her perch, pointing imperiously towards the trunk.

'This?' Veronica pulled out an extravagant ostrich-feather fan, opening it and swatting the air in front of her a few times.

'I hope there's a scene where I can use that?' Peony asked. 'It could make a feature of my eyes.' She held a hand in front of her nose, batting her eyelashes coquettishly.

'I'm not sure.'

Peony raised a perfectly plucked eyebrow. 'Ronnie, if there's scope for an opera cape in your wartime novella, there's scope for a fan.'

Bitsy glanced at Effie, positioned at the window again. 'What are you always looking for out there, Effie?' she queried. 'Devising an exit strategy?'

'Of course not—'

'Come over here,' Bitsy commanded.

Effie reluctantly crossed the room. No one ever said no to Bitsy, it seemed.

'Have you ever had a go on a rocking horse?'

'No.' What little wood ever drifted onto St Kilda's beach had always been put to better use than modelling racehorses.

'Well, now's your chance,' Bitsy smiled, patting the leather saddle on its back.

Effie looked at her in confusion. 'But it's a child's toy.'

'Lucky, then, that you're the size of a twelve-year-old girl. Some of us have big bones and can't share in the fun. Come along, hop on!'

Effie looked at the large black-and-white speckled horse. Its legs sat upon huge wooden bows; it had a long white mane of real hair, glass eyes, and teeth bared in a menacing smile. Effie wasn't sure she'd have gone near it if she were a child.

'Throw a leg over. Don't worry about being ladylike; it's only us girls here, after all. We can have a giggle, can't we?'

It wasn't being ladylike that Effie had a problem with; she simply couldn't understand the attraction of sitting atop this menacing wooden horse. Still, she was never one to show weakness, and she swung easily onto the seat, immediately grabbing the mane as the toy rocked forward, then back, under her weight.

She giggled nervously, catching Bitsy's eye as the other woman pushed her back and forth. 'See? Such fun, isn't it?'

The Midnight Secret

'. . . Aye,' Effie nodded after a moment. 'It is.'

The rhythm was soothing as she rocked back and forth, the fire crackling in the background, music playing through the gramophone, and she felt herself capture, again, another fleeting feeling of contentment in this strange new world in which she found herself. Fun. It could have different definitions, she realized; it wasn't just confined to scaling vertical cliffs.

'Do you ride, Effie?' Peony asked, watching from one of the sofas she had collapsed into. She always seemed perpetually exhausted, as if being upright, or awake, taxed her body.

'No,' Effie said, shaking her head.

'Oh?' Peony gave a small frown. 'That's odd, I was sure I heard you did. Didn't you, Bits?'

'Mm, yes, now you mention it,' Bitsy replied.

Effie felt her stomach pitch. She had been on a horse only once in her life and, but for the grace of God, it might have killed her. Lady Sibyl, Sholto's former fiancée, had pulled her mount into a full gallop across the Dumfries estate, knowing full well she was a novice. Sholto had been furious, and it had taken Effie hours to recover from the shakes, but there was no way they could know about that . . . Not unless someone had told them. Sholto had no reason to mention it, but . . .

Oh, God. Were these women friends of Sibyl's? The scandal of Sholto calling off his engagement to her in the summer had been reignited when word spread of his engagement to Effie instead, but Sholto had assured her it was old news, that no one would call sides. And yet . . .

'A little more?' Bitsy asked, pushing her a little harder. The pendulum swing increased, the horse tipping right to the very edges of the front and back bows.

Effie gave another squeal, but the delight had gone now, and she shook her head. Just a little harder and she would topple over, crashing face first into the table.

'Oh, yes, it's great fun!'

'No, I'd rather not—'

'Where's your spirit of adventure?' Bitsy laughed. 'I'll just give you one more push.'

'No! No, please!' Effie cried as Bitsy pushed harder anyway. She pulled back as the horse bowed forward to the very tip of the rails, falling back on her climbing skills and using her weight to counterbalance and reduce the dip.

'I say! What's going on in here?' a male voice asked loudly, interrupting them all. Effie's head turned towards the door – Gladly was standing there, Sholto coming in on his heel with a concerned look – but the movement of her body must have spun the toy on the wooden floor, because there was a sudden, splintering scream in her ear that made her jolt.

Effie turned back with a gasp to find Bitsy now thrown on the ground, clutching her foot.

'Bits!' Peony yelped, leaping from the chair and running towards her.

'My toes! She's broken my toes!' Bitsy sobbed.

'Let me see!' Peony demanded, slipping the shoe from her friend's foot. Already, through the silk stockings, Bitsy's pretty painted toes were swelling. 'Oh, you beast!' she cried, looking back at Effie. 'She's wretched! How could you do this to her? And after you hit her in the face, too! What's come over you, Effie?'

'I . . .' Effie stared back at her, appalled by this misrepresentation of events.

'You hit her in the face?' Gladly asked with a disbelieving

The Midnight Secret

tone. He hurried over to where Bitsy lay on the ground, weeping.

Effie looked at Sholto, seeing his expression change, a flush of embarrassment coming into his cheeks. '. . . I can explain,' she whispered.

There was a moment's silence, and in it she saw the gulf between them that he kept saying they could bridge. He blinked it away in the next instant.

'Of course you can. It was clearly an accident,' he said hurriedly, coming over and drawing her into him as she slid off the horse. He kissed her hair as they watched the others help Bitsy into the chair and Gladly examined her wounds.

'Well, I'm no doctor, but I've seen my fair share of crushed feet in the owners' enclosures. I don't think they're broken,' he smiled reassuringly. 'But you'll have a nasty bruise for a few days.'

'It was entirely our fault,' Sholto said. 'Barging in like that without knocking. We distracted you.'

Effie looked up at him, grateful for his tactful rescue but also hating that she needed rescuing at all. She was used to conflict and drama back home – usually with the men saying she couldn't do what they did – but here, she couldn't advocate for herself; it wasn't seemly. Sholto had to endorse her, defend her, protect her. Her word didn't count.

'Where are the others?' Peony asked.

'Drying off. It's raining buckets out there. The greens are turning into blues.'

Peony frowned. 'Hmm?'

'Rivers. Lakes, old girl,' Gladly said, getting up. 'Anyway, we came here to let you know Albie's invited us to Blair for cocktails this evening. Some Hollywood types have turned up unexpectedly and he needs to give them a show. I trust that will please you all?'

Peony and Bitsy both straightened up with looks of immediate interest.

'When you say a show—' Veronica piped up.

'Not that sort,' Peony snapped.

'Who's Albie?' Effie asked Sholto quietly.

'Son of the Duke of Atholl. Good sort, likes to fish,' he said distractedly, looking down at her with concern. 'Was everything all right just now, before we came in?' he murmured. 'I thought I heard you calling out. You sounded distressed.'

'No, I was fine,' Effie nodded, feeling the lie catch in her chest. But what else could she say? It would only worry him to hear that she'd detected real anger in Bitsy's actions. Had it only been retaliation for Effie hitting her in the pillow fight, or something else? Did Bitsy resent Effie for snagging Sholto because she was a commoner and he was such a prize? Or because he was a man who had once been betrothed to her friend?

They all knew each other, this set, moving between country houses and castles as easily as Effie had once wandered up and down the street in Village Bay; the only difference was scale. Perth, Edinburgh, Oxford, London . . . it didn't really matter, everyone was connected on their glittering, golden web. And Effie couldn't help but feel she was the fly, caught in the middle of it all.

Chapter Five

White turrets, a flag flying, a piper sounding into the night as the cars rolled up to the castle doors . . . These were the things Effie noticed as she slid down from her seat, slippery in the buttermilk satin gown Veronica had loaned her for the evening.

Sholto gave her his hand, so handsome in black tie dress – *titum*, he'd called it – and led her, with the others, inside. The entrance hall was panelled in oak, with a dazzling display of armoury on the double-height walls; colours hung from the gallery, a sixteen-pointer staring down at all visitors. Effie tried not to look impressed, following Peony and Bitsy's lead as they carelessly breezed through, but muskets, broadswords, targes and dirks arranged in symmetrical, geometric displays weren't usual where she came from. Her head followed where her gaze travelled: up, down and all around.

Sholto squeezed her hand, calming her nerves, as they passed through the corridors under the silent, watchful gaze of Atholl ancestors. She knew that for his sake she had to fit in.

'Hmm? The sixty-eight drawing room?' Gladly murmured with mild surprise as they were led on and on towards a room in the south wing. 'We don't usually get taken to the grand rooms.'

'Albie must really be putting on a show,' Colly drawled.

Effie couldn't imagine what, here, could possibly pass as *not* grand, but there was no time to comment as they were ushered inside.

'Ah, Gladly, you made it!' said a tall, pale man, breaking away from a group of four others standing before the vast oak fireplace. He looked visibly relieved to see them. 'Chaps, this is Gilbert Hay, the old chum I was telling you about. He lives down the road at Dupplin.'

'Why does he call you Gladly?' one of the men asked, pumping Gladly's hand vigorously.

'You'll see,' Albie smiled as Peony and Bitsy, who had taken extra care with their appearance tonight, sailed forward. 'Ladies, allow me to introduce Charlie Buck and Jimmy Cripshank, friends from the grand old U S of A. And also some pals from closer to home, Eddie Rushton and Archie Baird-Hamilton. Gents, Lady Bettina Cameron, Lady Peony Lovat, Miss Veronica Maudsley and—' Albie's gaze fell on Effie. 'I don't believe I've yet had the honour.'

'Miss Euphemia Gillies,' Sholto said, with a proprietorial hand upon Effie's waist that none of the men missed. 'My fiancée.'

Albie took her hand and lightly the kissed the back of it. 'Miss Gillies, I've heard wonderful things. A pleasure.'

'How do you do?' she smiled. He had kind eyes, which wasn't true of everyone she'd met; many seemed to hide guile behind manners, grit beneath polish.

'A pleasure to make your acquaintance, Miss Gillies,' Archie Baird-Hamilton said beside him. He was very tall, taller even than Sholto, with film-idol looks: brown hair, a chin cleft, deeply tanned but with freckles on the bridge of his nose. As with all the men in their group, he had an air of bemusement about him. Privilege, it seemed to Effie, bred a sort of softness into them; they didn't need to fight or struggle for what they had. But she caught a glint of something sharper in his eyes too.

The Midnight Secret

The girls already seemed to know Archie well, kissing him with bored familiarity, their eyes fixed firmly upon the international visitors. The men were all briskly shaking hands, but the Americans had a looseness to them which was at odds with the Scots' upright, almost military bearing.

'Colquhoun,' Tarquin said. 'Call me Colly.'

'Campbell,' Ferg nodded, openly regarding the Americans with suspicion. Their teeth were white, their smiles bright, and both Peony and Bitsy looked dazzled.

'Albie says you're in Hollywood?' Veronica asked as a cocktail was placed in her hand.

'Yes, but strictly behind the scenes, I'm afraid,' Cripshank replied.

'You're producers?' Colly asked.

Cripshank nodded. 'People think that it's glamorous, but ninety-nine per cent of the job is spent in meetings trying to secure finance.'

'But the other one per cent? Do you ever get to go on set?' asked Peony, who looked breathtaking in violet silk.

Cripshank's eyes settled upon her like a hand on a pelt. 'Of course.'

'Have you met Chaplin?'

'Indeed.'

'Is he a riot?'

'Surprisingly not.'

'How about Claudette Colbert?' Bitsy asked. 'Do you know her?'

'Sweet Claudie? I was the one who got her the deal at Paramount.'

'You did?' Peony breathed. 'She's so beautiful.'

'Sure,' he shrugged. 'The camera loves her, there's no denying it.'

'Do I sense a *but*?' Bitsy pounced.

'Not at all.'

Her smile was instantly coquettish. Confiding. 'Come now, Mr Cripshank, you're among friends.'

'Fine,' he shrugged, happy to be convinced. 'She's a swell girl and she photographs like a dream, but in person . . . Well, all I'm saying is, she's not a patch on you gals.'

Ferg Campbell's eyes narrowed in outright disdain as Peony gave a delighted laugh. 'You're just saying that!' she demurred.

'Absolutely not—'

'I'm a scriptwriter, actually,' Veronica butted in. 'Well, a writer . . . Playwright, really.'

'Is that so?' Buck asked, looking bemused at the abrupt turn in conversation. Veronica had little patience for flirting, mainly because no one ever flirted with her.

'Yes – we're putting on a production at Dupplin this week, in fact. You should come along.'

Peony gasped, although whether in delight or horror at the prospect wasn't immediately clear. Effie was too distracted to pay much attention. She was struggling to sip her martini without choking, for one thing; and she couldn't stop looking at the blond man, Rushton, standing laconically with one hand in his pocket. He seemed familiar to her somehow, and yet she couldn't place him. She'd met so many people in the past month – faces, castles, parties – they were becoming a blur. And he wasn't giving her much to go on; after the polite introductions he had fallen back, allowing the others to shine.

'Well, what's it about, this production of yours?' Buck asked.

'*Don't* ask!' Bitsy said quickly, rolling her eyes as she sipped her drink. 'I say, have you seen *Private Lives*?'

'Of course. We caught it while we were in London the other week. Terrifically novel premise . . . Have you?'

The Midnight Secret

'No, not yet. I'm *dying* to see it,' she sighed. 'I've been stuck here for eternity, it's beginning to feel.'

'It must be terrible, being held captive in these ancient Scottish castles,' Cripshank teased.

'Scah-ttish,' she mimicked, turning her attention to him now. 'You know, your accent is perfectly darling.'

'I might say the same about yours, Lady Cameron.'

She arched a plucked eyebrow. 'Bitsy, please. Tripping over titles is such a bore.'

'Bitsy, then.'

Effie watched their loaded sparring at a remove. Bitsy and Peony had very different tactics of seduction, but the results were always the same: men chased after them at every party they attended, and the day afterwards was always spent in deep discussion about the relative merits of their conquests. If Effie's own happy ending had been dependent upon her playing these games, she knew she would have been alone her whole life. She spoke as straight as an arrow – and as sharply too, when required.

The group gradually began to break up, the Americans luring Peony and Bitsy into conversation while Veronica, Colly and Campbell made small talk with Archie Baird-Hamilton and the reluctant Englishman, Rushton.

Albie turned towards Effie and Sholto with a look of relief, pulling a silk handkerchief from his breast pocket and mopping his brow.

'Everything all right, old boy?' Sholto murmured.

'Let's just say it's been a long few days,' Albie said under his breath. 'Keeping them entertained has proved . . . taxing. I had rather thought we'd be diverting ourselves along the lines of a fish from the river, a staff from the wood and a deer from the mountain.'

'But they have a different idea of fun?'

Albie made a low sound in his throat that Effie assumed to be agreement. 'B-H got here for support this morning, but even he's struggled to keep his game face on.'

Effie glanced over at the man in question. He was standing with a half-smile on his lips and his eyes slitted as Veronica opined on something, but detecting her stare, he glanced over.

Effie looked quickly away again.

'How much longer are they staying for?' Sholto was asking.

'Another few days.'

'So much for speeding the parting guest.'

'Yes, well – if everything comes off in the way I hope, it'll all be worthwhile.'

'Meaning?'

'They might be interested in hiring us—'

'Us?' Sholto frowned.

'The estate. As a location for several of their films. They think they have three pictures in the pipeline we could be suitable for.'

'I see.' The slight northward shooting of Sholto's eyebrows betrayed his surprise.

Albie pulled an apologetic face. 'Well, you know how it is, old bean, what with upkeep and taxes. The rates they're offering are not to be sniffed at.'

'Indeed,' Sholto nodded sympathetically.

'You know, you're both speaking almost without moving your mouths,' Effie observed with a wry smile, looking between the two of them.

'Boarding school, dear lady,' Albie grinned, openly smiling back at her. 'Survival takes many forms.'

'Oh, Effie knows all about survival,' Sholto said. 'We're in the presence of greatness in that regard.'

'Really? What is your great survival skill, Miss Gillies?'

Effie looked at Sholto, not sure that he would want her to

The Midnight Secret

reveal here, in polite company, that she could scale a cliff and wring a bird's neck. Had the conversation taken a wrong turn?

But he smiled back, waiting.

She looked back at their host and saw that he seemed genuinely interested. Could she really reveal something of her true self to him? It had seemed to her that being in 'company' meant doing the reverse.

'Well, I'm from St Kilda, you see. So I . . . I'm used to a more difficult way of life.'

'St Kilda, indeed?' Albie exclaimed jovially. 'I've heard a lot about the St Kildans in the past few months. More, I think, than in the rest of my life combined. I keep reading about you all in the papers! There's been the bother with that whatnot fellow of MacLeod's?' He clicked his fingers as he looked at Sholto, trying to recall the name.

Effie saw her fiancé's jaw tighten, as it always did when Frank Mathieson was referenced. He could only remember what the factor had tried to do to her, and not what had been done unto him. His anger was such that Effie was sure Sholto would have killed the man himself if someone hadn't beaten him to it. 'Aye, that's right,' she said quickly, knowing she had to divert the conversation in another direction. 'And I'm told the evacuation was reported as far away as—'

'I say! Did I just hear someone say St Kilda?' Charlie Buck called over, his neck craned with interest.

'Yes, Miss Gillies here is from the isle,' Albie said back.

'Is she, indeed?' Cripshank asked, sauntering over. Buck followed in his wake. 'Well, now, isn't that interesting?'

Was it? Effie looked at them blankly.

'Miss Gillies was just about to tell me her special survival skill,' Albie said, seeming pleased to have garnered the Americans' attention.

'Well, I . . . it's just that I . . .' She looked at Sholto again, still unsure he wanted her to reveal all this, especially as now everyone in the room was listening in. 'I suppose you could say I can climb pretty well.'

'How well?' Cripshank asked, his eyes gleaming with delight.

'Pretty well.' She knew better than to boast here.

'Could you . . . could you climb this castle?'

'Aye.'

'Without ropes?'

'Aye, but I never would. That was a rule back home. There's still a chance to save yourself if you slip on a rope. No man ever caught a cliff.'

The men's gazes travelled over her in disbelief. Her blonde hair had been brushed – not primped and set like Peony and Bitsy's, but it was smooth and shiny, like the satin dress that skimmed her body and highlighted her lithe figure. She looked more like a doll than a daredevil.

'You know,' Buck said. 'I believe you, Miss Gillies, of course I do – but to see it . . . I would pay good money to see that.'

'Well, if . . .' Albie began, his eyes bright.

'No,' Sholto said sharply, before clearing his throat. '. . . It's hardly the evening for it. We're not in our scrubs, after all.'

Effie glanced at the other women, who were regarding her with disdain. She had taken the men's attention *and* openly revealed her inferior roots – she knew it was doubly unforgivable. She glanced at Baird-Hamilton to see if he was appalled too, but his expression was inscrutable.

'Well, what were the chances of that, eh, Rushton?' Buck asked. 'Two St Kildans in the space of a month!'

'Two?' Effie looked between them, confused.

'Yes, we met one of your compatriots a few weeks back.'

'You did?' She caught Buck shooting a look towards Rushton.

The Midnight Secret

He was biting his lip as if holding back from breaking into laughter, but the amusement faded as he caught her eye.

Faint recognition flickered between them, a current not quite connecting.

'Yes, but their, uh, *survival skills* were quite different to yours,' Rushton said, breaking his silence at last. 'Far less . . . how can I put it delicately? Far less honourable.'

Effie felt heat ripple through her body. Who, that she had known, could possibly be regarded as dishonourable?

'What a sweet patootie, though,' Cripshank said, shaking his head in apparent disbelief at the memory. 'I've never set eyes on a finer-looking woman.'

Peony bridled at the comment, taking a step back and lifting her chin in the air. Immediately, Effie knew who it was they had met.

'Flora?' She looked between the men for confirmation. 'You met Flora?'

'Oh, you know her?' Cripshank asked, surprised.

Was he joking? 'Of course I know her. We were only thirty-six in number when we left home.'

'Ah yes, of course – the evacuation. What a crying shame all that was,' Cripshank said, shaking his head. 'We met her in Paris last month, right as she had everything laid out in front of her! The city was hers for the taking.'

'The city?' Buck pooh-poohed. 'Hollywood! And then the world! We were clamouring to sign her up! With a face like hers—'

'And the voice too, yes?' Albie interjected excitedly. 'I read about her show over there! The producer, George Pepperly, is an old mucker of my father's.' He looked at Sholto. 'Glasgow man. You must have crossed paths?'

Sholto gave a small shrug. 'I can't say it rings a bell.'

'What happened to her?' Veronica asked, looking rapt.

'She threw it all away. Just like that.' Cripshank clicked his fingers. 'Left the show high and dry! One night we were having dinner with her at Maxim's, making plans for a golden future in the movies. The next morning we're told she'd left the city and hightailed it back across the Channel with some swell.'

'Well, I wouldn't call him that, exactly,' Buck argued. 'Didn't you say he was a Boy Scout adventuring type, just back from some expedition?' he asked Rushton.

'*James?*' Effie gasped, recognizing the description immediately. 'He's *alive?*'

She couldn't believe what she was hearing. It was Flora's greatest wish come true! She couldn't imagine how her friend must be feeling. Their correspondence had been patchy in recent weeks; Flora had been so busy with the show and their only contact had been a telephone call from Paris; Flora had been in a fluster, wanting to know about Crabbit Mary fleeing to Canada with the baby . . . She remembered a man with an English accent had come onto the line to say Flora would call back, before the line had gone dead. Had that been James?

'It was you,' Rushton said, breaking Effie's train of thought. He was regarding her with a look of recognition. 'At the picnic on St Kilda.'

Memories stirred, shifting heavily like hibernating beasts, as Effie realized they had met before. The previous summer, he and James, his friend, had dropped anchor in Village Bay. James had paid Effie for a climbing lesson, and they had inadvertently interrupted Rushton's romantic picnic with Flora. Of course, with hindsight, she understood there had been nothing accidental about it; James had declared his love for Flora before they left – causing a terrible rift with his childhood friend – but he had remained undeterred, returning to the isle to propose just a few weeks later. Effie had scarcely paid either one of them any mind at the time, though. And of course, she herself now looked nothing like the tearaway in trousers who had scampered up and down the cliffs.

Everything had changed in the intervening fifteen months. Little wonder recollections were sketchy.

'What did you mean when you said her survival skills were less honourable?' she asked, her attention snagging on the more recent past. 'There's nothing wrong with singing.'

'Oh, of course not,' Rushton smiled, before qualifying, 'That is, clearly no lady would ever set foot on a stage' – he looked for, and found, agreement from Bitsy and Peony – 'and certainly not in the costumes *she* was wearing.' He cast them an apologetic look. 'But a life in showbiz isn't necessarily *infra dig* these days,' he shrugged, casual with the barbs. 'In fact, Hollywood has brought about a glamour that is positively aspirational, thanks to our friends here . . .' Both Cripshank and Buck grew an inch taller at this. 'So we certainly can't begrudge her that. I think we can all agree that with her face, she would have been foolish *not* to capitalize on it.'

Effie felt her blood begin to heat as she waited for his point, her animal instincts prickling, picking up a scent on the wind.

'No, what I was referring to was her unfortunate propensity to fall on her back for the first rich man to look her way. Not to be indelicate, but if that was what she was after, she could have done a lot better than Callaghan.'

Everyone – even Bitsy and Peony – looked startled by this sudden, casual cruelty, denigrating both Effie's friend and his own. Albie looked as if he was going to pass out.

'James Callaghan is a far better man than you!' Effie said in a low voice, holding back her temper, even though it was being buffeted by his taunts like a balloon in the wind. 'You're just saying that because she chose him over you. They were engaged! She loves him!'

'Does she really?'

'Aye, she does!'

'Eff . . .' she heard Sholto murmur, a blush of embarrassment in his voice.

But Rushton shook his head, a mocking smile on his lips. 'Then why was she standing in my Paris apartment a few short weeks ago wearing nothing but her negligée?'

Veronica yelped at the implied impropriety as Effie froze, her mind racing. Flora – in a negligée – in his Paris apartment? Was that true? She wanted to be loyal, but she couldn't say for certain that it wasn't. Flora loved James, Effie knew that, but she also knew her friend had supposed James dead. And she had been alone in Paris, with a man who had once courted her . . . Flora had never made any secret of her ambitions to marry up in this world.

'Now see here!' Colly said sharply, taking a step towards Rushton – but Effie was quicker. Her arm shot out before she could stop it, throwing her martini all over him.

There was another collective gasp, followed by a frozen silence as Rushton was forced to dry his face with the sleeve of his dinner jacket. At last the tension was broken by the sound of chuckling and Effie saw Baird-Hamilton smiling into his drink, amused rather than appalled.

Rushton looked furiously at him and then back at her, and Effie realized she was shaking. Horror at what she had done caught up with her. She'd lost control and revealed her true self – a wild creature, totally unsuited to polite society.

She couldn't bear to look at Sholto and see the mortification on his face. Out of the corner of her eye, she saw him set down his glass. Her cheeks flamed as she waited for him to speak.

'Good aim, darling,' he said, taking her empty glass from her and setting that down too before clasping her hand in his. Effie knew he could feel her trembling because his grip tightened in unspoken support. She risked a look up at him. His eyes were locked on Rushton's in silent challenge, daring the other man to pass another inflammatory comment. Just one. But none came. Everyone in the room knew Sholto outranked him.

Finally, Sholto turned to his friends. 'I say,' he asked Gladly, 'would you mind your driver running us back to Dupplin? I think we'll call it a night.'

Gladly smiled. 'Gladly, old fruit. Gladly.'

It was freezing outside as they waited for the car to be brought round. An owl hooted from the shadows of a nearby oak. Effie paced on the stone step, her hands balling into fists as her mind frantically replayed the disastrous events – Flora slandered; Effie herself losing her temper and confirming the women's worst opinions of her; Sholto forced to leave his friend's party . . . Oh God, had she done for Albie's financial hopes too? Would the Americans reject him outright now and take their splashy fees with them?

'Eff.'

She shook her head as she continued to pace, her despair growing with every passing minute. This would spread like wildfire through Sholto's far-flung set. Peony and Bitsy lived for scandal, and Effie had just handed one to them on a plate.

'Effie, stop.' Sholto placed his hands upon her shoulders, forcing her to look at him. 'What that man said in there was unacceptable about any woman, much less one of your dearest friends. If you hadn't thrown your drink over him, *I* would have, do you hear? . . . You've done nothing wrong.'

'Haven't I? *I* don't have the luxury of misbehaving, Sholto. People already expect the worst of me—'

'No one thinks that!' he protested. 'My friends are modern and liberal-minded. They take you as they find you.'

'When you're around, maybe,' she muttered, looking away.

'What does that mean?' He frowned. 'Has someone said something to you?'

'No.' Effie tried to turn away, but he held her gently in place.

'Was it Bitsy?' he pressed. 'I knew something was up between you earlier. Tell me what she did.'

'Nothing. It was just me getting it wrong.'

'Getting what wrong?'

She sighed, meeting his loving gaze. 'I thought the point of a pillow fight was to hit one another – but in fact you have to sort of *pretend* to hit one another.' A small frown creased her brow. 'And I don't know how to throw something with a bad aim.'

A smile curved his lips as he smoothed away her frown with his thumb. 'Your excellent aim is one of the many things I love about you.'

'No it's not,' she protested as he pulled her closer into him, protecting her from the wind.

'Yes, it is – albeit second to my love of your climbing ability. I had fallen for you before you even landed in the boat.'

Effie remembered the day she had raced Angus MacKinnon down the sea cliffs, launching herself into the smack with a reckless abandon that belied the fact she could not swim. She had been at her most feral, wild and free – and most herself.

He kissed the top of her head. 'For the avoidance of your many doubts, I'm glad you're not like the girls in there, Effie. Life with you is going to be infinitely more varied and exciting.'

The Midnight Secret

She looked up at him. He was an eternal optimist. 'Perhaps, but at what cost to you?'

'Effie—'

'I know – you think everyone's like you. You think they must love me because you do. But when they hear about tonight – me, a wildling in a castle, throwing drinks over a gentleman—'

'He was no gentleman!'

'But you know how it looks,' she persisted. 'Tonight I'll have lived down to their expectations. And what if it gets back to your parents? They might change their minds about me.'

Sholto's face fell at the prospect. '. . . That's not going to happen,' he said in a strangled voice. 'Besides, you're ignoring the context, Effie. I would have done exactly the same in your position, and anyone who dares bring it up with me will learn in short order that as far as I'm concerned, your actions tonight spoke to your character, defending your friend's good name. And you've got me, Gladly, Colly, Campbell and Atholl as witnesses. We'll not hear a word against you – or Flora.'

But Flora had already had her first taste of the dark side of fame. Not so long ago, *The Times* had run a headline – courtesy of Mr Bonner again – linking Paris's newest cabaret sensation with the murder scandal back on St Kilda. People assumed that was why Flora had vanished, leaving the show in the lurch. But in light of what she now knew about James's return and Flora's frantic phone call about Mary that night, Effie had to wonder . . . were they in pursuit of their child?

Sholto's chauffeur stopped the car in front of the steps and opened the door. Sholto handed Effie in before walking round to the other side.

'You know,' he said, settling himself as the driver pulled them away, 'we could just elope.'

Effie's head whirled at the suggestion. '. . . What?'

'Yes. We could run off to Gretna Green and do it right this minute. No one will be able to judge you once you're my wife. You'll be able to stop fretting, and we can begin to live our lives together properly.'

'But we already are, aren't we?' she asked him, reaching for his hand and admiring his handsome face in the moonlight. 'You said you wanted me to meet all your friends before the wedding.'

'Yes, but . . . you've met so many of them now as it is, and really, what does it matter what any of them think? *I* don't care! I just want you to be my wife once and for all.'

Effie laid her head upon his shoulder and sighed. 'Well, apart from the horror of robbing Bitsy and Peony of a grand wedding,' she deadpanned, 'surely your parents would be disappointed if we ran off to Gretna in the middle of the night? No mother should be denied the chance to see her son stand at the altar, especially when he's one of the scions of Scotland. Not to mention, they might hold *me* responsible for stealing you away like that. And what a start that would be to our life together! It would be like marrying under a curse.'

A small silence blossomed. '. . . You're right, of course,' he said finally, kissing her hair. 'I just want you to be mine, that's all.'

'I'm already yours,' she smiled up at him. 'But as you're so impatient, let's at least set a date.'

He cupped her face, kissing her gently. 'We will. But you're right. Let's stick to the plan and get through the rest of the Grand Tour first.' He widened his eyes jokingly at their nickname for their prolonged jaunt through Scotland. 'I must learn to be a patient man.'

'And I must learn to be a lady,' Effie murmured into the darkness. 'Starting tomorrow.'

Chapter Six

FLORA

Early December 1930

RMS *Empress of Britain*, **Atlantic Ocean**

'There you are. I was about to send out a Man Overboard call.' James bent and kissed Flora's forehead, his lips warm against her chilled skin.

Flora looked up at him from her huddled position in a deckchair, reaching for his hand and clasping it to her cheek as he sat beside her with a worried look. She was wrapped in the black coat they had bought her in Paris, her chin nuzzled into the plush fur collar, but she still wasn't warm enough. It was bitterly cold out here, on the top deck. Most of their fellow passengers were sheltering in their suites and she knew she ought to be doing the same, but she'd had an unstoppable urge to feel the wind and fresh air on her face. She had adapted quite easily to a life of riches, but a life spent indoors was more challenging.

She didn't know how long she'd been sitting up here alone, her gaze locked on the horizon. For almost a week it had been an unrelenting grey line; now they were in sight of land once more, and she couldn't tear her eyes away from it. Her earthly happiness lay somewhere in that indistinct grey smudge, and it was all she could do to sit out the final minutes until they docked there.

They had crossed an entire ocean at twenty-four knots – an impressive speed, but still nowhere near fast enough. By Flora's calculations, they were twenty-one days behind Mary. James had only shown himself alive ten days ago, but in that time they had left Paris, travelled back to England, headed straight to Southampton and now been at sea for five days. They hadn't wasted a single minute since they had learned of Mary and Lorna's emigration to Canada, and yet time was dragging with iron hooks. With every hour that passed, those two women were taking Flora and James's son deeper into the unknown. Wee Callum – she would never call him Struan, the name she had heard Mary give him aboard the HMS *Harebell* – was barely twelve weeks old, and already he was in a foreign country without his parents.

How could she ever have thought she could live without him? Paris had been a delirium, a dizzying whirlwind, exactly as she had hoped: Flora's every waking moment had been caught up with rehearsing and putting on the show. There hadn't been a second to think, much less feel. But here, in the languid splendour of the ocean liner, all she could do was lie around and think, sit and wait – and it was torture. She could scarcely sleep, and when she did, she always awoke with a gasp, her heart racing and the sound of a newborn's cries ringing in her ears. Her arms ached to hold him; her milk had long since dried up, but she felt still his heaviness in her womb, a footprint upon her soul.

James kept telling her they would make up the difference once they docked, that Mary and Lorna's head start would

The Midnight Secret

fall back once the realities of the immigration process kicked in. Third-class passengers had a far longer wait than first-class, for one thing; for another, the Depression had hit Canada particularly hard, and the authorities weren't accepting just anyone over their borders now. Not to mention that with a newborn to care for they would need to find lodgings, food, milk for the baby . . . Being on the road with a newborn would make them slow and conspicuous, he reassured her – Flora and James would catch them. But Flora was still terrified. How were they going to find two women and a baby in a city of 130,000 people? In a country of ten million? Canada was vast – they might go anywhere, change their names . . . The only advantage she could see was that Mary and Lorna had no idea they were being pursued.

'I've been looking all over for you.'

'I needed some air,' she apologized, seeing the worry in his eyes.

'Well, you've come to the right place,' he said with his usual dry humour.

The wind was growing ever more quarrelsome as they headed for land, and James shivered. He tried to hide it from her, of course; he was used to the cold after a winter spent on the tundra in Greenland. But he was wearing only his towelling robe, his dark hair still wet and slicked back after a swim in the pool.

'Let's go back to the room,' she said, swinging her legs off the deckchair, knowing he would stay here for as long as she did.

'You're quite sure? I'm happy to take some air.'

'Yes, I hadn't realized how cold I'd become . . . How was your swim?' she asked instead, threading her hand through his arm and clutching it tightly, pressing her cheek to his arm as they strolled along the deck: her in fur, him barefoot in his robe. One of the many things Flora could never have imagined when she lived on St Kilda was a swimming pool on board an ocean liner.

James gave a small groan. 'Unproductive. Digby Tucker arrived after three laps.'

'Again?'

'It's as if he's tipping the staff to keep him abreast of my whereabouts. Wherever I go, there he is. He's like a bad penny.'

'Oh no.' Digby Tucker and his wife, Mallory, were seated at their dinner table with the captain, and it was one of the other reasons Flora was so desperate to get off this ship. Tucker – 'a big noise in the shipping business', according to their new friend Dickie Grainger – clearly considered himself charming, but he was just a little too loud, his jokes a little too risqué for James's taste, and he always stared at Flora for a little too long. Mallory Tucker, by contrast, was almost silent and mealy-mouthed, permanently sipping gin cocktails – and she dripped with diamonds 'by day', which James had panned as *de trop*.

'Mm. He was bending my ear again about investing in the company. Says he wants to diversify.'

She squeezed his arm consolingly. News of James's transatlantic air-mapping expedition had spread fast, and everyone wanted in on the new venture. With a route now confirmed between Britain and Canada, aeroplanes were being touted as the future of commercial travel; even liners with swimming pools wouldn't be able to compete. 'Well, thank God we're almost ashore, and then we'll never have to see him again.'

They had reached the door and he opened it for her, allowing her to step through. Immediately the wind was denied access, whipping past with a howl, the air inside warm and comforting as they went down the stairs. Flora smoothed her black hair, aware she must look like a wild thing, but James reached for her and pulled her into him, stealing a kiss in the empty stairwell. 'You look beautiful,' he whispered.

Their ardour for one another was constant, a heat others could feel. She often caught envious looks from people who passed them on deck or in the dining room, her hand on his arm. She could tell there was a curiosity about them, the handsome couple who, unlike other first-class passengers, didn't spend their days socializing in the lounges or splashing in the pool. They were elusive, preferring to stay sequestered in their suite.

They had told their fellow guests they were honeymooners, and it wasn't exactly a lie – just what James called a 'scheduling issue'. They were engaged, of course, but he had registered them for the voyage as Mr and Mrs Callaghan for propriety's sake; and, although their mad rush to get here had allowed no time for a wedding ceremony, they had shared a private moment in Paris when he had slipped a thin gold band onto her finger with the words: 'With this ring, I *will* thee wed.' They would marry the first chance they had, but they also knew their time together as a couple was finite; once they brought their son home, life would change yet again into a different form, and they would be a family. To all intents and purposes, this was their honeymoon, even if it was cart before horse.

They talked endlessly into the night and through each day, sharing every detail of their lives during the year they had been separated. Mostly, Flora talked and James listened. There was a lot for him to learn about her secret pregnancy, Mary's lies and Lorna's duplicity. Flora knew she would never forget the look on his face that night in Paris, when he had discovered in the same breath that they'd had a son and then lost him. The circumstances that had forced her to give up their baby had been complex, indelibly intertwined with the fates and actions of others. James wanted to know about every conversation, every argument that had transpired between the St Kildans in his absence: Mhairi and Donald's illicit love affair, Mary's cold rage, Lorna's cunning, Frank Mathieson's murder. Anything that might yet impede the success of their mission.

The sound of a door opening just around the corner made them pull apart, but Flora saw the gleam in James's eye and knew they wouldn't be talking when they got back to their room. He took her hand and led on, turning onto their corridor.

James slid his key in the door and Flora's eyes ran dispassionately over the opulent decor as she entered: silk-covered chairs in the sitting room, a satin eiderdown on the bed, crystal glasses, fresh flowers in the vases . . . That was something she still couldn't understand – how were the staff producing new bouquets after five days at sea? But she didn't care enough to find out. The extravagant lifestyle that had, once upon a time, back in St Kilda, held her in its thrall now offered no comfort. All she wanted was her family reunited.

She unbuttoned her coat and draped it over a chair to reveal the deep berry crepe dress they had also bought in Paris before their hasty flight from the city. It had a belt at the waist, epaulettes at the shoulders and a silk lining that slipped over her skin as she moved. She turned to find James already moving towards her with a hungry look. Losing themselves in one another was one way to escape their pain, if only for a while . . .

A low, deep groan rumbled through the belly of the ship, stopping him in his tracks.

'What was that?' she asked, unused to the vagaries of transatlantic travel.

The Midnight Secret

They both instinctively turned to the windows, but from this vantage point there was nothing to see but grey skies over a grey sea.

'Are we . . . slowing down?' she asked, following James as he crossed over for a better look.

Outside the glass, the horizon held steady. Terrible storms had blighted central Europe, but here, further west, the weather had been on their side and the crossing had been uneventful.

'I'm not sure. Possibly,' he murmured. 'It does take these things several miles to stop, although . . . I don't see the tugs.' He stepped out onto the balcony, but returned moments later; there was nothing to see. 'I thought we were still a good few hours away from port.' He tightened the belt on his robe again. 'I'll go and find the steward. Ask what's going on.'

His hand was already on the doorknob when a crackle came through the speakers that were set into the ceilings throughout the ship.

'Ladies and gentlemen, this is your captain speaking.'

His tone was sombre. Flora and James exchanged an apprehensive look. They had dined at the captain's table and knew him to be a pleasant, avuncular man, but there was no lightness in his voice now.

'With regret, I must tell you that a case of tuberculosis has been confirmed on board by the ship's doctor, and another two cases are suspected.'

There was a pause. Too long. Flora could feel her heart beginning to race.

A heavy sigh whistled down the speakers. *'As tuberculosis is classified as a communicable disease, this means that under maritime law we are required to drop anchor in international waters for a period of thirty days. After this time, we can apply for free pratique to enter port for Quebec City. Until then, I'm sorry to say we may not dock, nor may anyone – under any circumstances – disembark from the ship. I must ask that all passengers remain in their quarters until the stewards have come round with further . . .'*

Flora stumbled back against the chair, her eyes wide with dawning horror. Had he . . . had he said *thirty days*? Anchored in open waters?

No. They were already twenty-one days behind!

She looked at James. Surely he would have a ready reply to this? He was a man of the world, a rich man. She had already seen how very differently things operated for those with money.

But her fiancé was staring back at her with the same expression of shock; his mouth was open, but no words were coming. How could this be happening? Every minute mattered. Their son, their baby boy, was somewhere in that landmass over there. They were so close to him – had they crossed countries, sailed a channel and an ocean to get here, only to fall short with a few miles to go?

Flora tried to find words, but all she could muster was a cry.

Chapter Seven

MHAIRI

Early December 1930

Oban

'You have another battle scar to add to your collection,' Donald murmured, his voice deep against her ear as he stroked her arm in the weak dawn light.

Mhairi stared at the burn – a deep purple slash just above her wrist. 'The cuff machine,' she said.

'Again?'

'It takes some getting used to.' She saw the redness of her palms even after a full night's sleep; her hands were inflamed, sore and cracked even though she had never been shy of hard work. Back home in St Kilda she had stood in the rushing burn in all weathers and scrubbed the linens on the mangle, but this was a different kind of labour, and she had come to the conclusion that industrialization didn't suit her. The first day she had walked into the laundry of the Regent Hotel, her jaw had dropped at the vast machines that automated the women's work: huge presses, rollers, irons and clamps filling the basement, the women standing before them ruddy-cheeked in their white cloth caps and pinafores as hot steam rushed out in plumes.

Still, she was lucky to have the job. Unemployment was on the rise, and she'd been in the right place at the right time, approaching the foreman's door just as one of the women had been let go. They badly needed her wage; once news had spread of Donald's arrest in the investigation into Frank Mathieson's murder, he had lost his job at the printworks. Several weeks had passed in which no one was prepared to take a chance on the suspicious St Kildan, and the two of them had grown increasingly desperate until finally he'd landed a job at the fish market, hauling ice and mending nets. It was something, but his earnings only just covered their rent, and they'd both grown thinner.

His arms, still so strong, tightened around her, his breathing slow as they dozed, savouring these last moments in bed before the harsh demands of the new day imposed themselves. They were together, at least. It wasn't how she'd imagined their happy ending would be as they'd walked out of the police station together, hand in hand, his bail posted and an alibi lodged in his defence, but it was still better than what they'd faced before: living far apart, both of them trapped in desperately unhappy marriages.

Mhairi never allowed herself to think of the future that had once, briefly, glimmered before them: buying a croft and raising their daughter together. They'd had the money, the evacuation was coming – but the dream had died when their baby had failed to draw her first breath . . . Sometimes Mhairi felt the loss like a hammer blow, knocking the breath from her body and making the world swim before her eyes as she remembered the sharp, shocking silence of that July night in Glen Bay. That was when the burns would happen – when her attention was distracted from the hot steel contraptions she operated by a worse hurt.

'We'll try again,' Donald kept promising her. Just as soon as he could get Mary to divorce him and he could make an honest woman of her. But neither of them knew when that would be. Mary had left for Canada with no forwarding address and Mhairi privately feared something that Donald appeared not to have foreseen: that his wife would draw out the entire process, maybe even refuse it altogether. After all, wouldn't it be the ultimate revenge for the spurned wife, to see them both thrown without honour?

She wriggled in his arms, turning around to face him. She cupped his face in her palm, staring into the blue eyes that loved her so. He had made vows before God to love and honour another woman, and this moment – lying in bed with him – was never supposed to have been hers. But no one could tell her it was wrong. She kissed him slowly, feeling his body awaken as their legs intertwined, the bed sheet twisting as they lost themselves in kisses, anchored not in a place, but in one another.

Mhairi fixed the braid, staring back at her reflection in the wall mirror. Her red hair had lost its summer fire, her tanned skin growing dull in the December rain; her body wasn't used to a life spent indoors.

From upstairs she heard the MacGregors shouting, the thump of a boot hitting the wall as she fastened the buttons on her coat and draped the shawl over her head. It was an eight-minute walk to the hotel, but the first two were always the worst. Donald had left an hour earlier to get down to the fish market in time; he had no idea of the gauntlet she ran every morning, and she had no intention of telling him.

She opened the door and looked out into the hall. Muffled voices rose up and down the stairway, a couple breaking into clear-voiced distinction as another door was opened on the floor below and footsteps stomped down the stairs.

Stepping out silently, she listened intently, waiting for the sound of boots to reach the ground floor and then counting – one, two, three . . . The front door of the building slammed shut, her own closing just a half-second after it.

Too late?

She waited, her breath held, before walking as quietly as she could down the stairs. She had learned where the creaks were on the split treads, but she was still unused to heavy boots and not as dextrous as she might have been, scuffing the toe on one of them so that it juddered loudly. She squeezed her eyes shut, bracing . . .

Mhairi turned the corner on the half-landing just as the first door opened, Lizzie MacGyver staring out at her with a hard look. 'Bitch,' she hissed, sending a gob of spit that landed at Mhairi's feet.

Coira Cameron, in the next flat, was already there, her arms folded across her ample bosom as she waited her turn. 'Harlot!'

Mhairi turned her face away, her feet moving faster as she gave up the attempt at stealth. She just needed to get out of here. The catcalls followed her down the stairs and all along the road as she pulled the shawl forward, trying to hide her face. But the names were thrown at her back all the way until she turned the corner.

'Homewrecker!'

'Slut!'

'Whore!'

There was no way to avoid it; the women had learned her routine and knew exactly when she left each morning. They

The Midnight Secret

thought they knew her story too, but there was no use in telling them the truth about Mary fleeing with the baby. It would only rob them of their sport. Her mother had always warned her, every dog sets upon the stranger dog.

Chapter Eight

FLORA

Mid-December 1930

International waters, East Coast Canada

Flora walked into the lounge, feeling eyes settle upon her as she surveyed the room. The faces were all familiar now – every evening she was obliged to socialize and make small talk with them at dinner, and it was always the longest three hours of the day.

She quickly found James seated at a table with Dickie Grainger and Bertie Sykes; the three men had become fast friends and met most afternoons when the wives were resting, to enjoy a gin and tonic over a game of poker. The men's days had come to acquire a rhythm on board a ship going nowhere. Their mornings were spent furiously swimming laps in the pool before lifting weights in the gymnasium; after lunch and a constitutional walk on deck or in the covered promenade when the weather was bad (which was most days), they came to the lounge either to read or play bridge, backgammon or in the younger men's cases, poker. After dinner, they danced to the live jazz band, drank cocktails and regaled the company

The Midnight Secret

with amusing anecdotes. They were all making a good fist of things.

Flora couldn't say the same of her own days. She had no desire to make new friends and she stayed in their suite whenever she could, writing in her diary, sleeping or staring at the wall, counting down the weeks, days, hours and minutes until they could get off this ship. She tried telling herself it could still be so much worse: they could have missed the passage from Southampton altogether and that would have been it for the year, no more transatlantic crossings till the spring. But she wasn't like Mhairi or, bless her soul, dear Molly: she had never been a convincing Pollyanna, and she could think of nothing but getting her son back.

James's face brightened as he saw her making her way towards him – a rare outing – and he pushed his chair back, rising to greet her. Dickie and Bertie did likewise. Flora noticed the Tuckers sitting at the next table – Digby Tucker reading a book, his wife doing some needlepoint embroidery on a hoop. Lurking.

'Flora,' Bertie smiled as James kissed her particularly flushed, cold cheek. 'You look refreshed. Another walk outside?'

His eyes darted to her hair and she realized she must be windswept.

'Aye. I can't be indoors so much.' In truth, it made her feel like a bird in a cage. Even pacing up and down the same straight stretch of deck day after day was enough to drive her mad.

'It's a joy to behold a woman in touch with nature,' Dickie sighed. 'My dear wife catches pneumonia if I so much as crack open the window. A snake could boil to death in our bedroom.'

Mallory Tucker leaned over slightly. 'I don't know how you

manage it, Flora. You must be as tough as old boots to survive the temperatures out there.'

Eyebrows lifted between the men at the interruption.

'Aye, I suppose I must,' Flora agreed. She had quickly decided on submission as the best form of defence while they were all sequestered here together; she had no desire to go into competition with the other women. She didn't debut a new hairstyle each evening, new jewels, nor even new clothes. She emerged simply to eat and then retreated to her room again, as quickly and quietly as she could. She wanted no attention at all, and yet eyes still followed her wherever she went.

'Darling, would you like a drink?' James asked, pulling out a chair for her as they all resettled themselves.

She shook her head. She didn't intend to stay. She had only wanted to see him for a few minutes. Although they shared the same grief, their ways of coping were very different: James needed to keep himself busy while she needed to keep herself small. It was different for her. He had never seen their baby boy's face, nor held him in his arms; he didn't know what it had felt like to walk off a ship and leave him in the arms of another woman, trying to do the right thing when it felt like the very worst . . .

'See any icebergs today?' Bertie asked, catching sight of her frozen expression.

'Not today, no,' she said, pulling herself back. Her sighting a few days earlier of a huge iceberg had caused a flurry of excitement on the upper decks and an unwelcome rush of company for her.

'Any ice floes?'

She sensed he was humouring her. Did they see her as eccentric, scanning the horizon for signs of any further

The Midnight Secret

obstructions to their destination? '. . . I saw a small one, but it was quite a way off.'

'But it was out to sea, yes?' James asked. He was looking at her, reassuring her that it wasn't the sea ice they needed to worry about. They were in another race against time, this one with the risk of being 'locked out' of their destination; they hadn't banked on a quarantine situation when they'd made the desperate dash to catch the final ocean crossing of the year, and now, with every day that passed, the St Lawrence River and estuary where they were due to dock was icing over. One day very soon – today, tomorrow, next week – it was going to become impassable. They could only hope and pray that they would make it through in time.

'Aye,' she nodded.

'Good. Remember, Iceberg Alley isn't our concern just now.' He winked at her, seeing the worry on her face.

'Tell that to the passengers on *Titanic*!' Digby Tucker quipped from behind, making them all startle.

'. . . Indeed.' James swapped looks with Bertie and Dickie.

Flora glanced over at Tucker, watching as he sank back into his book, even though it was patently clear he wasn't reading a word. A satisfied smile sat on his lips and the ceiling lights shone down on his bald head. He had no sense of embarrassment, it seemed to her, intruding on private conversations and butting in where he wasn't wanted. James had taken to referring to him as The Lurker, and Flora dreaded to think what Mad Annie would have made of him – she'd have given him short shrift for sure.

'I suppose the icebergs were two-a-penny for you on your Greenland expedition, weren't they?' Dickie asked James, picking up the conversation again. He had a particularly laconic way of speaking, as if his words were all threaded together on a chain.

'Yes. I would estimate we saw perhaps three hundred out there? But it's still a remarkable spectacle every time: watching them calve, the displacement of the water, the waves . . . The scale is just astounding. Spring's the time to see the action. You ought to take in a tour before heading home, seeing as you're out here already.'

'Mm, yes, sounds super in principle,' Bertie murmured. He rolled his eyes. 'Sadly I don't fancy my chances of talking the Long-Haired General into that particular trip. Her great-aunt was actually on the *Titanic*.'

'*Really?*' Tucker piped up with blatant curiosity.

'Oh dear,' Dickie frowned, ignoring him.

'Quite.'

'There's really nothing to fear,' James shrugged. 'The International Ice Patrol keeps a running tally these days on any and all icebergs that slip south of forty-eight degrees north.'

'International Ice Patrol?' Bertie frowned. 'Never heard of them.'

'It's operated by the US Coast Guard,' James replied. 'But it was set up on behalf of various maritime nations after the *Titanic*. It's explicitly there to safeguard ships from icebergs in the North Atlantic.'

'Ah, well, that may change things,' Bertie said, a little more hopefully.

Dickie cleared his throat. 'Tell me, Cally, seeing as you're the oracle on all things icy – what will happen if the St Lawrence ices up before we can get through? Where shall we go?'

'I should imagine we'll be forced to dock at St John instead,' James replied, glancing in Flora's direction. 'It's the winter shipping port for when the sea ice becomes unnavigable.'

The Midnight Secret

'Where is it?'

'At the mouth of the St John river. New Brunswick.'

'Ah. So quite a way south, then?'

'. . . Yes.' James didn't look happy at having to spell out the worst case scenario in front of her, and she sensed he held back his own fears from her. He put a hand on her knee. 'Don't worry, darling,' he murmured. 'They connected it by rail to Montreal forty years back. It's just a short hop.'

Flora looked back at him with dismay. Connected it might be, but it would be yet another diversion. Getting to Montreal was all she could think about. Montreal, then Quebec – her world was no bigger than that route. It was bad enough that they were sailing right past Quebec City to Montreal as it was. It felt like a cruelty to be within touching distance of the port where Mary and Lorna would have disembarked, but have to go another 150 miles further along. James was adamant they could drive the distance back within an afternoon, but that would mean buying a car – another thing to do! Everything was delay, delay, delay.

'. . . But I'm sure it won't come to that anyway,' James added as reassuringly as he could.

'What's so urgent that you chaps have to get to QC so quickly?' Bertie asked curiously, reaching for his drink.

James shrugged, his hand falling back. 'No urgency. We just want to get settled before the weather closes in.'

'Have you family there?'

James nodded, although it was another moment before he could reply. 'Exactly, yes . . .' he said, his voice suddenly choked. 'You? What are your plans?'

Bertie took a deep slug of his gin. 'Elinor's got cousins in Nova Scotia, so the original plan was to spend a few weeks doing the city loop – Montreal, Ottawa and Toronto – then head over there for Christmas. Of course, it's all been blasted to smithereens now with this dratted delay, so I dare say we'll have to cut a dash for the wilderness straight away.'

'Hmm, so St John might work out rather conveniently for you, then,' James mused. 'You chaps, Dickie? What are your plans?'

'We're heading straight for the border, skiing in Maine – Sugarloaf. Have you been?'

'To Sugarloaf? No.' James shook his head. 'Zermatt in Switzerland for me.'

'Yes, yes, very nice there,' Dickie agreed. 'I rather fancy tackling the Matterhorn one of these days.'

'Are you an Alpinist, then?' James asked.

'I've tried once or twice. Got halfway up Mont Blanc a few winters back.'

Flora sat in distracted silence, listening to how they discussed these far-flung places with insouciance. The world was far smaller for them than it was for her.

'I say,' Digby Tucker interrupted, leaning forward suddenly in his chair. 'Wouldn't it be fun if we were all aboard for the return trip in the spring?'

There was a momentary silence as the other men turned to him, riled that he made no attempt to disguise his eavesdropping.

'Well, I . . . sadly, I very much doubt we'll be heading back from here, that's the thing, you see,' Bertie demurred. 'Possibly Quebec, hard to say at the moment.'

'I should imagine we'll be in New York by then,' Dickie drawled unapologetically, moving slowly as he reached for his cigarette case. He was completely unhurried by life, and Flora liked him and his wife best of them all: Dickie didn't look at her with want, and Ginnie didn't look at her with envy. It was a marked relief to go unscrutinized for once.

The Midnight Secret

'What a pity,' Tucker pined. 'Callaghan? What shall you and your lovely wife be doing come the thaw?'

'Our plans are open-ended,' James said smoothly. 'It's impossible to predict, I'm afraid. We like to be fairly spontaneous.'

'Indeed,' Tucker nodded, falling back with a peeved look, seeming to recognize their reluctance to embed the acquaintance. 'Well . . . that is a shame.'

'You're travelling back from here, are you?' Bertie enquired, unable to restrain his politeness.

'Oh yes. Got our berth booked already. Mrs T is very particular about where she sleeps.'

Not particular enough, Flora thought to herself. She couldn't imagine how that woman could bear to lie next to him at night. 'Well, I think I'll have a rest,' she murmured; she had had quite enough small talk for one afternoon, and she had a wall to stare at and hours to count down before there was another dinner to suffer. They had another eleven days aboard before they were due to haul anchor and make their way landward.

She rose to standing, the men following suit as one.

'See you at cocktail hour,' Dickie said cheerily.

'Aye,' she smiled, 'I'll see you anon.'

She caught James's eye as she turned to leave.

'Actually . . .' he said, and she turned back to find him setting down his cards, disappointed looks growing on the other men's faces. 'I think I'll come with you, darling.'

'You will?'

'Yes. I'm feeling rather weary. A little shut-eye might be in order.'

There was a tiny pause and she felt loaded looks, as if no one believed they were going to be sleeping. She found Digby

Tucker's eyes on her again, his wife stitching by his side, oblivious. He gave a benign smile, but in the moment before his face could change, she saw something penetrating in his gaze that unsettled her – a surprising sharpness for a man widely considered a fool.

'Forgive me, chaps, won't you?' James asked, pushing back his chair.

'Not at all,' Dickie demurred with twinkling eyes. 'We'd be tired too if we were you,' he added under his breath as James slipped his hand into hers and led her out.

Flora sat at the desk in the writing room, her back to the room. She came in here most days to write letters that could not yet be sent. It should have been one of the upsides of the enforced delay, as it meant she finally had the time to write to her parents and tell them everything that had happened to her in the past year, starting from the day James had landed his seaplane in Glen Bay.

But every day, although she rewrote the same letter, she tore it up and threw it into the bin. How could she ever tell this story on paper – revealing to her parents that they were grandparents, but the child was gone; that James was alive, but they were still unwed? She had lied and lied for months about her situation, and with every new twist in the tale, it felt harder to start with the truth.

Only Mhairi knew about this latest chapter of James's return and their race to Canada. It was Mhairi who had picked up the telephone in Effie's hotel room in Oban, when Flora had called back the night James had found her in Paris – the same night Donald had been released. The others had been downstairs in the hotel bar with Sholto, celebrating freedom, when Mhairi had come up for a shawl.

The Midnight Secret

Flora had sworn her friend to secrecy that night. She was so terrified of losing track of her son in Canada, she didn't dare risk anyone else knowing that they knew the truth, at least about Lorna and Mary's relationship. Mhairi had been stunned, naturally, but Flora knew the secret would be safe until their return; and in the meantime, she had managed to send a telegram to her family telling them she was well and happy, without making mention of her flight from Paris.

But as she looked down at the latest iteration of the letter, she knew this was yet another one she would not send. The words, so bold in ink, might as well have been written in blood for all the horror they contained. The very least she owed her parents was to tell them this story face to face.

She heard footsteps coming into the room behind her, paying them no mind as she shuffled the sheets of longhand. But as she waited for the scrape of a chair, the rustle of a skirt, the gentle clearing of a throat before a pen began to scratch over paper . . . it didn't come.

She turned.

'Ah, Mrs Callaghan. What a pleasant surprise, finding you in here,' Digby Tucker said.

Flora closed her eyes briefly, trying to summon her manners as well as strength. 'Mr Tucker,' she said with a strained smile.

He was standing by one of the other desks and she saw, to her surprise, that the few ladies who had been in here when she'd arrived had since left. She wondered when, exactly; she hadn't heard them go, too lost in her own thoughts. 'Have you come to write some letters too?'

'Oh, no, no. I'm not much of a one for writing. My hand can never quite keep up with my head.'

Little could. He talked in a garrulous manner and laughed far too loudly.

Flora smiled but passed no comment; polite conversation with this man was the very last thing she needed, and she didn't want to encourage him to stay.

'Not a problem for you, I understand,' he continued, undeterred by her silence. 'My wife tells me you're a prolific writer. She says you're in here whenever she passes.'

'I do enjoy the solitude,' she said pointedly.

His fingers drummed lightly on the desk. 'You do not enjoy cruise life?'

'No, I do.'

'Really? You don't swim, play cards. You never dance . . .'

She wasn't going to tell him she hadn't the skill for the first two diversions, nor the heart for the latter. How could she enjoy herself when her baby son was out there, somewhere, without her? It was all she could do to eat, sleep, *breathe*, until he was back in her arms. She was living at a subsistence level, but it was none of this man's business. 'Oh dear,' she sighed instead. 'You make me sound very dour.'

'Forgive me, that was not my intention.' He drew a little closer, taking a seat at the nearby desk as he pulled out his cigarettes. He offered her one, which she declined. 'No, I suppose what I'm saying is, I sense in you . . . a sadness.'

She swallowed. 'Not at all. I'm deliriously happy, in fact – but thank you for your concern.'

Tucker lit the cigarette and smiled, his elbow on the desk, smoke curling into his moustache. 'Come, we are friends, are we not? A month spent in close quarters forces us to see one another as we really are, beyond just the social niceties. There's a melancholy to you, dear Flora – may I call you Flora?'

She stared at him. He already had.

'I sense something is gravely wrong in your world. I see the worry in your husband's eyes when he looks at you; I

The Midnight Secret

see how you scarcely leave your room except to eat; and when you do leave, you come here to sit alone.'

Is that why he had come here – to find her? 'I never knew I attracted such scrutiny.'

He gave a guffaw. 'Dear lady, are you quite serious? Queen Mary herself attracts less. It's not for nothing they call you The Enigma, you know.'

She frowned. 'Who does?'

'All the women. It's difficult to tell if they love or loathe you.'

Flora swallowed. 'You're making this up, Mr Tucker. I sincerely doubt they have any opinion on me whatsoever.'

He arched an eyebrow. 'Flora, you are beautiful yet reclusive. They want to look upon you and learn your secrets; they want to befriend you, but you deny them on every count. You hardly leave your room, and when you do, you won't leave your husband's side.'

She looked away. 'You exaggerate.'

'There's a palpable current of excitement whenever you enter the room,' he continued, undeterred by her refutations. 'Did you know every night, the women – my own wife included – do their hair and choose their gowns in the hope of outshining you? And yet they cannot.' He smiled. 'I think the very worst of it is that not only do you not notice, you do not even seem to care. You wear the same two dresses on rotation.'

She looked at him, picking up a pointedness to the comment. 'Only because we decided to come on a whim,' she murmured. 'There was no time to pack.'

He was regarding her closely. She sensed he was enjoying this privilege of staring upon her face with no one to disturb them. 'No valet, either.'

'As I said, we were rushing.' It was a glaring anomaly compared to the rest of the first-class passengers, who had come laden with trunks and staff. 'Besides, I never knew we were being judged, or that . . . that it was some kind of fashion parade.'

He laughed out loud at that. 'It's a cruise, my dear – of course it's a fashion parade! What else is there to do? Well . . .' His eyes flashed in her direction suddenly. 'Besides *that*.'

Flora startled, hardly able to believe he had said such a thing to her. She felt the mood shift in the room, his motives becoming clearer now. She had sensed his interest in her from the start, but she had never for a moment thought he would be so foolish as to attempt to act on it.

'Excuse me,' she said curtly, rising sharply. He shot to his feet too as she went to move past him, but it put him in her path, blocking the door, and she felt a sudden, visceral fear that he was going to trap here in here. She shoved him hard, so that he fell back against one of the desks.

'Mrs Callaghan!' he stammered.

'Stay away from me!' she cried.

'You have misunderstood . . . !' he called after her as she ran towards the door and out into the corridor. It was quiet – most people were now back in their rooms getting ready for drinks before dinner. Flora sprinted along the corridor, down the stairs, not stopping until her own suite was within sight.

James looked up from the bed as she burst in, out of breath.

'Flora?' he asked, dropping his book, immediately concerned. 'What is it?'

She stared at him as he got up and came over to her. How could she tell him the fear she had felt in that moment when

The Midnight Secret

she had thought Tucker was going to lay his hands upon her? It had reminded her of that night in Edward Rushton's apartment in Paris. *Let him have you*, Pepperly had counselled, thinking only of his money.

But Tucker hadn't laid a finger on her. He hadn't even said anything outright, merely implied a grubby little innuendo with his usual misplaced manner. For the first time, she checked herself. He hadn't chased after her, nor deliberately stepped into her path to obstruct her departure . . . Had he risen to standing from manners, not ill intent? Had she overreacted? Were her nerves so friable she had imagined something that wasn't there?

'N-nothing,' she murmured. '. . . I just felt like running.'

There was a pause as he pulled her into him. 'My wild island girl,' he grinned, kissing her hair. 'I might have taken the girl out of St Kilda, but I'll never take St Kilda out of the girl.'

Chapter Nine

MHAIRI

Boxing Day 1930

Oban

Debussy played over the wireless, Donald's hand clasping hers as he whirled her in sweeping circles around the room so that her skirt billowed out. She was still wearing her pinny, stained with gravy marks, and they were a little out of time, neither one of them sure if they were attempting a waltz or a foxtrot, but they didn't care; the perfection of the moment came down to its spontaneity, heart and sense of fun.

Donald's eyes fastened upon her and she marvelled, as she always did, at their blueness, the softness of his rough hands as he held her. These were the moments when she was reminded that life was good, that beauty lay within the small things: a shared smile, an unexpected dance . . .

They had been in their own feathered nest for almost two days now, and she didn't want even to open a window and let the outside world in. Everything she needed was within these four walls. The wireless had been his Christmas gift to her; he had spent weeks saving up, putting aside whatever

The Midnight Secret

pennies he could, reasoning that if the wild flowers she picked from the verges and the wood behind the town could bring beauty to their spartan home, music could add another layer too.

He spun her out, making her laugh at the unexpected move and catching her easily with his strong arms. He dipped her low – and kept her there, kissing her gently before the fire, just as there came a knock at the door. It wasn't unexpected, but Mhairi wished it could have come an hour from now. Or even a minute.

Donald sighed, pulling her back up and kissing her on the lips once more – but the tenderness of their private moment was already gone. He was nervous, she knew.

The knock came again. It had a percussive rhythm to it and, as Donald crossed the room, Mhairi, needing something to do, straightened the tablecloth. It was an old bedsheet she had washed and embroidered and she'd set a small posy of red campion in a glass. She looked around the space, trying to see it through a visitor's eyes: she had cleaned the windows so the glass sparkled, trying to let in as much light as possible, though the days were so short now anyway. The coal fire was heaped high and crackling so that the room had a rosy warmth. And of course, the mellifluous strings of Debussy soared, tipped and swayed in the background.

Donald looked back at her, both of them holding their breath, before he opened the door.

'David!' he exclaimed with robust pleasure. 'It's a fair treat to see you again.' Mhairi watched as the two men shook hands. 'Come in, come in.'

'I'm afraid I bothered your neighbours trying to find you. I ended two along by mistake,' David said, removing his hat as he entered their home.

'Easily done,' Donald nodded. 'I trust they were helpful?'

David's eyes darted over to where Mhairi stood. '. . . Aye,' he said.

'How are you, David?' she asked, greeting him with a sisterly hug. Flora's big brother had always felt like a brother to her too, and it was only as she set eyes upon him now that she realized how much she had missed him. Her loneliness here was like a hunger gnawing away at her all the time.

'All the better for seeing you, Mhairi . . . Both of you,' he added, glancing awkwardly at Donald. He wasn't yet accustomed to seeing them as a couple. The last time they'd all been together, Donald had been standing on the HMS *Harebell* with Mary and their newborn son . . . Mhairi knew David couldn't possibly comprehend the earthquakes that had shifted their world for them to have fallen into this new position. There was much to discuss, clearly – but not yet. Manners had to prevail over curiosity.

David looked down at the small package he was holding, wrapped in brown paper. 'A cake,' he said, holding it out to her.

Mhairi's eyes brightened.

'From my ma,' he added quickly, seeing her hopes rise and then fall back. 'She thought you'd like it for Christmas.'

She swallowed. '. . . How kind!' she said, trying to hide the disappointment that it wasn't something from her own mother. There had been no word from them since her parents had arrived on Harris for her wedding to Alexander McLennan, only to discover she had jilted him. Her letter warning them not to come had arrived too late, and while she didn't know exactly what Alexander had told them, there was no doubt he had painted her as the villain of the piece – a situation only compounded by Mhairi giving Donald his alibi for the night

The Midnight Secret

of the factor's murder, thereby revealing their affair. She'd known word of that must have reached back to Lochaline when her letters had started coming back to Oban stamped *Returned to Sender*. She had tried ringing the Lochaline telephone box across the lane from the cottages, hoping she could explain, but Christina MacQueen had told her in a frosty voice that her parents were 'out', and she had been met with a wall of silence ever since. Her family was ashamed of her, she knew. She had become that worst of things: 'a disgrace'. So David's telegram saying he would be visiting had given her hope that he might bring some token of affection from them: a letter, a blanket, a cake.

She carried the little package through to their small kitchen area as David shrugged off his coat and rubbed his hands before the fire. It was sleeting outside, a bitter easterly wind shaking the tailcoat of strong storms in Europe. He seemed nervous and on edge, the easy-going David of old left somewhere in the past.

Donald handed him a dram and they toasted good health, knocking back the amber nectar and letting it burn their throats. Mhairi had made a stew with plenty to go around and she pulled it out of the oven to stir, the aroma filling their small home. And it was a home. They hadn't much – not much more than they'd had in St Kilda – but there was heart here, comfort and quiet joys. She spent her evenings embroidering and stitching curtains and cushions from old pieces of laundry she rescued that had been tossed into the hotel bins. She saw David's eyes fall to the open doorway of the bedroom, catching a glimpse of their non-marital bed: clean sheets, but not clean enough without a wedding ring.

'How's the job at the Forestry going?' Donald asked, seeing the same.

David drew his attention back. 'Well enough. Da's making a good recovery from his accident.'

'I was sorry to hear of it. That sounded bad,' Donald frowned.

'Aye, it was a close call. He was lucky. There were lots of ways it could have been worse. We had a good surgeon in the end.'

'Thanks to Flora,' Mhairi piped up, closing the oven door.

'Aye. There were unexpected blessings for sure.' He looked at Mhairi. 'Have you heard from her?'

Mhairi shook her head. 'Not for weeks. It's my fault – we've been so busy these past few months. I've not had the energy in the evenings to sit down and write.'

'Mhairi's got a job in the laundry at the Regent Hotel,' Donald said. 'And I'm working in the fish market now.'

'Oh,' David nodded politely.

'It's not much,' Donald mumbled. 'But we're getting by.'

'Well, this is . . .' David motioned awkwardly to the small apartment. 'It's a wonderful home.'

Mhairi heard the nerves in the silence that followed. 'Well, it's not the Paris Ritz, that's for sure,' she joked. 'I think that's where Flora was staying, wasn't it?'

Donald nodded, although he could no more imagine the Paris Ritz than Buckingham Palace.

'It's going to make her rich, that show,' David smiled. 'Who'd have thought it? My sister, a star.'

'Oh, I think we all knew that would happen, one way or another,' Mhairi smiled. 'Flora was never destined for a small life.'

They could all, at least, agree on that.

'So what's the news back home?' Donald asked. Mhairi thought how strange it was that 'home' now meant Lochaline instead of Village Bay.

The Midnight Secret

There was a hesitation. 'Most are settling well. Your brothers are doing well in their jobs,' David said, looking at Mhairi. 'Angus is walking out with a lass called Bonnie from the village, the fishmonger's daughter. He seems fair smitten.'

'Surely not? I didn't know Angus had feelings!' she joked, but feeling a pang of sadness that she was missing out on seeing her brother's happiness. He'd always been a restless spirit back on the isle. 'Anyone for Fin?'

'Not yet, that I'm aware. He seems more interested in four wheels than two legs. Most evenings after work he goes down to the mechanic's and learns about oil changes and how to fit a new wheel. I think he'd prefer a job doing that than at the Forestry.'

'He was always clever,' she murmured. 'He needed more than climbing cliffs and catching birds.'

David grinned. 'And you'd be shocked at how big wee Rory is now. He's crawling about so fast, your ma can scarcely catch him!'

Mhairi bit her lip, holding back her emotions. It had always fallen to her to look after the younger ones, to help her mother with the washing and cooking. '. . . And how about Da?' she asked after a moment. She knew her father had struggled with his loss of position in their community after the evacuation. As the postmaster he'd had an important and central role in St Kildan life, but now he was just the same as everyone else.

'Och, well . . . quiet. You know how he is. Never exactly a big talker.'

'No,' she agreed, wondering if she was the real cause of his melancholy.

'He comes over most evenings to sit with my da, and they talk about the old days.'

They all felt the finality of that term. Their entire lives up to three months ago had been boxed away, guillotined away from the lives they were inhabiting now.

'And Old Fin? I was worried about him all alone, being set so far up the lane.'

'He's not alone,' David smiled. 'Jayne checks in on him every morning on her way to the factory. She's got a bike now, so she goes back at lunch to eat with him and then checks in again on her way past. He listens to the wireless in the meantime.'

'He has a wireless too?' Mhairi couldn't disguise her surprise. She and Donald had scarcely been able to afford theirs on two wages.

'Jayne bought it for him.' David's mouth had flattened into a line. 'Norman's doing very well at the Forestry. He's been promoted to deputy manager of the yard.'

'Already?' Donald said, surprised. 'That's fast.'

David sighed. 'Aye, I know, but the men seem to respect him, so . . .' His voice trailed off, and Mhairi watched him. His and Norman's relationship, never exactly close, had deteriorated sharply after Molly's death. They seemed so distant for two men who had once been on course – if Molly had only had her way – to become brothers.

'And how are things with you?' she asked gently. 'Are you . . . are you courting?'

He looked up sharply, as if the suggestion was offensive. 'Of course not.' He recognized his brusqueness and checked himself, taking a steadying breath, his fingers gripping the whisky glass more tightly. '. . . What I mean to say is, that's it for me. There'll not be anyone else.'

Mhairi stared at him, taken aback. 'You mustn't say that, David.'

'Why not? It's how I feel.'

The Midnight Secret

'It's only been just over a year. We all miss her – but you've got your whole life ahead of you. Molly wouldn't want you to be alone.'

'With respect, Mhairi, you don't know that. You don't know how it was with me and her. No one knows how it really was between us – the love we had . . . What we had together, we had to keep hidden.'

She watched him. 'And you don't think we, me and Donald of all people, could understand that?'

From the corner of her eye she saw Donald stiffen as she addressed what they were all dancing around.

David's head whipped up. 'It's not the same.'

'Because Donald was married, so our love couldn't possibly be . . . *true*, is that what you mean?'

David swallowed, but there was a flash of anger in his eyes too. '. . . Aye.'

'Things aren't always what they seem, David,' Donald said uneasily. He wasn't a man who found it easy to discuss emotions; like most of the St Kildan men, he preferred action over thought. 'Marriage is sometimes just a coat, putting a respectable face on something.'

'It wasn't how it looks,' Mhairi said. 'We tried everything to resist it – and it was never our intention to hurt anyone.'

'But you did! Innocent people were hurt—'

'Neither of them was innocent,' she said hotly.

David looked from her to Donald. Was he not going to defend his wife?

'Alexander McLennan is a pig and a brute,' Mhairi went on. 'You've no idea what he was really like. No one did. Only Donald.'

She saw the look of confusion cross David's face at her words.

'Then why didn't you say anything? Your brothers would have—'

'No. Some things can't be said.' She looked away, not wanting to say too much. 'And I didn't need them, anyway. Donald protected me from him.'

'But it wasn't his place. He should never have got involved. He was a married man.'

'Only in name,' Donald said flatly. 'The marriage had been dead for years, and if you were to ask her, Mary would admit it was as much a torment for her as it was for me. With or without Mhairi, it would have had to end. We couldn't have carried on as we were.'

'But you made vows before God. Y' canna ignore that!'

'Aye – and I made those vows with the best of intentions, but it was still a terrible match. Sometimes conceding defeat is the only way, David.'

'I disagree.'

'It was a bad marriage,' Donald insisted. 'There was no love there, and we each had good cause to leave. Whatever y' might have heard, I'd ask y' to remember that *she* was the one who left me. There's a good reason for that.'

'Such as?'

Donald looked across at Mhairi, frustrated. He could tell, but not without revealing other people's secrets too.

'David, surely you of all people can see that sometimes a marriage shouldn't be saved at any cost?' Mhairi said instead.

David frowned. 'Me? Why me?'

'Well, because of Norman and Jayne. You see how it is between them. Y' know the truth there. How is that a Christian marriage?'

David squinted back at her in confusion. 'Mhairi, what are you talking about?'

The Midnight Secret

'Surely you . . . ?' Mhairi faltered as she saw the look of bewilderment on his face. '. . . Did Molly never say anything?'

'About what?'

Donald and Mhairi swapped looks again.

'About what?' David pressed, as a silence billowed in the small room.

'Norman beats Jayne,' Mhairi said quietly.

David flinched. *'What?'* A disbelieving scoff escaped him. 'No . . . I would know. I see her all the time. She's my friend. I would have seen—'

'He hits her where her bruises can be hidden,' Mhairi said in a low voice. 'Flora told me.'

David didn't reply. He looked ashen, and Mhairi could see he was replaying moments in his head, belatedly recognizing signs he might have missed. He and Jayne had grown close after Molly's passing – but not that close.

'Mary and I weren't the only ones with a bad marriage,' Donald said quietly. 'But the difference was, we both wanted out. Jayne can't, or won't, leave Norman.'

David got up from his seat and walked the few paces across the width of the room. He turned back and did the same again, his breathing coming heavily.

'Another drink?' Donald asked, seeing his disturbance.

David nodded, and there was a silence as Donald poured. He handed over the glass and David downed it, seeming to savour the burn. '. . . Is he still doing it?'

'You're better placed to know that than us,' Mhairi replied. 'Flora tried to support her back home, but after your da's accident, when your family needed the money for his bills, she couldn't stay – not even for Jayne.'

He blinked, and Mhairi could see his eyes were watery. 'Who else knows?'

'I'm not sure. I think some might suspect.'

'Does Effie know?'

She shrugged. 'She went away to Ayrshire so quick after the evacuation. Flora told me Jayne made her promise not to tell anyone, but I think she needed to unburden herself. She only told me once she knew I was leaving for Harris; I suppose me going away too made it safer to confess the secret. Flora said she tried to get Jayne to leave him, but she couldn't get through to her.'

David dropped his face into his hand. 'How the hell didn't I know?' he whispered.

'David, you mustn't blame yourself,' Mhairi said, putting a hand on his arm. 'You couldn't have known.'

'Couldn't I?' he cried. 'I'm her friend. I should have seen it!'

'Not if Jayne was determined to hide it from you. You know how private she is. Her gift makes her . . . hide away. She can conceal herself in a room full of people.'

'Not from me!' he said. 'I can always see her!'

Mhairi didn't reply as he walked back to his chair and sank into it, clutching at his hair as he stared down at the floor. No one spoke for a long time.

'I'm sorry. We thought y' knew,' she murmured at last, glancing at Donald. 'We wouldn't have said anything otherwise.'

'Of course you should have! Do you know what he could do to her? He's twice her size!' David cried, looking back at them both. He had always been a mild-mannered sort, but Mhairi remembered that as a child he'd had his sister's temper when pushed.

'. . . David, I know it's hard to hear, but it's not for any of us to intervene. Flora tried and failed. And the truth is, if Jayne

The Midnight Secret

had wanted you to know, she'd have told you,' she said as kindly as she could. 'We have to respect her wishes. She's a grown woman – she'll do what she thinks is best.'

'And what is that? Staying with him till one day he hits her that bit too hard and kills her?'

'You think she should leave him?' Donald asked him.

'Of course she should.'

'So then, you see now that sometimes a marriage isn't godly? It can hide fouler sins?'

David stared back at him with blazing eyes as he realized the argument had come full circle. His elbows were splayed on his thighs, his head hanging heavy on his neck. He looked like a boxer in the corner of the ring. 'And what could have been so bad in *your* marriage to compare to a woman being beaten till her bones break, Donald? What could have been worth giving up your child?' David shook his head disgustedly. 'You let Mary go to Canada! She's taken your son halfway round the world. What kind of father would allow such a thing?'

Donald looked over at Mhairi again, their eyes locking. Everything came back to this. They couldn't tell David their truth without revealing Flora's. Their fates had been intertwined from the start, but with Mary – and Lorna – now gone to Canada, it was only a matter of time before the secrets became known.

Mhairi nodded at him reluctantly.

'The baby isn't mine, David.'

David blinked at him. '. . . *What?*'

Donald sighed, a low, whistling sound that carried suffering and pain, as he came to sit in the chair opposite. 'There's something you should know . . .'

*

'There's really no need,' David said, as Mhairi pulled on her coat.

'I'm in need of some fresh air anyway,' she said. 'I've been indoors all day.'

'Wishing you a merry Christmas,' Donald said solemnly as he shook David's hand. 'Thank y' for coming to see us. Tell the others we miss them.'

David nodded but struggled to find words back. What he had just heard – learned – would take some time to absorb and settle.

The door closed behind them, and neither David nor Mhairi spoke as they wound their way down the staircase. She instinctively moved in silence now, her ears straining for the click of latches; it was impossible to enter or exit the building without being observed, although God knew she had tried. She could only guess at the comments that would be trailing her tomorrow after they'd seen her walking out with another man.

It was still sleeting outside and they pulled their coats tighter at their necks as they walked along the narrow street towards the bus station. Coal smoke hung heavily in the air, every chimney puffing, the sandstone buildings blackened by soot.

'I'm sorry you had to hear all this from us,' Mhairi said, seeing how David had fallen into his thoughts. 'I know Flora would have wanted to tell you herself, but with Mary and Lorna taking off for Canada like that, and then the newspaper headlines on Flora leaving the show . . . I don't know if she's been in touch, but if your parents were to hear . . .'

'Aye, you're right. They'd have heard soon enough and they'd be fair worried.'

'Will you tell them?'

'I'm not sure.' He glanced at her. 'They've been through so much lately. Da's only just getting stronger and Ma's been on

The Midnight Secret

her last nerve for weeks. To tell them all this . . .' His voice broke. 'How would I begin to explain it to them? Flora secretly had a baby that Mary and Lorna then stole?'

'I know.' If Mhairi hadn't been there herself, she would have struggled to believe it. She put a hand on his arm. 'Flora had to make some terrible choices, David. It was difficult enough trying to hide her pregnancy until James could come back and make an honest woman of her. But when she heard he was dead . . . When her circumstances changed, she gave up her boy for *his* sake, so that he could take the McKinnons' name and grow up in respectability.'

David flinched, shaking his head in disbelief. 'And you? If . . . if what happened hadn't happened, would you really have given Mary your child?'

Mhairi closed her eyes, remembering the moment she had held her daughter in her arms, pink and perfect – her red hair, Donald's nose. Could she have done it? All her life, she had cared about being good, doing good, her good name. But if her daughter had only breathed, would she have followed through?

'Flora's stronger than me,' she said finally. 'I don't know if I could have been that selfless. But I do know I would have had comfort from knowing she would have been with her father.'

'Do your parents know? Is that why . . . ?'

She shook her head. 'No. It's bad enough with them thinking I jilted Alexander to take up with Donald.'

'They are fair upset about that,' he confessed.

'Aye. You can imagine how they'd feel about this.'

He was quiet for a moment, for they both knew there were no platitudes he could offer. 'It must have been so hard, having to hide everything.'

'Aye, it was. And I wish I could say it's better here and that we've got our happy ending, but . . . even though we're together, we're caught in limbo. We can't marry because Mary has fled without granting Donald a divorce. And of course, to the outside world, I'm the scarlet woman who forced out a mother and her newborn baby.'

'Ah,' he nodded. 'That certainly explains your neighbour's choice words earlier when I knocked on the wrong door. She has a vicious tongue.'

'They all do,' she groaned, reaching for his arm and looping hers through it as they walked. 'Thanks for not saying anything about that. I don't want Donald to worry.'

'He doesn't know?' he asked, surprised.

She shook her head. 'But I can manage. *I* know what they're saying isn't true, and that's all that really matters. Although sometimes I want so badly to tell them the truth about their sainted Mary! They think they're defending a good woman.'

David scoffed at the thought too. 'So why don't you just leave here? Leave them behind you and go somewhere new?'

'Because we can't. Donald may be out on bail, but he remains a person of interest. As long as there isn't another suspect with a strong motive for killing Mathieson, the suspicion is still on him. My alibi is the only thing keeping him a free man, and I think the police sergeant is convinced he can still build a case showing I'm a woman of disreputable character.'

'You? Mhairi MacKinnon? Does he have the first idea who he's dealing with?' David teased, but with sad eyes.

'Clearly not,' she shrugged. 'Either way, Donald's bail conditions mean he can't leave here, so we're stuck. Our fate is entirely bound up in Mary's actions.'

David stared at her. 'You've been through so much. You and my sister.'

'We've no one to blame but ourselves for our mistakes. Flora and I gave in to temptation, and we've both paid the price.'

The Midnight Secret

'But it was a far higher price than anyone should have to pay,' he said, shaking his head. They rounded the corner, passing under a street lamp, and she saw that he was wearing a haunted look that hadn't been there when he'd arrived earlier. '. . . Who else knew?'

'You mean besides Donald, Lorna and Mary?' Mhairi sighed. 'Well, we had to tell Effie . . . and unfortunately Frank Mathieson found out.'

David stopped in his tracks. 'Oh, no.'

'Aye. Of all the people . . . He thought he could threaten us with it – till Donald put him in his place. But of course it was still a risk, him knowing.'

David looked alarmed. 'Enough of a risk that . . . ?'

'No!' She shook her head quickly, knowing exactly what he was thinking. 'Donald didn't kill him, David. The police said he had motive, but it was Frank who attacked Donald on Boreray for daring to challenge him on the prices he was paying us. Frank was the one raging when Donald bypassed him with the sale of the ambergris. It was Frank who wanted *his* blood.'

But David looked unconvinced. 'So then, was it self-defence? It would be understandable, if Mathieson was harassing him one last time or threatening to go public about you—'

'Donald has alibis for the whole night now. I was with him after midnight. And Mary said in her statements that Donald was in the cottage with her all evening, during the birth. Which he was. If the story was going to work, the two of them had to be holed up in there together until Lorna could get back over with the baby.'

They crossed the wide town square. A Christmas tree had been erected in the centre and the lights twinkled, reflecting in the puddles. A sparrow was perched on the back of a bench; twists of red tinsel glinted in the windows of the hat shop.

'So then that means Lorna must have lied about her whereabouts to the police? She said she was in the cottage, when really she was over in Glen Bay with you.' He glanced at her. 'She's a nurse, an official figure, and yet she misled the police like that?'

'As we know now, she had plenty of her own secrets. This was her and Mary's chance to have a family and they took it. She wasn't going to let little white lies stand in the way of that.'

'And you really think they're . . . lovers?' he faltered.

'Well, obviously Flora had told me her suspicions on the telephone the night James came back, but when I told Donald, he was certain of it. He had put two and two together when the neighbours told him Lorna had been living here while he was in prison. She had told all of us she was returning to her family in Shetland. Of course, they all thought Lorna was just a friend helping her out with the baby, but . . . for him it all made sense. Little things he had seen before that he hadn't given much thought to at the time. Like seeing them holding hands, which might have been innocent enough. But when Lorna stayed over while he had his head injury, he heard sounds coming from the other room.'

'What sort of sounds?'

Mhairi arched an eyebrow and David immediately blushed. 'Oh.'

'Aye. He asked Lorna what they'd been doing but she told him he was delirious. Imagining things.'

'I see.' He looked ahead with a disconsolate expression, falling into his thoughts.

'What is it?'

'Nothing. It just makes you wonder, doesn't it, how well we ever really know our friends and neighbours. All those years we lived cheek by jowl, and yet I never once suspected

The Midnight Secret

any of these secrets. Not Mary and Lorna's. Not yours and Donald's. Not Jayne and Norman's . . . Am I such a fool?'

'David, you see the best in people. There's nothing wrong with that.'

'No? Not even when people are getting hurt? Norman beats Jayne! Someone murdered Mathieson. They stabbed him repeatedly in the chest, over and over.' He shook his head. 'The rage they must have had . . . ! Frank was a powerful man.'

'Aye, but he was tied up, remember. Or at least, he was when Flora and I saw him.'

He looked back at her. 'When did you see him?' he frowned.

'In the middle of the night, when we were coming back from the other side, after the birth . . . Flora could scarce walk. It took us hours.'

'Oh!' David flinched at the thought of his sister's suffering. 'Yes.'

'Lorna had gone ahead with the baby to take it to Mary while it was still dark, so she could get the neighbours over as witnesses . . .' Mhairi faltered as she thought back, remembering the horror of that night, Flora's pitiful cries as she had staggered over the moor. 'When we saw Frank, he was on the ground and tied up, just as Effie had left him. He was conscious, but barely. He'd got through most of a bottle of whisky.'

'Whisky? Where did he get that from?' They both knew the minister had been intolerant of any alcohol on the isle.

'Captain McGregor brought it over for Eff, with the money she'd earned guiding . . . It was all planned. She needed to keep Mathieson incapacitated until she could get off the island. She'd tied him up, but she'd left a knife nearby for him to free himself, and some water and oatcakes. It was enough to keep him going till the *Harebell* dropped anchor a few days after. Frank was out of it when we passed by, but definitely alive.'

'My God,' he muttered. 'All this was happening that last night.'

'I know. I keep wondering if we were the last people to see him alive. Well, I mean – apart from the murderer.'

They had arrived at the bus stop now. A few people were lingering, and several heads turned at her last word.

David stood in silence for a few moments and she could see he was thinking hard.

'What?' she asked, seeing his concern grow.

He lowered his voice to little more than a whisper. 'In the photos the police showed us, the ropes had been cut. Mathieson had got himself free.'

Mhairi shuddered at the thought of what the factor might have done to Effie if he hadn't been attacked. 'Okay.' She wasn't sure where he was leading with this.

'That suggests to me it had to have been a man who did it.' A dark look came into his eyes. 'A strong man – with a strong propensity for violence.'

Mhairi stared at him, sensing a hypothesis quickly taking root in his mind. 'Norman?'

'He's probably one of the few men who would have been able to go toe to toe with Mathieson physically.'

She blinked rapidly. She had never particularly liked Norman, but to see him as a murderer . . . ? 'He and Frank were friends, though. They were always together.'

'Precisely. And it's almost impossible for anyone to spend time with either one of them for more than ten minutes and not have some sort of disagreement break out. They're both bullies and they both like to be top dog. It would have been Frank on St Kilda, given his position with MacLeod. But once we were evacuated . . . I wouldn't be surprised if Norman began to overstep, would you?'

Mhairi remembered only too well Norman's grandiose

The Midnight Secret

ambitions. He had denied his own sister her happiness because he wanted her to 'marry up' like Flora and wed a rich man from the mainland.

David dropped his head lower towards her as he leaned against the wall. 'There's a theory that Mathieson was stealing from MacLeod, isn't there?' he asked. 'Effie said the police arrested the steward at Sholto's estate, and he confessed there were three of them in it. Him, Frank, and another.'

'Something like that . . .' Mhairi said slowly. 'Although I'm not sure if it's proven.'

'Well – what if the third man was Norman?'

'As far as I know, there's only this steward's word for that, and I wouldn't put much credence by what he had to say. Effie told me he even tried to implicate her in the thefts.'

'But just say it *was* Norman,' David pressed, a dog with a bone now. 'There's no honour among thieves; it would have been each man for himself. What if one of them double-crossed the others? They had a disagreement, it became a fight . . . We were only hours away from leaving the isle at that point. Norman would have known he had a good chance of getting away.'

'That's pure speculation David. We have no proof of any of it. Not that they were in cahoots together, nor that they fought . . .'

But David was looking at her with newfound conviction. 'It was him, Mhairi. I know it was. And I'm going to go to the police and tell them.'

'David, stop,' she said, catching him by the arm. 'You mustn't be rash. Until you can be sure.'

'Why are you so resistant?' He frowned. 'This would get Donald off the hook!'

'I know – and that's all I want. But if you make an accusation that can't be supported, who knows what Norman might do? If he doesn't come for you, he could . . . he could take it out on Jayne.'

For the first time, David slackened.

Mhairi went on. 'If there's anything Donald's experience with the police has shown me, it's that you need to have proof. And Norman must have an alibi or else they'd be looking at him too.' She shrugged.

David's eyes began to shine, a small smile growing on his lips. 'No, he doesn't.'

'What do you mean?'

'I don't know where he was the night of the murder, but I do know Jayne wasn't at home with him.'

'How do you know?'

'Because she was with me.'

'What?'

'Aye. Jayne and I spent that last night in the burial ground together, sleeping beside Molly's grave. We didn't want her to be alone.'

Mhairi's mouth fell open. For a moment, she had thought perhaps there was more to David's friendship with Jayne than anyone had realized. He was clearly protective of her . . .

'Don't you see, Mhairi? Even if he was at home that night, he can't prove it. Norman doesn't have an alibi!' He nodded. She could see that he was agreeing with the internal dialogue in his head, his instincts growing bolder.

'David—'

'I'm going to the police as soon as I get back.'

'David, no.'

'Aye. It'll kill two birds with one stone: clear Donald from the investigation, and protect Jayne. You know as well as I do that for as long as she's under the same roof as him, she's not safe. She's living not just with a monster, but a murderer.'

The Midnight Secret

'You don't know that! For all you know, he was at home all night, even if she was out with you. You've got to check with Jayne before you do anything. She'll know what Norman told the police.'

'It doesn't matter what he said,' he argued. 'Jayne can't possibly be his alibi if she was with me. And if he can't *prove* he was at home that night – then that, along with his reputation for violence, has to make him a person of interest or whatever it's called.'

Mhairi stared at him, seeing his desire – his need – for revenge. It was, after all, a dish best served cold. He wanted to point the police towards Norman for a crime he might not have committed, to punish him for one that he had.

'. . . Did you tell the police you were with Jayne that night?' she asked.

For the first time, David faltered.

'. . . Well? Did you?'

'No.'

'Why not?'

'Because she asked me not to. She said it could be awkward to explain. That people might . . .'

'So then, you lied to the police too?'

'. . . I was protecting Jayne, Mhairi. I was protecting her then and I'm protecting her now.'

Was he? Or was this vengeance for being kept apart from Molly in her final few months of life? Mhairi stared back at David, seeing for the first time how much he hated Norman – enough to put him in the frame for murder. She had always loved him like a brother, and he felt like blood to her, but he had been right earlier. How well do we ever really know our friends and neighbours?

Chapter Ten

FLORA

30 December 1930

Port of Montreal, Canada

The tugs pushed and pulled them into Montreal port, a crowd gathering along the quays to watch as the magnificent liner glided serenely to her berth a full month later than scheduled. She was conspicuous by her presence – no other ships were making the crossing now, with the Atlantic in full high swell. Flora looked out from her balcony, seeing the river was already thickly iced in places; they had been lucky to make it here and not be diverted south to St John. Canadian winters came in hard, even the St Kildans' cruellest season paled in comparison. The air was biting, the sky a shivering pale blue, unable to bring colour to its cheeks. Flora pulled her fur collar closer to her face as she continued looking down at the wharves.

She saw some reporters huddled in among the crowd, those distinctive round flashes catching her eye just as they had when she and her fellow islanders had docked in Lochaline, four months past to the day. Memories popped in her mind, blisters of a past hurt; she'd been so broken back then, mere

The Midnight Secret

hours after the birth, struggling to move, to hold herself together as she walked down the gangplank and away from her child. But everything had changed since then. Now she was preparing to walk down another gangplank to reclaim him, and this time she had his father, the man she loved, by her side.

Far below, the dockers were working at speed, looping ropes onto bollards as the *Empress* sighed to a stop. Flora had scarcely slept, waiting all night for the ancient groan of the engines far below in the belly of the ship that would tell them they were under way at last. The churn of the water was proof that finally this sleeping beast was awakened and they could make landfall. Their escape was coming in stages.

Yesterday, their papers had been approved on board. The doctor had examined them both and declared them free of disease; their personal effects had been inspected and found to be in order. Perhaps it was because they had so little luggage, compared to the other first-class passengers, that the immigration officers moved through with such haste, but the inspection had been perfunctory at best. James had told her it was a different matter entirely for those in steerage.

Now they were at port, finally, but still the wrong one: Montreal or St John, neither one was Quebec City, and they had another journey to make. A distance of 150 miles might be insignificant in a country measuring 4,700 of them, but for a girl who'd grown up on a rock only two miles long, it felt like going to the moon.

And yet the clock was ticking again, and that was something. It was mid-morning, the journey from their sea anchorage a short one. By dinnertime, God willing, they would be in Quebec City and their search could finally begin.

Impatience ferreted through her blood as she paced the

balcony, waiting for procedures to be followed. She heard the door close in their suite and turned to go back inside. James had been meeting Dickie and Bertie for a final drink at the bar; the men were well versed in cruising and knew the disembarkation process to be 'a bore'.

'I think they're going to be a while yet,' she said, slipping into the room and looking up to find James.

The blood pooled at her feet. 'What are you doing here?' she whispered.

Tucker was standing in the middle of the room, wearing his hat, his coat folded over one arm. 'I wanted to clear the air before our departure. It doesn't feel right to part under a cloud. I fear there was a . . . misunderstanding between us.'

She swallowed. She had scarcely seen him since their contretemps in the reading room a week and a half earlier. In fact, it seemed as if he had been going out of his way to avoid her, no longer lurking; even James had noticed, commenting that they'd managed to shake him off. For her part, Flora had convinced herself she had overreacted; her emotions were balanced on a hair trigger at the moment and she wasn't herself.

'It's quite all right, Mr Tucker. No hard feelings.'

She swallowed, waiting for him to leave as he continued staring at her.

'But, if you don't mind, James will be back any moment, so . . .' She pointedly looked towards the door.

'So?' He smiled, drawing his hands out wide, clearly not going anywhere. Not yet.

'Well, it wouldn't do for you to be in here when he returns.'

'Why not? Would he think we were engaging in something improper?'

There it was again, the slimy innuendo. It made her skin

The Midnight Secret

crawl and put her body on high alert. She was used to male attention, but she also knew when it crossed the line to something more threatening, and she saw now she hadn't overreacted the other day. And he hadn't come here to *clear the air*.

'Get out,' she said in a low voice.

'Come, now, Miss MacQueen, that's not how one welcomes a guest.'

Her heart beat faster at his use of her given name. She had never told it to him. 'It's Mrs Callaghan.'

He seemed to enjoy seeing her shock. 'Did you really think people wouldn't recognize you? A face like yours isn't easily forgotten, especially when *The Times* is hailing you as the toast of Paris one day and linking you to a murder the next. Of course, you were billed as Flora MacQueen, and to us you presented yourself as Mrs James Callaghan, so it wasn't immediately obvious to some of the guests at first.' He shrugged. 'But word always spreads fast. You know how people love to talk.'

She swallowed. 'I'm not in *hiding*, Mr Tucker. This is just a private trip with my husband.'

'Only he's not your husband,' he said matter-of-factly.

Flora felt herself grow cold. 'Excuse me?' How could he speak with such conviction?

'You're passing yourself off as man and wife when, in fact, you are not.' His eyes swept over the double bed. 'And I see you didn't even have the decency to book separate sleeping quarters. Do you think your dinner companions would have been so happy to share a table with you if they knew the despicable truth? You've drawn good people into your sordid deception.'

Flora stood still for several moments, hearing his disgust

and rage. Had he come here to shame her? Humiliate her? She held up her hand, showing him the sapphire engagement ring and the premature wedding band, but she was trembling and she knew he could somehow see straight through the lie.

He tutted and shook his head. 'Please – desist with the lies. You have been caught red-handed, no matter what you think those rings signify.'

'You know nothing about us,' she said quietly.

There was a long pause. 'Don't I?' She watched in horror as he pulled from his jacket pocket several folded sheets of paper. She recognized her own handwriting immediately. In her rush to get away from him in the writing room the other day, she had completely forgotten about the letter.

She saw the black look in his eyes as the smirk grew on his lips. It was a full confession to her mother – every transgression, every secret written down. He knew her private shame, her intimate history; he knew why she was here on this ship.

And she knew now why he was here in this room. He was going to blackmail her for his silence.

She took a step back as the threat asserted itself between them. 'Leave now, before James comes back.'

'Oh, I'm afraid he won't be back for quite some time. I saw him heading for Sykes in the Mayfair lounge, so I told your lover he was in the Observation salon. That should keep him busy for a while—'

The words were no sooner out of his mouth than he lunged at her, getting a hand to her thick coat before she could step out of the way. The weight of him brought them both down onto the carpet in a flailing mass of arms and legs. She wriggled and kicked desperately, but though he wasn't a tall man, he was portly and easily able to pin her down with his weight.

The Midnight Secret

'No!' she screamed, feeling the air pushed from her lungs. 'Help me! Help!'

He slapped her hard across the cheek, once, twice – the shock of it stunning her into momentary silence. She opened her mouth again in the next instant but he clapped his hand over it, his other hand tearing away her coat and clawing at her clothes.

His breathing was ragged, a wild look in his eyes as he overwhelmed her with his rage and lust. 'You've enjoyed toying with us all,' he panted, spittle on his lips as he got his hand under her skirt and tore her stockings. 'Flaunting yourself, making no attempt to hide your lewdness, staying in here for hours, for days . . .'

She screamed beneath his sweaty palm, but the sound didn't register. She shook her head from side to side, trying to free herself from his hand, but he redoubled the force through his arm, locking her into position, his eyes drilled upon hers.

'Everyone knows you showgirls are tarts . . . but we gave you the benefit of the doubt for marrying into respectability . . .' His hand was unbuttoning his fly now and she felt a tear of fury and fear trickle down her cheek onto the side of his hand. 'If I told the other men what you are . . . a *slut* . . . do you think they wouldn't be here too, doing exactly the same . . . ?'

She screamed again, pleading with him, but her cries were muffled vibrations against his palm and he laughed—

Until a roar subsumed him. Flora flinched as he was suddenly thrown off her, James hulking above them with a look she had never seen before. She scrabbled on the ground, pulling herself up, her legs in . . . trying to cover herself as James reached down and grabbed Tucker by the shirt collar.

'I'll kill you!' he yelled, punching Tucker hard, twice in

rapid succession, and pulling back his arm to deliver another blow; but the other man fell back so feebly, his head hanging back as if unconscious (though he wasn't), that James stalled with his arm poised in mid-air.

'James, don't,' Flora sobbed, hugging her knees now as she sat against the wall.

She couldn't bear to even look at Tucker as she lay half-exposed on the floor; her skin was still hurting from the pressure of his fingers as he had jabbed and pinched and probed her. She knew that if she were to look, her flesh would be reddened from his marks.

'No. Mercy's too good for him!' James snarled, his fingers flexing for the next punch.

'Please, James!' Flora cried, and he looked back at her. '. . . I just want him gone!'

'Did he – did he . . . ?' James's voice broke on the question.

'No,' she said, shaking her head. 'No. But I can't bear to see him.' She realized she was crying. 'I need him away from me.'

James gave another cry of rage as he hauled Tucker to his feet, still holding him by the shirt collar. He shoved him hard against the wall and pushed in close to him, eye to eye. 'I knew you were scum the moment I laid eyes on you, Tucker. Always oiling around us. I'm going to make sure everyone knows what you are—'

'No, James!' Flora cried again, getting to her feet now. 'You can't tell anyone! Promise me you won't say a word!'

James shook his head. 'He's a monster! He deserves to be vilified! People need to know what he is!'

'*I'm* the one who'll be shamed!' she pleaded. 'Don't you see that?' She took a few steps across the room, halting halfway. The thought of getting any closer to Tucker made her feel sick.

The Midnight Secret

'Flora, he can't be allowed to get away with this!'

'I know,' she said. 'But . . . not that . . . Please, James.' She implored him with her eyes. 'He didn't get what he came for! You stopped him.'

But James looked back at Tucker with fresh anger. He couldn't be mollified on this, no matter how she begged. 'I ought to throw you out of that window,' he snarled.

Tucker paled, seeing the murderous intent in James's eyes. 'Please . . . I'm s-sorry . . . I . . . I lost control of myself . . . Just l-let me go.'

'You think I'm going to let you go, just like that? Like you weren't just trying to rape my wife?'

Tucker didn't reply. She had been easy prey, but he knew far better than to correct James on the technicality.

Flora watched on. There was no competition between the two men. James could beat Tucker to a pulp if he chose; he certainly had just cause. Who wouldn't side with him?

'Give me one good reason I shouldn't break all your bones,' he snarled, twisting Tucker's collar even tighter in his grip, lifting him onto his tiptoes.

'I . . . I . . .' Tucker stuttered desperately. 'I have money . . .'

James shook his head. Tucker might be a rich man, but so was he.

'Connections, then . . .'

'You can't offer us anything!' His arm flexed in readiness to land the next punch.

'Wait!' Flora took another step forward as a realization came to her. James looked over with a frown. She took a deep breath. '. . . You said he's in the shipping business?'

James frowned harder, then nodded.

'Successful?'

'There's only his word for it,' James muttered.

'No, no!' Tucker cried desperately. 'It's true! It's a global company.'

Flora looked at him at last, her terror beginning to abate as he hung helpless in her husband's grip. 'So, then, your operations extend here?'

'Yes, across Canada. All over the world!' He was panting. James had not slackened his hold at all, but he looked over at her, beginning to understand what she was thinking.

'Tell me what it is you need!' Tucker whimpered. 'Whatever it is, I can arrange it for you . . . If you need someone to look the other way on a . . . on a shipment, I can arrange that for you. I can make that happen.'

He was shady all the way through, Flora thought. And, in that moment, this was the best thing that could have befallen them.

James slammed Tucker against the wall again, making sure he remained scared. 'We want a name.'

'Yes, yes, a name. I can do that . . . Wh-where?'

James's voice was low as he pressed his face towards Tucker's, eyes locked like the lion upon the antelope. 'Quebec City Harbour Commission,' he snarled. 'Immigration.'

'I won't be long.' James kissed Flora lightly on the cheek. They were in the lounge of the Clarendon Hotel, their single case left with the reception desk. They wouldn't be checking in if they could help it, but there was no guarantee James would be able to procure a car quickly.

That was his plan, to buy a car.

Just like that. Buy a car.

Flora's definition of luxury had changed. Once, it had been to *have* a car. Now, the luxury was the freedom it gave them to get on the road quickly and take their destiny into their own hands.

'You'll be all right?'

She was still pale and trembling, but no one could see the bruises that were beginning to purple beneath her clothes. To the casual onlooker's eye, she was simply another rich young woman off the last boat from Europe, one of many in fur coats and cloche hats. The men were in homburgs and puffing on cigars as their steamer trunks were rolled out on trolleys behind them. Flashbulbs had popped frantically as the first-class passengers walked down the gangplank, capturing the display of wealth for a nation caught in the grip of a depression. There had also been a frenzy of flashes for her; Flora's beauty had registered like an electric shock, the mass contracting as one as she moved slowly, her face downturned. James had sighed, still unused to the celebrity that came with that face, squeezing her hand all the harder as they were ushered quickly to the waiting taxi that had brought them here.

'I'll be fine,' she smiled, even though she felt terrified to be left alone in this new country. She hadn't known that the Canadians spoke French – or at least, that these east-coast Canadians did – although she did recognize some phrases from her time in Paris. James had ordered her sweet tea – for the shock, he'd murmured – and something to eat.

'I'll be back as soon as I can.'

'But what if you can't find one?'

'Money always talks,' he murmured, winking at her and making her stomach somersault.

She watched as he walked away, marching briskly through the revolving doors, heads turning at his handsome profile, his jaw set with a determined jut. No one could possibly imagine, she thought – watching them watching him – the purpose of his quest. They probably thought he was going to buy a pack of cigarettes. How difficult was it to buy a new car, twenty minutes after arriving in a new country?

She slid her thumb over the folded slip of paper. It had been torn from the notepad but it felt silky against her skin, a stolen whisper on a warm night. She could see the Canadian Pacific insignia through the back of the paper, feel the impressions made by the pen as the name had been written down.

She opened it up and stared at it: *Joseph Landon.*

Joseph Landon. Joseph Landon, she repeated to herself. It was a name she had never heard until an hour ago, but now her entire future – her entire life – depended upon it. This man had no idea of the importance he had suddenly assumed in their lives. There was no one more vital to their happiness than him. Who even was he? Where was he? What was he doing right now? She closed the scrap of paper again as reverently as if it were a prayer book and slipped it back into her coat pocket.

She had a name, and soon James would have a car. They would be on their way, with everything they needed for the next step of this pursuit.

At last, at very long last, their luck was changing.

Chapter Eleven

James returned with a car within the hour. It was a Ford Model A, painted deep maroon with black hubs and cream wheels. He had paid almost double what it was worth new – $1,000 was more than the average annual salary, and the owner had handed over the keys almost without question. Cash in hand didn't require an explanation. James had also bought a map and some pretzels in a brown paper bag, and they started out on the road less than ninety minutes after they'd docked.

Although it supposedly had a top speed of 65 mph, the car struggled to nudge past forty, and they drove for four hours before reaching the outskirts of Quebec City. It was large – far larger than Flora had expected, with tall factory chimneys in the distance speaking to heavy industry and rapid industrialization.

She looked on, mute and overawed that they were finally here. This was it. After a month at sea, they had arrived in the city that was Mary and Lorna's last known destination. They passed through historical city gates, along narrow streets and wide boulevards, roads chaotic with so many cars and trams that made Glasgow look like a provincial village in comparison. Flora sat straighter and pointed at an extravagant green-roofed building on top of the hill.

'What's that?' she asked.

James peered up at it and smiled, but he looked tired. 'Château Frontenac. Our bed for the night.'

She already knew it would be wonderful. Sumptuous. He had done – was doing – so much for her, getting them over here against all the odds, tackling every obstacle that sprang up in their path.

Her eyes fell again to his reddened knuckles, and she wondered how Digby Tucker was explaining his black eye to his wife. If James hadn't come back for his scarf . . .

'You're so pale, darling,' she murmured, reaching an arm across and stroking his hair.

He nuzzled her back. This morning's disturbance had shaken them both, even if it had led to a breakthrough of sorts. 'So are you.'

'I'm fine . . . I feel the best I've felt in months.' She refused to believe they were too late. She would not consider that this might be where the trail went cold, where their hopes might die. No one could go through all this, only for it to be for nothing – surely?

She looked out of the window, scanning for the tall cranes, railway tracks and grain silos that would announce the docks. Billboards flashed past, bearing slogans she couldn't understand. What if this Joseph Landon only spoke French?

'Do you speak French?' she asked him.

'Un petit peu,' he replied, but then, seeing she didn't understand, added, 'A little . . . Enough. Don't worry, I know how to make myself understood.'

The immigration hall was located on the Princess Louise quay, where all the Canadian Pacific Empress liners docked. The building was three storeys high and faced with barred windows,

The Midnight Secret

but beyond its sturdy walls there was only a flimsy chain-link fence as a barrier between this side, Canadian territory, and the other side by the water, where the passengers and immigrants disembarked.

James parked and Flora jumped out to get a better look. She had glimpsed the black hulk of a docked ship, and she gasped as she saw gilded letters across the hull: *Empress of Scotland*.

'That's it!' she breathed, taking in the sight as if it was magical. It had brought their child over here safely. 'James, they were on this very ship.'

James nodded, but his gaze was fastened upon the railway track that lay on the other side of the fence, between the ship and the immigration building. She knew exactly what he was thinking.

They headed for the main door, where a sign hung saying 'Welcome Home to Canada'. They stepped into a main hall, tall-ceilinged, bright – and deserted. Wooden benches ran the length of the room, some of them askew; there was a letterbox, a glass-windowed telegram cubicle, and a reception desk. 'No Smoking' was painted in large red letters on the wall; there was a sign for a foreign money exchange . . .

James's shoes sounded on the strip floors as they walked through. 'Hello?' he called, his voice ringing off into the distance. '. . . Anybody here?'

They moved into the next room. It was smaller, with numerous partitions for dividing the crowds that would pass through here in the summer months – men; women and children; Canadian nationals; British subjects; American citizens; foreign nationals. A row of cubicles was set into a wall, tubular structures like cages positioned in front of the cubicle windows as if to keep the immigrants set back. Glossy plaques were mounted above the windows: Intercolonial Railway; Grand Trunk Railway; Canadian National Railway; Canadian Pacific Railway. A door leading out. Passengers could literally disembark, be processed through Immigration and step onto a train – one of many lines – that would take them anywhere in Canada. They wouldn't even need to step foot in the city. The ease of dispersion in this vast country concerned her.

Behind them a door slammed, footsteps crossing the floor in the other room.

'Hello?' James broke into a sprint, disappearing through the doorway as Flora hurried after him. She stepped through moments later to find him in conversation with a man who looked more than a little startled.

'. . . pas ici! C'est interdit!'

Flora looked at James in panic. Did he understand a word?

'Oui, je sais,' James replied calmly. 'C'est tout bien. Je cherche un ami . . . Joseph Landon?'

'. . . Landon?'

'Oui.'

The man looked at James, then at her. They were both respectably dressed, clearly rich. She smiled and the man seemed to wilt a little.

'Il est là-bas,' he said, lifting his arm and seemingly pointing to the next building. 'Au deuxième étage.'

'Deuxième?' James clarified, holding up two fingers.

'Oui.'

'Merci. Merci, monsieur,' James said, taking his hand before the man could withdraw and shaking it with gratitude.

Flora smiled too as she passed him, hurrying after James across the empty hall. He burst out through the door where they had entered and crossed the road towards another building. Above the door, a sign read: 'Office of Immigration and Colonization; Harbour Commission'.

A woman looked up from her typewriter, frowning, as they walked in. 'Nous sommes fermés,' she said abruptly.

James hesitated. 'Do you speak English, by any chance?'

Her lips pursed. 'We are closed,' she said with a heavy accent.

'I'm looking for an old friend – Joseph Landon. I was told I could find him here. Upstairs.'

She sized them up, but James's casual reference to an old friend, his specificness of Landon's whereabouts, worked in his favour. 'Attendez,' she said finally, picking up a telephone and speaking rapidly into it. There was an agonizing pause. '. . . Il vient.'

'Merci,' James nodded. He had taken off his hat, and Flora could see he was trying not to wring it in his hands as he paced a few steps. Could it really be this easy, after weeks of obstacles and delays?

Several minutes passed, the woman typing with ferocious stabs on the keys, her eyes darting suspiciously towards them every few moments. Then came footsteps on the stairs and they looked up to see a man with curly, dark hair coming down with an expectant look. He stopped short as he took in the two strangers.

'Ah, Landon,' James said, immediately marching forward and offering his hand, so familiar as an old friend that the man instinctively responded in kind. He looked at them in bewilderment; Flora could see he was trying to place them. *Did* he in fact know them? 'Good to see you again. Old Tucker said we'd find you here.'

Tucker's name registered immediately. Flora watched

Landon's expression change as he looked between the two of them, seeming to get an understanding of the situation.

'Comment ça-va?' James smiled, aware of the typist watching them.

Landon withdrew his hand and slipped it into his trouser pocket. 'Can't complain, although the weather's a bastard,' the man replied in a broad Irish accent. 'How is Tucker?'

'Faring well. We just sailed over with him on the *Empress of Britain*.'

Landon's eyebrows shot up. 'She only docked this morning. You've made it to here from Montreal in a day?'

'Yes, we've a tight schedule.' James's gaze was steady, though there was an easy smile on his lips. He really was a social chameleon, able to adapt to anyone. 'We wondered if you fancied coming for a drink with us while we're in town?'

Landon hesitated. 'Well, I've a bit more paperwork to shift before I can get out this hellhole . . . Why don't y's both come up to my desk for a moment and we can talk over old times here for a bit?'

'Marvellous idea,' James said brightly, immediately following him up the stairs. He turned back to Flora. 'Come on, darling.'

Flora felt the typist's eyes upon her again as she delicately picked her way up the stairs.

The office was large but subdivided with partitions at each desk, overhead lights hanging low at intervals. Outside, the lights from the docks glowed, the sound of a train in the distance coming down the tracks.

'Looks like we caught you in the nick of time,' James said, making conversation as Landon led them over to his desk, set alongside the wall. 'Long day?'

Landon didn't reply; they were quite alone in the large

The Midnight Secret

room now and out of earshot of the receptionist. The pretence didn't need to be upheld. 'Why's Tucker sent you here?' he asked in a low voice.

'Let's just say he owed us a favour,' James replied, matching the shift in tone, his cordial smile now gone. This was business. 'He said you'd be able to help us with what we're looking for . . . for a fee, naturally.' James pulled his coat back and opened his jacket to reveal a slim wad of cash in the inner pocket. He had had his British pounds changed for dollars when they'd arrived in Montreal, ready for buying the car.

There was a pause as Landon regarded them both, sizing them up.

'This isn't a sting,' James said, reading his mind. 'You can trust us. It was Tucker who told us to find you. We're all friends. Mallory and my wife are inseparable.'

Flora tried not to shudder as Landon's gaze settled upon her more heavily. She doubted the man had ever met Tucker's wife, but James's comment had given him permission to look at her more closely, and no one ever seemed to pass up that opportunity.

'Tucker said you were the only man for the job.'

Landon looked back at him with a cautious look, flattered in spite of himself. 'What is it y'want?'

'Just to find someone . . . Well, three people, actually. They were travelling together. Two women and a baby. They came over on the *Empress of Scotland*.'

'And why do you want to know? What is it to you?'

'They're friends of ours – both widows – and we'd like to see them while we're over here.' James's voice was cool but Landon's eyes narrowed, sensing the lie.

'You've a lot of friends, it seems.'

'Indeed we have. But our circumstances are more . . . fortunate than theirs. We promised their families back home that we'd check they're getting on well in their new lives here.'

Landon clearly didn't believe a word of it, but he also looked like he didn't much care. 'What's the names?' he sighed, reaching for a pencil and notebook.

'Lorna MacDonald. Mary McKinnon . . . The baby is called Struan McKinnon.'

Landon tore off the sheet of paper and folded it, slipping it into his trouser pocket. 'I'll look into it – but that won't be enough,' he said, jerking his chin towards James's pocket.

'Of course not,' James said coolly, reaching his hand in and drawing out the cash. 'This is simply the advance. I'll pay the same again when you tell me their whereabouts.'

He held out the money, his gaze level.

Landon hesitated, then took it with a nod. 'I'll be in touch,' he muttered. 'Where are you staying?'

'The Frontenac.'

Landon sniffed, as if he'd guessed as much. Flora didn't drip in jewels like Mallory Tucker and James didn't have a Mediterranean tan like Dickie Grainger – but there was something in the cut of their clothes, or perhaps the gleam of their hair, that quietly spoke to wealth. She had been aware of it when she'd been on the other side as a barefoot wild isle girl, and in the course of her experiences in Glasgow, in Paris and on the crossing over here, she had gradually acquired a rich gloss.

'Then we'll meet at the Old Homestead hotel on Place d'Armes. Opposite the Frontenac. I'll let you know when.'

'As you wish, Mr Landon,' James said, tipping his hat.

'Thank you, Mr Landon,' Flora murmured. 'We're so grateful.'

The Midnight Secret

Landon watched as James led her back towards the stairs. By the time they stepped out into the night, it was raining, but neither of them noticed.

'It really is a castle,' Flora said, her eyes trailing over the bedroom's oak-panelled walls and heavy damask curtains. Turrets, turning staircases, tapestries . . . The Frontenac's atmosphere was so different from the silken froth and cool finesse of the Paris Ritz, yet it oozed the same sense of heritage and wealth. There were, she was learning, many different ways to be rich.

She looked back at James as he shrugged off his coat, remembering how they had first met on the shores of St Kilda, crowded by mountains and cottages. Their future – not least the idea that they would ever find themselves here, on the seventeenth floor of the hotel's main tower – had been impossible to predict as they'd stood barefoot on that golden sand.

'What is it?' he asked, sensing her gaze as he removed his hat.

'Nothing,' she smiled, drawing one from him too as he came over and took her into his arms. He kissed her tenderly, knowing she wasn't the firecracker she had once been, that a fissure ran through her now that hadn't been there before. She clung to him, resting her head on his chest. His heartbeat was the only steadiness in her life right now. She had no home; only him.

'Are you hungry?' His voice vibrated against her ear as he stroked her hair, and she nodded.

'Famished. But I'm too tired to dress for dinner,' she said, looking up at him. 'Can't we have something up here?'

He smiled. 'I'm afraid not.'

She pulled back. 'Oh.'

'There's something we have to attend to first. Paperwork and the like.'

'. . . Oh,' she said again. The bureaucracy of immigration was overwhelming to her.

'But I promise, champagne and sandwiches back here as soon as we're done, yes?'

She nodded, suppressing a sigh as he turned to open their trunk. The clothes they had been wearing in heavy rotation for the past five weeks lay folded in crushed layers.

'Hmm,' said James. He reached for the telephone on a side table and called reception. Flora wandered over to the window seat, hardly noticing his half of the conversation. 'Hello, yes . . . Callaghan . . . housekeeping services . . . if you would. Thank you.'

She glanced up as he came to stand beside her. 'They're going to send someone up to refresh our clothes. We can't go down in wrinkles.'

'No, I suppose not,' she murmured. All she really wanted to do was sit here and look out over the city where their son might, at this very moment, be sleeping. He could be anywhere down there: in a pram they passed on the street, on the other side of an open window . . .

'Darling, I'm going to pop downstairs to see if I can't get ahead with this dratted paperwork. Once they've attended to you, come down and find me, yes?'

Flora straightened up as James headed for the door. She'd been in a daydream. 'But . . .'

He was almost out of the room.

'James? How will I find you?'

'I'll just be downstairs,' he smiled, closing the door after him.

Flora blinked, before turning back to the twinkling lights

The Midnight Secret

of the city outside. It was dark now and she wondered whether anyone was looking up at her, silhouetted in the window of the city's landmark building.

There came a knock at the door several minutes later and she stirred reluctantly.

'Hello,' she said, opening up to a bellboy standing there.

'For you, Madame,' he said, holding out a large box secured with a blue satin ribbon.

Flora frowned in confusion. 'No, we asked for housekeeping.'

'Oui, Madame, for you.' And he held out the box towards her. 'From Monsieur Callaghan.'

'What?' Flora took it in bewilderment, watching as he turned on his heel and disappeared down the hall.

She closed the door and stared at the box for a moment. When had James had a chance to go shopping? They'd been together all day.

No, they hadn't, of course, she remembered.

He must have bought it when he'd gone to find the car, hidden it in the trunk and arranged for it to be brought up here for her as a surprise. The day had been long, intense and, in parts, distressing, but he showed her he loved her in a myriad of ways.

She took it over to the bed, slipping the ribbons off the corners with a smile.

Candles flickered in the oak-panelled room, moody shadows sloping over the floors as James waited for her before the desk that would serve as their altar.

His smile widened, climbing into his eyes as he took in the sight of her in the gown he had picked out for her: buttery ivory silk, cut on the bias, with lace cap sleeves and a short tulle veil on a mother-of-pearl comb. She had kept her long dark hair free, simply brushing it to a shine and accessorizing with the posy of dark pink roses that had arrived at the room a few minutes after the dress.

He had thought of everything. He always did. She had made only one adjustment of her own, a detail that was true to her.

She walked slowly towards him as somewhere a string quartet played. He looked so handsome in his new suit, and she marvelled at the way he always managed to surprise her. She had long since come to terms with the fact that their wedding would have to happen without her family in attendance; circumstances dictated prioritizing respectability over sentimentality or tradition. She had known they would marry at the first opportunity. She just hadn't realized he meant the *first* opportunity.

Her gaze, acclimatizing now to the small, formal salon, took in the Justice of the Peace standing on the far side of the desk, two witnesses standing off to one side. She laughed softly, wondering how on earth he had managed to pull this together when all she had done for most of the day was stare out of windows.

'You look even more beautiful than I dreamed,' he murmured as she stopped in front of him. His gaze flickered downwards. '. . . Did the shoes not fit?'

'Oh, aye, they did. But you said it yourself – you can take the girl out of St Kilda,' she whispered, wiggling her bare toes against the plush rug underfoot. '. . . But never St Kilda out of the girl.'

Chapter Twelve

EFFIE

Hogmanay 1930

The Gathering Hall, Portree, Isle of Skye

The room was a twirling mass, arms thrown aloft and skirts swishing as the ceilidh band played faster and faster. Effie laughed as she was spun by her dance partner. She'd had to check her dance card for his name, having forgotten it at first, and she'd been surprised to see he had put himself down for two reels with her.

'You're either a very brave man or a glutton for punishment, Mr Baird-Hamilton,' she had said. 'I was told by one dance partner he knew cows with more grace than me.'

'Ouch,' he'd laughed. 'Perhaps I should check my insurance first?' But the moment the fiddles had started up, he had taken her with a firm grip, spinning and placing her with assurance, sending her blonde hair flying and her skirt billowing like a parachute.

In the past six weeks she had learned all the great reels of the Scottish ball season – the Dashing White Sergeant; Hamilton House; the Foursome and Eightsome; Mhairi's

Wedding and others. The men had practised with her in the great hall at Dupplin whenever they weren't playing golf or shooting, which had been increasingly frequently after the snow had come in hard in mid-December. She was a quick learner but still very much a novice, counting the beats out loud and trying to remember the steps – but Baird-Hamilton was so well practised, carelessly chatting as he manoeuvred her to the music, that she almost forgot they were dancing.

She had recognized him instantly as he first came over, and she had braced for some kind of waspish or sly comment. She hadn't exactly esteemed herself at their first meeting, covering Eddie Rushton in gin, so it had been a surprise when Baird-Hamilton had shaken her by the hand for putting 'that odious man' in his place. She remembered his misplaced laugh in the silence that had followed, but even so, she'd assumed he must disapprove of her. And he'd been so watchful and reserved that evening, very different to the *bon viveur* here tonight.

The reel finished almost as suddenly as it had begun, with a vibrato on the fiddle. Everyone cheered, clapping wildly. These balls, the pinnacle of the Scottish social season, weren't so very different from the ceilidhs she had enjoyed at home. Yes, the dress code was more formal; here the men wore trews and kilts – any visiting *Sassenachs* in white tie – and the women were in gowns with tartan sashes. Women were supposed to glide as if on wheels, not bounce to the music; but the men still whooped and spun the women with abandon, hands on waists turning them faster and faster so that their chests heaved and their cheeks grew pink. As Effie was so light, the men would fling her one way then the next as she laughed, trying to catch her breath. Being fit, strong and light made her a good sport.

'Well, that was lively,' she panted as Baird-Hamilton led

The Midnight Secret

her back to her group, but they made slow progress through the crowd with so many bodies packed into the small village hall.

'Yes, that did get the blood up,' he agreed, unbuttoning his velvet evening jacket.

'Archie,' a red-headed woman smiled as she passed by him, nodding her head in greeting.

'Clarissa. You look beautiful tonight.'

'Thank you,' she murmured. 'See you for the Dashing White?'

'I'll find you.'

Effie watched the woman go. She couldn't imagine ever being so accepted into this circle that she too might one day carelessly weave in and out of the crowds, knowing everyone.

'And how was your Christmas, Miss Gillies?' he asked.

'Oh. Cosy, actually – which isn't something I ever thought I'd say about a castle,' she grinned.

'No?'

'We stayed at Dupplin with Gladly. We holed up in the snug most days and ate sandwiches and played cards and charades and backgammon. I'm dreadful at it. Even worse than at dancing.'

'Nonsense. You were a delight just now.' He cast a sidelong look and smiled. 'So you didn't see your families?'

'Well, the earl and countess were spending Christmas in the south of France, so it didn't make much sense to go back to Dumfries House.'

'. . . Indeed.' He cleared his throat.

'And my father decided to go back to Lochaline to see our old friends and neighbours. He misses them, especially with – well, with me spending so much time away from Ayrshire lately. I think he sometimes wonders why he moved there.'

'. . . I'm sure you'll be back in no time.'

'Aye,' she nodded, though their tour still had numerous invitations to tick off – MacLeod from tonight for a few days, then the Duke of Argyll . . .

'Brava!' Colly said as they rejoined the others. 'You didn't put a foot wrong!'

'Hmm. I think Mr Baird-Hamilton's toes might say otherwise,' she laughed, raking her hair back with her fingers to try to cool down a little.

'Codswallop. You were flawless, Miss Gillies. It was like dancing with a fairy.'

'Now I know you're lying!' she laughed, glancing over and finding Sholto still in conversation with his dance partner as he walked her back to her friends. She admired him from afar; he was always so proper and handsome, as unaware of the admiring looks that followed him as she was aware of the craned necks and wide eyes that greeted her entrance into every new room.

She looked back again to find Baird-Hamilton watching her, and she smiled. 'Thank you for looking after me out there.'

'Not at all. I've found there are few places more treacherous in the world than a Highland ball – sharpened elbows, rapier wit, heaving bosoms to take a man's eye out.'

She laughed again and he smiled, seeming pleased to have amused her.

'Well, it certainly looked from here like you were both enjoying yourselves,' Bitsy said archly from her perch on the tall stool. She was still sitting out most of the energetic dances on account of her 'terrible foot injury' at Dupplin, and her coolness towards Effie had dropped several degrees more since she had started seeing Eddie Rushton. He was due to

The Midnight Secret

return to California early in the new year, and as the day grew ever closer, Bitsy's mood was souring. It seemed no mention had been made of her going out to America to visit him. 'The two of you were beaming at one another.'

Effie flushed at the intimation, but Baird-Hamilton was unruffled.

'I suppose we were. I rather sense Miss Gillies and I are birds of a feather,' he replied, looking over at Effie for back-up. 'She's not afraid to take an evening by the scruff of the neck and shake every last bit of fun from it. If only there were more of our ilk, instead of so much mannered artifice.' It was a clear rebuke.

'Oh, Arch, there you are. Tell me, are you going to Monaco next month?' Peony butted in as she joined them all. Her dance card had been filled up within moments of arriving and she'd scarcely stopped for breath. She looked ravishing in dusky pink taffeta.

'Undecided. You?'

'Mm, I think so,' she sighed, eyes narrowed as if in intense concentration. 'I need some sun. Don't you remember how I loathe being cold?' She pinned him with what seemed to be a pointed stare.

Effie looked between them, confused.

'I do . . . But if you'll excuse me, I'd better find my next partner.' He bowed slightly, removing himself from the group without further ado.

Effie watched him go, wishing she could dance with him again. He seemed like the only straight shooter here, and it had been a relief to throw off the rules for a few minutes and just *be*.

'Hmm. Well, he seemed particularly pleased to make your acquaintance again,' Bitsy muttered.

'Did he?' Effie asked, sensing subtext. 'I thought he was just being polite.'

'Oh, don't fall for that,' Bitsy drawled. 'Our Archie has quite the reputation as a lady-killer. There's not a woman in here he hasn't had one way or another . . . Be very careful with him.'

Effie's mouth opened in surprise at the suggestion that he might be interested in her and, worse, that she might reciprocate. Flirtation and seduction might be part of their social language here, but she had no interest in learning it. 'I'm engaged! *Obviously* I'm not interested!'

'Ah, but that won't stop him,' Bitsy said dismissively. 'Old B-H relishes a challenge!'

Gladly approached the table and sweetly, wordlessly, handed her a glass of lemonade. She hadn't even had to ask. 'So what's going on?' he asked into the stiff silence.

'Just Effie catching certain eyes,' Bitsy said devilishly.

'I'm *not* catching anyone's eyes,' Effie defended herself. She didn't want gossip to start. 'I love Sholto.'

'I'm very glad to hear it,' Sholto himself said, suddenly appearing at her shoulder. '. . . Was it ever in doubt?'

'We're just teasing her,' Peony sighed, bored with the conversation. 'She just danced with B-H, so you know the drill . . .'

A small, disgruntled sound came from Sholto's throat but he passed no comment on the matter. 'What I want to know is, when am *I* dancing with you?' He pulled out her dance card and checked it, looking back at her with an aghast expression. '. . . You didn't leave me a single dance?'

'I didn't get a chance! Besides, you should have been quicker off the mark,' she shrugged. 'You're the one who knows how this goes, not me.'

'I'm a damned fool,' he drawled, his eyes dancing.

It was true she had been particularly popular this evening.

The Midnight Secret

The Skye Balls were held over two nights at the Gathering Hall in Portree, and this was the second. Last night she had mainly danced with the men in Sholto's closest friendship circle, but tonight that had opened up, and she didn't even recognize most of the names on her card: the Rt Hon Charles Arbuthnott, Mungo MacMillan, Viscount Lisle . . . What she did recognize was the look in their eyes as they twirled and spun her. Everyone wanted to experience for themselves the allure she must surely possess to have attracted a man of the calibre of Sholto Crichton-Stuart.

He turned her away from the others and reached down to kiss her cheek lightly. 'At least I get to take you home,' he whispered in her ear, making her shiver.

Wherever that was.

They were moving on tonight – Gladly and the others included – to Dunvegan Castle. They would all spend the first few days of the New Year with James MacLeod, heir apparent to the MacLeod estate and another of Sholto's oldest friends. *His* parents were away at the Isle of Bute. It seemed to Effie that one of the conditions of having a castle was never actually staying there, but visiting friends' piles instead.

'By the way,' Gladly said. 'I just saw MacLeod. He got here late. He's had to bring the boat down, would you believe? Apparently the roads north are impassable – there's much heavier snow further up – so he's going to sail us back.'

'Sailing in December?' she frowned, looking nervously at Sholto. 'Is that safe?'

He smiled. 'Freezing, but we'll manage. Don't worry – St Kilda's in open water but we're much more protected in the Minch.'

The first four bars of the next dance was played, their cue that the next reel was about to begin.

'Oh Lord, already?' Gladly groaned behind her. 'How's a chap supposed to finish a drink?'

'Which one are we doing now?' Colly asked with a sigh.

'Reel of the 51st,' Veronica said officiously. 'And you're doing it with me.'

'Oh, good,' he said flatly.

'Miss Gillies?' a voice asked. Effie turned to see a rotund, bespectacled man with sandy red hair. She had no idea of his name. 'Duncan Forbes. I believe I have the pleasure of this dance?'

The debonair Rt Hon. Archie Baird-Hamilton he was not.

'Wonderful,' she smiled, even though her feet were burning in her shoes. It was almost dawn, and they had been dancing all night. 'I'd love to.'

'Look after her for me, Forbes,' Sholto said, slapping him on the shoulder.

'She's safe with me, old boy.'

Sholto winked at Effie as she was led away.

'You're with me on this one, Sholto,' she heard Peony say to him, giving him her hand to lead her back into the middle of the room.

An hour and four reels later, they were almost done. Almost. It was approaching five in the morning, but still several hours off dawn; the sun didn't rise much before eight at this time of year. Effie was dropping. She was used to the night hunts back home, climbing sea stacks and catching gannets in the spring, but dancing all night took a different level of stamina.

'You look tired,' Sholto said, his hand on the small of her back as they reconvened before the final reel of the night.

The Midnight Secret

'Nonsense,' she rebuffed. 'That breakfast has refuelled me.' Gladly had come round with plates of hot kippers before the Eightsome.

Sholto wasn't fooled. 'Well, we'll be getting on the boat straight after this, so you can sleep all the way to Dunvegan. MacLeod's keen to get off quickly. If you head straight down to the jetty after this, Gladly and I will bring the trunk.'

'But how will I know which is his?'

'Ask anyone. They can point it out to you.'

She nodded as the fiddles gave their salutary warning. Sholto frowned as no partner came to claim her. 'Who's down with you now?'

She looked at her dance card. '. . . Viscount Lisle?'

'Oh, yes, I saw him over there somewhere.' Sholto's height made it easy for him to pick out faces in the crowd and he grabbed her hand, towing her through the bodies to where a stocky young man was finishing his drink. He seemed several years younger than Effie, she guessed.

'Lisle!' Sholto barked, after standing there for several seconds unnoticed.

The younger man stood to attention – before slumping again. 'Ah, Sholly, it's you.'

Sholto arched an eyebrow. 'How many of those have you had?'

'. . . T-two?'

Bottles, perhaps.

'You're swaying.'

'Nonsense. The room's just dizzy from all the dancing.' His words were a jumbled slur.

Sholto looked wryly at Effie. 'I need to find my partner for this – but he's harmless, honestly. Although *you* may need to lead *him*, by the looks of things.' He gripped the young viscount's shoulder hard. 'Look after my fiancée, Lisle, do you hear?'

'Yesh.' He swayed again.

Effie watched him with apprehension. Strip the Willow was one of the simpler reels, but it did involve a lot of turning. He didn't look as if he'd have the legs – or the stomach – for it.

'And when it's done, you're to accompany Miss Gillies here straight down to MacLeod's yacht, you hear?'

'Yesh.'

'What did I just say?'

'Accompany the ghillie to MacLeod's yacht.'

'Near enough,' Sholto muttered. 'Will you be all right?' he asked Effie.

'Of course.'

'I'll be . . .' He looked around to find Bitsy frantically motioning for him with a highly irritated look. 'Down there with Miss Sourpants.'

Effie stifled a laugh.

'See you on board, darling.'

The band played the first four bars as he darted through the room. The revellers had organized themselves into two long lines, men on one side, women on the other, and Effie took her position opposite her dance partner.

As the dance began, she had to reach for him and lead him into swinging her around. There was no doubt the young viscount had the muscle memory for the dance, but he lacked the physical coordination. He was supposed to swing Effie and then present her to each man in the line in turn, but as she swung round his neighbour and reached for him again, he missed her arm. Effie had to almost run around him to keep up with the music.

The Midnight Secret

When it was his turn to come back up the line, swinging and turning with the ladies, he was like a ball to skittles. It was a chaotic end to what had been an invigorating two nights, and many people were tutting at him by the time the last bar was played.

'Shorry,' he said afterwards as the dancers broke up into an emotional crowd, wishing one another festive greetings and swapping travel plans for the new year.

'It's quite all right,' Effie replied, eager to make her getaway.

'You're a good sport. I knew you would be.' He looked as if the room was still turning around him.

'Did you?'

'Of course. You're Sholly's fiancée.'

He really was very drunk. 'Yes. Well, it was a pleasure—'

'He must really love you.'

She gave a small laugh as she turned away. 'Given we're getting married, I should hope so—'

He made a long slurring sound. 'Not many men would give up their birthright for love. Certainly none of the fellows in this room, that's for sure.'

Effie halted and turned back, staring at him. '. . . What?'

He swayed. She had a sudden urge to shake him.

'Tell me – what did you mean by that?'

He blinked once, twice, but his eyes were vacant. 'The earl and the countess . . .' Was he going to pass out?

'What about them?' she demanded, feeling her heart beginning to pound. He was, to use one of Colly's favourite words, 'blotto', but that didn't mean he was talking gibberish.

'They said they'd disinherit him,' he shrugged. 'But Sholly chose *you*!' He held his hands out towards her in case she was in any doubt of who he meant.

Effie felt the room begin to spin around her. Was that . . . was that true? Had Sholto's parents refused to give their blessing for the engagement?

No.

She couldn't believe he would lie about such a thing to her! Sholto would never lie to her.

And yet . . . he hadn't been home in six weeks, traipsing from castle to castle, introducing her 'to the set' . . . She remembered their curious gazes every time she stepped into a new room. She had thought it was the class divide that fascinated them, and perhaps it was, to some degree. But if they all knew something she did not – that Sholto had walked away from his family, chosen her over them . . . He was the only son and heir, not only to the Dumfries earldom, but the marquessate of Bute as well . . . Was it any wonder she had held them in her thrall?

Oh God – had they all been sworn to silence? Did everyone know but her? She remembered Baird-Hamilton's polite enquiries about their Christmas plans just an hour previously as he tiptoed around a truth to which she was blind.

No. This couldn't be happening.

She looked around for Sholto in the crowd, but there was no sign of his beautiful golden head. She began pushing her way towards the door, leaving the swaying viscount in her wake.

It was freezing cold outside, especially for Effie, in just an emerald-green silk dress, and she shivered as she looked down the slope towards the water. A dozen or so yachts were moored along the jetty, just a few lights shining amid the pervasive darkness as the bay of Portree fanned out around them on three sides.

She ran down the steps towards the boats. People were

The Midnight Secret

already moving in groups towards them, laughing and talking as they walked in huddles, their capes and evening coats back on. Effie darted past, an emerald streak.

'MacLeod's yacht?' she asked a woman in marigold taffeta.

'What?' the woman barked, looking three sheets to the wind herself.

'Which is MacLeod's yacht?'

'Oh . . . There,' the woman pointed. 'Last but one over—'

'Thank you,' Effie muttered, taking off again, running until she stopped in front of a small, slightly battered-looking navy-hulled schooner. It was still dark, but a crack of sunlight was opening on the horizon past the Black Cuillin mountains. She could see someone at the far end of the boat, tinkering with the anchor chain.

'Hai!' she called out, her eyes looking everywhere for Sholto.

The man's head lifted as he heard her come aboard, though he didn't – couldn't – turn. 'Oh good, you made it!' he called over his shoulder. 'Jump on!'

A short, narrow gangplank had been laid across onto the jetty and was moving up and down off the surface with the roll of the waves beneath the boat. It would be disconcerting for anyone who didn't really know how to swim, but if a lifetime of cragging in St Kilda had given Effie anything, it was superior balancing ability. She slipped off her shoes, running easily over the walkway and jumping lightly onto the deck.

No one else was around, but she could see a light shining from a cabin below deck.

'I'll be right there,' MacLeod called again. 'Go down to the galley so you don't catch your death. There's some blankets down there. The wind's picking up, so I want to get ahead of it while we can.'

Effie hesitated. She really didn't want to talk to – confront – Sholto about what she had learned in front of all the others; she sensed Bitsy and Peony would take particular relish in showing they had been privy to information about her own situation. But she had only met their host briefly this evening, and she could hardly be the cause of a delay if he was so keen to set off.

She hurried down the steep, short steps into the warmth and braced herself to meet her fiancé's eyes. Would he see instantly that she knew? After all, she hadn't known that they'd been living under a lie for the past month and a half. She had taken him at face value.

Below deck she found a small kitchenette with bench seating and seemingly a bedroom space beyond a closed door. To her surprise, the others hadn't yet arrived, and she realized Sholto and Gladly must still be bringing down the trunks that had been put in the cloakroom on arrival. She had sprung into action too quickly – old habits died hard, clearly – and no doubt both men were getting caught up with drunken goodbyes.

Taking a breath, she tried to calm her shaken thoughts as she stood there alone. Perhaps it was no bad thing to have a few moments to herself. She knew she mustn't make a scene. She was angry that Sholto had lied, yes, but she also knew full well why he had. He knew that she would never have allowed him to give up his family, his home, his birthright . . . for her.

She sank onto the bench with a sigh. But now that she did know, what was she going to do about it? It hurt to think of the earl and countess rejecting her, even if she understood it. On a personal level, they had never been anything other than kind and friendly; the earl had often come into the collection

The Midnight Secret

rooms where she worked, and they would talk while she catalogued . . . Had it come as a bitter surprise to him? He had known she and Sholto were friends, of course. But had he been disappointed that his professional courtesy had been rewarded with her 'seducing' his son and heir?

Effie shivered at the thought and took a blanket from one of the benches, wrapping it around herself. Immediately she softened at the comfort; she was cold and so, so tired. She sat down, feeling the exhaustion hit her, the bones spreading in her bare feet as she could finally relax. She tipped her head back and drew another deep breath.

They would talk it out, find a way forward . . . wouldn't they? If Sholto wouldn't give up on her, then she wouldn't give up either, but they had to come up with some sort of plan for reapproaching his parents. She would never marry him without their blessing.

The boat swung a little, and she looked out through the porthole to see a fishing boat coming back into the harbour, a wake rippling behind it. The fishing boats had always made waves in Village Bay.

She closed her eyes, reassured . . .

Effie lay on the banquette, huddled in the blanket, feeling the rhythmic plunge and rise of the boat over the water. It was soothing, somnambulant. How long had she been asleep? She blinked several times, feeling the heaviness in her body and sensing she had been fast off for a while. She had always had an ability to nap for short periods; it was useful in lambing season, and of course when they went to Stac Lee to hunt gannets at night. But a full night of dancing was a different proposition and the boat had been like a cradle, rocking her to sleep . . .

The sun was sparkling on the sea past the little round windows, diamonds of sunlight glinting off the waves. She frowned. How long *had* she been asleep for?

Tightening the blanket around her shoulders, she carefully made her way up the steps. The wind grabbed at her as she emerged, her hair streaming backwards in lightning-strike blonde streaks and blinding her line of sight, her silk gown pressed back against her body and flapping loudly like the bedsheets on the washing lines at home.

MacLeod stood at the helm just ahead of her. He was reaching over to tighten a sail rope on a cleat to his right.

Effie gasped at the sight of him and immediately twisted to look back along the fore of the deck, searching for Sholto, of course, but Gladly and Colly too . . . Even Bitsy, Peony and Veronica would be a welcome sight right now.

But there was no one else aboard.

His task completed, MacLeod turned back and startled to see her standing there suddenly, a vision in blonde and emerald green. Immediately his expression mirrored her own.

'Wait—' Effie began, confused. This made no sense.

'Miss Gillies!' Baird-Hamilton exclaimed. '. . . What the devil are you doing here?'

Chapter Thirteen

'This isn't MacLeod's boat?' she gasped, staggering over to where he stood, trying to hold her hair back so she could see – but the wind was obdurate, tugging hard.

Baird-Hamilton looked bemused. 'Sadly not! His is far smarter than this old girl. I just use her for pottering about. Usually in summer, of course. But also when the roads are shot.'

They had to raise their voices to speak over the wind.

'But . . .' Effie looked around her in panic. How could this be happening? 'But I'm supposed to be on MacLeod's boat!'

'Yes, I guessed that.' A smile played on his lips, his eyes seeming to dance. 'If it makes you feel any better, I was expecting you to be someone else too.'

It didn't. Effie stared at him. This was a disaster.

'But not to worry,' he said after a moment, seeing she was distinctly less amused by their predicament. 'I've been caught on stickier wickets than this, I assure you.'

'Where . . . where are we?' There was a strong wind at their backs, the mainsail billowing at full reach so that they were flying past sea cliffs and coves, white seabirds diving and gliding on the thermals. It was a familiar landscape, and she felt a reflexive pulse of joy.

'In the Sound of Raasay. Beautiful, isn't it? There are always sea eagles over th—'

'We're heading south?' They were going in completely the wrong direction. Dunvegan Castle – Sholto had shown it to her on a revolving globe in Gladly's library – sat on a promontory on the north-west side of the isle, fronting onto its own sea loch.

'Indeed, but you see, the great – the very greatest – thing about this vessel, Miss Gillies, is that she turns around.'

He was teasing her, she knew, but she couldn't smile. What would Sholto be thinking? She had just disappeared into the night! Did he think her drowned? Lost? Would it occur to him that she had somehow ended up on the wrong boat?

'We have to go back,' she said urgently.

'I quite agree,' he said. 'But not till this wind has dropped, I'm afraid. These are force five north-westerlies. We're in the leeside here but if we were to round the Trotternish peninsula now, we'd be exposed to the full force of it. Far too risky.'

'But MacLeod's sailing it!'

'Yes. His yacht is ocean-going. I'm afraid the *Lady Tara* isn't up to those passes. Speaking of which . . .' He reached under the helm to a small stowage compartment. 'Put this on.' He handed her a bulky life vest, the same as he was wearing over his green velvet dinner jacket. 'Pass me the blanket while you put it on.'

She did as instructed, having to turn into the wind again to force her hair to blow backwards while she slipped it on. The dress plastered to her body as she fastened the jacket's ties. 'What's inside this?' she frowned, feeling hard ridges pressing against her ribs.

'Cork. Not comfortable, but if you fall in, you're guaranteed to bob.'

'Oh.' She looked back at him, taking back the blanket and clutching it around her again – this time as much for modesty

The Midnight Secret

as warmth. A gown by candlelight felt very much like a slip in daylight, and he was watching her with that intense look of his.

'Mr Baird-Hamilton—'

'Archie, please,' he corrected, looking pained by her formality. 'We have danced the Gay Gordons and Hamilton House together. That makes us dear friends.'

Was he ever serious? Effie wondered.

'Archie,' she sighed, trying to control her panic. With every comment, they were sailing ever further south. 'It's vital I get back to Portree. Sholto will think I've . . .' What *would* he be thinking, coming out and finding her gone? No word. No trace. 'He'll be worrying about me.'

'I'm quite sure he will, but he won't be in Portree now, I assure you. Once he's ascertained you're not in the water – and it's very protected there; bodies don't get far – he'll know there's some sort of mix-up and set off for Dunvegan before the weather gets worse. He'll have to; the winds are strengthening to gale force this afternoon, and with the roads closed, they can't afford to hang about.'

Effie stared at him. Was it true, that Sholto would have left her behind?

'Please don't worry,' he said calmly, seeing her continuing dismay. 'There's a telephone at my house. We can call Dunvegan from there and explain the situation. Once Sholto knows you're perfectly safe, we can wait out the weather.' He shrugged as if it was all very easy.

Effie clutched the blanket at her throat. 'Where is your house?'

'On Raasay. Not far. Here, take a pew beside me and get out of the wind. You look as if you're going to blow away.'

Reluctantly, she sat down beside him. What else could she do? The wind was at their backs, propelling them ever southwards, away from her one true north.

The *Lady Tara* slipped into the enfolding arms of a small bay, Archie expertly furling the mainsail, spooling out mooring ropes and dropping the anchor as Effie watched from her perch, decorative and useless. Boats remained an enigma to her: so many moving parts and mercurial conditions to account for. She far preferred the ancient immobility of cliffs to the sea.

'May I?' Archie asked, reaching out for the blanket. She hadn't let it go for a single moment on the journey over. He folded it and dropped it back into the cabin as she unfastened the life vest and stowed it in the space beyond the helm.

'Here, take my hand,' he said as he jumped onto the small jetty – but as in Portree, Effie alighted as nimbly as a fawn, drawing from him a smirk at her little rebellion. 'Then at least take my coat. I insist. This is no weather for bare arms.' He shrugged off the velvet jacket in a fluid movement and draped it over her shoulders.

It smelled of woodsmoke and moss, and she felt a pang of guilt at being enveloped in another man's scent.

She wondered briefly what her old friends would say if they could see her walking on a private jetty, a ball gown trailing behind her, with a man whose reputation preceded him. Flora, no doubt, would delight in the glamour; Mhairi would fret over the risk of gossip.

'That's your home?' she asked, looking up at the beautiful house towards which they were walking. It fronted onto sweeping snowy lawns and was built of pale honeyed stone, with tall floor-to-ceiling sash windows, a grey slate roof, gables, chimneys and a pillared portico. It was far less grand

The Midnight Secret

than Dumfries House, but still an elegant and imposing country house.

'Well, I'm the current owner, but it's more of a bolthole than a home. My uncle bought it just before the Great War. He was killed in the Battle of Amiens and I was his only heir, so . . .' Archie shrugged, as if it was merely a perplexing mystery that he should have come to find himself in possession of such a handsome home. 'Historically, however, Raasay House – and the island as a whole – belonged to a branch of the MacLeods. It was in their domain for centuries, and it rather feels they still have a hand on it.' He rolled his eyes. 'Certainly Jim MacLeod delights in telling me that I'm bunking in his boathouse.'

Boathouse?

'Oh.' She followed him along the path, through the grounds and into the house. The door opened onto flagged floors and dozens of wall-mounted antlers. Barley-twist chairs stood against walls and tables were laden with framed family photographs.

It was cold indoors, but she had seen smoke puffing from some of the chimneys, and a grey-haired woman emerged from one of the rooms at the sound of their footsteps. 'Welcome back, sir,' she said. 'Tea is served in the library, if you'd like to take the weight off?'

'I should think we would like that, Mrs Robertson. We've had a hard day's night,' Archie said appreciatively, flashing her a warm smile. He pulled at his bow tie and undid the top button of his shirt, stretching out his neck with the relief Effie reserved for taking off shoes. 'This is my friend Miss Gillies – Effie, my housekeeper, Mrs Robertson.'

'How do you do?' Effie smiled politely, receiving a restrained nod in reply. The woman's eyes darted up and down her in fleeting judgement. Too late, Effie remembered that Archie's jacket was still over her shoulders, and she quickly shrugged it off. 'Oh. Your coat.'

He handed it to Mrs Robertson, who looked quizzically at him. 'No Miss Bruce, sir?'

'No – a slight change of plan . . .' he muttered. 'I say, what women's clothes do we have here?'

There was a pause. 'None, sir. You requested a full clear-out after Miss Coutts-Fitzroy's departure—'

'Ah, yes,' he said quickly. 'So I did. Hmm.' He looked at Effie, resplendent in green silk at ten o'clock in the morning. 'We can hardly have you drifting about in that – you'll catch your death. It's usually colder inside this house than out. I'm afraid you may have to wear some of my clobber. Does that appal you?'

'Not at all.'

'Good sport. At least I'll be the only one to see, and I certainly shan't tell on you.'

'I'll lay out some things on your bed, then, sir . . .' the housekeeper said, turning to go.

'Actually, Robertson, Miss Gillies will be staying in a guest room.'

The housekeeper couldn't hide her surprise, although she looked like a woman not often startled. '. . . Of course. The – the blue room, sir?'

'Yes, why not? Everyone says it has the prettiest view.' He glanced at Effie. 'And draw a bath too, and get the fire going in there, won't you? Miss Gillies has caught a chill, I fear.'

'I'm sure,' Mrs Robertson said disapprovingly.

'It's a long story,' was all Archie said over his shoulder as he led the way into the library.

It was dark and moody in there, with ochre-coloured walls and oak bookshelves, several balding leather armchairs set

The Midnight Secret

before the fire. A writing desk stood behind a sagging linen sofa and a tiger-skin rug was spread on the floor.

Effie stared at it, riveted and horrified all at once. It still had teeth! Unpleasant memories of Lady Sibyl's pet cheetah surfaced in her mind; that had had sharp teeth too. What was it about the upper classes and their need for predators at hand?

'One of Uncle Bertie's trophies from India,' Archie explained. 'His father was Viceroy. Quite the hunter, I'm given to believe. Rather like you, I imagine?'

She looked at him as she settled herself in the armchair opposite him. A pot of tea and some scones spread with jam had been left on a tray on the small ottoman between them.

'Weren't you St Kildans renowned hunters?' he persisted as he began to pour. 'Wasn't the last Great Auk killed by one of your lot?'

'. . . How do you know I'm from St Kilda?'

He laughed out loud at her joke – the last time they'd referenced her heritage hadn't ended well for Edward Rushton. Effie couldn't help but grin at his infectious sense of humour.

'You know, you've had the *ton*, as they say, in more of a buzz than when Lord Tansey's wife was impregnated by their chauffeur. I shall be feted for this *coup de grâce*, hosting you here like this. Now I can get all the news.' His eyes danced with merriment as he passed her a cup and saucer. She wondered how he would react if she told him she had only just come into the full facts of her own situation herself. 'Of course, they'll all think I did this deliberately. Don't be surprised if they start a rumour saying I kidnapped you.' He sat back in his chair. 'I'm afraid I have a terribly low reputation. People always want to believe the worst.'

'So you're saying it's not deserved?' she asked, remembering Bitsy's warning.

'Oh, I wouldn't say that. But it's always more interesting playing along.'

Effie was growing used to his teasing. She wrapped her hand around the teacup, grateful for the immediate warmth. Tea and a fire suddenly felt like the greatest luxuries; she was delirious with exhaustion. A night spent dancing without sleep and a December sea crossing in little more than a nightie were taking their toll. 'Well, once I make that telephone call, all kidnapping stories can be laid to rest.'

'What a pity,' he tutted.

'May I?' she asked, her eyes falling to the telephone on the desk.

Archie looked back at her, smiling, but there was something else in his eyes too; a shadow of disappointment? 'Of course. Skye 2598.'

She got up and lifted the handset from its cradle. '. . . Hello?' she asked after a moment. She frowned, turning back towards him. 'There's no connection.'

He looked bemused, getting up and putting the handset to his ear as he pressed on the cradle.

There was a pause. '. . . Robertson?' he called.

The housekeeper was there within moments. 'Sir?'

'What's wrong with the phone?'

'Oh, yes, that. One of the telegraph poles came down yesterday morning. Cal Murdock skidded on ice in the tractor and hit it square on. Almost electrocuted half his flock.'

'Oh dear.'

'Aye, he was in a fair muddle. He's got an egg-sized lump on his head and was seeing double—'

'Yes, yes. When can they make the repairs?'

'Not until next week now. There's no more ferries before Monday on account of the winds.'

The Midnight Secret

Today was Thursday. Effie felt her stomach dive as Archie looked back at her apologetically. Sholto had no idea where she was – and now it would be another four days before she could enlighten him?

'I'm afraid we're not exactly a priority for the telephone board,' he explained, replacing the receiver.

'But I can't stay here till then,' Effie said urgently. 'I need to go back to Portree.'

'That would be pointless when all roads north are closed. We need to get you round to Dunvegan.'

'Then I'll find a way,' she argued. 'I'm used to bad weather.'

Archie looked bemused. 'I'm sure you are, and if my boat were any more robust, I'd take you up there myself . . .' He sighed. 'I'm sorry. I know this is all terribly bad luck.'

'What if we were to go now, before the winds *really* pick up?' she said desperately, turning to look out at the view. It was stunning, looking straight across the sound to Skye, with the Red Cuillin mountains – more sedate than their Black cousins – bumping the horizon. Effie refused to acknowledge the white horses already rearing in the open water, the bend and sway of the trees as the wind began to gust and moan. 'We could still do it.'

He shook his head, unmoved by her pleas. 'I'm reckless but not suicidal, more's the pity. I'll get you back there at the first break in the clouds. Until then . . . I'm afraid you're stuck here with me.'

A bath, a long sleep and a brief walk to inspect the fallen telegraph pole – confirming that they were indeed stranded – did much to improve Effie's spirits. She still couldn't help but fret about Sholto, but she took comfort in what Archie kept telling her: her fiancé would know she wasn't drowned, and he would guess that a mix-up had occurred. And at least she knew where to find him, even if he didn't know where to find her. All they had to do was wait for the winds to drop.

She stared at herself in the bedroom mirror, feeling conflicted by what she saw. It fit her perfectly, and yet . . .

Earlier, Mrs Robertson had left out a pair of Archie's trousers, a shirt and jumper for her to put on after her bath. The trousers were comically long and had had to be rolled up several times; he had cracked a one-sided smile of deep amusement at the sight of her as she had walked into the library. 'Like a glove,' he had quipped.

Luckily for Effie, she had worn the housekeeper's gumboots for their walk.

For dinner, however, he had had a brainwave, remembering his dinner suit from his schooldays. 'It must still be hanging somewhere in one of the wardrobes,' he had said to Mrs Robertson, who had simply nodded with the expression of someone who knew exactly where everything was hanging.

Effie tugged at the shirt cuffs and left the room, finding her host in his preferred fireside chair with a copy of the local paper on his knees and a tumbler of whisky in his hand. He glanced up and seemed to freeze as she saw a look of genuine shock cross his face – which was saying something. He didn't strike her as easily shockable. The dinner suit looked as if it had been made for her, but there was something . . . *confusing* about seeing herself, a young woman, her blonde hair spread over her shoulders, in such a masculine item of clothing. Wearing trousers was one thing, but an actual dinner suit? She still wasn't sure why they had to dress for dinner when it was just the two of them in any case.

'I couldn't do up the tie,' she murmured as his uncharacteristic silence stretched out.

The Midnight Secret

'No, indeed,' he said, getting up and coming to stand before her. 'There's a . . . there's a real knack to doing it . . . Tricky rascals.' He bent down and began tying the bow at her neck. It seemed an intricate process and she was very aware of his proximity as she stood there. Of course, they had danced together; she had already felt his hands on her waist, his hands gripping hers, but there was something . . . intimate in the stillness of this endeavour.

'No shoes, I see.'

'I'm a St Kildan, remember?' she murmured, looking diagonally away from him, not risking eye contact at these close quarters. 'And the choice was either my dancing shoes or Mrs Beeton's gumboots, so . . .'

'That really is sitting on the horns of a dilemma.'

There was another silence as she felt his fingers working against her throat.

'How old were you when you wore this?' she murmured as another silence bloomed.

'. . . Thirteen? Before I'd started shooting up,' he replied, his gaze dragging over her as he stepped back finally and admired the finished result. Barefooted but bow-tied, she saw the heavy rise and fall of his chest as a thick tension seemed to coagulate between them.

'Do we look like a pair of penguins?' she asked, needing to defuse it.

He laughed again. 'I fear we do! But take heart – if we can't make a lady of you, we'll make a gentleman for sure. You're a looker in a gown, don't get me wrong, but you do rather suit men's clothes.'

'I take that as a compliment,' she preened. 'I always wore my brother's clothes back home.'

'Did you indeed? Didn't your mother have something to

say about that?' He wandered over to the drinks cabinet and poured her a whisky, slowly unscrewing the bottle top with a distracted air.

'My mother died when I was ten. And my brother too, when I was fourteen.'

Archie looked taken aback. For once, there was no sign of a smirk on his lips. 'I'm terribly sorry to hear that.'

She shrugged. 'I didn't wear his clothes before that, obviously . . .' She rolled her eyes. 'He'd have scalped me.'

'What happened to him?'

'Climbing accident. The rope snapped.'

'Dear God, that's terrible.'

Effie was quiet for a moment. 'It was quick, at least.'

He came back over and handed her the drink.

'To absent friends,' he murmured. They clinked glasses, eyes locking as they both sipped their drinks.

'You must miss your home very much.'

'I do – especially as I haven't found somewhere to replace it.'

'Yes, you are currently somewhat nomadic, aren't you?'

She watched him, knowing that behind his discretion, he knew. They all did.

'Actually, I only found out last night that Sholto's parents don't want us to marry,' she said simply. 'He had told me differently.'

'Ah . . . Tricky.' He looked down at his glass, then back at her. Was his loyalty conflicted? He had known Sholto for many years. They had run in the same set since boyhood and even if they weren't as close as others, he wouldn't want to drop Sholto in it with a misjudged word. '. . . How did he take it when you told him he'd been rumbled?'

The Midnight Secret

'He doesn't know. I ran straight down to the boat to confront him – only to end up on yours instead.'

He nodded. 'Fate can work in mysterious ways, Miss Gillies,' he deadpanned.

She grinned back. He played to type a lot, she'd noticed. 'It isn't fate that I'm here. It's a simple mix-up. I asked a woman which boat was MacLeod's and she pointed to the wrong one.'

'Well, then, give me her name. I must thank her.'

She laughed, amazed that she *could* laugh about it. Last night, in the Gathering Hall, she had felt exposed and humiliated. Now, at least, she felt a little more perspective.

She peeled away and went to stand by the fire. It was distinctly strange to feel a tiger's pelt beneath her bare feet. Archie watched her bask in the warmth for several moments before coming back around too.

'I'm sure Sholto will have a plan.'

She looked at him, an eyebrow raised. 'There are a lot of castles in Scotland. I think he means for us to spend the rest of our days visiting every single one.'

'Perhaps he's buying time. He must believe he can talk his parents round.'

She shrugged. 'I did tell him they wouldn't accept it, but he wouldn't listen to me. When he insisted on going back to talk with them alone, I agreed only because I knew he would have to explain things. They were never going to welcome me with open arms . . . But I never imagined that he'd come back and lie to me.'

'You should be flattered. He refused to let you go.'

She shook her head, knowing he was right, and yet . . . 'He'll regret it, I know he will – if not today, then someday soon. It's too much to ask of him.'

A comfortable silence opened up which neither of them felt

in a rush to fill. Archie was holding his whisky tumbler in the palm of his upturned hand, the firelight making it sparkle. '. . . You know, we chaps are fishing in a small pond when it comes to wives, and Sholto – lucky devil – has found a wild creature from the sea. You're exciting and dynamic, Effie. Challenging too, I'm sure, but most certainly not a bore. None of the girls on our circuit are like you.'

'Oh, I know. And they hate me for it.'

'I refuse to believe it!' he said in mock horror.

She smiled. 'It's true. I get everything wrong. I'm too rough, too loud, too strong. Bitsy Cameron is adamant she's going to have a limp for ever because of me.'

'Whatever did you do to her?'

'Rode a rocking horse over her foot.'

'That could only improve her dancing,' he quipped, taking a sip of his drink. 'Look, if it's any consolation, the only woman I'm aware of who truly loathes, hates and despises you is Sibyl Wainwright – and of course she has good reason. We can't deny her the pleasure of pickling in her own resentment.'

Effie couldn't help but laugh. 'I would hate me too if I was her.'

'Oh, she'll get over it eventually. There are plenty of other bachelors lining up; she's coming into a fair fortune when her old man croaks. Although she is so very stuck on Sholto. I suppose he's just so pretty, isn't he?' He wrinkled his nose.

'Pretty? He's not a girl!'

'Coming from the girl wearing a dinner suit.'

She smiled. 'I think he's the most handsome man I ever met.'

'Thank you very much.'

'I wasn't trying to be rude.'

'No, you're like me – it just comes naturally.'

The Midnight Secret

She laughed, befuddled by his quick wit and refusal to play by the rules. From the moment she had set foot on the mainland, adapting had meant understanding what was and wasn't acceptable: wear this, don't say that; dance this reel, play this game; read this book, laugh at the right moment . . . But Archie Baird-Hamilton deliberately set himself apart from all that, not caring about the done thing. He was a gentleman rebel, a counterpart to what she herself had been labelled by Peony the other day: a noble *sauvage*.

She tried turning the conversation onto *his* love life instead.

'Who is Miss Bruce?'

He seemed surprised that she had remembered the name the housekeeper had mentioned earlier. 'She was my intended guest.'

'Was she the redhead we passed?'

'The Redhead,' he echoed, as if it were a proper noun. '. . . Actually, no.'

'What will have happened to her?'

'Well, I hope she's worked out by now that, clearly, I left without her,' he guffawed. 'Naturally, I assumed *you* were her.'

'I'm so sorry.'

'No, no. It was my own fault. Ought to have come down and checked, of course. I wanted to get ahead of the winds.' He took a sip of wine. 'Poor girl. I doubt she'll ever speak to me again.'

'I'm sure she will, once y' explain,' Effie said hurriedly.

He shook his head. 'She's quite spirited . . . It's probably for the best anyway. Would never have worked.'

'How do you know that?'

'Her husband's a crack shot.'

Effie's jaw dropped open as he smiled back at her with his eyes. '. . . Oh.'

Chapter Fourteen

Archie taught her to fish over the next few days. Not the kind of fishing she had known back home, sitting in a boat with ten men trying to catch ling, but the kind where they stood in a river up to their thighs and flicked a line in rhythmic waves over the water. It was freezing cold and tiring, and she could feel the iciness of the water through her rubber waders, but the first time she had a bite, she jumped up and down so excitedly that the pike wriggled itself off the hook again. When they could no longer ignore their hunger, they sat on rocks on the riverbank, smoothing away the snow to eat the pies Mrs Robertson had cooked for them and drinking tea from a thermos flask.

When they returned to the house in the afternoons, once the light had faded and after restorative hot baths, they met again in the library to talk, read the newspapers and play cards. Effie had been right that first day – tea and a fire really were the greatest luxuries. Archie had been right, too – it was often colder inside the house than out.

For three days there was no improvement in the weather. Northerly winds grew ever worse, squalling and quarrelling the skies, whipping the open water into a frothing cauldron. But on the fourth day, they awoke to blue skies and a sudden loud calm.

The Midnight Secret

Archie watched Effie as she came into the breakfast room. Mrs Robertson had hemmed his old trousers for her and it now seemed perfectly normal to see her in his shirts and jumpers.

'You want to go,' he said over breakfast: porridge, followed by grilled mackerel.

'Well, I do have to leave at some point. I can hardly stay here indefinitely, can I?' she replied. He said nothing, but there was an answer in his eyes anyway, and she knew he wanted her to stay.

She swirled the cream in her porridge, trying to ignore the sudden acceleration of her pulse, pushing down a feeling that was growing inside her. She loved Sholto. He was the love of her life; she knew that with every fibre of her being. But she also knew that there was an easiness between her and Archie that she had never known with anyone else. He was her in male form. The conversation was always unforced and they laughed endlessly. She didn't feel judged by him or lacking in any way. Even with Sholto, although she knew he adored her, there was a small but distinct dislocation between them; they couldn't ignore that they came from two different worlds, nor that to the important people in their lives, that mattered. Everything was just so easy with Archie.

'I don't trust it,' he said, staring out through the tall windows. The view was like a painting, almost unreal in its beauty, ever-changing. Effie could imagine the colours of autumn here, almost taste the salty tang of the summer breeze. Living on the water again reminded her of Village Bay, being shushed to sleep every night by the lullaby of waves breaking upon the shore.

'The wind's dropped,' she pointed out.

'It's unnaturally still. This could be the eye of the storm.'

She looked at him, knowing they were already in it. Last

night she had heard his footsteps in the hallway. They had stopped outside her room, his shadow visible as she stared at the tiny strip of light that came under the door. She had braced for the handle to turn, feeling her heart pound against the mattress, knowing what she would say if he did come in. She knew it would not be the first time he had visited a woman's room at night. But when she saw the shadow move and the light stream in unimpeded again, she understood it was the first time he had walked away.

Sitting here now, she sensed they both knew his secret. He longed for her; she could see it in the weight of his stare, hear it in the pauses between conversations. The things he didn't say were becoming louder than those he did. She knew he knew women, but he'd never known a woman like her. Something, something soon, was going to break, and it would either be his resolve or hers.

'All the more reason to act quickly, then,' she said, stirring her porridge. 'If we hold our nerve, we can still outrun it.'

'Why are you wearing that?'

Archie was sitting on the bench in the entrance porch, pulling on his gumboots. He wore a macintosh over his clothes, clearly anticipating poor weather despite the blue skies, and he rested his elbows on his thighs as she came through, barefoot in her emerald evening gown.

'Because this is all I have to wear. If I turn up at Dunvegan wearing your clothes, there'll be a scandal. You know, perhaps you should keep some women's clothes here?'

'For my next stowaway, you mean? . . . I'm not in the habit of collecting them.' His eyes narrowed as he watched her. 'I don't understand why it would matter if you were in my clothes.'

Didn't he? Even aside from his reaction to seeing her in his

The Midnight Secret

dinner suit, she had felt his eyes travelling over her every time he thought she wasn't looking. She knew that he liked seeing her in his trousers dramatically cinched in with a belt, his shirtsleeves rolled up her arms. He was covering her by proxy, his scent sitting upon her, as if imprinting himself on her. There was an intimacy to sharing layers, and she knew he knew it.

'. . . It's a matter of how it looks.'

'Ah . . . Well, we can't have that,' he said archly, looking at her with an expression she couldn't read. 'We all know how desperately it matters what other people think.'

There was an uncharacteristic bitterness to his words and she felt a fierce disappointment in herself. Caring about others' opinions was the antithesis of everything that happened between them here these past few days. They had both been their free, true selves. Mhairi had always cared far too much about reputation, but Effie had fancied herself free from all that. But it wasn't just her own good name she had to think about now – it was Sholto's too. He deserved her respect.

'Archie, you know what I mean,' she said as he abruptly got up. 'I'm engaged to Sholto. I have to consider how it reflects on him.'

His jaw balled for a moment. He was, in spite of himself, a gentleman. 'At least put on a jumper.' He grabbed a navy fishing jersey, rough but windproof, from a basket and held it out to her. 'I'll see you down there.'

He walked outside, and she watched as the door slammed shut behind him. A tension had already crept in between them, now that this interlude from both their lives was being forced to a stop. The friendship was being halted in its tracks. She belonged to another man, and he could no longer pretend she didn't.

She shrugged the jumper on over her dress and followed him, at a distance, down to the jetty. She hopped on board as he ran through his checks; it suited him to be busy, to neither look at her nor make small talk. She shrugged on the cork life jacket instead; it didn't rub against her ribs this time, thanks to the cushioning of Archie's jumper.

They cast off into the wind, Archie expertly tacking side to side up the sound, turning the huge helm with ease, his gaze dead ahead. Effie sat beside him, where she had sat on the way out, glancing up at him every few minutes and wishing he would talk to her. But what he wanted to say couldn't be said, and anything else wasn't worth saying.

'Look, seals!' she exclaimed after a while, spotting a colony sleeping on rocks.

He smiled, softening a little. He loved being on the water too much to hold a grudge, and he began pointing things out at intervals – the fin of a minke whale and then the eyrie of a pair of sea eagles high up in a pine tree, though there was no sign of the birds now.

Effie closed her eyes, her face angled to the sun and basking in its pale, wintry warmth. She didn't care that the wind made a tangle of her hair. She enjoyed the sounds of the boat: the rattle of the rigging, the flap of the sails, the sluicing of the water, her dress billowing in the wind.

She didn't notice immediately when the sun went in, but as they passed the wide mouth of Portree and came onto the shoulder of the Trotternish peninsula, the *Lady Tara* began to pitch. An army of white horses was galloping towards them, surrounding them on all sides, and she saw from the way Archie's eyes narrowed, the forward thrust of his jaw, that they were heading into the heavier weather he had feared. He glanced at her, catching her gaze. If he had been right about being in the eye of the storm, he was too gracious to say it.

Effie gripped the handrail, feeling the rain being carried in on the wind, striking her cheeks like glass bullets. But the strength of the coming storm increased dramatically as they sailed into Staffin Bay and headed towards the straits of Little Minch. They were fully exposed now to the northerly front, a merciless onslaught. These were the very winds that had always plagued St Kilda, alone in her solitary outpost in the ocean. Effie was no stranger to their wildness, but to experience them on a small boat, surrounded by rising waves . . .

'Stay low,' he shouted, his voice barely audible as the wind whipped it away. 'Don't let go!'

Water doused them, splashing over the sides every few moments. Archie widened his stance at the helm, his body bracing as he kept one hand on the wheel and with the other, adjusted the sail. Surprisingly, for all the discomfort they were enduring, she didn't feel frightened. She trusted his abilities as a sailor; he was skilled and fearless. There was very little this man couldn't do. He had been born accomplished.

She didn't feel frightened until she heard the crack. It was like a pistol-whip, sharp above the contralto wind, and she saw how quickly Archie's head snapped up, the look on his face as he studied the mast.

He visibly paled.

'What is it?' she asked, looking up too, but all she could see was a sail at full stretch, the rig clinking wildly on the pitch of the waves.

He didn't reply. He was struggling with the helm as the boat suddenly started to pull to starboard. 'We're losing the mast!' he hollered, and she saw the sail sag like a bellows without air, her eye catching sight of a deep crack – like the eye of a needle – at the very top of the main mast. It hadn't broken away – not yet – but the pressure from the sail was pulling on it, making it wider and deeper . . . It would give at any moment. Effie could guess what would come next: no mast, no sail, no control.

'What can we do?' she cried.

Archie stared up at it as he wrestled to keep the boat from turning in towards the coastline. 'I can't get up there,' he yelled. 'I have to keep my hands on this.'

Effie looked up too. It was high, but nothing to her. 'I can go!'

Archie looked down at her as if she was mad. '. . . *What*?'

'I can climb up there and strap it! Have you some rope?'

'Effie, no!'

'Arch, there's no time. You have to trust me. I am not some delicate flower.' Being so slight – 'a strip of wind', she'd always been called back home – had always meant she was agile and nimble. Here, a lithe body was prized only for wearing the latest fashions well, and she hated that she had been recast as fragile. Her strength, agility and skill on the ropes had defined her in St Kilda, but over here, no one knew or cared. It was as if her identity had been cleaved away. 'Just hand me some rope.'

Still he stared at her, and she saw desperation in his eyes. 'Effie, I can't! If anything were to happen to you—'

She looked back up and saw the crack breach and widen again, the sail tugging on it. 'You have to! Once it breaks, we'll lose the sail, and then we're both done for.'

With a look of disbelief that he was doing it, Archie reached under the helm and passed her a small loop of rope. Without hesitation she threw it over her head, the loop across her body.

'Help me up!' she said, reaching for his hand. The boat was

The Midnight Secret

rolling and lurching in the swell, buffeted by the wind as the slackened sail pulled them off course.

He grabbed her, hand upon hand, just as he had when they'd reeled in Portree those four nights back. Then he yanked her up from the bench, his other hand on the helm. The boat lurched as they were caught side-on by a wave and she felt the deck run out beneath her as she was thrown into the open expanse of the bridge. She was still too far away to reach the mast, their arms outstretched at full reach, but Archie didn't let go, gripping her tightly in no-man's-land until they eased into the trough for a few short seconds.

'Now!' she shouted, and he released her, watching as she sprinted the short distance to the mast.

'Dear God, Effie,' he cried, helpless now that she was out of his reach. 'Be careful!'

'Aye,' she replied, looking up the tall, narrow pole. It was slippery in the rain, no natural grip. She would have preferred a granite cliff-face, but at least there were some hand- and footholds: she could stand on the boom, grab the ropes . . . She hugged the mast like a monkey on a tree and, as she waited again for the *Lady Tara* to hit another trough, took one arm off to tuck her long skirt into her underwear. The dress being soaked through worked to her advantage, as it flapped less and clung in position up her thighs.

She felt the boat level out and sprang up instinctively onto the mast, hugging it between her arms and legs as she shimmied herself upwards. It was slippery, but she was strong and had expert balance. It didn't take her long to get to the top but she had to cling ever more tightly as she ascended, for the higher she rose, the greater the pendulum swing, side to side, of the mast.

She looked down and saw Archie watching with utter

horror as he struggled to keep the boat the right side of the wind. He looked so small from here, and from this vantage point she could see how truly vulnerable they were, the immensity of the sea roiling around them.

She made herself focus on the job in hand – panicking wouldn't help them now. Up close, the crack was worse than it had appeared from the deck. It was going to fail at any moment . . .

She set about strapping it with the rope, looping figures of eight to bind it tightly and hopefully minimize the breach. It wasn't a perfect solution, but it absorbed some of the strain. As she fastened off the end of the rope, she watched the crack closely as they continued to roll left to right. The sail was certainly better supported now that the mast had been strengthened. She could see the almost immediate relief for Archie on the helm as it stopped fighting him, but with these winds so strong and relentless, she couldn't risk leaving it and coming back down again. One particularly sharp gust might be enough to loosen the strapping, catch the sail at full throttle and send it all crashing down. There was nothing else for it.

'I'm staying up here!' she shouted down to him.

There was a pause as Archie processed her words. Could he not hear her clearly, or did he not believe her?

'Effie, no! That's enough! You've done enough! Get back down here.' He sounded desperate, his signature laconic drawl lost to the drama.

She clung to the mast, trying not to let fear take over. With every pitch it felt as if she would be dunked into the raging sea. 'I can't! It's too unstable!' she shouted back. 'Just keep going! I'm fine . . . I can hold on. We can do this!'

She saw him shake his head, but to argue was draining

The Midnight Secret

them both of precious energy, and he knew enough of her wild spirit now to understand she wouldn't be talked down. He stared ahead at the horizon, facing down the storm as the rain lashed and the wind moaned and the sea heaved. And Effie clung on, an emerald button on a conductor's baton – tick, tick, tick, marking time.

Chapter Fifteen

'Dear God, what a sight you made, steaming down the loch like that!' Gladly called up from the stone jetty, bundled in a mac and sou'wester as he wound the mooring rope around the bollard. The rain was still driving hard, the winds with no intention of letting up. 'We thought it was pirates coming to pillage us! MacLeod's gone off hiding all the family silver!'

Colly and Campbell ran down the path from the castle, fastening their coats too.

Effie, still atop the mast, closed her eyes with relief as she felt the *Lady Tara* stand steady at last as she was secured fore and aft. She would never forget the welcoming sight of Dunvegan Castle, sitting atop a rock at the head of the loch: ancient turreted towers and thick buff stone walls promising safe haven.

She would never admit it to anyone, but she hadn't known how much longer she could have stayed up there. As she had feared, the strapping was worked loose by the nudging wind; she'd had to re-secure it several times, gripping the mast with her legs as she worked with her arms. There had been nothing to hold her up there but her own muscles and willpower.

She descended slowly and carefully, lowering herself hand over hand until her bare feet touched the deck again. She was soaked through, her hair streaming rivers down her back, her dress now a second skin bunched around her thighs.

The Midnight Secret

'. . . What?' she asked, as she saw the two men looking at her with astonished expressions. 'Oh. I don't look much of a lady, is that it?' she asked, slicking her hair back and wringing it out like a towel.

'How the devil did you *do* that, dear girl?' Gladly asked, looking one part horrified, two parts impressed.

'It was fine—'

'How could you let her?' He looked at Archie, now three parts horrified.

'*You* try stopping her!' Archie replied, throwing out an exasperated arm. He dropped his hands on his knees and let his head hang; he looked spent too. He had been wrestling the boat on the stormy sea for hours. 'Besides, there really was no other choice. The mast was about to give and if we'd ended up in the water . . .'

'What in blazes happened to it?' Gladly asked, staring at Effie's makeshift strapping binding the masthead together.

Archie peered up at it too, still doubled over. 'I think it might be the spreader, or the forestay tension. I'm not sure till I can get up there and take a closer look.'

'Well, now's not the time. You look cream crackered, old bean.'

'I'll be fine.'

'Here, take my hand,' Gladly said, holding his out for Effie. For once, she accepted, stepping onto dry land with shaking legs. Her muscles were cramping and she realized her teeth were chattering.

Archie accepted help with disembarking too, just as Colly and Campbell reached them.

Colly tore off his coat and draped it over Effie's shoulders, but it was a case of bolting the stable door; she was soaked through, she couldn't possibly get any wetter. 'Hot bath, immediately,' he said, looking concerned. 'Pneumonia is no fun, let me tell you.'

Molly flashed through Effie's mind, and she winced in pain. It had been a year and a month now since her friend's death, but she still missed her with a visceral ache.

'Why on earth did you choose today of all days to make the journey?' Campbell asked Archie, looking flabbergasted as they began walking back.

Archie sighed. 'There was a break in the weather and we decided to take the chance on . . . outrunning the storm.' He didn't look at Effie, didn't throw the blame on her, even though it was all her fault.

She looked around her suddenly, realizing something now she was properly able to take a breath.

'And we couldn't flag you in advance to let you know we were coming. Telephone lines are down on Raasay so we've had no comms for days.' He looked at the other men. 'Has there been a search party out for her?'

'Oh no, not at all,' Campbell said, unperturbed. 'There was no mystery. Peony saw her getting on board—'

Effie's head whipped up. Peony had seen her getting on the wrong boat, knowing full well they were all supposed to sail together – knowing that Effie could end up alone with Archie – and hadn't spoken up to stop her?

'Sholto wasn't happy at the mix-up, of course, but at least he knew she was safe.'

Effie looked from one face to another. 'So, then . . . where is he?' Was he inside, too angry with her to come out?

The men all shared an ominous look.

'Ah yes, well, you see – losing you wasn't our only drama to contend with.'

She felt an immediate bolt of fear, far worse than anything

she had just experienced out on the water. 'What is it? What's happened?'

Gladly cleared his throat. 'Well, the thing is . . . that is . . . I'm sorry to say the countess, his mother, has had a stroke.'

'What?' Effie whispered. 'No!'

'I'm afraid so. She's alive, but it was a bad one. The prognosis is not good.' Gladly bit his lip. 'Sholly's gone back home to DH.'

Effie turned on the spot, hardly able to believe what she was hearing. She had thought clinging to a mast in a tempest had been the worst she would have to contend with today, but storm winds were still blowing. Sholto's mother had almost died.

The question was, were they to blame? Had Sholto's determination to marry her contributed to this – or even caused it? Effie had caught the look Gladly, Campbell and Colly had shared just now. Had Sholto said something? Had he thought the same?

'Is . . . is he coming back?' she croaked.

There was a marked hesitation as the men shared glances again.

'He asked if you would telephone him once you got over here,' Gladly said, his eyes kind.

'Aye, I must . . .' she breathed.

'But first things first. You're to do nothing before you've had a hot bath and warmed up,' Colly said. He was hunched over as the driving rain pelted him, quickly soaking through his clothes. She knew she ought to give back his coat; she had little need of it herself – wet was wet – but her mind was as scattered as her body was spent.

They rounded the head of the loch, staggering uphill towards the castle's rocky perch, past moss-addled rowan trees, silver birches and thick clumps of rhododendron. Now that they were closer, faces were visible at an upstairs window. Effie could just imagine Bitsy and Peony sitting there with sour expressions on seeing that she had not only returned but sailed in like a corsair.

They walked in, an impressive oak staircase immediately rising in front of them, a bull's head – motif for the MacLeods – mounted on the wall. The women appeared suddenly at the top step, so refined in their day dresses and stockings, hair set into neat primps. They stopped in apparent alarm at the state of Effie. The difference between them all had never been more acute now she had reverted to her natural feral state: barefoot, hair tangled, weatherbeaten.

Veronica moved first, running down the stairs and removing the dripping macintosh. Effie was shivering uncontrollably, the dress a sodden rag bunched around her bare thighs.

'Come, we've put you in the Lewis suite. There's a bath drawn. We'll get you warm in a jiffy.'

Effie nodded, even though all she wanted was to find the telephone and hear Sholto's voice telling her it was all going to be all right. But would it be? She had woken this morning to bright skies and optimism for her future, but everything had changed again, the ground no firmer beneath her feet than that heaving, swirling sea. First she had been taken from Sholto and now he had been taken from her. It felt like an omen, a karmic lesson being delivered that the world would not bend to their will. Love was not enough.

Veronica wrapped an arm around her, peeling her away from the men. She felt Archie's eyes on her back watching her go and she turned briefly, catching hold of his bleak look. This wasn't the ending either of them had wanted.

*

The Midnight Secret

'Sholto?'

'Effie.' She heard the sigh of relief in the word, as if she was comfort. Home. She closed her eyes and could see him, exhausted and tense in his library, just as she was exhausted and tense in the library here. She would give anything to see him right now, to hold him.

'Gladly just told me about your mother . . . How is she?'

There was a pause. 'Not well, I'm afraid. The doctor says she suffered a significant trauma. She's still with us, but . . . not as she used to be.'

Effie bit her lip, not quite sure what that meant, not wanting to press. His voice was right in her ear, but she felt the distance between them. 'I can come back,' she said in a small voice.

There was a long pause.

'. . . No.' The word was soft, its message sharp. 'I'm sorry. I . . .' She heard him take a deep breath and knew he was steeling himself to say what had to be said – the very conversation he had refused to have with her when he'd returned to Oban in November. 'It's just that . . . it's very difficult here at the moment, and the doctor has advised no . . . no undue stress.'

She closed her eyes, knowing *she* was the undue stress. 'I understand.' Her voice was a whisper.

'. . . Do you? I mean do you know I want you to be here, but that it's just . . .' She could hear his struggle to hold back his emotions. To do the right thing. Place head over heart. '. . . She's my mother.' His voice cracked and she saw in that moment the scale of his conflict, the very thing she had seen all along and he had sought to deny. He had thought he could turn his back on his family and choose his happiness over their wishes, but death hovered now, a spectral shadow casting them all into gloom. He could no longer run. He had to decide between them.

'Sholto, of course I do. I lost my mother when I was young . . . I would give *anything* for another day with her.' Tears were sliding down her cheeks but her voice was steady, if thick. 'You must be with her. You must.'

There was a long silence and she knew he was struggling for composure too. They both knew what they were saying: for as long as his mother lived, Effie must stay away; but there was no hope after death either, for to reunite would be to disrespect his mother's memory. He was checkmated, unable to move freely in any direction. Effie would never be good enough for his family, and his defiance in insisting otherwise had come at too high a price.

Neither of them spoke for several long moments as they listened to each other's breathing, reading their thoughts.

'. . . What will you do?' he asked flatly.

'You mean, where will I go?' She could hardly stay here at Dunvegan. James MacLeod was the consummate host, but his parents – good friends of Sholto's parents – would take an even dimmer view of her now, in light of the countess's illness. She could spend no more than a night here. 'Back home to Lochaline, I expect.'

But it wasn't home. She had spent less than a week there in total. It had been a landing point only; a springboard that had propelled her from St Kilda to Dumfries House.

'My father's there at the moment anyway,' she added. He had gone to stay with Old Fin for Christmas and Hogmanay, feeling strange about staying alone on the Dumfries estate with no sign of Effie. 'I'll call and tell him to stay.'

Sholto hesitated. 'He's very welcome to continue to make use of the cottage.'

She closed her eyes, feeling every pause, every polite word like a sabre swipe, though she knew Sholto was trying not to

The Midnight Secret

hurt her. On the contrary, extending use of the grace and favour property was a kindness, but if she was no longer working for the earl – and how could she now? – nor together with Sholto, then her father couldn't possibly remain there without her.

'Don't worry about us. We'll be fine,' she said quietly. 'But would you . . . would you send on our things?' She didn't think she could bear the prospect of returning to Dumfries to pack up. To be there and not see him . . .

'Of course. I'll have someone see to it straight away.'

She heard him flinch, his eagerness to help her in any way misplaced here.

Another silence bloomed. There was so much to say and yet words couldn't help them now. Feelings couldn't compete with facts. She had had no idea that his wink as he had left her with a drunk teenage viscount, back in the Gathering Hall in Portree, would be their last moment together.

Perhaps it was better that way. She never could have faced him and said goodbye; she would have clung to him and begged him to reconsider, even though she knew they were out of options and out of time. Events had overtaken them, and perhaps there was mercy in that.

'Goodbye, Sholto. I'll pray for her. I'll pray for you all.'

'I love you, Effie . . .' His voice broke. 'I'm sor—'

She replaced the handset, feeling the sob break free from her too. But the fates had spoken, the axe fallen. Their predicament could not be undone. She had known loss before.

She felt the sorrow rise up through her body in rolling waves as she staggered over to a high-backed library chair and sank into it, weeping pitifully at the loss of her only dream. She could see no future without Sholto in it. How was she supposed to smile again when her heart had been ripped from her body, still beating . . . ? How was she—

Behind her, the library door opened, a crescendo of laughter carrying down the hallway. Effie froze, knowing it would be Gladly or Colly or Archie looking for her; she didn't want anyone to see her like this, weakened and pathetic. She couldn't speak to them in this state, say out loud that the engagement was over, that she was going to slip back into the obscurity from which she'd come . . .

She waited for the door to close again – she was hidden from view here – but instead she heard footsteps coming in. She lifted her feet off the ground, lest they could be seen, huddling into a small ball. The chair backed onto the room from here; she would only be seen if her friendly hero insisted on walking all the way round to find her – but the footsteps stopped halfway along; she heard a light tapping on the book-lined wall behind her, the squeak of a hinge.

Effie bit her lip, realizing it must be her host, a man she scarcely knew, attending to private business in his own library. Immediately she felt like an intruder, her desire for privacy transformed into something more shady.

She didn't stir, even her tears slowing their march down her cheeks. She heard something jangling lightly before the hinge squeaked again and was followed by a click.

Footsteps, retreating.

Effie waited for the door to open again, but something . . . an instinct had her hackles up. As she heard the twist of the knob, she quickly peered around the wing of the chair.

What she saw made her blood run cold. It made no sense – there was no explanation at all that she could think of to account for it.

What was *he* doing here?

Chapter Sixteen

MHAIRI

5 January 1931

Oban

Mhairi could hear the children next door fighting. In her home, growing up, her brothers would never have landed more than two thumps before they would have been separated and scolded, but different rules applied here. The father was scarcely ever around – she'd heard he had lost his job when the distillery had closed and spent his days drinking in the pub – and the mother was either defeated or unbothered by her children's feral ways.

Mhairi hummed to herself, trying to drown out the noise as she plumped the pillows on their bed, the room cool and freshly aired. She smoothed the wrinkles out of the knitted blanket and refreshed the water in the glass of snowdrops, picked from the spinney around the back this morning.

She had been forced to make the walk there barefoot when she'd found her boots – left outside the door to dry after a heavy downpour – filled with dog excrement. Ordinarily such a thing would devastate her day, but this time she had merely washed them out and stuffed them with old papers in the hope they would dry before Donald got back.

He had no idea of the reign of terror the women had exacted over her in the two months they had lived here: her bedsheets mud-spattered on the washing line; 'slut' daubed in smuts on the front door; the butcher ignoring her at the counter; a dead crow left on her step; a smirking wall of silence from the women whenever she walked past. The gossip about her had travelled to the laundry of the hotel where she worked, killing off the green shoots of some fledgling friendships so that she had no one here at all but Donald. No friends. No family. No neighbours.

Of course, whenever she and Donald passed the neighbours in the street on Sundays, they were polite to *his* face, tipping their hats; but when she was alone, there was an unrelenting viciousness to their actions that took her breath away. And it would never stop, she knew that.

It would always be like this. The truth about their lives – their love story – would never be known and they couldn't escape here; David hadn't taken his suspicions about Norman to the police in the end. In his most recent letter, he had been despairing that Jayne had stopped him, refusing to admit to the horrors in her marriage nor to listen as he tried to explain his greater fears about what could have happened that final night. There was a part of Mhairi that had wanted him to do it anyway – anything that might get Donald off the hook once and for all – but, in her heart, she knew not having an alibi wasn't reason enough to put another man in the frame. Norman was a bad husband, that much was true; but a murderer? He could swing for it – and why? Because his wife hadn't come home that night and he couldn't prove he'd been in bed at home, alone?

The Midnight Secret

If David didn't understand why Jayne was covering for her husband, Mhairi did. In the absence of rock-solid proof, Jayne could take no chances. Sleeping outside beside another man that fated night, innocent though it had been, wasn't the sort of thing Norman would take well. A man who used his fists so freely didn't care much for the finer details, and Mhairi knew Jayne was simply making the sacrifices that had to be made to get through another day.

Weren't they all just surviving the best they could? Silence had been Mhairi's best form of defence living here, and she had thought she could bear it indefinitely; that had been her intention, certainly. There had been a saying back home: 'A man may do without a brother, but not without a neighbour.' And yet it wasn't true – within the four walls of their tiny home, she and Donald led a life of blissful happiness. Up until now, she had no need for more than she had with him here.

But everything had changed again, and that quiet refuge was no longer enough. Hard decisions had to be made.

She checked on the stew she had made him, pleased with the richness of the aroma. It filled their home, a perfect welcome after a hard day. She only wished she would be here to eat it herself, but she had been here once before and she knew, this time, what was coming. In a few weeks she would start to show and the neighbours' campaign would become vitriolic, if not downright dangerous.

She propped the letter she had written on the counter and walked over to the door, picking up the small case containing the few worldly gifts she owned – a change of clothes, a copy of the Bible and the photograph of herself and Donald, taken for a shilling at the market. She looked back into the room one final time, proud of the loving home she had created. A silk purse from a sow's ear, her mother would have said.

She wished it could have been enough – them against the world – as she slipped through the door and walked out. She didn't bother trying to be quiet this time, and the doors opened one by one, a low crowing rising up behind her as they saw the case in her hand.

'Good riddance!' someone yelled.

'The witch is leaving!' cried another.

Mhairi walked on, her head held high, unmoved by their jeers. She would not let them hurt her any more. She had already lost a baby once before and she wouldn't go through it again.

She knew Donald loved her, but he couldn't leave.

She loved him too – but she could not stay.

Chapter Seventeen

FLORA

5 January 1931

Quebec City

The room was low-lit and shadowy, red cloths thrown over round tables, people sitting on rush-back chairs and leather banquettes as waiters slunk through like cats. James surveyed the room, quickly finding Landon sitting in a corner. There was a newspaper in front of him, but he wasn't reading it. A tendril of cigarette smoke curled from his lip as he watched them approach.

'Mr Landon,' James said as they approached. 'Thank you for your note.'

Several days of silence had passed since their initial meeting, and Flora had grown increasingly terrified that Tucker had somehow 'got' to Landon and warned him off.

'Y' found it all right, then?' the man asked as they sat down opposite him.

'Indeed. A well-chosen spot.'

His gaze dragged over her like thorns as she fidgeted beside James, trying to control her nerves. She fiddled with the prized gold wedding ring that now sat beside her sapphire, the ultimate token of respectability. They were legitimately married at last, man and wife . . . and ready to become a family of three.

The moment was upon them.

A waiter came over and they ordered some red wine that would doubtless be too sweet or too cool, but drinking it was beside the point. They merely had to go through the motions to get to the reason for being here.

Landon seemed especially unhurried, watching the waiter disappear, taking another drag of his cigarette before he looked back at them.

'So,' he said finally. 'Your friends, the widows.'

'Yes.' James managed to make the word sound like a confirmation and not an eager question.

'It's not a straightforward picture.'

Flora felt her heart dive to her boots but forced herself not to outwardly react. She watched as Landon ground the cigarette stub into the ashtray, but she knew what he was going to say – they had boarded a train and disappeared.

'One of them's been quarantined. Typhus.'

Flora gasped so loudly that James had to take her hand in his own. 'Who?'

'Lorna MacDonald. She was infected on the crossing over. She actually passed the first two medical checks after disembarkation, but there was a query to the other one's papers—'

'Mary's?'

'Yes. Her paperwork was irregular on first inspection.'

Flora could guess why. Pepper had taken it upon himself to arrange her passport for her to travel over to Paris, but that had been a lucky exception. Upon evacuation, the islanders hadn't been issued with any formal travel documents. A census had been taken as they disembarked, and of course

The Midnight Secret

the minister had always recorded births, deaths and marriages in the kirk register. But passports and visas were down to each islander to sort for themselves . . . It would have been easy for something to go amiss for international travel.

'They were held in civil detention for a few days till it was all checked out, but in the meantime the MacDonald woman came down with symptoms. Lucky for us, or they'd have been stamped through.'

'So where is she now?'

'Ordinarily she'd have been sent to Grosse Île, the quarantine island thirty kilometres from here, but by that time it was cut off by the ice, and the only way in or out is by boat. She's in the isolation unit here.'

'. . . And Mary? Where is she while Lorna's being held?' James asked.

'She's currently in the Red Cross nursery with the baby.'

'Where's that?'

'Still in the Port. She can't go through without her companion.'

Flora and James looked at one another in disbelief. They were still in the city? The two women's misfortune was their good luck: paperwork and weather had conspired to keep them here in the city. If they had been able to go straight through when they'd docked, they could have been on a train within three hours and ended up who knew where?

Flora squeezed James's hand, trying to keep her excitement in check.

'. . . I don't understand. Why can't Mary go through?'

'She can't work with a newborn. The companion stated in her papers that she's a nurse and will be the financial provider. So until she's cleared from quarantine, the other one has to wait in civil detention.'

Detainment. Flora couldn't bear the thought of her child's first months of life being spent like this. He was seventeen weeks old, and six of those had been spent on board ship and in civil detention. Was it much different from a prison? Their hours regulated, movements restricted . . .

'But they've got money, haven't they?' Flora knew that Mary had stolen the money Donald had earned selling the ambergris.

'Not enough. Not under the new rules the government's bringing in. It hasn't been fully rubber-stamped yet but we've already been told to crack down. Things are bad here, and getting worse; we don't need more burdens on the state.'

'Is Lorna still unwell?' James asked. 'She must have been in over a month now. Either she's actively recovering or she's actively dying.'

Landon shrugged. 'I don't have eyes on the medical files, only the landing cards and papers. That's all I know.'

'What will happen to Mary and the baby if Lorna dies?'

'The mother won't have any way to earn, and they'll be deported on the first boat in spring.'

Flora was alarmed by the thought of Lorna dying – she was still a young woman. She would never forgive Lorna for what she'd done, but that didn't mean she wanted to see her dead.

The waiter appeared with their drinks and James sat back in his seat, deep in thought, as they were set down. He waited for the man to walk away. 'The nursery – can we go there?' he asked, keeping his voice low.

'No,' Landon said bluntly.

'Not even for an inducement?'

'It's next to impossible. They're not yet free citizens of

The Midnight Secret

Canada. They're in detention – that means they're being held in a secure space and guarded.'

Flora remembered the barred windows.

'The quarantine unit then?' James pressed, undeterred.

Landon scoffed. 'Even worse. You do understand they're trying to contain hazardous, highly infectious diseases that could lead to epidemics if they were to get into the general population? Authorized personnel is small and entry to the building is highly restricted. *I* can't even get in there, and I have access nearly everywhere.'

'Well, that's very useful to know, Mr Landon.' James glanced around the room quickly before reaching into his jacket pocket for the wad of bank notes and discreetly slipping them under Landon's newspaper. 'That's for the information you've provided so far,' he murmured.

'So far?' Landon enquired. But he didn't look disappointed.

'Yes. I have another proposition for you: get us a meeting with Mary.'

'I've already told you—'

'Next to impossible doesn't mean impossible. There's always a way.'

Landon stared. 'The risks would be much higher. I could lose my job—'

'I'll pay double.'

There was a pause, an angry flash of green eyes. Landon didn't like being pushed around, but he wanted their money. Flora could see him weighing up the odds. 'I sense you're a versatile man, otherwise Tucker wouldn't have pointed us in your direction.'

The fresh mention of Tucker made Landon look up. For all Tucker's personal shortcomings, he was clearly a skilled businessman, his interests reaching to every corner – and port – of the world.

'. . . All right,' he said finally. 'Meet me outside the immigration building on Louise Embankment tomorrow evening—'

'Evening?' Flora asked. 'Couldn't we go in the morning?' It was hard to imagine waiting another night and another day. She didn't know how long she could stand the unrelieved anticipation; every minute that passed felt like a month.

'The detainees are given access to the roof gardens between eight thirty in the morning and six in the evening. The guards and matrons patrol up there during those hours, and there are several hundred other immigrants who'd clock you as soon as you stepped outside . . . Meet me at quarter to seven, when it's quiet, and I'll arrange for her to be up there—'

'With the baby,' Flora urged.

Landon hesitated, and she knew she'd betrayed something of her urgency. Worse, her story.

She felt James's foot press against her own under the table and she sank back.

'With the baby, *if* that's possible. It might not be. It'll be dark and we won't have long before they count everyone in for dinner. Whatever you have to say to her, say it quickly.'

'Understood,' James nodded as Landon got to his feet.

Both of them watched him cross the room and disappear into the city's depths. Flora could feel her heart pounding so hard, she knew her body must be quivering.

When she turned to her husband, he was already looking intently at her, his eyes burning with hope. 'One more night,' he said, taking her hand and clasping it in his own.

'One more night,' she whispered back.

*

The Midnight Secret

Flora stared down at the reflection of the full-bellied moon shimmering on the black water of the docks. From the roof of the three-storey building, she had a clear view of the entire port: deep-water docks, huge storage sheds, miles of administration buildings, the slink of the railway tracks right up to the water's edge. There was no longer any traffic in the seaway – the ice had become fully impassable and the *Empress of Scotland* was now couched in her winter berth. At the height of the crossing season, this place would process several thousand immigrants a day, but now the lights shone on only a few wharves as some pre-docked grain ships were unloaded. She heard the whirr of cranes, the clanking of steel upon steel ... This was the epicentre of industrialization – which only made the garden in which she was standing all the more surprising. Thousands of plants were potted all around the vast roof space in a surprising antidote to the heavy industry that surrounded them, and all but disguised the fencing that kept the detainees prisoner here.

Flora was standing in a corner, hidden behind a large evergreen shrub; James stood alone in the open space as they waited for Landon to return with Mary. He felt it would be better not to startle Mary outright. If she saw Flora, she might immediately run. James was as good as a stranger to her, so they didn't anticipate her remembering him, or at least not outright; it had been eighteen months since his trip to St Kilda. That would give him time to start 'negotiating' with Mary, as he had put it. Getting their son back was a business deal that needed to be brokered.

She squeezed her eyes shut, trying to calm herself. It was snowing lightly, but she barely noticed the cold as the minutes ticked past. She could think of nothing but seeing her baby at last. How much had he grown? How long was his hair?

They heard footsteps, voices . . . a familiar scowl carried on words in a kindred accent. Flora looked up sharply as Crabbit Mary came into view, the same as she ever was. She drew a deep breath. Just like that, after crossing a continent and an ocean, Flora was reunited with her past.

Mary was holding the baby closely so that there was little to see of him from this vantage point, but he was bigger, so much bigger than when he'd last left Flora's arms, not even a day old. The world fell away. She could see his gleaming shock of dark hair, exactly as she'd remembered; she could remember the smell of it . . .

Instinctively she startled, impelled towards him, but James made a slight turn in her direction as if he anticipated her instincts, telling her to hold back. In that tiny gesture, he reminded her she was not out of mind, just out of sight. She had to trust him.

'. . . going to tell me what's going on?' Mary asked Landon, looking from him to James and back to Landon again.

As James had hoped, she didn't seem to recognize the well-dressed gentleman standing before her. She would assume him to be some sort of government official, perhaps. Something to do with her immigration application. Or perhaps one of Lorna's doctors . . .

Landon looked only at his paymaster. 'Make it quick. They'll be doing the dorm rounds shortly.'

James nodded. Landon sank back into the shadows, his footsteps retreating quickly on the stairs.

'What's going on?' Mary asked, looking more concerned now and clutching the baby closer to her bosom.

'Mrs McKinnon,' he said, stepping forward. 'Time is against us, so I'll be blunt. I've come to reclaim my son.' James's voice

The Midnight Secret

was cold, utterly toneless, as he stood tall. Even standing six feet away from Mary, he towered over her.

'. . . Your what?' she gasped.

'I am James Callaghan, the child's father.'

A moment of blankness was followed by gasping recognition. 'But . . . you're . . . you're dead!'

'Come now, Mrs McKinnon. We both know I'm nothing of the sort. That was the lie concocted by you and Miss MacDonald to put Flora into distress, induce the birth and convince her to give the baby up to you.' His words were brusque and unforgiving, none of his usual deference or polite euphemism.

Mary took several steps back, her mouth agape. 'I dinna' know what y're talking about.'

'Denials are pointless. We both know the truth. And the truth is you're in a sore predicament, Mary. If Lorna doesn't recover from the typhus, you're going to be deported back to the UK.'

Her mouth opened and closed as she tried to keep up with him. Flora could see Mary trying to work out how he could know all these things as she struggled to believe her eyes that he was actually standing here: that he had not only followed her to and found her in Quebec, but somehow negotiated a way in here to confront her.

'. . . She's almost well again,' Mary stammered. 'We'll be gone from here within the week.'

'Not according to my sources,' James lied.

'But she wrote to me last week.'

'Then perhaps she's sparing you the distress.'

Flora saw Mary's shock at the bluff. She wasn't sure what to believe. He clearly had these 'sources'; how else had he come to be standing here?

'Of course, once you're back home, I'm sure it wouldn't be difficult to persuade the police to take an interest in you. You stole the money to get here, after all.'

'It was our money! I'm his wife. What's Donald's is mine.'

'It suits you to be married to him now, does it? Even though you deserted him by coming here?'

Mary's eyes narrowed, and Flora could see her beginning to get to grips with the situation unfolding before her. If there was one thing she knew about the woman, it was that Mary had never been one to back down from a fight.

'And then, of course, you stole my child by deception and left the country with him. That's kidnapping. These are far more serious offences.'

'You can't prove them.' Mary's chin jutted defiantly into the air as she began to rock the baby in her arms, almost in a taunt. 'His birth certificate has *my* name down as the mother. His passport lists *me* as his mother. I've a registered nurse ready to testify on oath that she delivered *me* of this child the night before we evacuated. My neighbours in St Kilda saw me confined throughout the pregnancy, they visited me in bed holding my newborn. My neighbours in Oban will swear on the Bible they saw me with the child, day and night, tending to him as my own . . . Who's to say he's not mine?'

Her rationale was like a spray of bullets hitting them in the chest, one after the other . . .

'Donald. The other person whose name is on the birth certificate.'

'Pah!' she scoffed. 'He's a known liar and a cheat! He's gone on record to the police saying he deserted me in the hours after the birth to lie with that harlot! Why should anyone believe a word *he* has to say?'

James didn't reply and, as a silence stretched, Flora looked

The Midnight Secret

over at him in growing horror. They had banked on a strategy of surprise, intimidation, capitulation. *Say something else*, she willed him.

But what else was there to say? They *didn't* have proof. Lorna had constructed a cast-iron alibi in which their entire community had unwittingly served as witnesses. Flora and Mhairi themselves had gone to great lengths to hide their pregnancies on the other side of the isle, and none of the villagers had had cause to doubt Lorna when she said Mary's pregnancy was precarious and advised lengthy bed rest. There was no reason for the minister to have doubted that Mary was the birth mother when Lorna had told him she'd delivered the baby herself. The only person – besides Donald and James – who had ever known, *seen*, the truth was Frank Mathieson.

And he was dead.

'Tell me your price,' James said finally.

'What?' Mary looked bewildered by the question.

'How much to give up the child? Take a number, double it, I don't care. How much?'

There was a long silence. For a moment, Flora thought she really was choosing one. But then Mary began to smile. 'You think there's a number for this?' And she pulled the baby closer to her, kissing his head and nuzzling him affectionately.

Flora had to look away, her hand pressed over her mouth. It took everything she had not to leap out from her hiding place and rip the baby from Mary's arms.

'Do you really think I'll ever be able to buy myself another one of *these*?' she asked, angling the baby so that they could finally see his face.

James flinched as he saw his son's face for the first time – in the moonlight, in the snow, in a foreign country, in another woman's arms.

The baby squirmed, giving a sudden cry as he felt the cold upon his skin.

Flora thought she was going to throw up.

Mary pulled him back in again, soothing his cries by pushing her crooked pinky into his mouth. 'What do you think it's like, eh, for women like us? We're denied, always on the outside . . . But *your* mistake – yours and hers! – gave us an opportunity to be a family. A proper family! . . . And it'll never come again, we both know that.

'Just think what we had to do to get here. To get off St Kilda first and then all the way over here – enduring conditions animals wouldn't live in. Losing our freedom as we bide our time, patiently waiting to start living the rest of our lives together . . . No, there is no number. There's nothing more you can give me – not beyond what you've already given.'

A smirk played on her lips, and Flora burst forth from the shadows.

'You bitch!' she cried, flailing like a fury as the worst curse she knew fell from her lips.

Mary staggered back in fright as Flora lunged for her son, but James caught her, holding her so that she fell a few agonizing feet short.

'Darling, no!'

'Give him to me! Give him to me!' Flora cried as James struggled to restrain her.

'Well, well, Flora, y' came too, I see,' Mary gasped, recovering. Her eyes travelled over Flora's expensive coat, the plush fur collar. 'He made a rich woman of y' after all then, did he? Too bad he'll never make a lady of y'.'

'That's enough!' James barked, making both women flinch. Flora had never heard him raise his voice before. He stared at Mary with open disgust. 'Where's your compassion, woman? Can't you see how unnatural this is?'

'Unnatural?'

'Yes! A mother separated from her child! You tricked her! You told her I was dead and convinced her that she had no way of supporting the child!'

'And where's the compassion for *me*?' Mary demanded, the whites of her eyes showing, a vein in her forehead bulging as her rage finally surfaced. 'Who's ever cared about how I've suffered? Having to lie with a man who made my skin crawl! Having to endure his body on mine, when it was all for naught anyway? Who's ever cared that I've had to hide the only love I've ever known? That the world – and God himself – would forsake me and think me diabolical if they knew the truth of what I am?'

She took several steps away from them, seeing how Flora grew limp in James's arms, tears streaming down her beautiful face.

'I'm not moved by her wretchedness. She's a spoilt brat and always was, but she's your problem now. If she wants a baby so bad, then give her another one – but you're not taking mine. Because he *is* mine. The law itself says so, and I'm never giving him back! I'm all he knows and I'll die before I let you take him from me—'

And before they could even breathe, she had turned on her heel and was hurrying back down the stairs, disappearing into the building she had called home for the past five weeks.

'No!' Flora screamed, feeling her legs give out under her as her baby was taken away again. He had been there, *right there*, and she had still failed. She collapsed to the ground, feeling a wail erupt from her, an empty sound she had never known her body could even make, as James sank down beside her. His arms kept trying to scoop her up, but it was like holding water. She was undone, let apart at the seams. No stuffing, no shape, no form.

'Flora, no, my darling. This isn't the end,' he cried, his voice thick and split with distress. 'There's still more we can do. There's always another way.'

But she shook her head from side to side; she was unable to form words, but she knew Mary was right. There was nothing they could do to prove the baby was theirs. Flora had given him away and created a perfect cover story that even she could no longer disprove. These were the consequences of her own actions. She had no one to blame but herself.

Chapter Eighteen

There was no back-up plan.

From the moment they had left Paris, they had never once envisaged a future in which their child was not with them. Failure hadn't been an option. Chase, hunt, pursue, capture . . . that was how it was supposed to have been. They had thought justice was on their side. Truth and fact. But it was all for nothing without evidence.

The burden of proof.

James had taken it badly. He was used to doing business, where money was king, but that held little sway over a woman from a barter economy; and appealing to her better nature was pointless when, in all the years Flora had known her, Mary had never once been reasonable nor compassionate. Too late, he saw he should have offered a bribe for Landon to take the baby: snatch him back under a lie, as he'd been taken from them. Instead, they had lost their only advantage of stealth, and Mary would be on full alert now. She knew they were here and why. She wouldn't let the baby out of her sight for a second, and the patrolling guards and fences that were designed to keep her in were also now the protective measures keeping them out.

The if-onlys haunted them both. All the way across the Atlantic, James had bolstered Flora as she'd struggled with the slow passing of days. The idea of his son had still been notional to him: he had never seen his face or looked into his eyes, never felt his warm, drowsy weight in his arms. But standing on that roof garden and seeing the tiny length of him, the sheen of his dark hair in the moonlight – the scale of their loss, everything Flora had gone through back then and every day since, had finally washed over him too.

Finally, they were united in their grief. They couldn't sleep for more than twenty minutes at a time, barely ate. James had given Flora a brandy when they'd got back to take the edge off, but it had taken a lot more than one, and the bottle was soon half-empty as she cried and he lay in silence in ironed sheets.

Emotional and physical exhaustion overwhelmed them. James made one final visit to Landon, offering a small fortune to get him into the medical centre, but the Irishman was adamant it couldn't be done. They had nowhere to go, no other routes to follow.

Flora sat at the window now, feeling nothing and seeing nothing. The city was lost to fog, the noise of the buses and trams muffled like lovers' confessions under a blanket. She slumped against the glass, feeling the cool chill of the condensation against her skin. She didn't know how long she'd been sitting there . . .

Distantly, she heard a knock at the hotel door, but she ignored it. James was dozing; housekeeping could come back another time. They didn't care about clean sheets and fresh flowers right now.

But the knock came again.

And then a voice. 'Mr Callaghan?'

James stirred at the sound of his name, but Flora jolted at the accent.

The Midnight Secret

'. . . What?' He was disoriented but alert, off the bed within a moment and staggering to the door.

Flora twisted from her position on the window sill to get a better look.

'. . . Landon?' James's voice was deep with tiredness. 'What are you doing here?'

'May I come in?'

James stepped back.

'Mrs Callaghan,' Landon nodded, a small frown crossing his face as he took in their general state of disarray. Flora realized James was in only his trousers; she was wearing just her slip . . . Clearly they hadn't been expecting visitors. James had been at the door before either of them could collect themselves.

'You'll have to forgive appearances,' James muttered. 'We've been feeling . . . under the weather.'

Landon made a noncommittal sound. Flora noticed he was carrying a large brown paper bag.

'What can we do for you?' James asked.

'I've found a way into the quarantine unit.'

Flora gave a small gasp, but James's eyes narrowed. '. . . But you said it was impossible. The biohazard security . . . ?'

'Let's just say I've befriended a nurse there. We've had a couple of dates these past few days . . . I persuaded her to give me this.' He held up the bag, looking over at Flora as James took it from him and looked inside.

'It's a nurse's uniform.'

Landon nodded. 'Only Mrs Callaghan can go in. My . . . friend has given me her rota: shift changeover times, tea breaks . . . Plus the patient list. If we time it accurately, your wife can get in there and into the woman's room before the next shift starts their rounds.'

James looked at Flora with wide eyes, disbelief slowly marbling with joy. Could this really be happening? They'd been granted a second chance?

She pulled the uniform out of the bag: a white, mid-calf-length dress, white soft-soled shoes, a white cloth hair cap and a mask that looped over the ears, covering her mouth and nose.

'When can we go?' she asked, her voice little more than a breath. It hurt so much to hope. To become solid again.

'Can you be changed and downstairs in twenty minutes?' James nodded on Flora's behalf.

'Then I'll take you over there. You can follow in your car.'

He left the room quickly, and they stared at each other. Was this really happening? Flora began to dress, her heart racing, fingers fumbling on buttons as James began to pace and plot.

'We need to go about this the right way,' he murmured. They had never planned on Flora being the negotiator. James was better placed, not just as a businessman, but for being more emotionally removed. He had no history with these women. But Flora . . . she had once seen Lorna as a friend, had trusted her with her health and her baby's life, only to be betrayed in the most heinous of ways.

'You said that Lorna's not like Mary? That at heart, she's a good person?'

'She is . . . She *was*. But I don't know any more. I never would have thought Lorna could do what she did to me.'

'Love can make people do crazy things,' he said thoughtfully. 'But she's been locked up in quarantine for over a month now, with no contact with Mary beyond letters. That will have given her time to reflect while she's been all alone. She might well have been having regrets. Second thoughts.'

Flora shook her head. 'I doubt it. She's come this far.'

The Midnight Secret

'But if it wasn't her idea in the first place . . . she might have gone along with it because Mary so badly wanted a baby. We saw how determined she was about keeping him, especially if she can't bear a child herself . . . But that might mean this was never Lorna's personal crusade. If she wasn't the driving force behind it – *that's* our way in. At heart, she's a nurse. She helps people. She has a conscience.' He jabbed a finger at Flora, finding conviction in the plan. 'You never know – seeing you here and giving up the baby might be a relief for her. She might want to do the right thing but just not know how.'

Flora thought about what he had said, trying to contain her hopes. Even if all this was true and Flora could appeal to Lorna's better nature, could Lorna hold any sway over Mary? Last night, Mary had showed them her determination to be a mother: the child was lying in *her* arms, the paperwork in her name. She held all the cards.

But the lion was known by the scratch of his claws. And as Flora set the nurse's hat upon her head, she reminded herself Mary wasn't the only one with a sharp swipe.

Landon pulled up on the opposite side of the street to one of the wooden grain stores, James just a couple of feet behind him. Flora looked around at the empty docks as her husband cut the ignition. Small icy banks of dirty snow were heaped alongside the road, the sky hanging so low it almost bumped their heads. A bleak, depressive mood was hanging over the whole city, not just her.

They waited as Landon got out of his car and walked back to them. James wound down the window.

'That's it,' he said, nodding towards the grain store, a cigarette dangling from his lower lip.

James looked first at the building, then at him. 'It's a storage facility.'

'Was. It was converted a few years back. Clearly, we couldn't keep the sick in the same building as the healthy detainees.'

'No, I suppose not.' Typhus, typhoid, diphtheria, TB, cholera . . . all were highly infectious.

'Stay here. Don't leave your car,' Landon said to James. 'Your wife can follow me.'

James reached over and clasped her hand for a moment. 'You can do this,' he whispered.

Landon flicked the cigarette away and sauntered across the street as Flora shrugged off her overcoat – walking through the hotel lobby dressed as a nurse would have drawn far too much attention.

She hurried after Landon, who now stood by a door at the back corner of the building.

'Take this.' He pulled a patient file from his overcoat and handed it to her.

'What's it for?'

'Appearances.'

She opened it – empty.

He glanced up and down the deserted street to check no one was around. 'Right, this is what we're going to do. I'm going to let you in, and you'll find yourself in a long corridor. You walk along that—'

'Wait – aren't you coming in with me?'

He sighed, shaking his head at her. 'How would we explain me, a civilian, being in a restricted medical zone? You're the one in the disguise.'

Flora blinked, feeling her nerves peak.

'Just walk along the corridor until you see a staircase on the right. Go up two floors . . .'

The Midnight Secret

She listened intently, but her heart had gone into a gallop. Somehow, walking into an empty corridor felt more daunting than stepping out on stage in Paris to face eight hundred people.

'Take a left at the top. The room's halfway down on the right. Room 237. You got that?'

'Up the stairs. Two floors. Turn left. Room 237, on the right.'

He nodded. 'Very good.'

'What should I do if I see someone?'

'Keep your head down and hold the file against your chest. Remember, you look the part. There's no reason for them to suspect you.'

'But if they say something to me—'

'Nod in greeting if you have to, but don't speak. If they hear you're foreign . . .' He drew a line across his neck, which she understood to be a bad thing.

'. . . And you're sure it's . . . safe to see her?'

'She's three days off being medically cleared. No symptoms for eighteen days now.' He put a key in the lock and opened the door, handing the key over to her. 'Lock up again when you leave and put the key in the bag with the uniform. Leave it at your hotel reception for me to collect this evening. You've got ten minutes before they start making the rounds . . . Now go.'

Flora stepped inside. As he had told her, she was indeed at the end of a long corridor. If any of the doors running along either side were to open, she would be in plain sight with nowhere to hide. Quickly, she covered her lower face with the mask and hurried forward, clutching the file to her chest, her rubber-soled shoes squeaking on the floor. There was a strong smell of disinfectant and a pervasive silence. Quarantine meant isolation, but it was almost as if there was no one else here. Glass windows should have provided a view into the rooms, but most were obscured by curtains that had been drawn over.

She could hear voices up ahead and felt a rush of panic as she looked for the stairs. *Where . . . ?* She saw them and climbed the two flights, running up the steps two at a time. At the top, she took a left and scurried down the passage, scanning the room numbers.

Room 237. There it was, a card on the wall beside the door: *Lorna MacDonald, 31, Scotland. Dis. Empress of Scotland, 23/11/1930. Typhus.*

Flora stared at the words, seeing how they gave a summary of a woman she knew now from all angles. A woman with whom she had once laughed, talked, danced, gossiped in the burn as they washed clothes . . . A woman who was intelligent, educated and principled, but also overbearing, bossy and domineering; who had saved her fair share of lives, and been capable of extraordinary cruelty . . . A self-proclaimed old maid with no interest in marrying – because she was already, secretly, in love.

Flora held her breath as she looked at the doorknob. One turn and she would see again the woman who had tended her throughout her pregnancy and shown her the greatest kindness, before delivering her of a baby she would take.

It made her a monster, didn't it? James wanted to believe Lorna had goodness in her, but what woman could do that to another? For all of Mary's desperation to have a child, it was Lorna who had brought the plot to life: smiling as she lied to Flora's face, day after day after day. It was Lorna who had told her James was dead and held her as she cried. It was Lorna who had given her the herbs that induced her labour two weeks early.

She opened the door and peered in, feeling a jolt nonetheless

The Midnight Secret

as she saw the oh-so-familiar figure of Lorna sitting in a chair. She was quietly reading a book, a model of composure and self-improvement. No one could guess, just from looking at her, what evil she had done.

Flora slipped into the room, feeling her anger harden. 'Hello, Lorna.'

Lorna looked up, a frown already crumpling her brow as her ears caught the accent that told her one story, her eyes telling her another.

'Nurse Nanc—?' She stopped short as she caught a better sight of the nurse approaching her.

A silence exploded in the room as, slowly, Flora removed the mask to reveal her startling, astonishing face.

'This is a turnaround, is it not, Lorna?' she said. 'Me the nurse and you the patient.'

Lorna's eyes travelled over her in disbelief – that she was here, that she was dressed like this.

'You're only dressed as a nurse,' she corrected – she had always been so correct, so officious – but her voice still betrayed her great shock.

'Aye, but you're very much a patient, from what I've heard.' Flora perched on the end of the bed, setting down the dummy file as she took a better look at Lorna. 'Typhus is serious. You've had a hard time of it lately.'

She regarded her foe through narrowed eyes, taking in the changes since their last meeting. To all intents and purposes, it had been the night of the birth, for she had scarcely seen Lorna on the boat over to Lochaline the next day. Flora had been on all fours as she laboured, crying, wailing, moaning like an animal as Lorna had mopped her brow and shushed her. Lorna had been the one in control back then. She had held all the power.

How the tables had turned.

Lorna was thinner, her face pale and haggard, dark moons cradling beneath her eyes. Unlike the healthy detainees with their roof garden, she looked like she hadn't been outside for weeks. Her auburn hair had lost its rich colour, as if she was bleeding pigment, and there was an overall impression of *lack*. This crossing had come at a high cost to her, that was evident; she certainly hadn't set eyes on a swimming pool or a billiards table, or slept on silk sheets in a suite. She had suffered.

She sank back into her seat, seeing Flora's reading of her: pitiable and pathetic, she was diminished, no longer the woman who had quietly gathered a revolution on a small Scottish isle. Lorna looked away, but there was nothing to look at; the windows were set high in the walls, providing light but no view. '. . . You hate me.'

'Only appropriate under the circumstances, don't you think?' Flora replied. 'I had thought us friends once. I trusted you with my life, the life of my baby.'

'I would never have hurt or endangered either one of you.'

'How can you say that?' Flora asked coldly. 'You told me James was dead to trick me into giving him up. You forced me into a birth that my body wasn't yet ready for. And then you brought my baby on a transatlantic crossing, exposing him to dangerous diseases you yourself have been unable to fight off.'

There was a long pause. '. . . We had no choice.'

'Another lie. You just wanted to be sure I would never find you. You knew at some point James would come back and your lies would be revealed. You knew I'd come after you.'

Lorna nodded, admitting it. '. . . Of course. What mother wouldn't?'

The two women's eyes met then. *Was* she a mother? Did love alone make her so, or biological fact?

The Midnight Secret

A silence bloomed between them.

'Was it worth it?' Flora asked, feeling a vague pity she hadn't anticipated.

'... Aye. For a few weeks, we were a family. Just us, together, as we'd always dreamt.'

Flora watched her, wondering how she had been so blind to a truth that had been right in front of her all those years. Innocuous events were cast in a new light now – like the time she had seen Lorna and Mary holding hands around the back of the cottage as she had been talking to Effie at the bull house. Donald had just returned from Boreray after his fight with Mathieson, and she had taken the gesture as one of sympathy, a nurse's friendly care.

She wanted to hate Lorna, but the woman before her looked broken, nothing like the warrior she had known. Love had come at a high price.

'When did it begin between you?'

Lorna's brown eyes flashed in her direction. Had she ever told their story before? Unlike Flora, Mhairi, Effie and Molly's love stories, hers had had to live in the shadows, existing without a form. 'When Mary was sick. She was brought into the cottage hospital where I was working on the mainland.'

Flora remembered it. She had been a young teenager when Mary had fallen desperately ill and she vividly recalled the drama of Mary being carried from her cottage by the men and taken over to the mainland on Captain McGregor's trawler. She'd been gone several weeks in all, though it had felt longer at the time.

'... And you came to St Kilda the following summer,' Flora murmured, remembering the excitement as word had spread that a nurse was coming to live among them. Vaguely she recalled a bet between the mothers down by the washing burn – Christina had wagered Rachel a pocketful of crotal that 'the new lass' would start walking out with Norman Ferguson. It all seemed laughable now. 'You never said you knew Mary.'

'Of course not. We had to act as strangers.' Lorna's eyes simmered with bitterness. 'No one thought twice when we gradually became friends.'

'Did Donald know?'

She scoffed and looked away. 'I don't suppose it ever crossed his mind. He's not exactly a man of great imagination.'

Flora bridled on her friend's behalf. Mhairi loved the man in a way his own wife had never been able to. 'He deserved better than he got,' she said stiffly. 'He's a good man.'

'And us? Did we not deserve better too? To know love? Are we not good people because we were born this way and not that? No one would willingly choose this path, Flora.' She swallowed. 'Me moving to St Kilda was the only way for us to be together. A few stolen moments here and there was all we could ever hope for. It had to be enough for us.'

'So what changed that it wasn't?' Flora heard a hardness in her own voice that she didn't recognize.

Lorna swallowed. '. . . Molly's death,' she said finally. 'I took it badly, as you know. I couldn't accept losing a healthy young patient to something that is now avoidable. I began to feel enraged . . . frustrated . . . at the limitations of life there. It made me think about moving on.'

'And so you thought the entire community should go with you?' Flora asked angrily. 'What about Ma Peg and Old Fin, Robert Gillies and Mad Annie, who expected to live out their last days there? What about Mary Gillies, who buried five children there and had to leave them behind, their unvisited graves being mauled by the winds?'

The Midnight Secret

Lorna looked at her, unrepentant. 'I had all their best interests at heart. The world was moving on and St Kilda was being left behind.'

'St Kilda was *always* behind! But it was our home. You were just an incomer who came for her own reasons and then left for them too.'

'. . . I truly believed evacuation was the best choice for everyone.'

'You expect me to believe that?'

Lorna fell still, conflict running over her face like a spring storm. She looked tired, as if the words and the anger were draining her. 'I admit that . . . when I discovered Mhairi's . . . predicament, I realized it presented a unique opportunity. She was pregnant by a married man and she had two choices: disgrace or discretion. Mary had already discovered the affair anyway. Her assuming the baby as her own was a way for them *all* to recover the situation: it would be her husband's child, halfway to legitimacy. Mhairi would be spared the shame and could still go on to marry the farmer's son. It was a good plan for everyone,' she insisted.

An unspoken word hovered between them.

Until.

Until Mhairi had made one wrong decision. The 'sheep drama' that had killed Molly had had another knock-on effect: they had lost over sixty sheep that winter, threatening their ability to make their rent quotas when the factor came over in the summer. In trying to make up the shortfall and deliver that ewe of her triplets, Mhairi had lost her own baby – and put Flora in the spotlight.

It had been a game of dominoes. One of them falling and toppling all the rest.

Flora looked back at her, seeing the gleam of desperation in the other woman's eyes.

'No. Your arrangement with Mhairi was made with her consent,' Flora said in a low voice. 'She had made her choice and was prepared to live with it. *I* was never granted that mercy. What you did to me was cold and calculated. I had a fiancé on his way back to me, coming to marry me. We would have been a family and you knew that. That's why you stole it from me with lies.' Her voice broke under the strain of emotion. 'You know what you did, Lorna! It was *not* the same thing! It was monstrous, what you did! Monstrous! How can you live with yourself?'

'I'm sorry!' Lorna cried, the words pulled from her as if on a wire so that she slumped forward, her head in her hands. She began to sob. '. . . I'm sorry, Flora. What I did to you . . . it's haunted me . . .' She looked up with reddened eyes. 'But to have come so close to having a child of our own with Mhairi, only to have it ripped away again at the eleventh hour . . . Mary was beside herself. Nothing could console her! In the months leading up to the birth, we had dared to dream of a future that we *never* could have foreseen, and then it was gone again in the blink of an eye. It was cruel! Stepping back from that was . . . it was desperate! We both knew there would never be another chance for us.'

'So *I* was the sacrifice?'

'Look at you, Flora!' Lorna cried, her brown eyes wide. 'Everything's always come so easily to you. You'd have your pick of princes and kings if you wanted them! You could have as many babies as you like! Don't pretend things are equal for us when they're not!'

Flora stared back at her, seeing the wretchedness in the other woman's face. But desperation was no justification.

The Midnight Secret

'What you did was wrong,' she said flatly. 'In the eyes of God, of everyone, you have sinned.'

'. . . I know.'

'You have to put it right.'

Lorna's head whipped up. 'What?'

'You heard me. Put it right. Give back my baby.' Flora held her nerve as she got down to the bones of the confrontation. Lorna surely had no idea of Mary's win over them the other night: the burden of proof over morality was always going to have been Mary's play. But James had been right – the nurse did have a shred of conscience. 'James is here with me, in Quebec. He wanted to go straight to the police, but I've held him off. I asked him to let me speak to you first and give you a chance,' she lied. 'I know you're decent at heart, Lorna. And I . . . I can understand your motives, even if I can't forgive them. But if you give me back my child, I'm prepared to part ways without further recrimination. I'm sure you can see it's better to bend than to break. I don't want to see you and Mary jailed for this.' She saw the fear come into Lorna's eyes. 'You've made it all the way here – you can still build a life together. No one needs to know about any of it. I won't tell them. I give you my word.'

Lorna was breathing heavily as the words rebounded in her head: *police, jail, build a life* . . . 'But Mary,' she breathed, her head beginning to shake side to side. 'She won't—'

'I know. Which is why you won't tell her. Not till after it's done,' Flora said calmly. 'You and I know things were . . . chaotic in those final weeks back home. You weren't thinking straight, you were panicking . . . But you've had time to think in here and you know now that what you did was wrong. You can't outrun justice and y' know what will happen to you if we go to the authorities. You've a clear choice: lose the baby or lose everything. The two of you would never see each other again, they'd make sure of that. They'd make examples of you both. I know you understand it. But Mary? She's . . . Well, we both know it's hard to hold a conger by the tail.'

Flora saw the tears streaming down Lorna's face and held her tongue. She forced herself to hold back and wait, knowing her arrows had hit their mark. Her heart was pounding. Lorna was due to be released from here in three days.

Finally, Lorna nodded. 'I'll do it.'

'You won't tell her?'

'. . . No.'

'Because it's no secret if three know it,' Flora warned.

'I won't tell her,' Lorna murmured.

Flora felt her breath catch at the sweet, private victory. 'Then I'll tell James to hold off from his visit to the police. We'll be waiting for you three days from now, when you're all released from the Immigration Hall. There's a door to the trains beside the money exchange. Meet me outside there.'

'Right there?' Lorna looked panicked. 'Can't y' at least—?'

'No.' Flora cut her off. 'It has to be there. I won't risk you disappearing on us again. Your word is no good any more. You have to find a way to bring the baby out to me there, without Mary seeing, or we'll bring in the police.'

Lorna swallowed, then nodded. '. . . Aye.'

'Good,' Flora said, getting up. 'Then we're agreed.'

She stared down at the woman who had taken everything from her, wondering why it was she couldn't feel contempt, only pity. 'Three more days, Lorna, and then this nightmare will be over. For all of us.'

Chapter Nineteen

EFFIE

5 January 1931

Lochaline

'There was no sorrel but I found some nettles,' Effie called through from the small porch, gently patting her thigh to beckon Slipper and Socks to her side. She walked into the kitchen where Jayne was standing by the stove, the two dogs trotting by her heels. 'Will that do?'

'Aye,' Jayne smiled, taking the bunches from her. 'We'll make a chef of you yet.'

'I hardly think so,' Effie scoffed, sitting up on the counter beside her and drumming her bare heels against the cupboards. 'I'm better at the hunting than the gathering.'

'Talking of gatherings,' David said, looking up from his spot at the table where he was reading the paper. 'I was thinking of entering for the Lochaber Gathering in July.'

'Doing what?' Effie scoffed. 'And don't say tossing the caber, because *I'd* have a better chance in that than you!'

'You never give over with your boasting, do you?' he tutted.

'You might be strong for your size, Effie, but you're tiny and relative to me you're a pipsqueak, so don't push it.'

'I'll arm-wrestle you and we can find out,' she challenged, her eyes gleaming.

'Fine!' he shrugged, unbuttoning his shirt-cuff as she jumped off the counter and sat opposite him on the bench, arm already flexed. The puppies settled themselves by her feet.

Jayne tutted, grinning at their antics as they began to wrestle. 'You didn't say what you were going to enter in at the Gathering, David.'

'Thanks to Effie, butting in—' he said, as his arm suddenly went down.

'I win!' Effie cried.

'Wait, no! I wasn't paying attention! I was talking to Jayne!'

'Too bad.'

'*That* didn't count,' he said firmly, getting his arm back in position, his hand ready for her grip. 'Again.'

Effie beamed. 'Best out of three. But be prepared to lose.' She looked into his eyes devilishly as she resumed the position, his hand twice the size of hers.

'Piping,' he said as they began to push their palms against one another.

Effie frowned, confused. 'Eh?' Her arm went down.

'I win,' he grinned.

'Wait, no!'

'What? You were distracted?' he teased.

'Oof,' she muttered, eyes narrowed. '. . . Right. Final one.'

'But you don't know how to play, do you?' Jayne asked over her shoulder as they began again.

'Not yet. But Roddy MacRae has offered to teach me. I came across him mending his chanter reed the other day and we got talking. It's something that's always interested me. I love the sound of them.'

'Aye,' Jayne agreed. 'I mean, don't get me wrong, the fiddle and Old Fin's accordion are the sounds of home, but there's something so haunting about the pipes.'

'That's what I think,' David replied to her without taking his attention off Effie; she was staring into his eyes as if preparing to reach in and pluck out his soul. She was the Effie of old – or desperately longing to be, reviving the version of herself with an unscarred heart – but she could see he was wholly unperturbed by her intensity; she was his little sister in all but name and he was used to her competitive ways. 'Obviously I wouldn'a be entering with any hopes of winning anything, but it would give me a target, something to strive for.'

'Don't be so sure you wouldn't. I think you'll be a natural,' Jayne said.

'You do?'

'Aye. You always excel whenever you apply yourself to something. See how well you've done with growing the kale this winter?'

Effie's eyes swivelled between them. Did they even remember she was here, mid-competition? 'Only because you helped me with the transplanting.'

'It was you,' Jayne demurred. 'You've got green fingers – and probably fast nimble pipe-playing ones too.'

Effie saw the smile grow on David's face at the compliment and knew this was her chance. She went to swoop his arm down suddenly and she was halfway there when he locked back in and froze her attack. She felt her muscles strain as he grinned infuriatingly back at her, their arms at an impasse. His effort level was significantly lower than hers and she realized, for the first time, that he was humouring her. That he could easily win this if he so chose.

Just then she heard the creak of the garden gate, footsteps coming up the path. She saw another expression come into her opponent's eyes as he glanced over at Jayne, still working quietly by the stove.

Effie took her chance, slamming his hand down upon the table – 'Yes!' she cried victoriously, but David didn't appear even to notice.

The puppies pulled themselves up to sitting position, eyes on the door as Norman appeared a moment later, frowning with displeasure at the curious scene in his kitchen. 'David, what a surprise to see you here. Again,' he muttered sarcastically.

'Evening, Norman,' David nodded. 'I was helping Jayne set some mousetraps.'

'Well, of course. There's always something she needs help with, isn't there?'

Effie glanced at David and saw him biting his lip, holding back hot words. It was true he was always over here, but so was she. There was now at least one bicycle per household and all the villagers darted in and out of each other's homes like dragonflies, just as they had in the old days. Since returning from Skye, she had moved back in with her father to their old cottage down the lane; Sholto had arranged for their possessions to be brought back up to Lochaline and his driver had personally driven her father up here. They were a community once more and it was almost like old times. Almost.

Jayne turned from her position at the stove, her gaze searching for something on Norman. '. . . Did you remember the pork chops?' she asked.

The Midnight Secret

Norman winced, giving a hiss of irritation. 'Me? . . . '

'Aye, I asked y' to pick them up on y' way past this evening.'

'Why are y' adding to my list of things to do, woman? You know how busy my days are at the minute! What's wrong with you getting them?'

Effie flinched. She could see he'd been to the pub after work – everyone knew Norman was the first to the bar and last to leave most evenings – and there was a brazen, eyeballing quality to Norman's stare that reminded her of Frank Mathieson on the night of the storm. He was unpredictable and belligerent. Slipper, leaning against her right leg, whined softly.

'Because the butcher explained yesterday there would be a delay with the delivery, and you agreed to pick them up on your way home.'

'. . . Well, I was working late. Being Deputy Manager comes with added responsibilities.'

'I know that, but—'

Effie's eyes slid over to David – perhaps they should go? – but he was watching the married couple intently. He looked like a cat about to spring.

Jayne sighed. 'Never mind. I've some leftover lamb scrag I can use.' She turned away.

The air seemed to suck out from the room.

'Why are y' so huffy?' Norman demanded in a low voice, stepping closer so that he was right behind his wife. 'It's hardly m' fault!'

'I'm not huffy.' Jayne was standing very still.

'Well, y' sound it.'

Effie watched as Jayne slowly turned and forced a smile. '. . . Really, Norman, it's fine. It's no bother, I can use the lamb just as easy.' She wiped her hands on her pinny and put a hand softly on his chest. 'Why don't you take a bath? You must be tired after y' long day.'

He stared at her for a moment, seeing how she wouldn't rise. He glanced back, as if remembering they had an audience; Effie felt herself shrink a little under his gaze before he gave a huff of irritation, exiting the room with a mutinous look. Norman's arrival home in the evenings was always her cue to leave and set to preparing dinner for herself and her father. David would usually stay until his mother blew the whistle down the lane, calling him home for his dinner.

There was a small silence, David watching Jayne as if expecting her to fall. She gave another of her weak smiles.

'It's been a big step up, moving into management,' Jayne murmured to them, looking embarrassed by the scene they had just witnessed.

'Aye, of course,' Effie nodded quickly. She glanced at David again for agreement but he was silent, staring at his hands on the table, his jaw balling like a pulse.

Effie saw Jayne see it too, watching him with a worried look.

'. . . Did I tell you they want him to go on another business trip again soon?' Jayne asked as she saw Effie watching her.

'Oh?'

'The last one went so well—'

'The one to Skye?' Effie asked.

'Aye. They're talking about Perth this time.'

'Are they now?' Effie hadn't forgotten her shock at seeing Norman in the library at Dunvegan. He had no idea she had been there, of course, and she'd kept her mouth shut, but it had sat in the back of her mind like a worm ever since, curled up and solid, impossible to ignore.

'What exactly does he do on these trips?' she asked.

The Midnight Secret

'Consults with the estate managers, he says. About forest management.'

'Ah,' Effie nodded, none the wiser. Did that explain his presence at Dunvegan? He'd been meeting with MacLeod's estate manager to discuss planting trees, or cutting them down? But even if he had, why had he stolen into the library? She had seen and heard the way he crept about in there: furtive and stealthy. And it wasn't as if he had been waiting to meet someone there. He'd been in and out within minutes.

'Which estate in Perth, do you know?' she asked.

'I'm not sure, he hasn't said. Probably several.'

Dupplin? Effie wondered. Or Blair Atholl? She wondered how many castles and estates there were in Perthshire. The lairds were all connected to one another, old friends and foes through historic allegiances and rivalries that spanned back through the centuries. Of course, the MacLeods, Hays and Atholls were all in the same circle – but was it just coincidence that Norman should be attending their estates on business, or something more sinister? A deputy manager of the Forestry Commission had no place being in any of their libraries.

Jayne stared down at the bunch of nettles on the counter. 'These won't work now; not with lamb,' she said quietly. She seemed to Effie suddenly very small. 'I'd best get some rosemary.'

'I can get it,' David said, getting up.

'No,' Jayne said quickly, stopping him.

'But—'

'It's fine, I'll go. It might be better if . . .' She looked ashamed suddenly. 'I'm sorry, but it might be better if you aren't here David, when he comes back down. He's tired and . . .'

She looked at him imploringly.

'. . . Of course,' Effie said quickly, seeing Jayne's

embarrassment. 'I need to be getting back anyway too. Come on, David.' She jumped up, the dogs too.

But David didn't move. He was staring at Jayne as if she had just had an argument with him and not her husband.

'David?' Effie said, tugging on his arm and having to all but drag him out. '. . . See you tomorrow, Jayne,' she called over her shoulder.

The garden gate slammed behind them, marking their departure, and Effie looked up at David as they started on their way down the lane. It was dark but they were used to that, their eyes adapting quickly. 'What was that all about?' she asked him as they drew away from the cottage, the dogs running ahead.

'Nothing,' he muttered sullenly.

'Well, something's got your goat. Couldn't you see poor Jayne was mortified? Sometimes people need their privacy, David.'

'Privacy?' he scoffed. 'Being alone with him is the very last thing she needs.'

'He's her husband.'

'He beats her!'

Effie swallowed, looking back quickly to check Norman hadn't overheard. '. . . I know, so you said,' she said in a low voice. It had been a shock when he had confided it to her, after Mhairi had told him on his visit to Oban at Christmas. 'But if Jayne won't admit it, then we have to respect her wishes to deal with him her way. You saw her in there just now – she knew exactly how to calm him down.'

'But what about the times when she can't? Do we wait until she's dead, or half dead, before we do anything?'

'David, I know she's your friend, but you can't live in her kitchen just in case it gives you a chance to stop anything.'

The Midnight Secret

He shook his head. 'How did I never see it for all those years?' He sounded incredulous. 'Why did Molly never say?'

'Perhaps she didn't know.'

David scoffed again, angrily. 'She lived in the same house. She knew, Eff.'

'Well, if she did, she never said anything to me either.'

They were quiet for a bit as they walked, their eyes roaming over the gentle heathered hills. Effie had seen a red stag earlier, forced down from the snowy summits.

'Well at least she'll have a few days' peace if he does go away on another of these business trips.'

'*Business trips*,' David muttered sourly, shaking his head and looking away.

She looked up at him sharply. 'What does that mean?'

'Surely you've heard the rumours about him and Fiona MacDougall?'

'The blacksmith's wife?'

'Aye. The lads in the yard say they've been at it for weeks. Supposedly she "visited her sister" the same week Norman went to Skye.'

'Oh, poor Jayne,' she whispered, feeling her cheeks burn with shock. Not just beaten but betrayed in every way. 'And everyone knows?'

'All but you and her, it seems,' he said grimly.

They had reached Effie's cottage now and they stopped at her gate. The light was on in the front room, her father sitting in his chair by the fire, whittling a stick. She turned to look directly at David, recognizing the mulish expression on his handsome face.

'If you're thinking of doing what I think you're thinking . . . don't. Don't tell her.'

'But if she knew he was humiliating her like this—'

'It's none of our business. It's their marriage. Jayne's no fool.'

'No, but she's naive! And too loyal. She's too good for him. Even when he beats her black and blue, she defends him! Doesn't she see she's protecting him by staying silent?'

Effie put her hands on his arms, seeing his agitation. 'David, if you want to be her friend, you'll trust her to do what's best. She married him for better or for worse.'

'And she's got worse than she could have dreamt!'

'You've got to *trust* her.'

David shook his head. 'You don't understand, Eff! He's a dangerous man. Far more dangerous than you think. It doesn't stop with wife-beating with him.'

Effie looked at him, alarmed. 'What do you mean?' she frowned.

He looked away, raking both hands through his hair, squeezing his elbows in front of his face. What wasn't he saying?

'. . . David?' she pressed.

He stepped back suddenly. 'I've got to go.'

'No – what did you mean by that? Tell me! David!' she called as he strode away, arms swinging.

'I'll see you tomorrow,' he said, disappearing into the darkness so that all that remained with Effie was the fading sound of his footsteps and a feeling of dread.

Chapter Twenty

MHAIRI

6 January 1931

Lochaline

The bus door opened with a hiss and Mhairi stepped down into a puddle. She waited where she was as the door closed and the bus pulled away with a groan, continuing on up the lane until it summited the low hill and disappeared down the far side.

Mhairi stood at the small junction and looked at the row of white houses, gates askew from where the children blew in and out like autumn leaves, lights shining from almost every window. Bicycles were propped against the walls and buckets sat beside the coal boxes, ready to be filled. Her own house lay at the end of the row and she saw the rosebushes her mother had been so excited about planting, now in the ground ready for next summer; a small ball lying on the grass . . .

Mhairi walked slowly up to the gate. It creaked on the hinge – she had forgotten that – and she was halfway up the path when she saw a face appear at the upstairs window. Even silhouetted, she recognized her little sister Red Annie at a glance, and she could almost hear the girl's gasp through the glass.

She disappeared in the next moment, and Mhairi had scarcely got to the front door before it flew open and Annie was leaping into her arms. Mhairi laughed, dropping her bag as she hugged her sister back. She was braced for a cold reception and she was surprised at how comforting a child's hug could be. She nuzzled her face in Annie's hair, so like her own, and smelled within it all the scents of home.

By the time they pulled apart, the others had heard the commotion and were gathering at the door. Wee Murran stood there holding a wooden train toy, an impressive scab on his knee; Christina, the next oldest after Mhairi, had a book in her hand. Her big brother Fin, holding three-year old Alasdair on his shoulders, pushed a new pair of spectacles up his nose.

'Hello, everybody,' she said quietly, her eyes searching for her parents in the background but finding no sign of them.

There was a pause and the younger ones looked over at Fin, as the eldest assembled there and therefore the default authority.

'You'd better come in,' he said, stepping back so the others could do the same.

Mhairi followed him through to the front room. The fire was lit, even though they had radiators, and she set down her bag, taking in all the changes accrued during her absence. A framed needlepoint she suspected was Christina's handiwork decorated a corner of the wall. There was a small bookshelf half-filled with books, and a rug had been laid on the floor, which was currently covered with wooden building blocks.

Fin put Alasdair back down on the ground and he toddled

The Midnight Secret

over to them as Mhairi set down her bag and shrugged off her coat. She was aware of the way Christina and Fin were looking at her, as if she had two heads, and she realized David must have told them what she and Donald had revealed to him on Boxing Day. They hadn't sworn him to secrecy on the matter and he was no tittle-tattle, she knew that; he must have done it in the hopes of somehow pleading their case with her parents and the rest of the community.

'Mhairi, we weren't expecting y—' Fin began.

'I didn't give warning,' she replied, just as a commotion in the hall made them turn and Mad Annie burst through, followed a few moments later by Ma Peg.

'So it's true, then,' Mad Annie said breathlessly, looking at her with wild eyes. 'You're back.'

'Aye.'

The air in the room seemed to roll around their heads, thoughts jostling for space, everyone looking at her with stunned expressions that gave her an indication of just how they had received David's revelations. She wondered when exactly he had told them. The day after he got back? This morning?

Annie looked like she wanted to say something, to do something . . . her body lurching forward a little before she caught herself and pulled back. Mhairi knew a slapped cheek was the least she deserved.

'Well, lass,' Ma Peg breathed, shooing the children away so she could get to a chair and sit down. She looked back at Mhairi with aged eyes. She had seen plenty of scandals in her lifetime; but did anything amount to the horror of Mhairi and Flora's secrets? 'What a thing, you coming back unannounced like this.'

Mhairi swallowed. More sounds were coming to their ear – the squeaky hinge of the gate, footsteps on the path, the front door hitting the wall – and she knew the entire village would be here within moments. One of the children must be running from door to door, spreading the news.

Two puppies shot in, ears up, noses down, as they investigated the commotion.

'Mhairi?' Effie gasped, bursting through a moment later, looking worried and excited all at once. 'What are you doing here? Why didn't you tell me you were coming?'

But there was no time to reply. More familiar faces were coming through, young and old, all wearing the same look – except for David. He came in with wild eyes that told her he'd sprinted here too.

'Mhairi?'

'Hello, David,' she said quietly, offering nothing more. She was waiting now for her parents to arrive, since it was clearly their judgement that would determine everyone else's response. They were holding their tongues – even Mad Annie, just – and a silence fell over the room as it filled up with more and more bodies. Mhairi felt as if she was in court, waiting for the judge to pass sentence.

Her parents were the last to walk through. Her mother's eyes were already wet as she came in. Her father was pale. They were followed by Christina MacQueen, wheeling Flora's father, in his chair. His injured leg was still bandaged. Norman, Jayne and Old Fin were further up the lane and it would be several minutes before they made an appearance, though Mhairi didn't doubt they would.

Rachel looked her daughter up and down with haunted eyes, taking in the young woman's slender body, and Mhairi could see she found it scarcely possible to believe that she had birthed a baby. Her own child had lost a child and she had hidden it all behind a ridge, a shawl and a stoical smile.

The Midnight Secret

Finally, the room stilled. Silence fell like a black curtain. Everyone waited.

'. . . I know I've let you all down,' she began in a small voice, her eyes darting between them all. 'You expected better from me and I failed you . . .' She swallowed, feeling the quiver of emotions in her chest at the coming words she knew she had to say. 'It was never my intention to fall in love with Donald. He was married and I know what that makes me. I have wrestled with my conscience since the very first moment and no one could hate me more than I have hated myself. I ought to have married McLennan and done my duty and I'm . . . I'm sorry that I couldn't go through with it.'

David's head dropped at her words, Effie blanching, for she too had lived through a similar fate. Mhairi saw a tear trickling down her mother's cheek, although she stood as frozen as the rocks on the St Kildan hills.

'I tried my best not to lie to any one of you and, in going over to the other side, I was trying not to deceive you but to spare you from the shame of my actions.' Her eyes moved slowly over the gathered faces and she saw in them sorrow marbled with pity, but disgust too. She could not sugarcoat the egregiousness of her actions.

'. . . Donald and I tried to make things right, as best we could, and we were resolved to stand by our . . . our decision to be apart and give up the baby. But . . . I lost my daughter . . .' Her voice broke on the words, her mother slumping too. 'And I have come to accept that it was God's will. It was just punishment for my sin. I knew Donald was a married man. I deserved my fate.'

'Mhairi—' David said, taking a half step forward from where he stood pressed against the wall.

'No, David,' she said, stopping him from stopping her. 'I need to say this. All of it.'

He fell back, looking pained by her self-censure.

'But Flora's only sin was her . . . haste. Timing. It was wrong, aye, but James was coming back to marry her. The scandal would have been erased the moment they were wed. She did not deserve to have her baby stolen under a wicked lie. *No one* deserves that. ' She tried to stand a little taller. 'Flora and I sinned, we don't deny it – but we were not the only ones. Lorna is not who you believe her to be.' She saw the look of consternation cross Ma Peg's face at the unexpected mention of the nurse's name. She stalled for a moment. 'Nor Crabbit Mary either.' She swallowed. 'They're lovers.'

A collective gasp whistled around the room and she realized David must not have revealed this final secret. Had it been a scandal too far for him? None of these were his stories, after all.

For a moment Mhairi felt her nerve fail her as a murmur of protest broke out and the children were quickly shooed from the room, but she was here to speak the truth, no matter how dark or unpalatable it may be.

'I'm sorry but it's true. They manipulated us both in different ways . . . And tricked Donald too.' She looked down, playing with her fingers, which were interlaced in front of her.

'When I went to Oban, it was to do the right thing. I could not stand by as he was jailed on account of a lie. It was Flora, not Mary, who gave birth to a baby that night, and when Mary forsook his alibi, I had no choice but to come forward and tell the truth – that he had been with me after midnight.'

She saw her father turn away, but her mother stood motionless, tears tracking down her cheeks.

The Midnight Secret

'And when he was freed, I could not pretend I did not love him still. I have always been, I hope, a dutiful daughter, but we had suffered greatly during our time apart and, in the end, I chose to live with shame than to live without him. Of course we cannot be wed – Mary has seen to that, fleeing to Canada without giving him a divorce.'

Ma Peg flinched at the word and Mhairi stared down at the floor. Was her message falling on deaf ears? Had coming back been a terrible mistake?

'I don't expect you to understand, much less to forgive, and I know you must be wondering why, then, I am here.' She bit her lip before she looked up again and stared at the opposite wall. It was impossible to meet anyone's eye.

'I have left him, not because I do not love him. I do and I always will – but he cannot leave Oban and it was no longer safe for me to remain there. The neighbours harass me daily, believing themselves to be defending Mary. I would have tolerated it, as I have these months past, but it would get worse in the coming months, once they realized . . . and I will not lose another baby.'

She pressed a hand to her belly as another collective gasp whistled around the packed room. Her mother staggered backwards, her father catching her with strong hands.

'You're with child?' Christina MacQueen cried.

Mhairi tried not to show her fear at their startled response. It was just as she had anticipated. She took a sharp intake of breath, steeling herself. '. . . If you cannot bear the shame of me coming back here, I understand. I'll go somewhere new and tell them I am a widow. I know I do not deserve to be happy. But my baby does.'

She stared into the room, her chin held high as she looked for the horror in their eyes. Her mother was openly weeping now. Christina too. Her father's eyes were red-rimmed, though he could not look at her. At some point, Norman and Jayne and Old Fin had come into the room, and Mhairi caught the look of sympathy in Jayne's soft brown eyes. She knew what it was to be on the outside.

Mhairi looked at David, who was ashen and stunned that she had confessed every last secret.

For several moments no one stirred.

'It'd be a scandal,' Old Fin muttered, shaking his head. 'It's bad enough already with some of the rumours flying about us.'

'Aye,' Norman sneered, his arms folded across his chest.

'What rumours? Who?' Archie MacQueen asked.

But the old man would not be drawn, clamping his thin lips together with a furious look. Murmurs erupted, the veneer of composure breaking down as everyone began to stir from their silence.

Effie spoke up first. 'I'll stand by you, Mhairi,' she said staunchly. She was used to being talked about too.

'Me too,' David nodded, but dissenting noises rose up, subsuming them both.

'A disgrace!' someone cried from the back.

'We'd be dishonoured,' Old Fin muttered again.

'Oh? And who here can cast the first stone?' Ma Peg demanded, getting suddenly to her feet and quelling them all into a hush again. 'Not you, Fin. I'm the only person in here old enough to remember you as a youth – and you were lucky, not good!'

Mhairi startled at the unexpected comment, others too, looking back at the elder with surprise.

'Aye,' Mad Annie chimed in. 'I've a long memory too, and I know which wedding dates and birth dates got smudged in the register.' She gave a narrow-eyed look. 'For what else was there to do?'

Still there were shakes of heads, but Annie was never one to be denied.

'And are y' so short-sighted y' don't remember poor Kitty's fate, dashing herself upon the rocks for fear of the shame? Is that what you want for her?' She waved towards Mhairi, who well remembered what had happened to Flora's cousin Kitty. 'You'd rather see her *dead*?'

At the question Rachel rushed forward, throwing her arms around her daughter so fiercely that Mhairi didn't have time to lift her arms as she was caught in a tight embrace. Was this really happening? Her mother pulled back and looked into her eyes. Mhairi saw no anger there, only sorrow. She had been braced for the slap; she didn't anticipate the hand upon her belly.

Everyone fell silent.

'. . . My baby's going to have a baby?' her mother whispered.

Mhairi nodded, feeling her tears run again. 'Aye, Ma.'

Rachel lifted her hands and clasped Mhairi's face. '. . . Then we'll get to do it together this time. You and me, my girl, the way it should be.'

Chapter Twenty-One

FLORA

8 January 1931

Quebec City, Canada

They walked through the lobby holding hands. It was a bright, beautiful morning, sunlight falling through the window in deep, dazzling shafts onto the oak floor, James and Flora's steps as light as if they were partially suspended on wires.

Heads turned as they passed, people instinctively smiling at them, and Flora wondered if they could sense their wellspring of joy. This was it now. Nothing could stop them. Mary and Lorna were being released within the hour and they wanted to get into position early. Landon had been paid 'a retainer' to keep an eye on the paperwork pertaining to their release. If Lorna relapsed, or if Mary tried . . . *something*, anything . . . they wanted to know about it.

But the days had drifted past with a blissful ease and now all the shadows had cleared. James had taken Flora shopping the previous day and they had bought a crib and blankets, baby clothes, nappies, infant milk and bottles. Everything was

The Midnight Secret

being delivered this morning and the concierge would send it straight up to their room.

Flora felt nervous. What if she had somehow forgotten how to mother her child? It had all come so naturally on the night of his birth, her body flooded with the impulses to bond them to one another, to feed him and protect him. But that was a tide that had long since gone out. Her milk had dried up within a fortnight of leaving St Kilda, and hers wasn't a face he knew. Would he cry for Mary?

Probably.

James had gently warned her to expect teething troubles. This wasn't a fairy tale but real life. They would make mistakes and get things wrong, but they would learn fast. He was already on the hunt for a nanny and a house to rent over the winter, somewhere they could settle down till the spring thaw.

They walked quickly down the steps to the courtyard, where their car had been brought round. Flora was carrying the fine shawl she had bought to wrap the baby in; that would be her first act of reclamation. She had even slept with it last night so that it would smell of her. The second would be to rename him. Both she and James associated the name Struan with the heartache of this period, and giving their baby the names they chose for him, as his birth parents, felt like a natural and healing next step.

James opened the car door for Flora and she slid into the seat. She pressed the baby blanket to her face, trying to detect her own scent. She wanted to know what he would smell.

But as she looked up and out of the window, she froze.

James had stopped, midway across the front of the car, and was standing alert as a gundog as Landon crossed the courtyard towards them.

Why was he here?

Flora didn't stir as she watched the Irishman approach and begin to talk to her husband. Her heart felt as if it might leap from her chest, her limbs leaden and holding her back from moving out of the cab into the space where his words would wound her. Because she knew they would. James was raking a hand through his hair. He glanced back at her, making eye contact through the glass. He looked sick.

Despite her instinct for self-preservation, Flora opened the door and got out shakily. She couldn't endure another delay. Landon's voice was a low murmur, the words indistinct but solemn.

'. . . body was found this morning. There'll have to be an inquest—'

Her hand gripped the car door. '*Inquest?*'

'Flora—' James began. He wore a haunted look that tore the hope from her in an instant.

'My God,' she gasped. 'Who's dead?'

Chapter Twenty-Two

EFFIE

21 February 1931

Lochaline

Effie came down the hill on the bike, her trousers tucked into her socks, hair flying as she sailed on the straight into the village. Slipper and Socks were far ahead, of course, just black-and-white streaks enjoying their flat-out run. It was one of the joys of having come 'home' to Lochaline, being reunited with her young dogs. They had been company for her father in her absence, but there was no denying she felt less herself without them trotting at her heels, just as her shoulders now felt forever bare without her loop of rope.

'Morning, Effie!' Ishbel MacDonald called as she passed on her way back from the bakery, her basket filled with warm bread.

'Hai Ishbel!' Effie waved cheerily at her new friend as she sped past. They sat next to one another on the looms, and Ishbel's bright smile and infectious warmth was one of the only things that had got Effie through her first few weeks at the factory. The manageress, her old foe Mrs Buchanan, had taken great delight in making Effie crawl to get her position back; no one could have been more pleased at her fall 'back to earth' as word spread that her engagement was now broken off. Effie made no mention that Sholto had tried his best to persuade her to accept a generous annuity that would allow her and her father to live comfortably, but if she had never accepted charity back home, she wasn't about to start over here. Unfortunately, the enmity between the two women only grew and, more than once, Effie, at boiling point, had declared she would 'rather starve than lick that woman's boots'. But Ishbel had a way of talking her down and their days together at the looms passed quickly. It was only the nights, when Effie was alone with her thoughts, that were long.

She pulled on the brakes, hearing the squeal of the rubber as she swerved to a dramatic stop and jumped off, placing the bike against the greengrocer's wall. Her father had taken a liking to rhubarb and she was only too happy to get some for him; Saturdays could feel endless sometimes, with no cliffs and no Sholto.

She went inside and bought half a pound and a bottle of lemonade as a treat with her coins. Emerging again a few moments later, she turned to call for the dogs, whistling through her fingers when she caught sight of them on the jetty, being petted.

Her hand dropped down as Archie Baird-Hamilton smiled back at her. He was sitting on a fishing crate, clearly waiting for her.

Effie walked over, feeling dazzled that he should be here. She had thought she would never see him again after leaving Dunvegan – she had fled the very next morning, before he had come down for breakfast. It had been cowardly, she knew, and she hated herself for it, but she hadn't known how to say goodbye to him as well as Sholto.

The Midnight Secret

She couldn't deny it was good to see him again, with his easy smile and those dancing eyes . . . A moment passed as they took in the differences of two months' passing. Archie's hair was perhaps a little longer; she herself was back in boys' clothes.

'What are you doing here?' she asked at last.

'It's a nice day for a sail,' he said. 'The weather's been so gloomy lately. I thought I'd make the most of this bit of high pressure.'

'You sailed here? All the way from Raasay?'

'It's not so very far when you come down through the Kyle of Lochalsh.'

Effie blinked. 'But how did you know I'd be here?'

'I didn't. This is all a very happy surprise.'

Her eyes narrowed with open suspicion. Surely it was far too much of a coincidence that he should have moored in the very harbour village where she lived?

'Honestly. I wanted to test out my new mast.' He motioned to the *Lady Tara*, docked alongside.

'Oh!' She studied the pristine foremast, remembering the horrors of that passage – and all that had come after it. '. . . Well, it certainly looks a lot better than the last time I saw it.'

'Indeed.' He looked up at the mast too, both of them remembering it all. Loaded looks, weighted silences, easy conversation and long shadows in the hallway.

'How long have you been sitting here?'

'Long enough to see you're a demon on that bike.'

She laughed, feeling embarrassed that she'd been caught in her feral state again; it seemed he rarely ever saw her at her well-mannered best. 'Oh. Aye . . . Well, it's great fun, I like it a lot . . . I've never had a bicycle before.'

'That's a criminal oversight.'

She laughed again. 'I know.'

A small silence bloomed as he watched her. '. . . Well, seeing as we're both here, do you fancy a potter around the sound? I'd be glad of the company . . .' He wiggled his eyebrows playfully. 'And you have provisions.'

'Not really. It's rhubarb, for my father.'

'Ah. Well, as luck would have it, I do have some sandwiches with me.'

She arched an eyebrow. Was that a coincidence, too?

'Do you have plans for today?'

'No—'

'Fine. Then what say you we feast on sandwiches and lemonade on the water, and I'll drop you back here in a few hours.'

Effie looked at him. His arrival was the only exciting – only happy – thing to have happened to her since her return. She had been determined to make a good fist of it all and not mope – her situation, desperate as it was, was unalterable, and she knew she had to face that – but the only way to suppress her sadness had been to fall into a sort of numbness instead. If she didn't cry much, nor did she laugh. 'All right. So long as the dogs come too.'

'Salty sea dogs – what could be better? What are their names?'

'Slipper and Socks.'

Archie chuckled.

'They're siblings,' she explained with a smile.

'Come along, then. Let's get out there.' He got up and hopped aboard, but instead of holding out his hand, stepped back and waited for her to follow. Meeting his gaze, she understood that it was a sign he knew her and accepted her, even if she wasn't a lady.

The Midnight Secret

She jumped aboard, followed by the dogs, and turned her face to the sun, feeling the shadows fall behind her.

'What's that?' she asked, her knees hugged to her chest as she sat in her usual spot beside Archie at the helm.

They had been sailing for a couple of hours, the sail dancing with the wind. To her relief, the water was reassuringly flat and calm, the Isle of Mull lying to their starboard side.

'Duart Castle. Owned by the MacLeans.'

'Friends of yours?'

He smiled. 'Naturally.'

Effie watched him thoughtfully from the corner of her eye. He knew everyone, was wanted at every party; women flocked to be on his arm. And yet there was something enigmatic about him. Not quite reclusive – but elusive. Absent at some times and remarkably, unexpectedly present at others. Now, for instance. She could never have imagined, as she'd woken up in her cottage that morning with her father sleeping on the other side of a sheet wall, that she would be sailing the Sound of Mull with him today. He was easy company, not given to unnecessary chatter; he valued silence as much as good conversation.

'So how are the others? Have you seen them?'

'Well, Gladly's very glum. Everyone's sort of disbanded. The girls have shot off to France. Colly's driving around Europe, I believe; he's got notions of racing the Mille Miglia this summer. Campbell is . . . Hmm, I'm not sure what Campbell's up to. London, probably.' He glanced at her and she wondered whether he was going to make any mention of Sholto, but he offered nothing more.

She looked down at her hands, composing herself. 'How long did you spend at Dunvegan after I left?' she asked.

'Only a few hours. I left the boat there. MacLeod got his man to organize the necessary repairs and I fetched her back a few weeks later.'

'But weren't they talking about throwing a party?'

He looked further out to sea. 'I wasn't in the mood for socializing.' He glanced at her. 'A broken boat can do that to a man.'

She nodded, but they both knew it wasn't the boat that had lowered his spirits. Her hand fell to Slipper's head and she ruffled him between the ears. Socks lay at Archie's feet in a display of trust as well as affection that did not go unnoticed by her; he was the more guarded of the two. She had spoilt Slipper early on with her eager cuddles.

She lay back on the bench with a sigh, folding her arms behind her head, and watching with a melancholy nostalgia as the seabirds wheeled above them. There was something about rolling over the water, listening to the flap and tug of the wind, that soothed her spirit. It wasn't St Kilda, but there were so many similar sights and sounds that it brought her back to herself somehow, in a way she hadn't known since the evacuation.

She closed her eyes, feeling the boat's gentle rise and fall align with the dogs' snores, the wind rippling over her as Archie cut a path through the sound with skilful insouciance.

If not for her broken heart, she could have almost passed for happy.

Chapter Twenty-Three

EFFIE

14 March 1931

'What is this?' Effie asked, standing at her garden gate.

Archie Baird-Hamilton smiled. 'I'd hoped we had civilized you enough to know, by now, that it is a car.'

'Ha ha.' She stuck her tongue out at him. 'I've never seen a car look like that before.'

'Understandable. This is a fresh-off-the-factory-line MG C-type. Do you like it?'

'I don't know yet. Why is it shaped like that?' The car was painted baby blue. There were no running boards, no roof, and the exhaust seemed to run along the side. The seats were slung low and the back end was curved and pointed like a wasp's tail.

'It's a sports car. Faster and zippier than the usual trundlers on the roads. Great fun. You'll love it.'

'Oh, will I?' She arched an eyebrow as he stepped aside and opened the door.

'I know your thrill for adventure Gillies. Hop in. We're going for a drive.' She saw the confidence in his eyes that she was going to get in beside him, his hand in his pocket, staring her down with his steady gaze.

'What if I've got plans?'

'I am your plans. You see me on Saturdays.'

'I don't *see* you on Saturdays,' she protested. 'It just so happens that I *have* seen you on *some* Saturdays.'

'The past three on the trot,' he countered. 'When does it become a habit, do you think?'

She looked back at him. It was true they had spent the past few Saturdays together: after surprising her at the harbour that first day, he had done the same again the following week, asking if *she* had deliberately come down again to the village to buy rhubarb in the hope he would be there! She had denied it, of course. The third weekend, he had been standing on the jetty with a bicycle of his own and a picnic pannier. Now she had opened her cottage door to find him standing outside. He was getting closer and closer every week.

She stared at the rope that was coiled and slung over his shoulder. Another provocative move.

'There are some mountains further along the road I thought you might like to see,' he said, following her gaze.

Effie glanced towards the low rolling hills that brought the horizon forward here. Since coming back to Lochaline, she hadn't gone further than a mile's radius from the cottage. She was like a spider on a web, tracking between the far points of the factory, neighbours' houses, the shops and her cottage. After a brief, exhilarating moment of expansion with Sholto, her world had become small again, scarcely larger than she had known in St Kilda.

'I want you to teach me to climb. After all, I've taught you to fish and sail. It's about time you returned the favour,' Archie quipped, his hands stuffed in the pockets of his trousers. He had a raffish, boyish quality, teasing and playful, and it crossed Effie's mind that he was like herself in male form.

The Midnight Secret

She heard footsteps approaching up the lane, just beyond the trees, and wondered what the neighbours would think about this gentleman and his blue sports car stopped on the lane. Word had already begun to circulate in the village about her 'Saturday outings'.

Was it Mhairi, coming for a morning chat over a cup of tea? Since her dramatic – and brave – return, the villagers had enfolded her in a protective embrace; it was now commonly held that she had already paid 'too high a price', and the two girls had become closer in the past few weeks than at any time since last summer.

'G'morning,' she heard the person – a man – say as he came past the trees up to the car.

'Good morning,' Archie replied jauntily.

'Norman,' Effie said in surprise. He looked rough – unshaven and unkempt, his clothes crumpled – and he was heading back towards his cottage, not from it. Effie felt her stomach drop at what it implied.

She saw the subtle understanding in Archie too. From everything the Dupplin girls had implied, he too was a man who had spent many nights *not* at home. The difference was, he wasn't married.

'Effie,' Norman nodded, throwing her a suspicious look in return, as if it was her behaviour that was questionable. He had always been good at turning the tables. 'Going somewhere?'

'Climbing lesson, for me,' Archie said, cutting in as if he recognized Norman's game. 'Archie Baird-Hamilton, how do you do?' He offered his hand.

'Norman Ferguson, Robert and Effie's neighbour.' His eyes were red-rimmed and bloodshot; Effie could only guess at the amount of whisky he'd had the night before.

Archie looked at him more closely as their hands pumped. '. . . I say, have we met?'

'No.'

'You look very familiar.'

'. . . Hmm, no.' Norman shook his head thoughtfully. 'I'd remember a car like that.'

'Actually, it's new. I only took delivery of it yesterday . . . But I definitely feel I've seen you.' Archie was regarding him closely. 'I'm good with faces.'

'Y' must be confusing me for someone else,' Norman shrugged, looking keen to move on.

'Norman's the deputy manager at the Forestry Commission,' Effie supplied helpfully. 'Perhaps you've seen him there?'

'No. Never been there.'

'Well, I'm afraid I don't get out much. Now, if y'll excuse m—'

'Oh but, Norman, what about your business trip?' Effie said, a thought suddenly occurring to her. She knew of one place where the three of them had been – unwittingly – gathered before. She looked back at Archie. 'He's being modest. Norman's got a big job; he was sent all the way out to Skye a few weeks ago.'

She felt Norman's stare land upon her like an iron sword, heavy and cutting.

'Skye? Is that so?' Archie asked with renewed interest and scrutiny.

'Aye, he consults to the big estates.'

'Of course, that's it! I saw you at Dunvegan!'

'No—' Norman rebuffed.

'Yes, yes! I remember – I saw you talking with MacLeod on the steps.'

There was a long pause, Norman's red eyes still and

The Midnight Secret

unblinking in their sockets. 'Oh, aye, MacLeod . . . that's right,' he said slowly. 'I'd forgotten about that. I did stop in, now y' mention it . . . I was passing and—'

'Just passing? You weren't working there?' Effie asked innocently, even though her curiosity was fully piqued.

'No. Just passing . . . I was returning Frank Mathieson's belongings to the Laird.' He looked back at Archie. 'You'll have heard about what happened to his factor?'

'Yes; yes,' Archie nodded. 'Who hasn't?'

Effie steadied herself, knowing she mustn't react, although every mention of Frank Mathieson – even though he was dead – still made her heart leap like a salmon.

'Well, he was – I suppose you'd say we were friends. He had no next of kin that I was aware of, so . . .' Norman shrugged. 'Returning his personal items to MacLeod seemed the next best thing to do.'

'Very decent of you,' Archie nodded. 'I'm sure he appreciated that. The family's been very cut up about it all. Terrible business.'

There was a brief silence as everyone ruminated on the unsolved murder.

'Well, enjoy y' climb. Effie's the expert for sure.' Norman tipped his head towards them, his gaze lingering on her ever so slightly, before he turned and continued up the path.

'Huh,' Archie murmured, watching him go. 'What an extraordinary coincidence.'

'Isn't it?' she agreed. She supposed Norman's explanation made sense. He and Frank had been friends, or at least, the closest thing to one that either man had ever had, for they were both lone wolves.

And yet, he'd been in the *library* . . . It still snagged in her brain.

Archie looked over at her. 'Before I forget—' Effie watched as he reached into the car and held out a brown paper bag. 'For your father,' he smiled. 'Can't have him going without.'

Her father had already wandered up the path to Old Fin's, but she took the rhubarb with a smile; they had become a weekly habit too. 'Thank you. I'll put them inside for him,' she said. 'Let me get my rope as well.' And she turned in to the house, forgetting all about Norman Ferguson and his good and bad deeds.

The single-track road was winding, swooping through deep purple-clad glens, past lochans where grey herons stood motionless in the shallows. At one point, Effie thought she saw a golden eagle soaring high, high above them, but she couldn't be sure. She pointed it out to Archie but their driving goggles restricted their peripheral view and it was gone in the next moment.

She liked the feeling of the wind in her hair; it was a recurring experience when she was with him, and she knew she didn't have to worry about how the tangles looked to him afterwards. They parked on a small track that led off from the main road, somewhere between Claggan and Alltachonaich. The mountains had quickly grown in might and magnificence as they moved further inland and Archie informed her they were in the heart of the Highlands now, the nation's very highest mountain Ben Nevis just a hop, skip and jump across the waters of Loch Linnhe.

He left her to pick the mountain they should scale and she chose one which reminded her a little of Mullach Bi back home: a path wound up the gentler south face, with a stepped series of bluffs and slopes they could navigate

The Midnight Secret

back down if his climbing skills didn't match up to his sailing prowess; they couldn't afford an accident. They had passed no more than four other vehicles on the journey out here, and she didn't want them to become stranded in this wilderness.

Archie took her instruction well. He was a man of action, highly physical and strong, and as she showed him the different knots and rappelling skills, he advanced quickly. She liked that he showed no inclination to reject her wisdom or advice just because she was a woman. He treated her like an equal in every single way.

'I know what you're doing, you know,' she said later as they picnicked on a ledge, eating their favourite sandwiches and apples. She was back in her element, her muscles aching, and it was the happiest she had felt in weeks. She felt him turn and look at her, though she stayed staring dead ahead, looking again for the eagle.

'. . . Good,' he murmured. 'It wouldn't be very effective if I was the only one who knew it.'

His frankness always surprised her. 'But you know it can't work. You know I love him.' She glanced over in time to see him wince.

'Yes. But I also know you can't be with him, so . . .'

'. . . So, what – you're going to wait?'

He shrugged. 'Unless you're playing a waiting game with him.' He caught her gaze with his direct stare. 'Is that what you've agreed? Wait until the countess dies?'

'No! God, no.' She shook her head quickly. 'How could we possibly? That would be disrespectful . . . knowing it was the last thing she wanted.'

He watched her, seeing how she swallowed hard on the truth, a bitter pill. 'I'm sorry they can't see what I can. You deserve a lot better, for one thing. But I won't pretend it isn't what I want . . . or that I don't have hope.'

His words were bald but honest and she liked him all the more for it.

'And if I told you I see you as a brother?'

He gave a surprised laugh, though he winced again too. He was quiet for a moment. '. . . I wouldn't believe you.'

'But—'

'You still love Sholto, Effie. I accept it's better for you to bracket me like that while you still have feelings for him. But I do believe that in time, you'll recognize what's really here.'

'And what if I don't stop loving him?'

He turned and looked straight at her, hearing the forlorn note in her voice. She wasn't being argumentative; some days she really did fear she was never going to know peace and happiness again. 'At some point you will. The heart needs something to beat against.' He shrugged. 'One thing I learned early on,' he said, 'is that we have to accept things as they are and not how we want them to be. And you're in a bad spot. I feel for you both, I do.'

'. . . But not so much that you're not going to chase me?' she said wryly.

He caught her gaze in his and held it. This was no game. 'I can't help how I feel any more than you can. And if I thought you had a shot of being accepted by them and living happily as his wife, I'd stand aside.' He said it so matter-of-factly, enduring his heartache as she endured hers. 'You love him, I know, but the truth is, he needs you to be something you're not and I don't. I see you for everything that you are, because it's everything that I am. We're both outsiders, that little bit too wild. We're the same.' He glanced over at her. 'I know you can't love me yet – but we both recognize something fundamental in one another. Just don't insult me by pretending we don't.'

She swallowed. '. . . I wouldn't.'

He nodded, looking away. 'Which is why I'll wait.'

They drove back with aching arms and trembling legs, much like their storm odyssey in the *Lady Tara* as they had sailed down Loch Dunvegan.

'Such a funny coincidence,' Archie murmured as they drove back towards the setting sun. The sky was marbled peach and plum, high-vaulted above them like an Arabian tent. 'Seeing that neighbour of yours in Skye.'

'Norman? Aye, it was.'

'I knew the second I laid eyes on him that I'd seen him before. He's a handsome fellow. Striking.'

'He's certainly that,' she mumbled, thinking of poor Jayne living with a beautiful monster.

Archie must have picked up on her ambiguous tone because he glanced over. 'You don't like him?'

'I'm friends with his wife. She's a lovely woman,' Effie said as diplomatically as she could.

'Enough said,' he grinned. 'Poor MacLeod, though, being lumbered with Mathieson's possessions. I'm sure he would have wanted to burn anything that belonged to that man. He's every bit as troublesome in death as he was in life.'

'How do you mean?'

'Well, the police have suspicions that Mathieson was stealing from MacLeod. A rare book of theirs turned up at Dumfries House, where one of his cronies worked.'

'I know about that.' Frank Mathieson himself had given the book to Effie, although it was pure coincidence that she had brought it to Dumfries House.

'Well, what you won't know – what nobody else knows, because the family is keeping it strictly on the QT – is that the losses run deeper than one valuable book.'

'What do you mean?' Effie frowned.

Archie regarded her for a moment. They both knew the information he was sharing was privileged, reserved for the aristocracy's inner circle only. Finally he said, 'Have you heard of the Sir Rory Mor horn?'

'The what?'

He chuckled. 'It's a mouthful – and one of the most totemic Clan MacLeod artefacts. Right up there with the Fairy Flag and the Dunvegan Sword.'

Effie shrugged, shaking her head. 'I've never heard of any of those things.'

'No, you wouldn't have; they're of little concern to most other people. But the horn is absolutely fundamental to Clan MacLeod lore.'

'Why would a horn be so important to them?'

'It's no ordinary horn; not to the MacLeods, anyway. It's an ox horn from a wild bull that a MacLeod chieftain, several centuries back, slew on the way home from a night of carousing.' He grinned at her, clearly approving of the story; it was the kind of anecdote that should be stitched to *his* heels. 'It's why the bull is now the motif for the MacLeods – an emblem of their strength and virility – and it's been tradition ever since that every new chief must drink claret from it, in one pass, to prove his manhood. Some historians date the horn back to the sixteenth century, but there are others who date it right back to the tenth. Either way, it's ancient – and it disappeared last summer.'

'*What?*' Effie stared at him, feeling her heart begin to thud.

Archie nodded. 'Why do you think MacLeod's been kicking

The Midnight Secret

up such a stink about getting to the bottom of what happened to his factor? He's hoping that if they can discover who killed Mathieson and why, they may stand a chance of being able to get the Mor horn back before anyone even knows it's gone. Ever since the Dunvegan book was found in the possession of Mathieson's accomplice at Dumfries House, MacLeod has been convinced the two of them had a black-market racket going.'

'But why . . . why would anyone want an old book, or a h-horn?' Effie croaked, trying to make sense of the distant memories that were surfacing. Events that had once seemed innocuous were taking on a new complexion in the light of this revelation.

'Because the Scots have been flung far and wide over the past century, thanks to the Highland clearances – and now, of course, there's this economic depression starving the rest of them out. There are thousands of MacLeods, Campbells, MacLennans, you name them, settled in Australia, Canada and America. Some of them have done very well for themselves in their new frontiers, and you wouldn't believe what they will pay now for a bit of their heritage.'

Effie stared dead ahead, hardly able to believe what she was hearing. Images were rushing at her . . . What had she done?

She felt Archie's hand on her arm. 'I say, are you feeling all right? You look as if you've seen a ghost.'

'This horn,' she said. 'Is it . . . is it capped with a silver rim and stamped with small marks?'

'Why, yes . . .' Archie did a double take as they flew over a humped bridge. 'Wait, Effie – how the devil did you know that?'

Chapter Twenty-Four

MHAIRI

17 March 1931

Lochaline

The bell rang and the clacking looms came to an abrupt halt. Mhairi pushed back on her chair, glancing around the factory floor as the women stood and began unceremoniously streaming towards the doors, buttoning their coats as they talked.

It was late afternoon but the sky was already the colour of damsons, and bright lights glowed from the shop windows and terraced houses along the street. Figures streamed past in silhouette. It would be several weeks yet before the days grew longer and they could step out into daylight.

She saw her mother and Christina up ahead, heads bent in conversation – as ever – as they began to make their way up the hill, towards home. Effie had called in sick from the telephone box that morning, driving Mrs Buchanan into an apoplectic rage. She'd said a death certificate was the only sick note she would accept and that there would be no job waiting for her on her return this time! But Effie wouldn't care. She was already halfway across Scotland, having set off beside Archie Baird-Hamilton in his blue sports car with a look in her eyes that Mhairi knew only too well. Would she be back?

Mhairi wasn't sure, but today at least, it suited her to walk alone. Donald's most recent letter had come yesterday and it had sat in her skirt pocket all day, next to her skin as she worked, his words memorized and playing on a loop in her head as she worked the treadles. He had begged her to come back to him, over and over, in every way it was possible to ask, and she had cried reading it. But nothing had changed; their circumstances remained as impossible as Effie and Sholto's. The universe was against them.

The path summited the low hill and began to wind left, heading back towards the coast. Mhairi felt the breeze on her face, the growing heaviness in her belly. She was still not showing in her clothes, but when she bathed at night, she could see her body falling more easily into a rounded shape this time, as if her baby girl had laid the path for this child.

'Mhairi!'

She looked back to find David coming up the track from the Forestry. Behind him, her brothers Angus and Fin were walking too, both of them long-legged and striding out – but she knew they would head left, back into the village, when their path met the road. It had quickly become routine for the men to have a pint after work.

Not David, though. Never him.

She stopped and waited as he jogged over, his shirtsleeves rolled up, his cheeks reddened from another day of exertions.

'Another day done?' she asked as he pulled up beside her with a puff.

He took off his cap and ran a hand through his dark hair. 'Aye, though they all look the same.'

There was complaint in the comment. Back on St Kilda, chores had been decided by the men at their daily parliament outside Old Fin's and set according to weather, season and need. Here, the jobs were mundane, repetitive and performed for profit. They did the same tasks day in, day out and the future was beginning to look like a very long, straight road.

'I hear Effie's taken off again.'

'Aye,' Mhairi grinned. 'This morning. Mrs Buchanan had a fit. She thinks Effie's the devil herself come to torment her, even though she's the only person who's been doing any tormenting. I don't know how Eff's put up with it, honestly; I've never known her so mild.'

'Well, she's not been herself since the break-up.'

'Aye,' Mhairi smiled. 'It made me fair happy to see some of her old spark back in her when she told me her plan last night.'

Mhairi was still intrigued as to what was going on. Effie – supposedly sworn to secrecy – had been discreet, telling her only that she had some information that might be helpful to one of Sholto's friends.

'And is any of that "spark" down to the man driving her around in his sports car, do you think?'

Mhairi sighed. 'I'm not sure. It's far too early for her to think of anyone else in that way yet. She truly loved Sholto.' In spite of Effie's stoic insistence that she was looking to the future, Mhairi still felt guilty using the past tense. After all, she wasn't with the man she loved either, but her love for Donald was nowhere near ending.

'Mm,' David agreed. 'First love cuts the deepest, that's what they say. It scars the heart.'

Mhairi glanced at him, hearing something in his tone that she couldn't quite place.

The Midnight Secret

'Still, this new fellow seems like a bright prospect too,' David continued. 'The toffs really have a soft spot for her, don't they?'

Mhairi shrugged. 'I think her spiritedness appeals to them. They like novelty, and let's face it, there's no one quite like Eff.'

'No, there isn't,' he grinned. 'Norman looked like he was chewing a wasp when he was talking about that car.'

'Effie doesn't care about cars.'

'I know, but this one sounds like a daredevil too. Y' never know – Effie might actually have met her match this time.'

Mhairi swallowed. Was he right? Was she confusing first love for everlasting love – not just for Effie, but herself too? Effie was facing facts, but Mhairi . . . she was as anchored to Donald as she'd ever been.

'Don't look so sad,' he said, knocking her affectionately with his arm. 'I'm only playing . . . I know you and Donald are the real thing. Everyone does.'

They had been brought in from the cold now that the full truth had been revealed. Mhairi and her mother had talked at length about the love affair – how it had begun, Alexander McLennan's abuses, and how Donald had tried to protect her from him. The pendulum of public opinion had swung fully in their favour, and it was Mary and Lorna who were now vilified. The St Kildans had rallied around her, but also the MacQueens, who had lost their grandson on account of the women's deception and lies, which had left their daughter bereft. The only brightness on their horizon had been a telegram from Flora – finally – telling them that she had been reunited with James, and that they had married in Canada. She had written that she had 'much to tell' when she returned, little knowing that everyone already knew.

'Have you heard from him?'

'A letter came yesterday.'

'And how is he?'

Mhairi sighed. '. . . He's not doing well. He's so alone; he hasn't the heart to go to the pub with the others after work. He just sits in the flat.' She glanced at David. 'I'm worried he's going to come up here.'

'But he can't,' David frowned. 'His bail conditions—'

'I know. I keep telling him that, but . . . he's desperate. I'm worried he'll do something rash.'

'You've got to make him understand that he has to wait. It can't be easy remaining under police caution, but it won't be for ever.'

'It's been four months now, though.'

'Aye, so any day now they'll surely release him from enquiries. They have no proof—'

'They're sticking with motive. They believe they can put a case together on that alone.'

'You gave him an alibi, remember? They can't disregard that because it's inconvenient to them. Trust me, they're just throwing their weight around because they've not got anyone else on the hook.'

She glanced at him, Norman's name a spectre between them.

'Did you try talking to Jayne again about . . . your suspicions?'

He winced. 'Aye, I tried. I told her it's about letting justice be done. Both of us going to the police and telling them we are each other's alibis doesn't mean she's incriminating Norman. If he's guilty, then the truth will out. It *should* come out. And if's not, then there'll be nothing for them to find.'

'But . . . ?'

The Midnight Secret

'She won't do it. She says he wouldn't be able to prove he had been at home alone all night, and she knows for a fact he didn't do it.'

Mhairi tutted. 'She can't possibly know that.'

'Of course not. She's just frightened of him and what he'd do if he found out she was with me that night.'

Mhairi looked at him, hearing the bitterness in his words. He hated Norman, she knew that – he resented everything the man had done to keep him and Molly apart in the months before she died, believing his sister could 'do better' than David. There was no doubt David and Jayne had become good friends after Molly's death, united by grief, but since moving back to Lochaline, she had noticed something else too. It was something she kept trying *not* to see, but couldn't help recognizing – because she too had once been in love with someone who was married. She knew how it was to go years seeing someone in a certain light, only for something to shift so that they were recast in a golden haze. Did Jayne know?

Did David?

Their white terraced houses were in view now, the neat walled front gardens running down to the track, the smart new telephone box sitting proudly on the other side. Lights glowed in the windows of the smaller property wedged between the MacQueen and MacKinnon houses, where Mad Annie and Ma Peg lived; they looked after the children after school while Christina and Rachel finished their shifts at the factory.

'Come to ours,' David said, opening the gate for her. 'Ma made some batter for drop scones this morning.'

'Drop scones, you say?' she smiled, needing no further persuasion.

They walked into the house. The younger ones were playing

upstairs, and they found his mother prodding the fire in the front room and throwing on a bucket of coal.

'Ah, Mhairi,' Christina smiled, straightening up. 'I'm just about to make some scones. Will y' have one?'

David grinned. 'Aye. I told her already.'

'Good! We need to feed that baby up,' Christina smiled, rubbing Mhairi's arm affectionately as she passed her and went into the kitchen. They followed, David kicking off his boots as his mother poured batter onto the cooking plate. The drop scones sizzled as she reached for the pile of post left on the table and sifted through the envelopes.

'Oh, look! A letter from Flora!' she exclaimed delightedly. They could all recognize the handwriting immediately.

'What does she say?' David asked impatiently as his mother tore it open and excitedly began to read.

But Christina rapidly paled, the joy fading from her eyes as she went.

A faint burning smell came from the stove. The scones only took a matter of moments to cook – but Christina was oblivious as she looked up at them with a stricken expression.

'What is it?' David asked, seeing his mother's distress. 'What does she say?'

'She says . . . I canna believe it . . .' Christina's voice was pale and thin as she glanced at the sheet of paper again. '. . . She says Lorna is dead.'

The words ricocheted around the room as Christina staggered to the chair.

'That can't be,' Mhairi whispered, feeling the world tilt beneath her own feet. She hated the woman for what she had done to Flora, but she also couldn't deny the nurse had always done everything in her power to help Mhairi and her baby.

'But what happened to her?' David asked.

The Midnight Secret

His mother looked back at him with haunted eyes. '. . . She killed herself.'

They all recoiled. David spun on his heel, clutching his jaw and rubbing it hard. '. . . When? Why?'

Christina looked again at the letter. 'Flora says she and James found them both in Quebec, with the baby. They were detained at Immigration. Lorna had fallen ill with typhus on the crossing.'

'Typhus!' Mhairi echoed. It had done for many an islander in years past.

'They confronted Mary first, appealing to her better nature—'

'*What* better nature?' David scoffed.

'. . . But Mary said they have no proof the baby is theirs. All official paperwork has her down as the mother . . .' Christina looked over, aghast, at Mhairi. 'Is that true?'

Mhairi blinked. She hadn't kept up with the 'technicalities' of the plan beyond helping Flora through the birth. She had scarcely been able to get herself through as it was, grieving her own dead baby and leaving Donald. 'It must be.'

Christina looked away, staring into space, her chest heaving with pain. Just when she thought the situation couldn't become worse, it did.

'Ma?' David prompted, restless to know more.

Christina looked back at the letter. 'Flora says she confronted Lorna about what she'd done instead. She says Lorna had the decency not to lie about it . . . and that . . . she agreed to hand the baby back to them when she was due to be released from quarantine, three days later.' She pressed a hand to her mouth as she stared down at the words. '. . . Her body was found in her room that morning. She'd stolen some pills from the infirmary.'

Mhairi pressed her eyes shut at the thought of it.

'I can't believe she would do that to herself,' David mumbled.

But Mhairi could. She knew what it was to live with shame, but this had been of another order. Lorna couldn't live with the guilt of what she'd done. She'd done a terrible thing, but it didn't mean she had been a terrible woman.

She looked at Flora's mother, so helpless in a kitchen thousands of miles away. '. . . Does that mean Mary's still got the baby?' Mhairi asked her.

Christina nodded. 'Aye. And with Lorna dead, it's her word against Flora's that the baby is hers. My girl has no proof to say otherwise.'

David's hands balled into furious fists. 'So what's she going to do next? She can't just give up. Mary can't be allowed to get away with this!' he said angrily. 'Surely James can do something? He's a rich man. They can buy anything! Babies. Justice.'

Christina's eyes tracked over the page. 'Mary's being deported back. She wasn't allowed through without Lorna to provide for them financially . . . Flora and James will be on the boat too. Oh, they're coming home!'

But Mhairi closed her eyes in despair. Flora had gone all that way, only to end up empty-handed?

Lorna had been the nurse to deliver Flora of her baby, an eyewitness who was respectable and upstanding, a pillar of the community. She could have undone her wrongs and still slipped away into a new life with Mary – not a perfect ending, without the baby, but a happy enough one at least.

Instead she'd chosen to fall deeper into the lie, taking her secrets with her to the grave.

Chapter Twenty-Five

EFFIE

17 March 1931

Dumfries House, Ayrshire

Effie sat low in the sky-blue car, her goggles on and hair flying like Medusa's snakes as they roared over the graceful hump of the Capability Brown bridge. They swept through the estate at speed like a tropical typhoon in the heathered Scottish countryside. Effie felt her heart accelerate as this small pocket of land, which had briefly been a home to her, revealed itself once more.

Archie glanced over at her as the great house came into view. It was gracious and elegant, and to her eye when she had come fresh from St Kilda seven months ago, it had seemed like a palace. But she had grown since then, and she knew now it was an exercise in neoclassical restraint. Grand, yes, but also very much a home.

She looked up at the tall windows. Was Sholto in one of the rooms, still hidden from her, just as her approach now was unknown to him?

Archie's fingers tightened around the wheel, his driving

gloves so new they still creaked. He had insisted on driving her here, even though she had told him she was perfectly capable of taking the train. She knew this was a test. There was every chance in coming here that she would be standing between the man who loved her and the man who wanted her. But it wasn't a question of who she wanted. It was a matter of who she could have. She had been lying to herself that she'd only come here with one mission in mind; the frantic thud of her heart was making it plain this was not neutral territory for either of them.

He hit the brakes, sending gravel flying as they careened to a flamboyant stop, and Henry the footman stepped forward with a blank expression – which slipped as Effie removed her goggles.

'Hallo, Henry,' she smiled, pushing back her tangled bright blonde hair.

'. . . Miss Gillies. Welcome back to Dumfries House.'

His hesitation revealed his profound shock, and she knew word would be below stairs before she could achieve what she had come here to do. She wondered if Fanny, Billy and Mrs McLennan would want to see her; they had been her first new friends on the mainland and she felt still the tension of being caught between worlds here: upstairs or downstairs? Where did she belong? And with whom?

Seven months later, she still didn't know.

'Thank you, Henry. This is Mr Baird-Hamilton.'

'I wondered if I might have an audience with Sir John,' Archie said, taking charge.

There was another uncharacteristic, stunned hesitation. '*Sir John?*' the footman clarified.

'Yes. I was told he and Lady Rosemary have been staying here during the countess's recuperation?' Archie said briskly, pulling off his driving gloves with a bored air.

The Midnight Secret

'Indeed, sir,' Henry nodded, recovering himself.

'Tell him I have some information he will want to hear – pertaining to . . . er, recent losses.'

'Of course, sir. Please follow me.'

He led them into the house Effie now knew well; she had walked, or rather run, these corridors barefoot, slept in a bed upstairs and eaten dinner at the servants' table below stairs. They passed beneath the family portraits that had once seemed so austere. Now, as she looked on those faces, all she saw was Sholto's eyes or his nose or the curve of his top lip – or that blonde cowlick that wouldn't stay back, no matter how often he combed it . . .

Was he here? In his bedroom or in the pantry, wheedling Mrs McLennan for a pie? Driving down the long avenue or riding on Taliska, his favourite horse? She felt her senses reach out, straining for a trace of him: his scent lingering in the hall, a stray hair on a coat, muddy boots, a familiar shadow glancing on the wall . . .

Their footsteps echoed, sounding into the far reaches of the long corridors as Henry led them to the blue drawing room. It was where visitors were usually escorted, not the parlour where the family preferred to gather.

'I shall inform Sir John of your arrival,' Henry nodded, leaving them in the grand space with a nod of his head and a flash of his eyes in Effie's direction.

Archie unbuttoned his coat and took off his cap, raking a hand through his hair. His cheeks were flushed from their drive, his eyes as bright as if he'd run here. He paced, restless, as they waited for their audience. Was it irony or fate that MacLeod was to be found here, in the crucible of Dumfries House, and not at home in Dunvegan?

Effie stiffened as she heard the soft closing of a door further up the hall, then footsteps sounding – but they were travelling in the wrong direction. Her heart fluttered, sparrow-like, darting and alert, too frightened to land, searching for Sholto in every corner and every shadow.

She crossed to the windows and stared out over the grounds. Every patch held a memory for her: the fountain, the night of the party when Sibyl's cruelty had been revealed; Stairs Mount, where she and Sholto had picnicked between the trees while pretending they could simply be friends; the ha-ha where her runaway horse had bolted and only Huw Felton's quick thinking had saved her.

Huw. She wondered, for the first time in months, about the gamekeeper. It was he who had given her Slipper and Socks, and mended the hole in her heart after losing Poppit. She had been a poor friend to him in return, their fledgling companionship suffocated by her desire for Sholto, even though on paper they made the better match. He was *still* the better choice. The differences between her and Sholto were every bit as apparent now as they had been at their first meeting; and even Archie – a soulmate who went toe to toe with her spirit – hailed from a different pedigree that he couldn't quite outrun.

And yet, she couldn't settle for less just because she came from less. Her heart had always been wild and defiant. She would rather be alone and free than captured and tamed by the wrong man.

She watched the gardeners pruning the rose garden, their bodies bent as they worked in the weak spring sunshine. The trees and shrubs were still bare, pointing spiky fingers towards an unflinching grey sky, but tiny buds were swelling at their tips; they were tender and hesitant amid the frosts but the sap was rising, even if it was unseen. Life was beginning anew after the bleakness of winter.

The Midnight Secret

She heard the crunch of gravel and looked over to see an unfamiliar sight: a wicker chair had been set upon large wheels, the small figure sitting within wrapped in blankets and scarves. A young woman was walking behind, pushing the wheeled chair along and talking animatedly to the invalid.

Effie blanched as she recognized Lady Sibyl's rail-thin silhouette. Her sharp bob poked out beneath a cloche hat, a belt slung low over her coat. When had she returned? Effie wondered in dismay. At the very first klaxon call of the countess's illness, proving herself a worthy daughter-in-law? Had Sholto called her for comfort?

Either way, it was clear Sibyl's feet were back under the table again.

Tears pricked at Effie's eyes, but she swallowed hard and willed them back down, knowing this was right. All was for the best. It was the proof she had unwittingly been searching for from the moment they had arrived – an answer given without a question having been raised. Life had returned to its proper form. All the chess pieces were back in position on the board.

She sensed Archie's sympathetic look on her back. He knew as well as she did what it meant.

The door opened again, and the earl walked in with a bemused look.

'Archie!' he began, his hand already outstretched before he caught sight of Effie there too, standing by the window. His arm dropped in surprise as Sir John followed him into the room with a similarly wry look.

Effie had never met Sir John in person before but, as their landlord, he had ruled the villagers' waking lives back on St Kilda. Everything they did on the island – weaving, milking, catching birds for oil – had been done to fulfil their rents. The rather unassuming-looking man who now stood before her didn't seem, somehow, to match the enigmatic figure of their collective imagination.

There was a momentary silence as the two older men adjusted to her presence, and she realized Henry must have announced only her companion. It was Archie, after all, who had requested the meeting.

'Miss Gillies. This is a surprise,' the earl said courteously, albeit coolly.

'Hello, sir,' she nodded, making no move to advance towards him. She knew she represented a threat to him, just standing in this room. Had she been the catalyst for his family's implosion? Did he blame her for his wife's collapse? He was visibly thinner and more grey-faced than when she'd seen him last, the strain of the past few months sitting upon him like a threadbare coat.

Behind him, Sir John had recovered himself enough to shake Archie by the hand.

'A drink?' the earl asked, looking back at him. Effie realized Graves had slipped into the room too and was standing by the door. He was the consummate butler – always unruffled, ever loyal – but she saw his disapproval of her in the tilt of his chin. Did he perceive her as a threat, too? How could a poor island girl, no more than a strip of wind, seem so formidable to one of the grandest families in the land?

'A warming tot would be appreciated,' Archie murmured, sending the butler gliding over to the drinks cabinet. 'We had a blustery drive over.'

'Oh?' It struck Effie that the earl looked more interested in his use of 'we' than in the driving conditions. 'Where have you come from today? Not Raasay, surely?'

'Lochaline. Morven Peninsula.' Archie put a hand in his pocket. 'Have you been over that way?'

The Midnight Secret

'Mm, yes,' the earl nodded distractedly. Effie remembered his visit to her cottage when he had first come to offer her the job on the estate. How he must have rued that offer since! 'Bluey MacLean . . .'

'Mm,' MacLeod intoned too, looking sombre. '. . . He's having a dratted time with the roof. Duart's got more leaks than No. 10.'

'Mm.' The men nodded in commiseration for Bluey MacLean's damp castle, but moments later their gazes slid towards Effie again like water down glass, with one question in their eyes: what was *she* doing back here?

'Mind if I smoke?' Archie asked. He peeled off and turned a languid loop, strolling the room as if enjoying everyone's silent torment. But then, he was a maverick; he loved a little chaos.

He began talking about the winter storms on Raasay and the bother they had caused, bringing down a number of trees.

'Not to mention your mast!' MacLeod exclaimed as Graves returned with their refreshments. 'The *Lady Tara*'s fixed now, I understand?'

Archie nodded. 'Jimmy got me straightened out in no time,' he replied, inclining his head in a token of thanks to MacLeod's son. 'He knew a fellow.'

'Glad to hear it. I've scarce been home this winter, but I'm given to believe your dramatic approach down Loch Dunvegan has already entered local legend.' MacLeod's gaze flitted over Effie with open suspicion again. 'The lady of the loch, they're calling you, Miss Gillies.'

Effie had to bite her tongue from saying she was no lady.

'Rightly so,' Archie grinned. 'If it hadn't been for Effie's bravery, I daresay we'd have capsized and gone under.'

Eyebrows were raised by his casually familiar use of her given name.

'Well, then . . . to your very good health,' the earl mumbled as he raised a small toast.

It was true the dram was warming. Effie felt the small, hot bullet travel down her throat and into the very centre of her; until that moment, she hadn't realized she was shivering. She tried not to think of the quietly mannered scene still playing out behind her back: wheels on gravel; blankets in a biting wind; a frail body and a lithe one; duty and promise. The best thing she could do now was to say what she had come to say and get away again as quickly as she could. There was nothing to be gained from seeing Sholto again. He wasn't the reason she had come here – at least, that's what she had told herself – but he was the reason she would run.

'So.' MacLeod cleared his throat and regarded Archie with a quizzical look. 'I'm told you wish to discuss something important. Shall we take this into another room?'

'On the contrary – it's Effie who's got news for you.'

'Wh-what?' MacLeod blustered.

Archie motioned to Effie to take the floor as he stepped back with a look of pride.

Anticipation billowed, and she saw the wary look on both noblemen's faces as they tried to guess at her motives for being here. It hadn't crossed either of their minds that she might be here to help.

'I know where the horn is,' she said simply. 'The Rory Mor horn.'

MacLeod gasped, looking first astounded, then furious. 'And how the devil would you know about that?'

'Because I found it in one of the cleits back home. On St Kilda.' She looked curiously at him, wondering why he looked so angry when she was giving him good news. She glanced at Archie, who gave her a nod of encouragement; he was used

The Midnight Secret

to bluff and bluster. 'It was in a tumbling-down cleit that none of us villagers used. It had been the property of a family that emigrated years back, and it had stayed empty. Maybe that's why Mathieson used it.'

'Mathieson?' MacLeod queried.

'Aye. I had noticed that he kept lurking about it whenever he came over but never paid much heed – until I was cragging on the rocks a few days before the evacuation and I saw him coming out, all suspicious.'

MacLeod's frown deepened. 'Suspicious how?'

'Looking around him, as if checking no one had seen him. He didn't see me, of course, so when he went back to the village, I went over and had a look inside to see what he was up to. And that's when I found the horn. It was hidden beneath a dead lamb, so I almost missed it.'

Sir John raised himself to his full height, wearing a look of consternation. 'Let me get this straight – you're saying you saw my factor, Frank Mathieson, put the Rory Mor horn into the cleit?'

Effie shook her head. 'No. I only found it in the cleit he'd visited. I can't swear an oath that *he* put it there,' she shrugged. 'But, as I said, we never used it, and I do know it couldn't have belonged to any of the islanders. The most valuable things we owned were Old Fin's accordion and his gold sovereign he kept up the chimney.'

'I see.' MacLeod shared a cautious look with his host. 'And where is it now, the horn?'

'Still on St Kilda.'

MacLeod caught his breath, as if steadying himself. 'In the cleit?'

'No. I moved it.'

'What! Where? Why?'

'I moved it somewhere else. I could tell from the silver that it was valuable – and from the way he'd tried to hide it, I knew he wasn't supposed to have it.'

'So you intended to blackmail him, I suppose?'

'Now steady on,' Archie said sharply, a flash of anger upon his face. 'Effie's come here to help you. Not to be insulted. *She* isn't the one who stole from you.'

There was a tense pause before MacLeod conceded. '. . . Forgive me, Miss Gillies. I misspoke . . . but *why* did you decide to move the horn?'

Effie blinked, her cheeks burning from the slight. She couldn't explain it without telling them everything Mathieson had done – and was threatening to do – to her. And that wasn't something she had shared even with Archie. She never wanted to think of it again; she wanted it all dead and buried. With Frank.

She swallowed, speaking slowly. 'I didn't know what the horn was or why he cared about it; I only knew that he did. It was important to him. By hiding it somewhere else, I figured it would give me . . .' She struggled for the right word.

'Leverage?' Archie guessed, watching her closely.

She nodded and a pause followed. '. . . He wasn't a good man. He had threatened me and my friends, all in different ways . . .'

She saw MacLeod's features darken.

'I thought that by taking something that was valuable to him and hiding it, it might give me something to barter with, if things took a bad turn again.'

Her words settled like stones in the room: *a bad turn again.*

'And did they?' the earl enquired, looking concerned.

'. . . Aye.' She saw a flash of alarm pass over Archie's features.

The Midnight Secret

'Can you elaborate?'

'I'd rather not, sir,' she said stiffly. It was none of their concern what Frank had done to her or the lengths to which she'd had to go to escape him. They didn't need to know that she had suffered his mouth and hands upon her as she'd plied him with whisky – bought with the shillings the earl himself had given her for guiding him around the isle – until he had all but passed out. They didn't need to know she had tied him up with ropes but left him with a knife to free himself, and enough food and water to tide him over till the *Harebell* dropped anchor. They didn't need to know that the horn had been her final bargaining chip if all this had failed – and it so nearly had, for somehow he had got himself free.

'. . . But I can tell you he became very agitated when he saw it was gone. He started scouring the hills, saying he had to do inventory checks for you' – she looked at MacLeod – 'and make sure all the cleits were empty.'

'I never requested such a thing,' MacLeod protested.

'No. Only I knew what he was looking for – I just didn't know why it mattered so much.'

There was a long silence as they absorbed the revelations.

'So, in effect, you took the horn as an insurance policy?' the earl said.

She shrugged. 'I don't know what that means, sir.'

'Your actions suggest you felt a strong element of threat from Mr Mathieson.'

She jutted her chin up, but passed no further comment. She had said all she had to say on the matter.

He watched her thoughtfully. 'Thinking back to our time on the island, I do recall Mathieson being brusque with you. Certainly rude . . . intimidating, even.'

MacLeod cleared his throat. 'You know, I've since heard

from some of the island men that he had been inflating the rents and keeping the extra for himself.'

'Really?' The earl arched an eyebrow with mild interest and great disdain.

'And now we hear he'd been threatening the women too,' MacLeod mumbled. 'Dear God, with every new report the man somehow confounds my low estimations.' He shook his head. 'I ought to have trusted my instincts and fired the fellow years ago.'

Archie took a deep, pondering breath, looking troubled by the revelations. It was more than she had shared with him beforehand. 'Well, all that really matters now is that we know the Mor horn is safe.'

MacLeod gathered himself. 'Yes, yes. It's all that really matters.' He looked at Effie. 'Miss Gillies, do you remember where you hid the horn?'

'Of course, sir.'

She watched as MacLeod and the earl swapped looks again. Slight smiles gradually flickered into life on both of their faces, as if they were somehow hatching a plan in silence. Old friends, able to communicate without words.

MacLeod shrugged. 'Well, it might be rather fitting to go back one last time,' he said in reply to an unspoken suggestion. 'Ink the deal, so to speak.'

Archie narrowed his eyes. '. . . Deal?'

The earl smiled. 'John has sold the archipelago to me. We agreed it over lunch yesterday.'

Effie's eyes widened as she looked between them. 'You've sold St Kilda, sir?'

'Well, it's not much use to me now, with only sheep living on it,' MacLeod replied. 'And this old boy is so very keen on his birds. He's got a grand plan for designating it as some

The Midnight Secret

sort of safe haven for seabirds.' He shrugged, as if it made no sense to him. 'But I suppose we could have some sort of official handing-over ceremony. Kill two birds with one stone, eh?'

The earl looked amused. 'I'm not sure that's quite the phrase I'd use in this instance, John.' He looked over at Effie again, pausing for several moments before he spoke. 'Miss Gillies, you've done a very gracious thing, coming here today with this news. I know that it can't have been easy,' he added.

Effie swallowed at the admission. 'I'd have come sooner had I known what it was I'd found, sir.'

'You'll be rewarded, of course,' MacLeod said quickly.

Effie bridled. 'That's not necessary, sir. I'm just glad to have been able to help.'

Archie smiled at her as the earl and clan chief exchanged another look.

'So, Miss Gillies, how exactly will we find the cleit in which you've hidden the horn?' MacLeod asked. 'There are a great many of them.'

'Oh, it's not in a cleit.'

'Where is it, then?'

'The last place anyone would think to look. I needed to be certain he wouldn't find it.' She let her mind fall back into the landscape of her girlhood – the velvet smudge of grassy moors, the grey stone cottages smiling along the street like giant's teeth, the towering cliffs harassed by thousands of fluttering white birds. She had left so much of herself behind there. To climb the crags one last time . . .

'How will we find it?'

'You won't.' Her eyes flashed with steel. 'I'll have to show you.'

*

'Effie!'

The word was a low hiss. She turned in the hallway to see Fanny's head peeking around the doorway of one of the servants' staircases. Effie had excused herself to freshen up before the journey back, although the way Archie's eyes had trailed after her as she left the room suggested he didn't believe her.

She hurried over. 'Fanny!' she beamed, surprising the maid by embracing her; she too, it seemed, didn't quite know to which world Effie belonged. 'I hoped I'd see you!'

'Come in here so we can talk without been seen,' the maid whispered, looking furtively around as Effie slipped into the cool, shaded corridor. Fanny closed the door quietly, taking a good look at Effie in her new clothes. She was still clad in trousers and woollens, but they were the clothes Sholto had bought for her on their Grand Tour, and hung differently to the homespun garb in which she'd first arrived at Dumfries House seven months earlier. '. . . You look so well!'

'Do I?' Effie asked ruefully. 'I don't feel it.'

Fanny gave her a pitying look. 'We've all been keeping up with y'r adventures!'

'There's been a fair few, I suppose.'

'Do y' know what they're calling you over on Skye?' Fanny giggled.

'Aye, I did hear,' Effie winced. 'And it really wasn't as dramatic as they're making it sound.'

'I'd bet it was!' the maid laughed. 'Mrs McLennan says drama follows you like a shadow!'

Effie chuckled; the cook had always been the first person to prop her up after one of her disasters and was forever trying to get a hot meal inside her. 'How is she? How's everyone? I've missed you all.'

The Midnight Secret

'No, you haven't! You've been living in castles with the aristocracy!'

Effie reached for her hand, not wanting to think about any of that. 'Honestly – I've missed you all. I so hoped I'd get to see you when I came here today.'

'Poor Henry was beside himself when he came down earlier, saying you'd roared up in a fancy car with Archie Baird-Hamilton, of all people! What the devil are you doing with that rascal? You know his reputation, don't you?'

Effie didn't care any more about Archie's reputation with the ladies than he cared about her humble background. 'I've been told it many times. But he's been a perfect gentleman to me.'

Fanny chuckled, shaking her head. 'Don't be fooled. It's all an act.'

Was it? Or was he misunderstood? Underestimated? She had sensed his hunger for her on Raasay, but he'd not acted on it. He'd been honest and true to his word, and although she didn't know if she could learn to feel for him what he felt for her, she was grateful to have him in her life. Sometimes she felt as if their Saturday outings were the only thing keeping her going during the long weeks spent sitting indoors at the factory loom, weaving tweed. It made her despair to think this could be it for her – a life spent caged, married to the grocer's son or a Forestry man or the postie. She didn't care a whit about money, but she cared about spirit. She would always fight to live a life of adventure, and Archie, for everything else that he might be – rascal, playboy, cad – was the same.

'Barra says he was a frequent guest at her previous lady's house parties,' Fanny said with a scandalous glee. 'And that one time, he visited three ladies' bedrooms in one night . . . The hallboy was counting.'

'Oh.' Effie nodded, remembering Archie's apprehensive look as she had left the room just now. She wasn't the jealous one in their relationship. 'Well, he and I are just friends. I'm not looking to fall in love again.'

'No.' Fanny looked at her with wide eyes.

'. . . Is he here?'

The maid shook her head sympathetically. 'Edinburgh. He went a few days ago. I'm not sure when he's due back.'

'Oh.'

'I think he needed a change of scene. It's been a bleak time.'

'Aye.' And it was all her fault. She thought of Sibyl, manning the fort in his absence, caring for his mother like a dutiful prospective daughter-in-law. 'I saw the countess earlier. She's in a wheelchair?'

'She's very frail now, but the worst of the danger is passed. There's still a long road ahead, but they're quietly hopeful she'll make a good recovery. Good enough, anyway.'

'I hope so,' Effie nodded. 'That would be wonderful.'

Fanny reached a hand out to touch her arm. 'He misses you so much. He never says anything, certainly not around any of us, but I can see it in the way he walks. And he's so quiet now. Always polite, of course, but . . . it's as if he's had the stuffing pulled out of him. We'd none of us ever seen him so happy as when he was with you.'

Effie felt a lump stopper her throat, tears immediately pricking at her eyes. It always amazed her how quickly they could appear from one moment to the next. 'Well . . . it just wasn't supposed to be,' she said in a choked voice. 'A blind man could see that.'

'But you made each other so happy.'

Effie pressed her lips together, trying to hold back her emotions. 'We can't always have something just because we want it.' Her voice sounded strangled as she made herself say words that sliced her like knives, and she knew that in spite of all the reasons they were wrong for one another, there was one overarching reason they were right: her heart spoke to his. Sholto wasn't her perfect match, and she wasn't his equal, but the love that bonded them was true and pure. Their differences might overwrite that truth, but they would never subsume it. She could see that now. 'There are other things . . . and other people . . . to consider.'

The sound of voices rose on the other side of the door. Fanny's eyes widened. 'Y'd better go,' she said quickly. 'Before they catch us talking.'

Effie wiped her eyes quickly. 'I'll write. I'm in Lochaline now, not so very far.'

Fanny opened the door and peered out. The magnificent reception hall was still clear but the men's voices were carrying as they came down the hallway. Fanny disappeared back down the staircase into the servants' corridor as Effie stepped out onto the flagged stone floor, composing herself.

She was looking out of the windows across the rose garden when they turned the corner a few moments later.

'Ah, there you are,' Archie said with evident relief. 'I was beginning to think we might have lost you.'

Effie looked back at him with reddened eyes and a sad smile – that told him he had.

Chapter Twenty-Six

FLORA

15 April 1931

RMS *Empress of Britain*, international waters

They were sailing into the sun, chasing a golden horizon they could never quite catch. Flora stood on the middle deck, feeling the wind bring colour to her china-doll cheeks. This winter had been especially hard and cruel, leaching her world of all colour as kindness and goodness had become lost concepts. She had taken Lorna's death badly, retreating to her bed for several weeks as she saw they had finally come to the end of the road in getting back their son. There was no consolation to be had, not even in knowing that Mary had been denied the love of her life and the promised land of her dreams.

She had still won. Flora's baby lay in *her* arms, loved *her* face; and with every day that passed, those facts only became more true.

James had leased a beautiful mansion on Rue Saint-Denis as they waited for the sea ice to thaw, but Flora had rattled around it, wraith-like, and eventually they had moved back

The Midnight Secret

into the Frontenac. He had immersed himself in work, channelling the pain of their personal loss into business gain as he developed and refined the plans for his new transatlantic air company. She had no such diversion to occupy her mind. All she could think of now was returning home to the family and friends she had left behind.

All around her, the laughter of the leisured class tinkled like sunlight upon water; some were playing shuffleboard, tennis and even golf, others strolling the long deck as they promenaded up and down, stopping to talk to those lying out on their deckchairs.

To her relief, there was no sign of the Tuckers, although James was vigilant, scanning the dining room every night for a sighting of them.

On the deck below, the third-class passengers were taking some air too, though the sun couldn't fill the high-sided space flanked by bulkheads and lifeboats. She watched from above, seeing how very crowded it was, with none of the activities laid on for the upper class, but people made their own amusement – playing cards, reading palms, children hopping and skipping . . . Scuffles would often break out, arguments erupting over a wrong look or a stolen bread roll.

She stood here every day hoping for a sighting of her son. She was rarely noticed – they never seemed to look up – and she came out, whatever the weather. She didn't feel the cold, she didn't care about the wind, but only yesterday James had forced her back inside, telling her there was nothing to miss: Mary wouldn't bring the baby out in the driving rain.

She was torturing herself, she knew, but she would gladly bleed for the sabre swipe of a glimpse of his face. He was almost eight months old now and he was growing bonny and fat, with ruddy cheeks and two teeth that she could see when he gurgled with laughter. Flora thought perhaps he was teething, for sometimes he would drool and grizzle and Mary would give him her knuckle, as she had that night in the rooftop garden. She would watch as Mary walked in figures of eight, making wide loops around the deck as she sang to him, or else stopped to talk with the other mothers and their bairns. She actually smiled and laughed, and Flora realized she had never seen her look happy before. It pained her to think that although Mary was a bad woman, she was not necessarily a bad mother.

The door below opened and Mary herself came out at last, as she always did. She was a St Kildan – she needed to be outdoors. Flora caught her breath. She had been standing here since breakfast, waiting for her to emerge, and she strained for that first look. Mary had dressed the baby in green knitted woollens today; if the St Kildan women could do anything, it was knit, and her boy had no shortage of clothes to wear. Still, the wind was biting and could nip among the twist of the stitches, making him protest. A little arm shot out, his pink fist splaying before balling tight again as Mary hushed him, making the first of her turns.

Flora knew a proper coat was what he needed. Felted wool, perhaps a velvet collar, like the one she had bought in her excitement back in Quebec when she had still believed she could undo the past. She hadn't had the heart to throw it – any of it – away, the clothes she couldn't give him like the love she couldn't give him.

She frowned as an idea came to her.

Unless she could.

Chapter Twenty-Seven

JAYNE

16 April 1931

Lochaline

Like a cat on a sun-warmed wall, the evenings were beginning to stretch. Every afternoon now, as the women swarmed into the factory yard, shadows fell upon the cobbles beneath a gladdening sky. The hills were resplendent, clad in their magnificent yellow gorse blossoms, and the trees were filling with returning birds: Effie had so far spotted willow warblers, tree pipits, yellow wagtails and wheatears.

Jayne quietly waited her turn in the queue at the butcher's, eyeing the cuts laid out behind the glass and wondering which her husband would want for his dinner tonight. Ahead of her, Mhairi, Effie and Ishbel were laughing about Mrs Buchanan's skirt being caught tucked in her undergarments all afternoon and how no one had cared to mention it to her. It was a petty victory that put a smile back on Effie's face. She had been listless ever since returning from the day trip with her new gentleman friend last month, and his blue sports car had been conspicuous by its absence ever since too. But, although the girls laughed here and there, they rarely smiled. Effie, Mhairi and Jayne herself – none could really claim to be happy.

Mhairi stepped backwards, standing on Jayne's foot. She was beginning to show now and her balance was a little off.

'Och, Jayne, I'm sorry!' she apologized. 'I didn't see you there!'

'Not to worry,' Jayne smiled.

'Hai, Jayne,' Effie said in surprise, turning too.

'Have you heard anything more on the visit back, Eff?' she asked, moving the conversation away from her invisibility.

The news that the Earl of Dumfries had bought their island home was all the former villagers had been able to talk about for weeks. Jealousy was rife that Effie would be going back with the lairds to St Kilda for a formal handover ceremony.

'Not yet.'

'I heard people are asking the size of the boat,' Mhairi said as they shuffled forward in the queue.

'What boat?'

'The earl's, of course. How many passengers can he take?'

'How should I know?'

'Did you never go on it?' Ishbel asked.

Effie shook her head.

'But you saw it,' Mhairi pushed. 'When it was anchored in the bay last summer.' Mhairi had been sequestered in Glen Bay, on the other side of the ridge, by then, but Flora had kept her up to date with all the news from her fleeting visits back to the village.

'That wasn't the earl's boat, it was MacLeod's,' Effie corrected. 'And I saw no more of it than anyone else.'

'Oh,' Ishbel said disappointedly. 'What a pity.'

'Why do they want to know, anyway?'

The Midnight Secret

'Others want to go back with you,' Jayne said simply. It was all Old Fin could talk about when she went to sit with him at her lunchtimes. 'They don't think it's fair you should get to go and not them, just because you . . . well, because of your relationship with Sholto.'

Effie stiffened. 'But I don't have a relationship with Sholto.'

Jayne felt a swell of sadness as she took in the young woman's doleful expression.

'So then why have you been invited?' Ishbel asked. It didn't make sense.

Effie blushed, and Jayne had a feeling she was holding something back. She quickly changed the subject. 'Anyway, no matter – but I think they're going to write to the earl and ask to go along too, just so you know.'

'Aye . . . thanks, Jay—'

'*Fight!*'

The word cracked like a gunshot and a sudden contraction rippled through the crowd of women in the butcher's shop. It was as if an energy bomb had been dropped. The hairs on the back of Jayne's neck stood up and she felt a tingle of dread. Her stomach lurched. Fights always made her sick.

'They're fighting!' someone cried again.

'Who is?' someone from the back asked.

'Brodie MacDougall and Norman Ferguson.'

Jayne felt the blood still in her veins as everyone disgorged onto the pavement to watch the drama unfold. She felt as if she was moving through treacle, the shouts and roars distant to her ear as she stepped outside to witness the flailing of fists.

She knew exactly why they were fighting. She had heard the rumours about Fiona MacDougall and her husband, even though everyone thought she was unaware. They thought her too foolish to know where her husband slept on those nights he didn't come home, or why he smelled of perfume when she owned none. But she knew everything. She knew so much more than he knew.

She blinked at the frenzied spectacle. Her husband was a tall man and powerfully built, with strong shoulders and muscled arms. His opponent had none of his physical prowess – but he had fury on his side. Being cuckolded could make a lion of a lamb, and she watched as MacDougall landed several direct hits on her husband's planed cheeks. Norman's piercing blue eyes were bloodshot, and there was a deep cut above his brow already bleeding that she would need to tend to later.

The men, on their way to the pub after their own long shifts at the Forestry, were gathered around in a loose huddle, as if keeping the warriors penned in like fighting cockerels while they cheered on the action. As if this was exciting. Fun. *Funny.*

Was Fiona MacDougall here? Was she watching as the two men fought over her? Jayne lifted her head, casting a hollow-eyed gaze around the faces that had not once considered her in the fracas. This was a three-way drama. She wasn't even in the equation.

But someone was staring at her. His stillness matched hers, conspicuous amid the twitching, baiting mêlée: hazel-green eyes, as sorrowful as her own, watching her from across the street.

She saw his sympathy for her predicament – his pity – and it was even worse than being overlooked.

Jayne wrenched her gaze away with a gasp. She saw Effie's bicycle propped against the butcher's wall and she grabbed it, throwing her leg over and beginning to pedal. It was an uphill climb, but fury propelled her. Being humiliated could make a betrayed wife fly.

'Jayne?' she heard Effie call, turning a moment too late to

The Midnight Secret

stop her. But Jayne didn't stop. As she glanced back, she saw David following her, chasing in silence.

Her breathing became ragged quickly; she could scarcely see through her tears, but she wouldn't stop or slow down, her muscles burning, her lungs squeezing as she left the scene – left him – far behind her and took the path for home.

On the lane, she passed Mad Annie in her front garden, staking runner beans in the beds she had dug out that week. 'Jayne?' the old woman asked, a frown creasing her wizened brow, as Jayne whizzed by in silence.

She passed the Wee Gillies' place too, further along, finally reaching her own threshold twelve minutes after she had left the fight in the street. She threw the bicycle down on the ground and ran through to the kitchen, running the tap and splashing the water on her face as she gasped to catch her breath.

She let the water run, her hands splayed wide on the counter and her head hanging as she gulped for oxygen. Minutes passed. The physical exertion of getting back here had extinguished her tears – she couldn't cry and pedal uphill at the same time – and all she felt now was bitter, stinging humiliation at her husband's indiscretions having been so publicly aired. She knew Fiona MacDougall was not his only lover, and she also knew she wouldn't be his last. Norman hadn't touched Jayne once since they had arrived in Lochaline. It was both a mercy and a blessing, for back home his nightly attentions had been difficult to bear. And yet . . . it had also shown her how very unwanted, undesired and unseen she was to her husband. Now that Norman had choices, she was nothing more than his housekeeper and cook. She had been able to bear the shame of her inadequacy when it was private, but there was no hiding from it now. Everyone knew. David had seen with his own eyes that she was an unsatisfactory wife.

The sound of the gate creaking on its hinges made her straighten up just as the door was thrown back and David himself filled the doorway. He was breathing heavily. Had he really sprinted the whole way here? She had expected him to fall back, to give up. 'Jayne—'

'Don't!' she cried, as he came into the kitchen he knew so well. He sat at that table every evening, more often even than Norman, so that now she had come to regard the chair as his and not her husband's. 'I don't want to hear it! I don't want your pity!'

Anyone but his.

She turned away, but she felt him watching her. She always could. His gaze had become her silent companion over these past few months, always there.

'Well, too bad,' he said in a hard tone she didn't recognize as his. 'You've got it. Everyone pities you now! Is this what you wanted?'

She turned back in shock that he was being so cruel. Norman, yes, she expected nothing else. But David . . . ? 'How can you ask me that?' she gasped.

'What else am I to think? Why else would you stay when you know what he's been doing? Everyone knows, even the kiddies in the playground!'

'Stop it! I want you to go.'

'No!' he said curtly, stepping further into the house instead. 'What will it take, Jayne?' he demanded. 'When will you admit what he is and leave him?'

'Never! I can't!'

'Yes, you can! He uses you! He abuses you! And now this? He's humiliating you!' His eyes were flaming. She had never seen him so enraged. 'God almighty, Jayne, where's your self-respect?'

The Midnight Secret

'Stop it!' she cried, putting her hands to her ears; but he crossed the space between them and took hold of her wrists, lifting them away again in the next moment.

'No, it's time you listened to me! I'm done with playing things your way,' he said, holding her still as he stood before her, toe to toe, staring down with an anger she had never seen before. His eyes travelled over her and she saw the pity rise again in his eyes. 'Jayne . . .'

She turned her face away in shame, trying to hide her face. 'Don't look at me!' she sobbed. 'Please just go! Leave me alone!'

His grip tightened around her wrists. 'You know I can't do that!'

She whirled back to face him. 'Why? Because you're going to confront Norman? You're going to save me?' Her sarcasm was biting and cruel, she knew that, but she couldn't help herself. Something inside her had snapped and she had lost control. She felt wild. Animalistic.

She yanked her arms out of his grip, surprised that he offered no resistance as she pulled away. Such a move with Norman would have resulted in a solid backhand to her cheek.

'Aye. I am,' he replied, growing ever more calm in the face of her hysteria. 'I can't stand aside and watch this any more. I won't. I won't let him hurt you.'

She stared back at him in bewilderment, tears streaming down her cheeks, her vision bleary, as he continued to stand here. '*Why?*' she cried. 'What do you care?'

'You know I do!' His voice cracked. '. . . I've loved you for months now.'

The world fell still. She'd never heard the word 'loved' directed at her before.

'I've only stood by for as long as I have because I was trying to respect your wishes! I tried to believe that your marriage was sacred – even if it was flawed; that it was not my business to intervene, no matter how hard it was to have to stand on the sidelines and watch.' His jaw balled, a flickering anger surfacing with the memories. 'But he's made it clear tonight there's nothing sacred in this union. There's no marriage left to save.'

She stared at him, hearing the simple truth she had tried so hard to deny. She had been an outsider her entire life, misunderstood and abandoned by her father, and she had fiercely cleaved a new identity to being Norman's wife and Molly's sister. But neither one of those was true any longer and, as she looked back at David, she understood to whom she really belonged. It had been obvious for weeks, but she had refused to see it.

She rushed forwards, pressing her mouth to his and tasting her own tears on his lips. His arms tightened around her immediately, holding her close, keeping her safe, as she felt an incredible power surge between them. It was so strong, even the force of her visions paled in comparison. The rest of the world ceased to exist. There was nothing but them and this moment.

Her hands were in his hair, his hands on her back, her waist, her hips . . . hitching up her skirt as they staggered backwards towards the table where he always sat, to the corner she thought of as his.

Where he would make her his.

She trembled, afterwards, in his arms, her legs still wrapped around him. He kissed her face as if she was something beautiful and rare. She had never known it could be like that, the act; that her own body was capable of such pleasure, or that

The Midnight Secret

she could make those sounds – and make those sounds come from him too.

She looked up at him, seeing the tenderness in his eyes as he cupped her face.

'I've wanted that to happen between us for so long,' he said in a low voice. 'I thought it never would.'

'Me too,' she whispered; and it was true. It was David's face she saw as she drifted off to sleep at night; his face that haunted the other dreams she kept private and which sometimes woke her, panting, in the middle of the night as Norman lay beside her (or didn't). But in her waking hours, she had never allowed herself to think of him as anything other than a friend. As he sat at this table, chatting away and reading the paper while she cooked; as he walked her up the lane on the way back from work; all the time, she told herself that he was her friend, Molly's fiancé, and nothing more. It was impossible to believe he would see her in any other light than as Norman's little, mousey wife. She could scarcely believe he saw her as a woman at all.

But somewhere between here and St Kilda, as the months had passed and they forged a new, humdrum life on this small Scottish peninsula, things had gradually changed between them. She felt his eyes on her back as she moved around the kitchen, saw the way he bristled whenever Norman was near. He left notes in her prayer book at church, telling her to wait for him so they could walk back together when Norman went 'fishing' afterwards. Their friendship was played out in clear sight of everyone, but it had a downy underbelly now; something gentle and soft had been growing in the quiet moments.

'I love you, Jayne.'

'I love you too,' she whispered as he kissed her tenderly again.

A sound outside made them both start, and they looked over to see the front door was still open. It was only a squirrel leaping from a branch, but if anyone should be passing . . . Only Old Fin lived further up the track, and he didn't often make the walk down, but if anyone should be going to visit him . . .

Fear intruded on their privacy and instinctively they drew apart, correcting their clothing and smoothing away any dishevelment that betrayed the passion that had overcome them.

Still, as David buckled his belt, his eyes caught hers; he seemed so languid and happy. 'So . . .' he smiled. 'What now?'

'What now?'

'Aye, how do we play this? When should we tell him?'

The room contracted.

Jayne slid off the table, pushing back down her skirt and smoothing her hair carefully with her hands. She glanced back at him, feeling a heavy pulse beat through her veins. Her equilibrium was settling again, her cool steadiness returning as a physical distance opened up between them. 'Tell him what?'

David's smile faltered. 'That you're leaving him.'

There was a pause.

She turned away. 'I . . . I'll need to pick the moment carefully.'

He was watching her again, his eyes upon her back, reading her. 'What about now? You could pack and be ready to leave by the time he comes back. We can tell him together and then go. I don't want him laying a hand on you.'

She gave a shocked laugh. *'Now?'*

'Aye.'

'And where am I to go?'

'To ours,' he shrugged. 'Where else?'

'To yours? You honestly believe Archie and Christina would be fine with a married woman coming to live with them? With you?'

He hesitated. 'Well, I'll need to explain things to them, obviously . . . but everyone knows what Norman is. And after today, who would blame you for leaving him? I think they'd be more surprised if you stayed!'

She looked at him. It was all so straightforward for him. He wanted to launch straight into 'happy ever after' – but she was another man's wife, no matter how bad a husband Norman might be.

'I need to consider things, David. It's not as simple as you're making it seem.'

He caught his breath, picking up on her growing coolness. 'No, it is simple, Jayne. It's as simple as it could possibly be. He doesn't love you. He doesn't respect you. He doesn't protect you. I'm sorry to be blunt, but y' need to see things for what they are. You're at a crossroads and y' have a choice to make. We both know this day has been a long time coming.'

His words hurt her even though she knew they were true. 'That's as may be, but as I said, I'm not leaving right now. I have to think.'

'But what is there to think about? Do y' really want to continue living in fear? He's got y' so broken down, y' think it's normal to be hit and to be hurt! But it's not. And you and I both know he's far more dangerous than people realize.'

She looked away. How many times had he brought this up with her? 'If you're referring to Frank—'

'Of course I am. Norman's the only one who doesn't have an alibi for his whereabouts that night. You lied to the police for him, and it's an innocent man, Donald McKinnon, who's taking the heat for it!'

'David, I've told you before, whatever Norman's faults, I know he didn't kill Frank.'

He threw his arms up in exasperation. 'You *don't* know that!'

'Yes, I do! I assure you, it will make no difference if I tell the police he didn't come home that night.'

'It would make all the difference in the world to Donald and Mhairi!' he snapped.

Jayne swallowed. 'Aye... Maybe,' she conceded. 'And I'm sorry they've been caught in this – but that isn't on Norman. The police will only waste their time redirecting their energies to him. I know he isn't the killer.'

He stared at her, that pitying look coming into his eyes again. 'No, it's not that. You don't care whether the police waste their time. You know you could have Donald taken off the hook of suspicion like *that*' – he clicked his fingers – 'but you don't want Norman knowing you were with me that night, because you're afraid he'll see what's really between us.'

She stared back at him, knowing he was right. She'd been too frightened to face her feelings for him before now, not only because she feared they were unreciprocated, but because they had existed far longer for her than they had for him. The terrible, shameful truth was that she had been drawn to him even when Molly was still alive. To have witnessed at such close quarters a love she had never known with her husband . . . it had made her want that love for herself. It had made her want him.

'It's a risk I can't take,' she whispered. Norman would kill her before he let her leave him for another man. For David, of all men.

The Midnight Secret

David shook his head, a small, scoffing laugh falling from his lips as he saw her intransigence, her refusal to remove herself from this place of fear. 'I don't understand you, Jayne. Here, you are ignored and overlooked and downtrodden; you live in terror of his moods and his fists. You deserve a better life than this, and I want to be the man to give it to you! But you won't come with me.' His voice broke on the frustration of it all.

'I'm just asking for some time, David. I know you love me and I love you back, but . . .' Her voice trailed off. How could she explain that it was safer to stay here than walk out with him into the sunlight? She only knew how to live in the shadows.

A silence stretched as she stared at the floor.

'Well . . .' he muttered, looking disconsolate. 'You'll be sure to tell me when you've finally had enough, won't you? Maybe after the next woman he fights over. Or the next broken bone.'

'David . . .'

But he walked past her and out through the open door, where a squirrel scampered on the garden wall and the world continued to turn.

Chapter Twenty-Eight

JAYNE

20 April 1931

Lochaline

Old Fin had brought his accordion and sat on the stool, playing it beside the fireplace in Ma Peg and Mad Annie's front room. There was scarcely room for Mhairi to swing her long red hair, but the children were all playing upstairs, and most of the men had spilled into the garden to smoke their pipes and take in the sunset.

Food was set out on trestle tables – pies and sliced roast beef and a colourful custard trifle that had got everyone excited – as the women sipped on sherry. Most of them were wearing their Sunday best dresses, cut in colourful florals with lace collars, and had styled their hair with set curls. Jayne took in the scene from beneath lowered lashes as she carried through a plate of bacon roll-ups. The guests of honour hadn't even arrived yet, but the party was in full swing, a buoyancy to the villagers' collective mood that she hadn't seen since their waulking the tweed ceilidh almost eighteen months earlier.

So much had changed since then. They had left their

The Midnight Secret

homeland and made new lives here. There had been much sorrow along the way – Lorna's death was still a bitter shock to everyone, in spite of the betrayal of her actions; Effie (though she put on a brave face) was still numb from her split with Sholto; and Mhairi, although blooming, bitterly missed Donald. But tonight they were celebrating their small successes. Archie MacQueen was finally off his crutches, Mad Annie had been made captain of the local bowls club, and more important than anything, one of their own was finally returning.

'Just put it down beside the gammon there, Jayne,' Ma Peg said, leaning back to inspect the edible offerings, one arm clasped below her bosom as she nodded with pride. The party had been her idea.

'When do you think they'll get here?' Jayne asked, rubbing her hands nervously. She felt unaccountably chilled for such a warm evening, a growing heaviness in her arms from carrying all the plates through, but she preferred to help with the setting up rather than stand around talking with the others. Although everyone smiled and behaved as normal, she knew what they must be thinking after the fracas a few days earlier. David had been right; she was weak and pathetic. They must pity Norman, being burdened with such a wretched and pitiful wife.

'Any minute n—' Ma Peg began, glancing at the clock on the mantlepiece, just as a cheer outside rose up and the children began stampeding down the stairs. 'Well, talk of the devil herself,' she laughed, clapping her hands together gleefully.

Through the windows, Jayne could see the high shine of a glossy black motor car, the men immediately gathering around to admire it as Christina and Archie MacQueen climbed out first. They had gone to the guesthouse where the Callaghans were staying earlier this afternoon; they had wanted to see their daughter privately, before the rest of the village.

Jayne smiled, startling slightly, as she caught sight of Flora's beautiful face again through the glass. It was easy to forget just how very lovely she was – those appled cheekbones, perfectly tilted eyebrows – and of course those flashing green eyes so like her brother's. Her glossy black hair had been cut into a fashionable bob back in the autumn, when she had made that fateful journey into Glasgow, but now it was growing out and fell more softly around her face – more like the island girl they had all known so well.

There was still no baby in her arms that Jayne could see from here. And in her eyes there was an ancient tiredness, as if her soul had become as old as the mountains.

Behind Flora, James was shaking hands with the men and accepting compliments on the car. Motor cars had become a source of intense fascination and admiration among the village men since their relocation here.

Jayne watched as David stepped forward from the mass to hug the sister he adored. They had both changed since their last meeting. Flora was thinner, and David . . . Jayne caught the quizzical frown that crossed Flora's face as she looked into his eyes. She asked him something and he nodded, but Flora looked sceptical, although the moment quickly passed.

Jayne turned back towards the table and stared down at the feast. It was all everyone had to offer. There were no riches here, but they had community, support, love and friendship. They would continue to give to one another, as they always had.

She leaned on the tabletop, feeling the heaviness increase in her bones again, and suddenly she knew what it really meant. It wasn't down to carrying plates.

'Please, no,' she whispered vainly in the empty room. '. . . Not now.'

The Midnight Secret

She closed her eyes, her face raised to the ceiling as she felt the tingling start up, golden shimmers sparking in her blood, flashing behind her eyelids.

She saw grey . . . Grey and red . . .

Her breathing came more heavily as the vision, indistinct at first, began to develop clarity. Green flickered at the edges of her mind's eye. She turned her head. What was she seeing? . . . Who?

People had started spilling back into the house again, the inevitable procession towards the heart of the home. Somehow, Jayne pulled herself out of the trance. It felt like swimming out of a whirlpool, resisting a force that wanted to suck her downwards, away from the light . . .

'. . . married us at the hotel! James had arranged everything.' Flora's distinctive voice carried through from the hall.

'But I always thought you'd have a cathedral wedding!' Mhairi replied.

'So did I,' Flora laughed. 'But we'll be sure to have a grand reception party to make up for it. We'll have a cake and flowers, and Ma's going to help me choose a dress to wear—'

Suddenly Flora's voice became crystal clear, and Jayne turned to find her standing in the doorway. 'Jayne!' she exclaimed delightedly, rushing over. 'I was wondering where you were!'

Jayne was startled by the comment – nobody ever wondered as to her whereabouts – as Flora threw her arms around her. 'How have you been?'

For a moment, Jayne couldn't find her voice. She felt wretched, but compared to what Flora had suffered these past eight months . . . 'Tremendous. Though life here has had none of your glamour or excitement.'

It was the wrong thing to have said, of course.

'If there has been excitement, it's all been the wrong sort,'

Flora said, pulling a face and reaching for her friend's hand. Jayne knew Flora's parents would have told her that everyone knew. There were no more secrets among the St Kildans.

Well, almost none.

Jayne's eyes looked for David again, but he was nowhere to be seen. He was keeping his distance with the same diligence he'd once kept watch in her kitchen. He'd not left a note in her prayer book, nor met her on the path to walk home since. She cooked in her kitchen alone, silent, staring at the spot on the kitchen table where he now wasn't but where their ghosts still played. She'd lost not only the man she loved, but her best friend.

The room had filled rapidly again, everyone pouring drinks and the children hovering around the food now that the party had officially started. James was looking overwhelmed but pleased as he was brought into the villagers' fold and greeted as one of their own. Everyone wanted to hear about his near-death experience in Greenland.

'Flora, you've returned!'

Jayne heard Norman's voice and turned to see him walk over to greet Flora too.

'Oh my goodness, Norman!' Flora laughed as she took in the sight of his black eye, cuts and bruises. 'Have you been fighting bears?'

'Something like that,' he grinned.

Jayne tensed at his light-hearted volley. As if it was all fun. *Funny.* He had no shame before her. He hadn't apologized for what had happened, as if it hadn't happened to her as well as him. He had come back that evening expecting his dinner on the table – of course there had been none; she had never been served at the butcher's, after all – and he'd given her no account of how he had come by his injuries as she tended to them.

The Midnight Secret

She could no longer pretend to be ignorant, to turn the other cheek, even though it had served her so well till now. He knew that she knew – and still he didn't care. His wanton disregard for her feelings was so blatant, she felt completely frozen inside. Dead.

'And what's this I hear about a return to St Kilda tomorrow evening?' Flora asked, as Effie came over with a glass of sherry for her.

'Ah, well, now there's a story,' Effie said with a roll of her eyes.

'Is it on account of good news between you and Sholto?' Flora asked hopefully.

Effie's smile slid off her lips. '. . . Not exactly.'

'Oh, Eff,' Flora said, reaching a hand to her arm. 'I had hoped . . .'

'We have to face facts, Flora. We're from different worlds.'

'But—' Flora opened her mouth to protest to the contrary, Jayne knew. After all, she had married a rich man. Then she seemed to think better of it and simply nodded. 'Pa says there's quite a crowd going over with you now?'

'Aye, seems so. Me, Mhairi, Angus, Fin, David and Mad Annie . . . Old Fin wants to go too, but Ma Peg say he's not up to the crossing.' Effie shrugged. 'We'll see.'

'Are you going, Jayne?' Flora asked her, bringing her into the conversation.

Jayne glanced at Norman. '. . . Eh, no. No, there's no need,' she murmured.

'What's need got to do with it?' Flora asked. 'Don't you want to see the old place again?'

'We have to work,' Norman said sombrely. 'Can't afford to miss the wages.'

'Norman's been made deputy manager at the Forestry,' Jayne said, just as David squeezed past their group in the crowd. He must have heard the small boast, for his gaze tangled with hers, and she recoiled at what she saw in his eyes: dismay was turning to something closer to disgust.

'Is that so?' Flora asked with an impressed look. 'You're going places in the world, Norman.'

'Perhaps not as far – or as fast – as y', Flora,' Norman admitted, looking irritated by the concession that her light dimmed his. 'Still, it's something to pull us up by the bootstraps.'

'And so what's the occasion for the trip?' Flora asked, looking back at Effie.

'The earl has bought the archipelago from MacLeod.'

'Has he now? Well, I'm not surprised he wants shot of it after all that's happened with Mathieson.' Flora rolled her eyes in disdain. It didn't matter that the man was dead; her contempt for him lingered.

'Aye, so they're having a handover ceremony of sorts.'

'And they invited you?' Flora looked quizzical.

Effie nodded.

'But why you specifically, Eff? If you and Sholto aren't together . . . ?'

Effie hesitated. It was the question everyone had been asking her and she'd been hedging her answer for weeks. '. . . Let's just say I'm helping them with finding something.'

'Oh, don't tell me,' Flora groaned. 'He needs a precious bird's egg for his collection and only you can find it?'

'Not the earl. MacLeod. And no, he's looking for something else.'

Beside her, Jayne felt Norman straighten up. 'Like what?'

'I can't say,' Effie replied enigmatically. 'I've been sworn to secrecy.'

'Och, give us a clue,' Mhairi pleaded, pressing her hands together in prayer.

'I wish I could, but I gave my word I wouldn'a say a thing till it's safely recovered.'

'But you can tell us!' Norman insisted.

'My word is my bond,' Effie shrugged. 'I'm sorry.'

'. . . Ridiculous,' Norman muttered, stalking off.

Flora grinned. 'He's as grumpy as ever, I see . . . Ah, sorry, Jayne. No offence intended.'

'None taken. He's the man he always was.'

Except that wasn't true. Norman had become worse since moving over to the mainland, leaning into all his vices and darkest corners. Variety had given him opportunities, choices – and he wasn't making wise ones.

Jayne watched her husband cross the room to get another drink. He stood almost a head taller than the other men, so he was easy to follow. He stopped at the table beside David, who glanced across as he was putting a slice of pie onto his plate. Jayne saw Norman say something to David in a rare show of sociability, but to her astonishment David put down his plate and walked away, leaving Norman hanging, mid-sentence.

Norman looked astounded for a moment, a black look darkening his handsome features. Then he glanced round to check whether anyone had seen. Quickly she turned back to the women's conversation as she felt his gaze settle upon her.

'– when I left, there was no indication she was going to do what she did. She was . . . she was calm. We didn't part on hostile terms.'

Lorna? Jayne leaned in as Mhairi put a hand on Flora's arm.

'Y' mustn't blame yourself,' Mhairi said. 'You did nothing wrong going over there after her; they took your baby under false pretences. Following them was the only thing you could do. *She* was the one who had to live with what she'd done, and . . . well, perhaps the fact that she couldn't live with it speaks to some scrap of humanity left in her after all.'

Flora nodded, seeming to find comfort in her friend's words.

'There's no excusing what she did to you, but you and I both saw her kindness too. She wasn't a complete monster. Not like Mary.'

'Talking of whom – what's become of her?' Effie asked.

'Don't worry, she's not coming tonight. She knows she'd not be welcome here.'

'Wait—' Mhairi looked stunned. '. . . You mean she's *here*? In Scotland?'

'Aye. She's in the guesthouse we're staying in, down the road.'

Jayne watched Mhairi's hands fly to her belly. She was showing clearly now, her shame there for all to see, although the St Kildans made sure she suffered no waspish comments in the village. But if Mary would only grant Donald a divorce . . .

'So,' Effie was looking pained. 'The baby . . . ?'

'He's with her too.' For the first time since she'd come through the door, Flora's happy demeanour slipped. '. . . We've come to an arrangement.'

'An arrangement?' Effie frowned.

Flora gave a deep sigh. 'We've had to accept we can't prove that . . . that Struan is actually ours. All the paperwork – his birth certificate, passport, the evacuation census – it's in the McKinnons' names. It's Donald and Mary who are down as his parents. Lorna could have stood as our independent witness, but . . . well, that chance went away with her.'

Flora's face had fallen. Everyone could guess at the depths of the suffering she must have endured these past eight months while trying to get her baby back.

The Midnight Secret

Jayne shifted her weight apprehensively. She could feel the tingling growing more vigorously throughout her body, and she knew that soon she wouldn't be able to move at all. The vision wouldn't be denied; she would have to submit . . . get out of here. If anyone were to realize what was happening to her, they would understand immediately what it meant. A party would never disband so quickly . . .

'But what's to stop Mary disappearing again? What's to stop her getting on another boat?' Effie asked with concern.

'James has struck a deal with her. A financial one. Without Lorna, Mary has no one to look after the baby and no way to earn. She has the ambergris money she took from Donald, but that won't last for ever – so James is going to pay her a very generous wage to live beside us. Without proof or witnesses, we can't change the paperwork saying the baby is ours; and Mary won't let us adopt him back either. So our only option is to pay for her to stay in our lives with him. James is going to buy her a flat in the same square as us in Glasgow, and we'll have daily access and visitation rights to Struan; but we can't call him ours or have him actually live with us.'

Colours splashed in front of Jayne's eyes: Grey. Red. Green . . . She saw a hand upturned, the fingers curled.

She took a step back.

'And . . . is that going to be enough for you?' Mhairi asked, looking appalled.

'What other choice do we have? We can have some of him or none of him.' Flora shrugged. 'On the boat back here, we upgraded her to a first-class suite and gave her a taste of the kind of life we could offer her and the baby.'

'I'll bet she bit your arm off, did she?' Mhairi sneered.

'Aye. Once we made her see she had no other viable options.'

Jayne felt her panic growing as the edges of the room began to blur. 'Won't you excuse me?' she murmured. 'I just need to see to something . . .'

She turned away from the group quickly, pushing through the crowd. She needed to get outside – gulp down some fresh air, find somewhere she could be alone. But there were so many people, bodies everywhere. Was that why the force seemed stronger than usual – because the victim was here, close by? She had wondered why she hadn't envisaged Lorna's death. Jayne's gift had always encompassed their community members, and she had only been able to conclude that the distance between them at the time had been too great.

By that same reckoning, someone here was going to be dead within days.

She staggered outside, around the back of the house. Everyone else was in the front garden, which enjoyed the sunset views, and she leaned against the wall, dropping her head back as she felt the vision unfurl now, unimpeded. It was so clear and bright—

'There you are!'

God, no. She was pulled back into the moment.

'What are you doing out here? What's wrong with you?'

She opened her eyes to find Norman bearing down on her.

'Nothing. I just needed some air,' she mumbled. '. . . A little too much sherry.'

The face began to bloom in her mind's eye, the eyes still black sockets.

'And people wonder why I'm embarrassed by y',' he tutted, looking disgusted. 'Get home before you make a spectacle of yourself.'

'Aye . . . I will,' she murmured. How could she get him away from here? The consequences of her last vision had been

The Midnight Secret

severe for her. If he realized what was happening, he would want to know whom it concerned, and that was a boundary she would never cross. 'What . . . what is it you need?'

'From you? Nothing,' he snapped. 'I just came to tell y' I'll be going to St Kilda after all.'

She frowned, confused. 'But the wages . . .'

'My salary's good enough that I can forgo a day's work, and I don't know when the next opportunity will come up. I'm going to take the chance, seeing as they're offering the trip for free.'

It made no sense. He had shown absolutely no interest in returning home when the idea of a wider village return had first been suggested by the men in the pub. But this wasn't the time to discuss it. She just needed him to go.

'I agree . . .' she slurred. 'You should go.'

'I wasn't coming to ask y' permission, woman! I'm telling y' as a courtesy. That's all.'

A courtesy? As if he were a gentleman? The very idea made Jayne want to laugh, but she was beyond that point now. Besides, he had already gone.

Her body slumped as the image finally bloomed in her mind, with or without him. It offered no time, no place, no why, no how. But she had a face.

And another terrible secret to keep.

Chapter Twenty-Nine

Jayne sat on the rock, the letter on her lap as she looked out across the silvered water. It had been delivered yesterday, though in all the haste for the preparations for Flora's homecoming she hadn't opened it till she'd come home last night. She still wasn't sure why it had come to her, and she had stolen away from her bed before dawn to come here to think better – for this had become her new favourite spot, the secret place to which she could remove when things became too much with Norman. She'd never even brought David here.

David.

She missed him so much she ached. He wouldn't meet her eyes at all last night and she had felt a gaping loneliness at being in a crowded house and ignored by the only person who truly mattered to her. She missed his easy conversation and lazy smiles, watching their shadows walk ahead of them on the path on the way home each evening. But amid the gentleness of their everyday encounters, she also remembered the passion that had erupted between them that afternoon in the kitchen, stunning them both. She couldn't forget it.

They could have had everything together. Been everything to each other.

But she had blocked her own happiness.

She understood why he was angry. From the outside, she

The Midnight Secret

knew her actions made no sense, but no one, not even he, could ever truly understand what happened inside her head. The burden of her so-called gift held her apart from everyone else, irrespective of her own desire to fit in. It was a curse to know more than she should, prefiguring death while the victim lived.

Only this time, things were different. She alone knew something and, although she couldn't change the outcome, time was on her side. She could make a change for good.

She had been awake all night, debating her next move as Norman slept beside her. He had come in late, stinking of beer and almost collapsing into unconsciousness, still wearing his clothes. Did she dare to act?

It would require her to be bold, defiant and brave – all the things she wasn't – and she didn't have long to decide. The sun was already rising. If she was going to get there and back in time, she would have to leave now.

She watched a pod of dolphins slip through the waters of the sound, untroubled by anything other than where to find their next meal – and she suddenly understood that she had a greater destiny than that. Simple survival wasn't enough. If she couldn't stop death, she could at least help others to truly live.

She got up from the rock and began walking.

There was one thing she could do.

Nine hours later, Jayne sat by the bus window, her fingers grasping anxiously at the cloth of her skirt as the small green bus wound its way along the coast road and back into the village's main street. She had been certain they would get here too late, for timings had been tighter than she had imagined, the distances greater. She wasn't a woman of the world, not like Effie, who had travelled through Scotland, or even Mhairi – and certainly not like Flora, who had crossed half the world.

But the ivory yacht was still moored at the quay, its sails wound in around tall masts as a crowd gathered to wave them off. Jayne was amazed at how familiar it was to her eye, though it had been almost a year since she had seen the boat last. Memories rushed at her as she was reminded of Effie – ropes looped over her shoulder and wearing her brother's clothes – marching the earl and his son up and down the slopes in the hunt for birds' eggs; the striking slashes of the semaphore cut into Boreray's turf after Donald's fall; Lorna gathering everyone around as she shared the news of the evacuation; Flora streaking over the hills with a red shawl at her waist, keeping a secret . . . It had only been a few days, and yet all those events had transpired while the yacht lay at anchor in Village Bay last May. And their consequences stretched into the present, even now.

More than anyone could possibly know.

The bus stopped outside the greengrocer's and the doors opened.

'Ready?' she asked her companion.

'Aye.'

They disembarked, casting around for the St Kildan faces as they moved into the crowd. Jayne found Norman easily, across the way, talking to one of the fishermen, but she kept her distance. He would only be angry to have discovered her gone this morning. Christina and Rachel were talking with Mad Annie. The shift at the factory had just ended and all the women were bustling around as if they were sending their sons off to war, not waving cheerio to neighbours who would return in two days' time.

The Midnight Secret

MacLeod's skipper, reading the winds and weather forecast, had estimated a sailing time of roughly eight hours. They would be travelling through the night, hoping to make landfall soon after dawn tomorrow. All being well, they would cast off again tomorrow evening to return here the following morning. It would be gruelling, even on a luxury yacht.

MacLeod himself had arranged to travel over with the earl and his minister on the Dumfries boat, to make room for the villagers on his own, but even then there weren't enough berths for everyone. Many of the villagers would have to sleep where they lay. But no one was complaining. The excitement of returning to their homeland had been building for days and was now approaching fever pitch. They would sleep on spikes if they had to.

Jayne saw a flash of red in the crowd. 'Mhairi!' she called.

The young woman turned, her jaw dropping open as she saw who was standing beside Jayne.

'. . . Donald?'

In an instant, tears were dropping down her cheeks as he pushed his way through to her, scooping her up and turning her round and round, Mhairi cupping his face in disbelief. Seeing how their eyes locked, Jayne was reminded again of how David had looked at her. Bodies echoing souls.

'But how . . . how are you here?' Mhairi cried. 'I don't understand!'

'Jayne came down to Oban on the first bus this morning,' he said. 'She's changed her statement. I'm officially off the hook!'

Jayne saw Mhairi gather the breath to squeal, but she reached forward hastily and pressed a finger to her lips. 'Not yet,' she whispered. '. . . You must keep it to yourselves till we return.'

'But—' A look of concern tracked into Mhairi's grey eyes.

'If anyone asks, just tell them Donald is no longer a person of interest in the investigation. There's nothing more that needs to be added just yet.' Jayne glanced across to check Norman was still out of earshot. Donald and Mhairi followed her gaze, understanding the implications for her husband – and for her, should he discover the change to his alibi status too soon.

'I understand,' Mhairi whispered solemnly. 'We'll not breathe a word.'

'Donald?' Fin MacQueen asked. '. . . Are my eyes playing tricks?'

The others came over too as word spread fast through the crowd. It was good news – and at the perfect time too.

Jayne looked for David, finding him standing with his father, hands in his pockets and nodding as Archie gave him instructions for something or other to do when he got back to the isle. Many of the villagers wanted something checked, replaced, repaired while they were over there. Mary Gillies had given Mad Annie some flowers to place on her babies' graves.

Jayne watched as David scuffed at the ground. She wished she could go over and stand with him, talk easily as they once used to; but everything had changed now, and she didn't think she could hide it. She couldn't risk people seeing the breach that had opened up, lurking between them like a blood river.

Her eyes found Mhairi and Donald again, standing together as he was welcomed back into the fold, and it seemed to Jayne that no one found it strange to see him now with his arm around a woman who not his wife. It was as if they could see that the love that existed between them was truer than the false bonds of marriage that had trussed him.

The Midnight Secret

She looked over at David again. Would the same have been true for them? Would their friends and neighbours have accepted their love, as well as that one? Or was there a limit to their forgiveness, to the amount of shame any one community could absorb?

With Mary back in the country now, there was at least hope that Donald could finally get the divorce he craved from his wife. If Mary's motherhood could be bought, perhaps his freedom could be negotiated too. Or would it suit Mary to hold them hostage, casting Mhairi as the scarlet woman and staining their child with the slur of illegitimacy? That would be the spurned wife's final act of revenge, wouldn't it?

Not that it mattered now. Whatever Mary did or didn't do, the dice had already been rolled, and everything would play out exactly as the fates decreed.

Jayne already knew it.

And soon everyone else would too.

Chapter Thirty

The water glittered sugar-pink as the rising sun nosed above the horizon. Jayne sat on deck, her knees tucked into her chest, feeling the wind ripple through her hair. She had untied her signature braid, wanting to feel free in the elements. Unbound.

She wasn't alone. Most of the villagers were up here, too – David, Donald and Mhairi, Angus and Fin MacKinnon, Effie, Mad Annie – unable to sleep through the plunge and roll of the Atlantic, too excited to risk missing the first sighting of home. Only Norman remained below deck, sleeping in MacLeod's feathered bed.

He had been displeased to find her on board. He'd been irritated enough by her absence at breakfast that morning, having woken from his drunken stupor to find nothing ready for him; but to miss two lots of wages, he had argued . . . Jayne had simply shrugged, saying that she wanted to see her home again too. It was a defiance that had not gone unnoticed, and she knew he intended to punish her for it at a later time. For now, at least, she was safe in company.

She watched the horizon, a line that never tilted although the boat cut and carved through the water in sweeping arcs, powered by billowing sails.

'Is that . . . ?' Donald asked suddenly, getting to his knees to peer more closely. 'Is that her?'

The Midnight Secret

The villagers followed the direction of his pointed finger. Sure enough, a pale, indistinct haze could be just made out: a shadow in the distance, growing in density and form as they drew closer.

Jayne never took her eyes off it, her heart thudding faster, harder as they ploughed through the waves. Destiny was calling – she could feel it.

'There she is!' Mad Annie cried, pulling her handkerchief from her shirt pocket and waving it as if she expected St Kilda to wave back. Everyone else cheered and waved too. Even though they knew it was ridiculous, they had to do something with their hands. Like an old dog getting to its feet on its master's return, their island home steadily reared up, blotting the horizon once more.

It took another two hours from that first tentative glimpse for their home to fully rise from the sea. Noble and majestic, St Kilda's ragged stone walls emerged cathedral-like, a black diadem from the blue. Drawing closer still, they saw the stacks standing like sentries in the sea as the waves battered them with huge, heaving run-ups, the scattered landmasses of the archipelago – Dùn, Boreray and Soay – clustering around Hirta like huddling sheep. And as they slipped into the kelpy basin of the underwater caldera, the skies grew thick with seabirds, and the soundtrack of their past came to their ears. There were none of the lilting melodies of the songbirds on the mainland; rather a savage cacophony of strangled shrieks and murderous cries. The sounds of home.

Jayne saw Effie sitting erect, her rope looped around her waist as she eyed the cliffs that had once been her playground. Angus threw a cheeky comment her way – some kind of bet, it seemed – and in the next moment Effie was shaking his hand with an intense expression.

'Norman, you're awake!' Angus cheered as a dark, tousled head appeared at the top of the steps.

'How was I supposed to sleep over the racket y're making?' Norman muttered, coming to sit beside Jayne. His breath was sour and he looked rough – his black eye had yellowed, the cuts still crusted with scabs. 'You'd think they'd never seen the place before.'

David glanced over at the two of them, looking away again before she could catch his eye.

'If you're so unmoved by coming back, Norman, why did you bother coming at all?' she asked. It was provocative of her to be so direct. Confrontational, even. But she reminded herself that she had to be bold, brave and courageous, because she had to know – why *was* he here?

Norman regarded her. 'You've quite a mouth on y' at the moment, Jayne,' he said loudly. 'Have y' got your monthly curse?'

David's head whipped around as she felt her cheeks flame. She quickly looked away and Norman chuckled, his objective achieved.

They were sailing past Boreray now and the crew began hauling in the sails, slowing their speed so that they curled into Village Bay at a declining clip. Immediately the waters calmed, the wind dropping as the cliffs encircled them with a loving embrace, welcoming them home. The villagers gathered at the bow rails and Jayne caught her breath as she had her first sight of the village, the stone cottages standing there just as they'd left them, forgotten foot-soldiers still in formation on the battlefield.

A collective silence blanketed the boat. Tears pricked her eyes as she saw their own ghosts: Mad Annie sitting on the wall, knitting . . . Ma Peg carding on the stool in her

The Midnight Secret

doorway . . . White sheets flapping in the wind down the long allotments that stretched all the way to the beach . . . Angus and Fin patching a roof . . . The men hauling the smack . . . Children running barefoot around the cleits . . . Chimneys puffing and golden squares from windows on moonlit grass . . . Effie dangling playfully on a rope . . . Mhairi and Flora dancing on the sand . . . Lorna washing bandages in the burn . . . Molly and David kissing on a path . . . And Jayne herself, sitting on the rocks as the sun went down, a silvered silhouette upon which bruises couldn't be read.

She saw it all, the lives they had lived here, and it seemed to her their laughter still echoed around the glen, hymns sounding in the kirk, their shouts forever red-hot in the snow.

Another yacht was already at anchor, shadowy figures on the beach telling them that the lairds and their minister had arrived in advance. One head glinted like a nugget of gold.

Beside her, Effie startled. 'No,' she whispered. 'What's *he* doing here?'

Jayne felt the sand between her toes as she waded in to the beach, her skirt gathered about her legs. Everyone up ahead was already shaking hands with MacLeod and the earl, the minister clutching his Bible and ready to work. There was a celebratory atmosphere ashore, as if this was more than a transfer of deeds.

Effie was right beside her. Jayne saw the way Sholto swallowed at her head-down approach, taking care not to get her rope wet nor meet his eyes.

'Did you not know he was coming, Effie?' she asked quietly.

'No.' The word was a breath, without shape or hope, and Jayne could hear the pain in it. Would Effie have come if she'd known? '. . . How does he seem?'

'Nervous . . . He's watching you.' Jayne tried to talk without moving her lips.

They stepped out of the water and towards the dignitaries waiting for them on the shore.

'. . . And this is Mrs Ferguson, Norman's wife,' Donald said, introducing her as Sir John offered her a hand.

'How d'you do, Mrs Ferguson?'

'Sir,' she nodded, seeing David was watching on. Norman was on the beach already too, trousers still rolled up to his knees, his hands on his hips as he looked up at the glen.

'And Miss Gillies, who you . . . already know,' Donald faltered.

Effie stopped before them with a sigh and a nod. 'Your lordships.' She was wearing her brother's breeks again. Nostalgia, perhaps? Or just practicality?

'Effie,' Sir John said warmly. 'Our guest of honour!'

Effie frowned, as did Norman, who had turned back to watch. 'I wouldn't say that exactly, sir,' she demurred.

'Oh, I would. It's thanks to you we're all gathered here today.'

'Really?' Donald asked, curious. 'And why's that, then?'

Everyone listened keenly. The exact reason for this homecoming hadn't been made explicitly clear, beyond Effie helping them to find something – but MacLeod just tapped the tip of his nose. 'All in good time, I promise.'

'Hello, Effie,' Sholto said.

Effie looked across at him. '. . . Hello, sir.'

Sholto winced at her formality. Everyone did. Jayne saw a sharp look of pain cross his features as Effie began walking up the beach towards the grassy allotment of her old home. For a moment no one else stirred, but then they disbanded too, making straight for the cottages they knew so well. Norman led the pack.

The Midnight Secret

'Shall we proceed to the kirk then, gentlemen?' the earl's minister asked. 'We can offer up our blessings while the villagers reacquaint themselves.'

Both Sholto and MacLeod looked agitated, watching Effie as she stalked away across the grass, but reluctantly they nodded. '. . . Of course.'

Jayne headed for her home, her spirit soaring as she trod barefoot on the lush grass – everyone had left their boots on the boat – her senses assaulted by the intensity of being back. She could taste the salt on the breeze, could feel those familiar winds tussle and tug at her hair. The heavy slump of the waves and the cries of the birds crowded her mind, pushing out all other thoughts so that she could almost forget what was coming.

The door of number two was still closed. She had assumed Norman had gone ahead to come here, but as she pushed it, she felt the air of desertion she remembered from that last morning here. Complete abandonment. No one lived here; no one had ever loved here, either.

She walked in and stared at the bare rooms, where no visible trace of the Fergusons remained. They were devoid of furniture but not of memories. No one would ever know he had thrown her against that wall or kicked her against that door as she'd tried to escape. The tin bath where he'd once held her head under the water was no longer tipped upside down round the back.

She stood at the doorway to Molly's box room, the place where she had died. Closing her eyes, she tried to feel her presence; but nothing lingered. The girl's spirit was free now, far from here, and it was another presence Jayne felt instead – the darkness, like a black smoke that billowed behind her and wouldn't come free now, not till *it* was done. She knew they were on borrowed time, that the clock was already running down.

It would be soon, she knew that. The visions came with a hyperbaric pressure system that steadily ratcheted up inside her body. She could feel the moment building as the elements came together, and she had felt a sharp surge as she stepped onto the sand here, onto the grass – the very grass where it would happen.

She went back to the doorway and leaned against the wooden frame as she always used to, watching the activity of her neighbours. Angus and Fin MacKinnon were checking the metal ties that kept the roof strapped down in high winds. One had seemingly come loose, and they were tightening it in tandem. Mad Annie was sitting on the wall, smoking her pipe and kicking her legs as she looked back in at her cottage, as if it was a child she couldn't decide was in need of a hard hug or a good scolding. David was sweeping Ma Peg's doorstep, a promise he must have made to her. It had always been one of his chores, and Jayne supposed old habits were hard to give up.

Much like loving him.

She looked across at Lorna's cottage, right at the very end of the street. It stood slightly apart, with the blackhouses either side she had once used as medical stores and a clinic room. The roof was in poor order from its more exposed position and the cottage had a forlorn, melancholic air, as if aware of its owner's fate.

David stepped back inside and Jayne felt seized by the urge to talk to him. If she couldn't adequately explain herself, at the very least she had to apologize for rejecting him in the moment he'd offered her everything.

She strode quickly along the familiar path, knowing the pitch

The Midnight Secret

and size of every slab. She glanced in the windows of number five, the Wee Gillies' old home, as she passed, catching sight of two figures in the bedroom. She'd not seen Effie since she'd all but run away from Sholto on the beach. Jayne had assumed he had gone to the kirk with his father and MacLeod, to endure the official ceremony the lairds were insisting upon, but . . .

Her feet stopped. No, it wasn't Sholto she'd seen. And as her mind played back the glancing image, she heard sounds. She knew all too well what a struggle sounded like, and she ran back into the cottage.

'Where is it?' Norman growled.

'Norman!' Jayne gasped in utter horror as she stood in the bedroom doorway. 'What are you doing?'

He turned, and she saw the black look in his eyes she knew all too well. He had Effie caught against the wall, her arm pinned awkwardly behind her back. She was whimpering in pain as he turned her arm at the wrist a little, threatening to break it. Jayne knew exactly how much that hurt. He had done it to her many times over the years, but to see it so graphically being inflicted upon someone else . . . Upon wee Effie, of all people. She was strong, but she had no chance against a man of Norman's size.

Norman bared his teeth, unconcerned by her interruption. 'Get out, Jayne,' he growled again. 'This doesn't concern you.'

But Jayne's body wouldn't obey his commands. Not this time.

'Leave her alone. Let her go.'

'I said get out! Don't make me make you regret waking up this morning!'

She felt herself start to shake. His threats, so familiar, provoked a reflexive response in her now. She knew when to run, and this was it . . . *Turn around. Go.*

She stepped forward. Two steps.

Norman's eyes narrowed at the defiance. A confrontation had been brewing between them for days now, and she knew exactly the consequences of provoking him like this. Until now, she had known there was safety in numbers – he wouldn't beat her till they were home – but if he was doing this to Effie, he wouldn't hesitate to strike her in front of Effie too. Neither one of them was safe.

Slowly, Jayne raised her hands in a gesture of surrender. 'Just tell me what it is you want from her, Norman,' she said in her calmest voice.

'She knows what!' he sneered, twisting harder on Effie's arm and making her cry out.

'Do you, Eff?' Jayne's voice quavered on the question, but she knew she had to pacify her husband. He was like a cornered rat, never more dangerous than he was right now. To have thrown off his veneer of respectability like this, to expose his true self to one of their neighbours, could only mean one thing – he had nothing left to lose.

'I'm not telling him anything!' Effie gasped through gritted teeth.

She cried out as he wrenched her arm around, holding it at a grotesque angle so that Effie's knees buckled and she fell to the floor.

'Effie, tell him!' Jayne pleaded. 'Whatever it is, it's not worth this!'

'You don't know that,' Effie whimpered.

'I do. *Really*, I do . . . Please just give him what he wants . . . Please. Trust me. Whatever you've got, give it to him.'

Norman pressed his face up to Effie's ear. 'Listen to her,' he sneered. 'She's talking sense for once.'

The empty room echoed with Effie's laboured breaths. She

The Midnight Secret

was panting hard as she tried to withstand the pain, but Norman kept twisting her arm just a little bit more, a little bit more . . . Once more and he'd break her arm.

'Fine,' she gasped. 'Fine!'

'Where is it?' Norman whispered menacingly.

A tear slid down Effie's cheek. '. . . In the inky pool,' she gasped. 'I put it in the inky pool.'

Jayne watched as Norman's entire body softened, the tension lifting off him at last. She had no idea what Effie had hidden, but the inky pool was over in Glen Bay, a curiously dark, small pond in which the water glistened black like an oil slick. No one could account for the phenomenon, but the villagers' best explanation was that the grease or lanolin from the sheep and birds, cleaning themselves, somehow made its way into the water courses and pooled there.

Norman released Effie's arm with a savage push, throwing her forward so that she sprawled across the floor. Jayne lunged for her, getting down on the ground and drawing the girl into her arms and a fragile safety; for the first time, she saw Effie had a nasty graze on her cheek.

Her husband stared back at them both, his chest heaving as he began to calm himself down. 'Not . . . a . . . word,' he threatened, pointing a finger at them both.

'Of course not,' Jayne whispered before Effie could respond, squeezing her with her arms a little tighter in silent warning. 'I never do. You can trust me, Norman.'

He stared right into her soul, seeing everything broken and frightened inside her. 'Aye, but make sure *she* understands it too,' he growled. He cast his attention onto Effie once more. 'Things can always get worse, little lady. For you *and* y' loved ones. We all remember what happened to Poppit, now, don't we?'

Effie flinched, and Jayne could feel her shaking in her arms – but it was with rage, not fear. Effie was a fighter. 'I'll make sure she understands, Norman,' she said quickly.

There was a silence as Norman ran a hand through his hair and adjusted his shirt, then he strode out of the cottage. For several moments, neither woman stirred. It was hard to believe what had just happened – their joyful homecoming tarnished in this way, violence erupting in the middle of a peaceful day.

Effie wriggled out of Jayne's arms. 'We need to stop him,' she gasped.

'No.'

'Aye, Jayne! We can't let him do this!'

'Yes we can. Just let him go. Let him do what he needs to do. It doesn't matter.'

But Effie misunderstood. 'How can you say that?' She looked at Jayne with an expression of utter disbelief, and Jayne knew what she was really thinking; it was what David hadn't been able to understand either. Why had she stayed with Norman all these years? But there was no easy one-word answer. Survival took many forms.

'What is it he's gone to get, Effie?'

Effie turned away, rubbing her sore arm. 'It's supposed to be a secret.'

'And so is this,' Jayne replied, watching her. 'What is it Norman wants so badly that he'd hurt you like this?'

But Effie shook her head, not listening. 'How could you make me give it up to him like that?!'

'Because it was the only way to make him stop,' Jayne replied simply. 'What is it he wants?'

Effie sighed and dropped her gaze to the ground. She looked exhausted. '. . . The Sir Rory Mor horn,' she said finally.

'. . . What's that?'

The Midnight Secret

'It's a MacLeod artefact. Mathieson stole it last summer and hid it over here. The theft was kept a secret. Superstition or something.'

Jayne closed her eyes, her own suspicions confirmed at last. If Frank Mathieson had stolen the horn but the theft had been kept a secret, then there was only one way Norman could have known about it: her husband was the third man the police believed to have been involved in the smuggling ring. She remembered the final days and nights on the isle, when the two men had been roaming the hills, examining every cleit as a so-called inventory check for the landlord . . . That last night when he hadn't come home at all.

'Norman killed Frank,' Effie said, watching Jayne as she got to her feet.

'No.' The word came out before Jayne could stop it.

'Aye, Jayne,' Effie said pityingly. 'I know it's hard to hear. He's still your husband even if he is a brute, but there's no honour among thieves. Norman's a thief – I saw him creeping around MacLeod's library at Dunvegan. I reckon he was looking to see if the horn had been found and brought back. He must have thought Frank had double-crossed him or gone back on his word, and they got into some kind of fight—' Her voice broke as a memory surfaced. 'I met him coming back from Glen Bay the morning we left – when he killed Poppit. He was the very last man on the island, don't you remember? He was making sure no one found the body.'

Jayne shook her head. 'No,' she repeated.

Effie raised an eyebrow. 'I know. Donald's only here because you finally told the police Norman didn't come home that last night.'

'Did Mhairi tell you that?'

'No, David . . .'

'Hello?' A knock came at the door. '. . . Effie, are you here? I must talk with you.'

Both Jayne and Effie froze at the distinctive voice sounding through from the kitchen. A moment later, Sholto appeared in the bedroom doorway. He took in the sight of them both: the fear on their faces, Effie's grazed cheek and dishevelled clothes. 'My God, what's happened?'

Jayne looked over at Effie. She could see, as Effie met the blue-eyed gaze of the man she loved, that it was all over for Norman now.

'. . . There's something we need to tell you.'

'He can't fight all of us,' David said, his eyes blazing as the men gathered around him.

He could, Jayne thought to herself, looking at them too. They weren't a large group: Sholto, Donald, Angus and Fin. Jayne wasn't convinced the earl, MacLeod or the minister could really be counted on for fighting prowess, but at least they represented authority and made up numbers.

She watched from her perch on the wall. Effie had given a comprehensive and clear account of what she knew to be true, and there was nothing Jayne could do to change those facts. Norman had been exposed at last for what he really was.

David kept glancing over at her, though he was leading the chase, powered by a rage that long predated today's revelations. Several of the villagers had caught sight of Norman already heading over to Glen Bay. The men had agreed to head over to the inky pool and confront him there; he was a big man, and an angry one too, but even he, they believed, couldn't overpower nine others. They had Effie's rope for immobilizing him. He could be stowed in the hold until they were back on the mainland, and then they would call the police for his arrest.

'Onwards, then!' David cried, leading the march towards the Am Blaid ridge. Only Mad Annie and Mhairi – who wasn't taking any risks – hung back as they started up the steep slope. They covered the ground quickly and easily; eight months in a gently undulating landscape couldn't undo the muscle memory that came from decades of hiking this ground, not to mention ancestral heritage. They were fit and strong, the inclines familiar beneath their bare feet, and the village men, along with Sholto, quickly pulled ahead of the earl, MacLeod and the minister.

Effie, beside Jayne, kept throwing her concerned looks as they strode out, as if she expected Jayne to sink to the ground at any moment.

'I see him,' Angus said as they reached the saddle of the ridge. He pointed out the white dot of Norman's shirt, bright against the grass. 'There.'

Jayne looked down on the glen. MacLeod's brown-fleeced ancient-breed sheep now grazed the slopes and it looked a very different scene to that of a year prior. Even here in this remote outpost in the Atlantic, life moved on, it seemed.

She caught sight of her husband striding forth, unaware as yet of the chase. She thought of his coming rage as her betrayal was revealed to him – a secret not kept after all. But now she knew that the blows he was saving for her would never land.

David turned back. 'Stay here,' he commanded the women, but his eyes were upon her alone.

'Not likely,' Effie muttered, going wide as the village men streamed down the other side of the ridge, coming for Norman fast and breaking into a run. They wanted the element of surprise. It would be far easier to overpower Norman if he didn't see their approach.

Jayne ran after them too.

The inky pool was set below a rocky outcrop on the far north-westerly side of the bowl. It couldn't be seen from above, as the bluffs dropped away out of sight so that the moor seemed to extend in an unbroken sweep down to the sea. But the villagers knew it well. They could find their way there in the dark if required.

It had been clever of Effie to hide the horn there, Jayne thought. The cleits were the obvious hiding nooks and, even though there were two thousand of them or thereabouts, Frank and Norman between them would have been able to cover enough ground in those final few days and nights to find the horn. Jayne could imagine their growing anger and mistrust of one another on that final night, as the last cleit had given them nothing.

She watched as the gap was steadily closed on her husband – David was in the lead, Angus close behind – and felt her heart pound ever harder, knowing this was their goodbye. Not face to face, but at a remove. Norman would never hurt her again.

He was coming round to the bluff now and she saw him stop and look down into the inky pool, trying to perceive the horn from a height. For several moments he stood still, his head moving from side to side as he studied the dark depths for a lighter spot.

Suddenly his body became taut, alert as a hunting dog pointing towards its quarry. He moved sharply sideways. Had he found it? He straightened abruptly and she recognized his delight – she could read him, even at a distance. Norman was readying himself to claim what he'd come for.

The Midnight Secret

This was his final victory, she thought, watching as David and Angus advanced. They were perhaps a hundred feet away now, speeding silently over the grass. They were hunters, all of them – Norman too, for he turned suddenly, detecting the lion stares trained on his back.

'Halt there, Norman!' David cried. 'Don't go any further!'

Norman froze as he saw their number heading for him. As he saw *her* racing over the grass and realized the game was up.

There was only one person he didn't see.

He began to laugh, a maniacal laugh that became a roar as he railed up at the heavens. Jayne stopped in her tracks at the scale of the rage within him now that he didn't need to be quiet any more. Now that he didn't need to hide what he really was.

How had she survived him?

'Don't do anything foolish, now, Norman!' Angus warned as he took up the flank. He was the only islander close enough in size to match Norman one on one.

Norman watched as the other men spread out, taking their positions on the moor. He couldn't get past them to reach the boats, and behind him there were only cliffs. It was over. His threats towards her and Effie had failed and he'd been exposed. There was no getting off this island. There was no way out of this.

'Just give it up, Norman. We know everything,' David panted, slowing to a walk now. He was less than six feet away from his foe – the man who had denied him twice over: first Molly, then Jayne herself. 'We know what you did. You killed Frank.'

Jayne saw the look of surprise that crossed her husband's face, but it was only momentary. He was still calculating a getaway.

'And what do *you* intend to do, David?' Norman jibed, seeing that David was unafraid. 'You're going to be the one to stop me, are y'?'

'Aye.'

'Come on then, big man!' Norman jeered, drawing him in. 'Land one on me! Let's see if y'can take a point off me.'

But David only laughed. 'I don't need to take points off you, Norman,' he said with a cold smile. 'I'm taking your wife . . . She loves me.'

Jayne felt her heart quail as David spoke a truth she had thought would never see daylight. Perhaps he had thought the same. But his tactic worked, as Norman, completely wrong-footed, looked over at Jayne in utter disbelief. It had never crossed his mind that she might betray him. He hadn't thought her *capable* of anything beyond mere existence. Simple survival. She was just a thing to him.

'It's true, Norman,' she cried out. 'I love him! And I hate you!'

Let those be her last words to him, she thought, trembling as she saw the rage gather anew in his body. If they were alone now, she knew he'd kill her.

'You bitch—' he spat.

'Don't call her that!' David growled, stepping forward as Norman pulled his hands into fists, getting the reaction he wanted. He drew back to throw one of his heavy punches – unaware of the figure emerging behind him: Effie, climbing onto the rocks.

'I've got it!' she cried triumphantly, her wet hair slicked back, her clothes sodden, holding up the horn. She must have slipped into the pool unnoticed behind him.

Norman turned, but something happened; Jayne couldn't see what. He caught his own foot, or he slipped in his haste,

The Midnight Secret

unbalanced by his warrior pose . . . All she saw was his arms beginning to wheel. His broad, powerful arms that had inflicted so much damage on her, turning uselessly in the air, unable to right him. Unable to stop his fall over the ledge.

He disappeared from sight in the next moment – gone, just like that – down towards the black-water pool.

Jayne knew he had hit the rocks before she rounded the hillock and saw his arm outstretched, his hand upturned and fingers curled as blood slowly seeped into the grass.

Effie screamed, stunned by what had happened so quickly, right in front of her.

But Jayne was utterly silent, feeling the dark shadows curl away from her heels at last, now that the dream had come to pass.

Chapter Thirty-One

It took several hours for the men to bring Norman's body back from Glen Bay. Strong in life meant heavy in death, and they had to carry him in rotating shifts. Jayne spent that time sitting with the minister as they prayed together in the kirk and discussed what would come next. He reassured her there were enough witnesses to the accident – and she understood from his tone that he meant enough witnesses 'of repute', namely the lairds – for the death not to be considered suspicious. Registering Norman's passing back on the mainland would be a matter of paperwork, that was all.

That was all.

She had decided he should be buried here beside Molly, his dear sister and – Jayne believed – the only person in the world he had ever truly loved. The coffin cleit had been the only cleit not cleared before the evacuation, so there was enough wood to nail together a casket. Donald, Angus and Fin were leading that task; David and Sholto were digging the grave.

She sat now on the rocks, staring – as she always had – at the seabirds diving for their fish suppers; but her hands were idle now, no knitting with which to soothe her restless spirit.

She heard voices and knew the girls were approaching. Effie and Mhairi had been fluttering around her like butterflies

The Midnight Secret

ever since it had happened, bringing her water to sip and holding her hand. Everyone was in shock. For all their anger at what Norman had done – and what he had been revealed to be – no one had wanted this. They'd never imagined for a moment that their hunt would end with a kill.

They kept looking to Jayne, supposing the shock to be all the greater for her, never realizing that she'd had several days to process what was coming. To plan for it. Everything was all so neat and tidy, the mystery tied up at last, but she had been determined Norman's death would not be in vain. Changing her statement to the police had been only the first part of it.

'We knew we'd find you here,' Mhairi said, sitting beside her and resting her head on Jayne's shoulder.

'But of course,' Jayne smiled. 'Where else would I be? This was always my safe spot.'

She caught the girls' surprised looks at her plain words. She'd never been so candid before. To declare this a place of safety was to imply that elsewhere was not. But there was nothing to hide any more. Everyone knew now that her home had harboured hidden horrors and that her husband had ruled with an iron fist.

'Are they ready?' she asked, understanding why they had come to find her. The sun was beginning to make its descent in the sky, the day folding down on its drama. The hours had slipped past amid blood, sweat and tears.

Effie nodded, squeezing Jayne's arm sympathetically. The minister had found himself an unexpectedly busy man today.

'Very well, then,' she said, gathering her skirt and rising. This had to be faced. Walked through.

Effie and Mhairi flanked her like bridesmaids, each woman holding her hand as they walked back to the village, the long grass brushing their bare ankles. Jayne felt the smoothness of the stepping stones against her soles, the wind in her unbound hair, her body soothed by the elements of home.

They walked wordlessly along the street, past their old homes where the doors stood open once more. They turned into the narrow path between the Big Gillies' and Ma Peg's, emerging round the back just below the burial ground. Its circular stone walls stood untouched by the storms that had blown through this past winter, just as they had for all the generations before; the winds could find no corners to catch here. Though the isle was now abandoned and the cleit roofs would, in time, fall in and the cottage doors would rot off their hinges, she knew this would always be the last place standing. She had sensed it that last night as she lay in its ancient embrace under the stars, with David above ground and Molly below. It belonged to the people and the wilds; an inside, out.

The men and Mad Annie were assembled in a solemn crescent either side of the minister, a Bible in his hands and Norman's coffin at his feet, lying ready before the fresh grave. The men's cheeks were still pink from their labours and she saw grief in their dry eyes as she took her position on the opposite side of the grave.

A silence fell upon the already muted company, eyes falling earthwards, hands clasped across still bodies.

'. . . Almighty God, Father of all mercies and giver of all comfort . . .' the minister began.

Jayne closed her eyes, aware of the proximity of the island girls, closer now than she had ever allowed them to get when Norman was alive.

Was it over?

Was it really over?

The Midnight Secret

'. . . casting all their care on you, they may know the consolation of your love . . .' the minister intoned.

She opened her eyes to find David watching her. She had walked through the valley of the shadow of death. But a light was shimmering on the other side.

It was over . . .

Almost.

Chapter Thirty-Two

Jayne stood in the small garden that fronted the guesthouse. She had been invited in, of course, but what she had to say wasn't for just anyone's ears.

'You wanted to see me?'

She turned, facing the figure silhouetted against the porch light. 'Aye.'

There was a pause as she waited for the inevitable.

'I was sorry to hear of your loss.'

'Thank you,' Jayne replied.

She hadn't come here straight from the yacht. She had known that news of Norman's death would spread like wildfire – another St Kildan tragedy, another scandal on the tiny outer Hebridean outpost – and she had wanted to let it get ahead of her. 'I know you'll be wondering why I'm here, so I'll get straight to the point . . . I wanted you to know that I changed my witness statement two days ago.'

'. . . Oh?'

'Aye. I went down to Oban and told them Norman never came home the night Frank was killed.'

There was another pause. 'And why should y' do that, after all this time?'

'Because it wasn't fair to Donald that he should continue to be kept under suspicion when I knew he hadn't done it.'

The Midnight Secret

'I see.'

'I was afraid of Norman for a long time, you see, but I realized there was no longer any reason to give him an alibi. Not once I'd had the dream that he was going to die.'

A silence stretched as her intimation was absorbed: she had foreseen Norman's death.

Of course she had. She always did. Everyone knew that – they just didn't always remember it.

'. . . Well, it's just a pity we didn't see what he was capable of till it was too late.'

'Aye,' Jayne sighed, her gaze never wavering. 'We think, because we've lived cheek by jowl all these years, that we know each other so well. But everyone can hide a secret. Even out there.'

'I suppose that's true enough.'

'Flora did it. Mhairi too. Lorna, God rest her soul – and you, of course . . . I know what you did, Mary.'

The older woman's eyes flashed. 'Everyone knows! . . . It's not a crime to want a child and not be able to bear one—'

'But it is to steal one.'

'I never stole the bairn! She placed him in my arms.'

'Only because you and Lorna told her that James was dead. You made Flora believe she was in a desperate position, with no way to support the child. Just as you now have no way to support him, without Lorna.'

Mary bristled with barely contained anger. 'A solution has been reached which we all can live with, and that's all I have to say on it. You don't have to like it. It's nothing to do with you.'

She turned to leave.

'Isn't it?'

Mary turned back. 'And what does that mean?'

'I've just told you that I know everything.'

'So? Everyone knows and I don't care if they all hate me!'

'I'm not talking about the baby.'

Mary fell very still then, the hostility in her eyes beginning to give way to something else. Fear.

'I know it was you.' Jayne didn't so much as blink, her gaze steady. 'Norman didn't kill Frank. You did.'

She wasn't doing this for the sake of her late husband's reputation. Norman had ruined that all by himself. History would not remember him kindly as the villagers' stories were passed down through the generations, and it would serve no purpose to enlighten others about his innocence in one matter when he was guilty in so many others. But Jayne could still help those who would otherwise remain trapped by the false notion that he had killed the factor.

'And how have y' come to that conclusion?' Mary's voice was quieter now.

'The same way I knew Norman wouldn't be coming back here with us. I saw it before it happened – and *as* it happened. I was sleeping out in the burial ground that last night. You walked right past me, Mary.'

There was a pause. 'I have multiple witnesses who say I was in bed that night – in no fit state to walk to the kitchen, much less all the way over there to kill a man!'

'Do you really think those statements will stand? Do you think Christina MacQueen will support you, now she knows you stole Flora's baby? Or Rachel, knowing you tried to take Mhairi's? Annie's more likely to kill you. Ma Peg, Effie – everyone hates you. And of course, Lorna, your lover, your witness, your ally and alibi, is dead.'

Mary's breathing came hard, but she was a fighter. She knew how to come out swinging. 'It's about what can be

The Midnight Secret

proven! No one will believe you because of a *vision*! They'll think you a witch before they think me a killer!'

'You may be right there,' Jayne nodded. She knew people were either sceptical of her gift or superstitious about it. 'And it's true, the visions aren't always clear. It can take me time to understand what I'm seeing. I don't always see everything – or everyone – in the death scene. But in this instance, I had some help.'

Mary's eyes narrowed. 'Help?'

'Were you aware that Lorna had written a confession before she died?'

'. . . What?' The word was a croak.

'She sent me a letter the night she took the pills, saying that she had delivered Flora of a child and not you. She admitted to prematurely inducing the labour and then, after the child was born, carrying him all the way back here to place him in your arms. She wrote that she told you Frank had seen her as she passed by with the baby crying, that he already knew Flora and Mhairi were pregnant and that he was going to tell the world what you and she had done.'

Mary gasped, trying to keep pace with the revelations. 'No – that's not true . . . She would never betray me like that.'

'She couldn't live with what you'd done! To take a baby was one thing – but to crack a man's skull, to stab him? She had never agreed to be part of a murder!'

Mary's eyes were wide as she saw her future narrow to a small, black point.

'You're going to swing for this, Mary. You killed Frank Mathieson in cold blood. While he was half trussed up and drunk, unable to properly defend himself.'

'No!'

'Yes. The letter proves it. I've already told the police I was out here that night, with David as my witness – but they don't know yet what I saw: Lorna coming back with the baby; the shouts I heard first. Mathieson threatening to tell everyone the baby wasn't yours!'

'It must have been her that did it, then!' Mary cried desperately. '. . . I was in bed! People saw me—'

'You were in bed long enough for people to see you with the baby – as Mhairi helped Flora back home. She could barely walk, but *you*, Mary, when you came out later, you were up and down the hill in no time. You could have run it. You silenced Mathieson before he was in any fit state to act and I saw it.'

Mary stared back at her with an empty expression. Jayne could see that all hope had gone from her. She had no allies, no defence.

'. . . What are you going to do?' she asked finally.

Jayne took a breath. 'Let Norman take the blame.'

She let the comment hang in the air.

'. . . *Wh-why?*' Mary breathed, stunned.

'Because he's dead, and it really doesn't matter now if people think that one cruel man killed another cruel man.'

'But why would you do that?'

'Because you're going to do two things for me in return.' Jayne looked her in the eyes. 'You can still have a chance to live, Mary.'

Just not happily.

Epilogue

13 May 1931

Rose Cottage, Dumfries House

'May we come in?'

Jayne peered around the door of the cottage bedroom. It had been crowded with bodies all morning, the women fussing excitedly – none more than Mad Annie, who loved a wedding – as the men waited downstairs with Robert, admiring his vegetable garden and the views back towards the Big House. But now the guests had gone ahead and Effie was standing alone, staring at her reflection in the mirror, just as Jayne had done five years before.

It had taken them all a while to get used to the sight of their 'strip of wind' in white chiffon and ribbons, satin slippers on her feet. For someone who had got through the first eighteen years of her life trying to ignore that she was a girl, it was bewildering enough to see herself as a bride – but to wear a crown . . . Fanny had called it a 'tiara' as she had come up from the Big House to do Effie's hair, carefully pinning it in place, shooing everyone out so she could 'work in peace'.

'Oh!' Jayne gasped in admiration as Effie turned towards her with a nervous look.

'Does it look all right?'

'All right?' Jayne beamed, her hands fluttering to her heart. 'Effie, you're a vision!'

'Let me see!' Flora cried impatiently behind her, pushing the door wider so she could get through. 'Oh! You're like a princess!' she gasped, her hands rushing to her mouth.

'Well, she is marrying a future earl,' Jayne laughed as Flora and Mhairi came further into the room.

'You're like a fairy!' Mhairi exclaimed, lifting the gossamer veil and letting it billow and flutter back down.

Effie blinked back at them, her eyes wide. 'Am I dreaming? I feel as if I'm in a dream.'

'It's better than that, Eff,' Mhairi said, taking her hand and clasping it tightly. 'It's the life you were always supposed to have.'

The four of them stood for a moment, the bridesmaids matching in peach silk and carrying posies of miniature cream roses.

'. . . How did we end up here?' Effie asked, the question coming out as a half laugh, half sob. But her tears were happy ones.

Ever since the earl had invited her to sail back on his yacht 'as his honoured guest', Sholto hadn't left her side. He had put duty before self when the hour of need had come, but his mother, caught for a time in what she called 'a living death', didn't want the same for her son – and she had finally urged him to win Effie back. She had seen Sholto become a shell of himself in those few months after the split, robbed of all joy or interest, and when he had escaped to Edinburgh rather than stay while Lady Sibyl had 'been passing' – refusing to return until she had left again – the countess had known a society match could not be forced. For the earl's part, he had

The Midnight Secret

been impressed by Effie's willingness to help their dear friends, the MacLeods, even after she had been shunned, and he had seen that 'a rich heart lay beneath her poor coat'. And, after all, he had always had a soft spot for her 'spiritedness'; her growing legend at Loch Dunvegan had delighted him.

'It's at the year's end that the fisher can tell his luck,' Jayne shrugged.

'You're saying we've had a good year?' Effie laughed, the others too. Had they ever suffered so much? And yet it was a year to the day that she had first met Sholto, catching that glimpse of him strolling down the street – before, an hour later, she was leaping into his boat on account of a wager, and it had all begun.

'I'd say it was worth it in the end,' Flora smiled, reaching for Jayne's hand and drawing her over to stand with them. 'You know, Jayne, when we were plucking the birds last summer, I said to Eff and Mhairi that we would always be St Kilda girls, no matter where we ended up: Dumfries House, Lochaline, Glasgow or Paris or Quebec . . . it doesn't matter. We're sisters, all of us.'

Jayne felt the warmth in her words. Soon Flora would be her sister in deed as well as spirit, and Jayne couldn't help but think of the girl she had first loved as her own. Losing Molly had been a desperate blow for the village, a tragedy for Norman and David, and a personal catastrophe for her. All their worlds had unspooled in the aftermath: Lorna might never have found support for the evacuation had Molly survived; David would have become her fiancé, not Jayne's . . . Sometimes the guilt caught up with her that she was living the future Molly had been denied. But David argued the opposite: that their love held Molly within it, keeping her memory close.

'I also said that what we three did, only we three would ever know . . . But it's what we *four* did that only we four will ever know.'

'Aye,' Mhairi nodded, reaching for Jayne's hand too. 'What you did for us . . .'

'It was the only possible happiness that could come from so much wickedness,' Jayne replied.

Mary had disappeared, as agreed, as soon as the paperwork for the divorce and the adoption had been finalized. No one knew where she had gone and no one cared. She was exiled.

Jayne's world, by contrast, had opened up like a flower. It contained colours and textures now; it brimmed with life. David loved her, she had friends – true friends – and she felt safe for the first time in many years.

She saw Mhairi's hand settle on her rounded belly. She and Donald were to be married quietly within weeks, and would be relocating here to settle down in full respectability. Donald had accepted Sholto's offer of a position as gamekeeper of the estate when Huw Felton took employment with the Duke of Argyll. Effie fretted that she was responsible for driving him away, but Sholto said it was for the best if he really couldn't let her go. Archie Baird-Hamilton had conceded defeat with good grace, at least, sending them a wedding present before slipping away to the wilds of Kenya.

They heard the sound of hooves on the ground outside and Flora ran to the window. 'It's here,' she said excitedly.

Effie gathered her long skirts and walked carefully out of the bedroom and down the narrow cottage stairs. Her father was waiting alone in the front room for her. He was wearing his Sunday suit, and someone had put a rose from the garden in his buttonhole.

He caught his breath as Effie stepped into the room, ethereal

The Midnight Secret

in white, the diamond tiara glittering in her hair. It was another few moments before he spoke.

'Y'r mother would be proud, lass,' he said finally. 'As I am.'

He gave her his arm, and together father and daughter walked out of the small cottage into the spring sunshine where the horse and trap was waiting. The earl had offered his Bentley to bring them down the short drive to the Big House, but Effie preferred to feel the wind on her face in her last moments as a single girl. She would have walked if she could. Only Flora's horrified interjections that she would ruin the dress had persuaded her that a pony trap was a suitable compromise.

Jayne, Mhairi and Flora helped Effie negotiate her long, delicate gown around the steps before they climbed into the back and sat on the low wooden bench seats.

'Not forgetting these rascals,' Robert said, clicking his fingers – and Slipper and Socks, with peach satin bows around their necks, jumped in beside them. 'Stay there,' he commanded in his gruff voice, ruffling behind their ears before closing up the back and taking his place beside his daughter.

The driver shook the reins gently, and the horses began their slow walk along the track towards the chapel. No one spoke as they took in the glorious sight of Dumfries House basking in the sunlight; the gardens were in full bloom, the water spouting from the fountain refracting the light so that diamonds seemed to twinkle in the air.

It felt like an ending, even though they knew it was the first of many beginnings. Flora and Mhairi's aside, Jayne herself was going to walk down the aisle for a second time after David had proposed in her kitchen.

Too soon, they were passing through the old stone wall of the chapel grounds where ancient yew trees stood fatly like

Mrs McLennan's steamed puddings. The young flower girls and page boys were clustered around the chapel door, waiting restlessly with the mothers, Rachel, Christina and Big Mary, though they all fell still as they caught sight of Effie as a bride.

'Oh!' the women exclaimed as one, exactly as the bridesmaids had done, as the trap rolled to a stop and the passengers disembarked, dogs first.

'What a vision y' are,' Christina smiled, stroking Effie's cheek tenderly.

'The most beautiful bride,' Rachel chimed too.

'Is he here?' Effie asked nervously as Mhairi and Flora arranged her veil.

'Is he here?' Rachel laughed. 'The poor man's been pacing the floor for nigh on twenty minutes now! He got here early!'

Jayne came around and put the floral posy in Effie's trembling hands as Flora and Mhairi carefully pulled the veil forward. 'There,' she said with satisfaction, covering the bride's hands with her own for a moment to calm her. '. . . Are you all right?'

Effie nodded, although she looked terrified. 'I just . . . don't feel quite myself,' she mumbled.

'Wearing the veil down can be disorienting at first,' Jayne said calmly. 'But it's not for long. Only while you walk down the aisle – then it's pulled back again.'

Effie nodded, but Jayne knew her friend would far rather be in breeks and holding a rope than all this. She supposed the tiara might feel alien too.

'Hurry now,' Big Mary said, shuffling the children into position behind Effie. 'The minister's waiting.'

'We'll sit at the back in case they misbehave,' Rachel said hastily as the organ started up inside the chapel and the doors were opened.

Jayne, Mhairi and Flora positioned themselves behind Effie

The Midnight Secret

as heads turned, everyone smiling, particularly as they caught sight of the dogs standing at Robert's heel. All the St Kildans were seated on the left, Sholto's family and friends on the right, the estate staff lining the walls.

Robert offered his daughter his arm and they walked forward a few steps into the small porch. Jayne could already see Sholto standing at the end of the aisle, tall, golden and utterly in love. The relief on his face as he saw his bride was palpable. His pride too.

'Ready?' Effie's father said nervously under his breath, as the introductory music ended and the first few bars of Pachelbel's Canon in D Major sounded. He began to move . . .

'No!' Effie said suddenly.

Jayne felt her stomach lurch. *What?*

Some of the guests heard it too. A look of horror dawned on their faces and concern rippled through the pews. Sholto startled.

'Effie!' Jayne whispered desperately, as there was a pause – and then Effie grew smaller as she slipped off her satin shoes, her bare feet pressing to the cold stone floor and connecting her to the moment. The place.

Her new home.

Sholto – watching her, understanding her – beamed.

And the bride beamed back. '*Now* I'm ready.'

Acknowledgements

So here we are. At the end. If I'm being honest, I wasn't completely sure this day would ever come. This has been my first attempt at writing a series and, as with any creative endeavour, you have to learn on the job. So what have I learned? For one thing, writing contemporaneous stories is the hardest way to create a series (good call, Karen) – editorial decisions made in Book One have to stand throughout the later books, too – but I've never been one to shirk a challenge and I have absolutely *loved* it. Coming back into known scenes from other angles and perspectives has been fascinating to me, layering facts and building intrigue and developing characters beyond just one viewpoint. I know that I will definitely write more series in the future but, even if they're written sequentially or more loosely within a world, they will be published back to back so that we don't all have to wait for so long. My mother has been furious with me for the past four years after the cliffhanger at the end of Book One, so I really hope the reveals and answers in this final instalment will mean she forgives me at last!

I'm so sad to be saying goodbye to the girls. They've lived in my head for four years and I'm not sure they'll ever fade. As you know, they are completely fictitious characters, but I have been meticulous in my research throughout to ensure

The Midnight Secret

I've depicted their life on St Kilda – and their wider worlds – as honestly and truly as I can. It has been such a privilege to revisit a lost land and have free rein in my imaginings to bring it back to life briefly on these pages. It's been a joy to be reunited with all the characters in this final book and, even as I was editing, I was wanting more time with them all – but there are other worlds to discover and I'm so happy with where we're leaving them: all together, with full hearts, smiles on their faces and bare feet!

Thank you all for coming on this journey with me. Your love for the series absolutely sustained me when I felt daunted at the beginning of each new book, wondering how on earth I was going to tie it all together. I had to get to know each character page-by-page and go digging for their stories – nothing came fully formed – but I knew I couldn't let you down. You trusted me to give you answers, as well as adventure, and I hope you're reading this now feeling utterly satisfied. As ever, come and find me on socials and give me your thoughts. I'm always keen to hear what lands and what doesn't.

As you know by now, there's a mighty team of brilliant people standing behind me. I write the stories, but they fashion the books. Together, we have put out twenty-eight beauties in fifteen years. It takes patience, respect and trust. Each new book is agonized over – endless edits; title deliberations that can take months; does the cover shine and the shoutline sing? We all care hugely about making each one the best it can possibly be, and the team at Pan Macmillan is absolutely top-flight: James Annal, Melissa Bond, Chloe Davies, Stu Dwyer, Claire Evans, Lucy Grainger, Ellah Mwale, Natasha Tulett and my copy-editor, Camilla Rockwood – you are not only brilliant at your jobs but such good eggs, too! Working doesn't feel like work with you. Thank you all for absolutely everything.

To my commissioning editor, Gillian Green, and publishing director, Lucy Hale, thank you for having the trust in me to broaden my creative wings. You both inherited me at a time when the St Kilda idea was just a buzz in my brain, but your confidence infected me with the belief that I could do it. And at last I have. I will be forever indebted to you for that, and to Pan Macmillan more widely for seeing something in me when my first ever manuscript landed on a desk in Kings Cross.

Finally – Amanda Preston, my agent extraordinaire. We're so aligned we have the same wardrobe! Two words only for you: Never. Retire.

Karen Swan is the *Sunday Times* top three bestselling author of more than twenty-eight books and her novels sell all over the world. She writes two books each year, which are published in the summer and at Christmas. Previous summer titles include *The Spanish Promise*, *The Hidden Beach* and *The Secret Path* and among her winter titles are *Midnight in the Snow*, *The Christmas Postcards* and *All I Want For Christmas*.

Previously a fashion editor, she lives in Sussex with her husband, three children and two dogs.

Follow Karen on Instagram @swannywrites,
on her author page on Facebook,
and on Bluesky @swannywrites.bsky.social.

The Secret Path

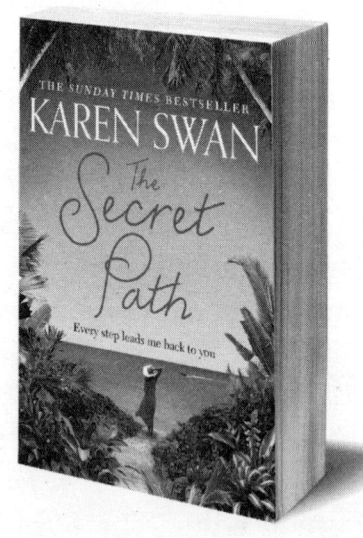

'Deliciously glamorous, irresistably romantic!'
Hello!

An old flame. A new spark. Love can find you in the most unlikely places.

At only twenty, Tara Tremain has everything: she's a trainee doctor, engaged to Alex, the man of her dreams. But, just when life seems perfect, Alex betrays her in the worst way possible.

Ten years later, she's moved on – with a successful career and a man who loves her. But, when she's pulled back into her wealthy family's orbit for a party in the Costa Rican jungle, she's flung into a crisis: a child is desperately ill and the sole treatment is several days' trek away.

There's only one person who can help – but can she trust the man who broke her heart?

The Hidden Beach

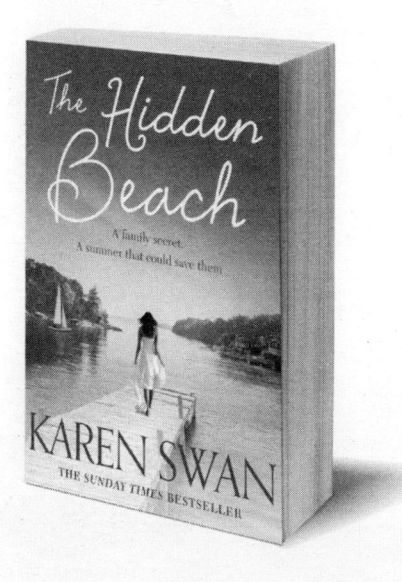

'Novels to sweep you away'
Woman & Home

Secrets, betrayal and shocking revelations await in Sweden's stunning holiday islands . . .

In Stockholm's oldest quarter, Bell Appleshaw loves her job working as a nanny for the rich and charming Hanna and Max Mogert, caring for their three children.

But one morning everything changes. A doctor from a clinic that Bell has never heard of asks her to pass on the message that Hanna's husband has woken up. But the man isn't Max.

As the truth about Hanna's past is revealed, the consequences are devastating. As the family heads off to spend their summer on Sweden's idyllic islands, will Bell be caught in the crossfire?

The Spanish Promise

'The perfect summer read'
Hello!

The Spanish Promise is a sizzling summer novel about family secrets and forbidden love, set in the vibrant streets of Madrid.

One of Spain's richest men is dying – and his family are shocked to discover he plans to give away his wealth to a young woman they've never heard of.

Charlotte Fairfax, an expert in dealing with the world's super rich, is asked to travel to the troubled family's home to get to the bottom of the mysterious bequest. She unearths a dark and shocking past in which two people were torn apart by conflict. Now, long-buried secrets are starting to reach into the present. Does love need to forgive and forget to endure? Or does it just need two hearts to keep beating?

The Greek Escape

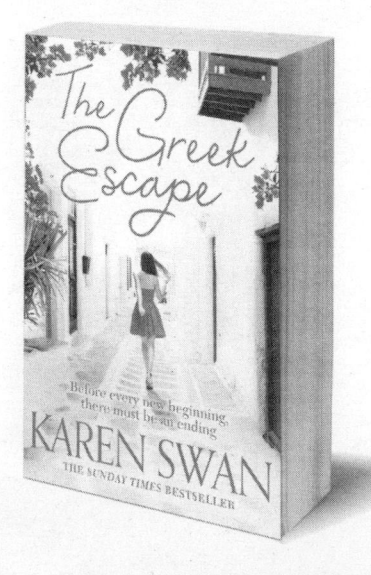

> 'A beautiful setting and steamy scenes – what more do you need?'
> ***Fabulous***

Set on an idyllic island, *The Greek Escape* is the perfect getaway, bursting with jaw-dropping twists and irrepressible romance.

Chloe Marston works at a luxury concierge company, making other people's lives run perfectly, even if her own has ground to a halt. She is tasked with finding charismatic Joe Lincoln his dream holiday house in Greece – and, when the man who broke her heart turns up at home, she jumps on the next flight.

It doesn't take long before she's drawn into the undeniable chemistry between her and Joe. When another client's wife mysteriously disappears and serious allegations about him emerge, will she end up running from more than heartbreak?

The Rome Affair

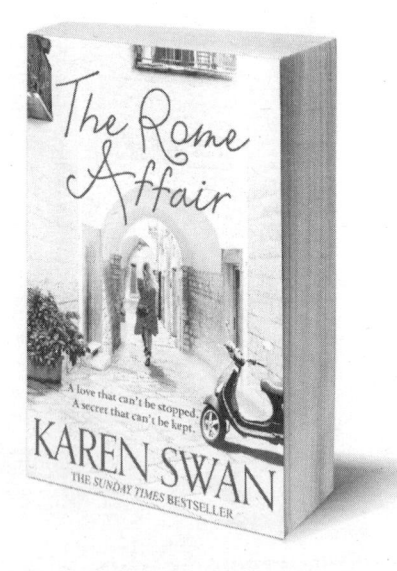

'**Enthralling and magical**'
Woman

The cobbled streets and simmering heat of Italy's capital are brought to life in *The Rome Affair*.

1974 and Viscontessa Elena Damiani lives a gilded life, born to wealth and a noted beauty. Then she meets the love of her life, and he is the one man she can never have. 2017 and Francesca Hackett is living la dolce vita in Rome, forgetting the ghosts she left behind in London. When a twist of fate brings her into Elena's orbit, the two women form an unlikely friendship.

As summer unfurls, Elena shares her sensational stories with Cesca, who agrees to work on Elena's memoir. But, when a priceless diamond ring found in an ancient tunnel below the city streets is ascribed to Elena, Cesca begins to suspect a shocking secret lies at the heart of the Viscontessa's life . . .

Summer at TIFFANY'S

'Glamorous, romantic and totally engrossing'
My Weekly

A wedding to plan. A wedding to stop.
What could go wrong?

With a Tiffany ring on her finger, all Cassie has to do is plan her dream wedding. It should be simple, but when her fiancé, Henry, pushes for a date, Cassie pulls back. Meanwhile, Henry's wild cousin, Gem, is racing to the aisle for her own wedding, determined to marry in the Cornish church where her parents were wed. But the family is set against it, and Cassie resolves to stop the wedding.

When Henry lands an expedition sailing the Pacific for the summer, Cassie decamps to Cornwall, hoping to find the peace of mind she needs to move forwards. But, in the dunes and coves of the north Cornish coast, she soon discovers the past isn't finished with her yet . . .

There's a Karen Swan book
for every season . . .

Have you discovered her winter stories yet?

www.panmacmillan.com/karenswan